The lightest touch on her quivering eyelid was like butterfly wings, hardly anything at all. Her lashes fluttered against his thumb. She could feel the closeness of his palm, her head full of his scent. He feathered the tips of her eyelashes and followed their edge to the bridge of her nose—tracing a long line down and resting a hush on her lips.

Like a kiss.

Her eyes opened. She stared straight into Ink.

He dropped his hand.

"Thank you."

They were both surprised when he said it.

Ink stood up, backing away cautiously—Joy kept her eyes on him as he moved, step by step. It looked as if he might do something, as if he wanted to maybe say something more, but he waved a hand and stepped forward into the breach, disappearing as he'd come.

Joy stared at the space where he'd been, doing everything in her power not to touch the side of her face.

DAWN METCALF

INDELIBLE

·THE TWIXT· BOOK ONE·

HARLEQUIN®TEEN

Recycling programs
for this product may
not exist in your area.

ISBN-13: 978-0-373-21073-2

INDELIBLE

Printed in U.S.A.

To Maestro & The Pigtailed Overlord,
Mommy loves you!

ONE

THE MUSIC BEAT HARD AGAINST JOY'S RIBS. SHE COULD FEEL the rhythm in her chest and the bass in her teeth. The Carousel spun slowly, crammed with mirrors and frantic dancers. It was dark. It was light. It was dark. It was light. Joy felt the music call to her, dizzying and loud.

"Isn't this great?" Monica shouted next to Joy's ear. They stood just inside the nimbus of carnival lights and techno grind. Behind them, the Tilt-A-Whirl roared.

Joy nodded. "It's wild!"

"Well, come on, wild child! Time for fun."

Monica loved fun. And Joy loved her for it. Despite the craziness of the past year, Monica had stuck by her, so even if Joy wasn't too sure about going to the spring fair among several dozen rabid cool-hunters prowling the Carousel on the Green, she wasn't about to ruin it. Instead of ballroom dancing classes or community theater-in-the-round, the Carousel was attempting to become Glendale's hottest indoor/outdoor scene. People pumped their fists in the air and smartphones caught the rave on glowing screens. Joy checked hers for the time.

"Well, fun better get started. Dad's only letting me stay out till eleven."

Monica snorted and smoothed the edges of her razor-cut bob. "You'd think you were the one who skipped out." Then she winced and whispered, "Sorry."

Joy shrugged. "'S'okay."

Lots of parents split after their last kid went off to college. Mom could've waited two years before running off to L.A., but by then, her twenty-six-year-old graphic artist, Doug, might have been considered too old for a cougar like her. As she'd tried to explain before she left, she had "needs." The memory still brought an embarrassed ache, but no tears. Joy had cried herself out months ago. Nowadays, she half expected Mom to reappear when her boy-toy turned thirty.

"Come on." Monica tugged Joy up the incline. "Party's wasting!"

They held hands and jumped onto the crowded dance floor. The old hardwood shivered, rotating slowly on merry-go-round gears. The Carousel was packed, but Monica nabbed a spot beneath the peeling brass ring—the only original piece left after the horses had been auctioned off. Joy edged toward the speakers as the Carousel turned. The town fair fell into purple shadow rimmed in fairy lights.

Joy moved her hips and shoulders, enjoying the thump of the music. Closing her eyes, she felt strangers' laughter bubble up inside her as if it were her own and she popped her heels to the beat. Her ponytail brushed the back of her neck, alternately sticky and cool. Hands ringed in glow bracelets and Under 18 wristbands clutched empty cotton-candy cones and miniature teddy bears. The air smelled of hot sugar, cooking oil and sweat. Distant roller coaster screams echoed somewhere out in the glow of a thousand twinkling carnival lights. It was like swimming in a dreamworld, floating in noise.

Joy wound her long arms over her head, stretching her spine. Her hipster jeans hung loose. She'd gotten a lot thinner since Mom left, her abs tight under stretched skin. Mom would have noticed and made her change clothes. The thought brought Joy dropping back to earth, feeling heavy and solid as she sank into her shoes.

No! This was *not* going to be like last year. Those days had been too long and the house too quiet. She'd become a total stranger. She was officially over it. This was spring, a new beginning in a brand-new year. This year, things were going to change.

Joy checked her posture and her attitude as she spun on the shifting floor. She shuffled toward Monica, who had lightly rebuffed some blond boy and was now glancing over her shoulder at the guy on her left. Joy wasn't surprised. Monica liked jocks. Or, as she liked to put it, "big strapping jocks," and Mr. Wide Shouldered Crew Cut in Tight Pants definitely fit her type.

Joy pushed away some stray hand. The floor chugged with the beat.

"Chocolate-vanilla swirl?" Joy shouted.

Monica raised her hands and whooped, "Oh, yeah!"

Monica was more the color of classic grand pianos than chocolate ice cream, but she was always game for showing off. Linking fingers, the two of them slowly undulated their hips, bending lower and lower as they sank to their knees, hanging on to one another for support and inching back up the same way, laughing. They got some applause and even a few appreciative hollers. Joy grinned. Eleven years of gymnastics came in handy once in a while. It'd been over eight months since she'd quit, but she missed it. She missed it like laughing. She missed it like this.

They slapped high-fives before going solo. Monica made her play for Mr. Wide, his large hands sliding down onto her hips. She nodded to Joy and laughed, the black lights on the undercarriage making her eyes and teeth glow an unappetizing purple. It made Joy secretly want a breath mint.

Joy turned away, gazing out at the crowd. Flashes of color and jerky movements made everybody look strangely the same—no one was boy or girl, black or white, freshman or senior. They were all one big glom. Joy usually avoided the Carousel's Under 18 scene, but Monica had said that there was a new DJ and Joy had to admit that he was really good. The guy was backlit in the gutted central pillar filled with concert notices and band stickers, the giant headphones over his ears making it look like he wore a Viking helmet. Her eyes skipped over faces, trying not to linger too long. She didn't want company—she just wanted to dance and forget about Mom and Dad and her brother, Stef, away at U Penn.

She turned a one-eighty, swishing her fingers as the music switched over. Joy lifted her face to the ceiling and watched the colored bands of pink and green spin. She turned counterclockwise, making herself dizzy. Searing neon afterimages blinked in her brain. That's when she saw the all-black eyes.

At first, she thought it was a trick of the light, but everyone else's eyes had that purplish glow while these stayed flat-shadow. Joy stopped, confused.

A lean guy with spiky hair stared into the crowd with his strange, dark eyes. Shaggy bangs fell forward into his face, the back cut close behind his ears and neck. The girl next to him could have been his twin—shorter, with a heart-shaped face, matching hair and whiteless eyes. They stood on the edge of the dance floor, looking like black thistles against a field of psychedelic blooms.

Goths, Joy figured, with freaky contacts.

He stared, unblinking. His eyes swallowed everything. And when they found her, it felt like falling.

The Carousel turned, but those eyes stayed with her.

Joy adjusted her feet and tried to put the boy out of her mind. The music tracks dovetailed and the view slowly changed. Lightbox signs hawked caramel apples and funnel cakes. Crayon-colored chair swings spun in and out of sight. Monica had disappeared somewhere with Mr. Wide. The music dipped and surfaced, vocals skating up and down scales. Joy's eyes flicked to the mirrors, the black lights, the brass ring, but an itch kept pulling her gaze over her shoulder. The platform circled, and she saw him again through a sea of indigo limbs.

He stared at her. Joy glanced away, pretending not to notice. She rotated in place, rolling her hips slowly as the floor crept clockwise, not realizing that she was flirting until she'd circled beyond his sight.

Joy considered him from the safe zone behind the DJ booth. The guy's shirt looked expensive and his vibe was lurkish, intense. He had a sort of animal grace, even standing still, and his serious expression was a sharp contrast to his pretty, boyish face. On the next pass, she wondered if he'd still be there, staring at her.

He was. But it wasn't a nice stare.

Joy's stomach dropped as he headed straight toward her. She looked down at her shoes, a hot, awkward prickle crawling over her cheeks. He wasn't dancing his way closer or being in any way subtle—he was marching right at her, stepping smoothly onto the rotating platform and pushing gently but firmly through the crowd. His attention was relentless. Joy backed farther into the throng.

She scanned the club for Monica, feeling those eyes on the back of her neck. She was afraid to turn around. Didn't this break some sort of dance floor etiquette? If Joy ignored him, maybe he'd get the hint. But she really wanted backup.

"You."

Joy was surprised that his soft voice cut so cleanly through the noise. It didn't sound as if he'd shouted, and she was too surprised to pretend she hadn't heard him.

He was within arm's reach—dancing distance—but he wasn't dancing. His thistle sister stood as close to him as static cling.

Joy closed her eyes, feigning boredom. She'd gotten more details in that second brief glimpse: smoky shirt, dark pants, heavy chain dangling to his back pocket—*so* Goth! Joy projected a pointedly obvious *no*.

"Hey, you," he said again in the simple way that sliced through sound. Joy glared at him. She didn't like to be rude, but she would if she had to. She didn't need this. She kept her arms moving, trying to keep things casual. Colored lights flashed off tent tops, stuffed animals and sweaty faces, making it impossible to see where he was looking with those blacked-out eyes.

He took a step closer. Joy smelled rain on the breeze.

"You can see me?" he asked.

Joy stopped dancing at the patently stupid question.

"Yeah. Why?"

A strange look passed over his face, determination that looked like regret. His arm rose at the shoulder, snaking out in a short burst of speed. Bright lights licked the edge of something sharp in his hand. Joy flinched and fell down hard. She skidded on the floor and banged against knees.

Cupping a hand to her eye, she inhaled a scream, but it

stuck in her chest. What had just happened? There'd been a flash. It was bright. Had he cut her? Was she bleeding? People backed away. The floor kept turning. Joy could feel it shudder.

Monica appeared beside her. "You okay?" she gasped, voicing the panic Joy was just starting to feel. "What happened? Joy?"

Her eye hurt. A lot. Every time she tried to look up, she blinked rapidly over a pinprick of pain. It felt like a splinter.

Through the blur, Joy saw the Goth girl's hand bright against her brother's shirt, shoving him back into the crowd. Her voice had that same slicing clarity.

"Well, now you've done it."

Joy wanted to get up and grab them, but the twinge in her eye and an icy fear pinned her to the floor. Slippery tears wet her palm.

"He cut me!" Joy said in accusation and disbelief. Her words caught fire to those nearby, passing quickly from person to person in the breathy excitement of a night on the Green gone bad. Staffers descended. Rent-a-cops were called. There were shouts to remain calm, shut off the music, man the gates, but by the time any of it happened, the two Goth kids were gone.

Dad drove her home from the E.R. with a neat patch over one eye and a bottle of numbing drops in her hand. The scratch on her cornea was clean, but kept flipping open, so the nurse had taped her eyelid shut. Joy's pleas to stay home for the next three to five days had not met with success. There was a text from Monica and a message from Mom. Dad hadn't called her, had he? Joy frowned and shut off her phone.

"I'm glad Monica called," her dad said. "It was the right

thing to do." Joy didn't say anything as she gazed out the window. There was a long pause. "You *sure* you weren't drinking?"

"Dad, Monica's the treasurer of S.A.D.D., for Pete's sakes. She's like the poster girl for prevention," Joy said. "Besides, no alcohol at Under 18 Nights." She rubbed her eye patch.

"Stop that," he chided.

Joy dropped her hand. She and Monica had agreed not to say anything about what had really happened. Monica hadn't actually seen the guy and if Dad found out, he'd never let Joy out of the house again. Their story was that something had dropped from the ceiling, but it didn't explain the shaky feeling that had stayed with her hours later.

Like looking into those all-black eyes.

She picked at the tape with her fingernail. "It'll take me forever to do my homework," she complained.

"Fortunately, you have the whole weekend to do it," he said. "It's still Friday night—" he glanced at the clock "—well, Saturday morning, and there's plenty of time. Just do a little bit every few hours." He glanced left and right quickly as he ran a yellow light. "If you have a test, I could quiz you."

"No tests," Joy said. "But this totally blows my weekend."

He frowned. "You had plans this weekend?"

She didn't, but he didn't have to sound so surprised. She *might* have had plans if she'd had a life.

Dad seemed to sense that he'd stepped in it. "How about after the first pass at your homework, I take you to the mall for ice cream?"

Joy grimaced. "Looking like this?" She pointed at her face. "No, thanks."

Her dad sighed and kneaded the steering wheel. "O-kay," he said. "How about this—you invite Monica over since she's seen you already, and I'll pick up a pizza and then vacate the house? Girls' night in and Dad's gone out?" Joy tried not to brood over her father's idea that the greatest gift to her was being absent. She twiddled the eyedrops in her lap.

"That is my final offer," he added.

"All right, fine," Joy said.

"All right," her father agreed. "Fine."

Joy turned her head fully to study his balding profile in the window. The streetlights etched the worry around his eyes and the pinch of his lower lip. She sighed against the headrest. He was trying so hard. Neither of them were good at the reaching-out thing; they'd left that stuff up to Mom. But Mom was gone, and Stefan was at college, and everything had changed. Dad was the only original piece of her family she had left. Joy needed him to be the one thing that stayed.

She smiled. "Thanks, Dad."

He smiled back.

Not only was there pizza, but her father had left a carton of ice cream in the freezer with a Post-it note that said *Study Break*. Picking out the chocolate chips while dancing to satellite radio, Joy had to admit that Dad wasn't half-bad at spoiling her. She'd heard that she could expect it now that her folks were officially divorced, but this was the first time it had tasted like victory instead of leftover Chinese takeout. To Dad, dessert was love, or the next best thing. Every time he bought her a treat, Joy felt obliged to have some right away. It was Dad's way of saying "I love you" and her way of saying that she knew.

Fortunately, she liked ice cream—unfortunately, not mint chocolate chip. Mom would've known that. Stefan was the one who liked chips. Joy sighed as she made a little wet stack of brown rectangles for her brother, who wasn't there. Mom was gone, Stef was gone, but she still had ice cream and pizza and Monica. Hooray!

Joy vaulted over the couch and landed smoothly on the cushions, repositioning herself for maximum pillow access. There were a lot worse things than hanging with Monica at home watching classic chick flicks. Having Dad stick around while they watched *When Harry Met Sally* came to mind. She was actually glad that he was going out. He'd been haunting the house ever since the divorce papers were signed.

"I'm off," Dad called from the hallway with a jingle of keys.

"Night, Dad," Joy said, bouncing her feet in time to the music. She waved her mismatched blue polka-dot and pink-and-purple socks. "Have fun."

"You, too," he said. "Emergency numbers are on the door."

"Yeah. Okay."

"And don't be afraid to call the cell."

Joy leaned back and enunciated pointedly: "Good. Night. Dad!"

"Okay, okay, I'm going." His hand rested on the doorknob. "Call me if you need anything."

"Dad!" she warned.

"Bye!"

The door clicked closed. Gone.

Joy spent a few minutes clicking around the TV. Channel surfing was hard on her eye, so she shut it off, figuring she'd save it for the movies.

Hauling herself out of the couch, she went to double-cut the pizza into long triangle strips. Monica only liked to eat pizza that didn't smudge her lip pencil and Joy had adopted the habit. Now she didn't eat pizza any other way. She put her playlist on shuffle and grabbed a couple of plates.

She was singing and sawing the pizza slicer deep into grease-soaked cardboard when the phone rang. It was Monica on caller ID.

"Hey, there," Joy chirped, shouldering the cordless phone.

"Hey..." Monica hesitated.

Joy stopped slicing. "What's up?"

"Please don't kill me or make me out to be the worst friend in the world."

Joy laughed and lowered the volume. "Well, with an introduction like that, how could you go wrong?" she said, switching ears. "Spill."

"Gordon asked if I could meet him at Roxbury downtown." Monica paused, sounding unsure. It was weird. Monica was cocky and confident when it came to boys asking her out. She'd be the first to say that she'd had lots of practice. "And since we got interrupted last night by, well, you know..." Several things clicked together.

"Gordon's the guy?" Joy asked. "Mr. Wide from the Carousel?" She put down the pizza slicer.

"Yeah." Monica sounded guilty, maybe even shy. "But I told him I had plans tonight."

Joy filled in the blanks. "Plans that maybe you could get out of?"

"Only because you're my very best friend."

Joy smothered the pathetic feeling that she'd be home alone with a patch over one eye and too much food for one person. Monica sounded so hopeful. "This must be some guy."

Monica's voice warmed with relief. "I'll let you know!"

"Spare me the details," Joy said as she placed one of the plates back on the shelf. "Go have fun, and remember—don't be stupid."

"I know. No Stupid. Sorry it's last minute." Monica's voice slowed, clearly wanting to sound torn. She wasn't fooling anyone, though. Gordon won, Joy lost. Score one for Team Penis.

"Are you sure it's okay?"

"Yeah, I'm sure," said Joy. "Rock the Rox for me."

"And you go enjoy some Joy time."

"I'll try," Joy said, but Monica had already cut her off with "Bye!"

Joy hung up the phone and sighed. The last time she'd watched this movie, it'd been with her mom. There was a tight, hollow feeling in her stomach and a dry twinge in her eye. She brought her plate of pizza to the couch, tucked herself under the afghan and thumbed the remote to Play.

Well, she still had ice cream and pizza.

Hooray.

She fell asleep in the middle of *Nick and Nora's Infinite Playlist* and woke to the sound of scratching. Joy sat up, clawing at the unfamiliar obstruction over her eye. Then she remembered: Weirdo in the club. Knife. Scratched cornea. Her fingers came away from the latex weave as she adjusted to the idea of being awake.

Alone. Dark. Ditched by Monica. Decent movie. Cold pizza. The TV was a blue screen. The clock said 2:18.

The scratching came again.

Joy threw off the afghan, removing the warmth from her body. The condo felt chilly and very, very empty. The automatic thermostat was set for sixty-two. Energy-saving mode. She shivered and got to her feet, accidentally knocking cold pizza slivers onto the floor. Grumbling, she knelt and tossed them back on the plate, ruffling the thick carpet with her hand to mask the stain.

Making her way to the door, Joy wondered if Dad had lost his keys. Why didn't he just knock? Her brain waded through the fuzz. That didn't make sense. She yawned. It was late. Or early. She was too tired to think straight.

The scratching came again. But it was coming from the kitchen window.

Turning around, Joy squinted. The sky outside was a patchwork of blue-orange low-glow. The wind was blowing through the backyard. She could hear it whistling outside. Maybe a branch was scraping the glass?

There was a long, drawn-out *scrrrrrrrrrrrick!*

A large shadow with glowing eyes loomed in the dark. The eyes were shaped like arrowheads and fiery, electric white.

Joy stumbled.

The eyes slanted in amusement. There was a scratch at the glass again.

Joy's back hit the wall, her whole body tingling. The kitchen phone was still on the couch, impossibly far away. So was her voice. So was her breath. She stared, quivering.

A large palm pressed flat against the glass, thick fingers ending in points. There were only four of them. The hand flexed and dropped into darkness, but the eyes were still there, burning.

Joy blinked her one eye over and over, gripping the edge of the sliding closet door. She couldn't be seeing what she was seeing. She wanted to hide behind the coats, but she didn't dare let the thing out of her sight. If it didn't stay where she could see it, it could be anywhere.

Wake up, she told herself. *Wake up, Joy!*

The eyes narrowed. The claw reappeared and thumped dully against the glass. Once. Twice.

Joy could feel her head shaking. *No no no no.* Her fingers gripped the fake wood. *No—go away!*

The heavy hand retreated and reappeared as a fist. It struck casually, with a little more force. The window shivered. Sealant creaked. She watched the hand draw back again and slam down, spiderwebbing the first double pane.

Joy screamed on the third impact. Screamed again when the web spread. Her heart skittered as a single gray talon tapped the splintered glass, skipping on a shard or jag, white light shimmering as the finger drew words:

Joy stared at the words as they slowly flickered and died. The eyes and their owner faded from sight.

She wanted to move, bolt for her room or the couch or the phone and 911.

Smack! A bulbous nose plastered itself against the window. Joy shrieked and grabbed the flashlight out of the closet. She threw it at the broken window, knocking the light over the sink. The hanging lamp swung wildly, throwing erratic light and shadow.

The monster laughed, lips peeling back over fat brown

tusks, and slid its tongue recklessly over the shards. The mouth opened wider. Its tongue curled and shot forward, shattering a waterfall of glass.

Joy sprinted for the couch. Laughter followed her like a rusty saw through wood. She dove, clearing the cushions, tucking smoothly into a tight, upward crouch. Her fingers shook as she grabbed the phone and dialed, botching the numbers. Joy hung up, swearing, and glanced back at the window.

Nothing.

She froze.

Joy glanced around, breathing hard.

Where was it?

She squeezed the phone, shaking, refusing to let go. Behind the patch, her eye burned, salt tears stinging. She was dreaming. Wasn't she dreaming? She'd been watching old movies. She'd fallen asleep. It could have been a nightmare.

Joy peeked over the couch into the kitchen. The window wasn't webbed in shattered glass. It reflected nothing but shadows and the light above the sink.

She sank back and blinked her one good eye, feeling her heart pound. Had she just woken up? Had she grabbed the phone, half-asleep? Her body tingled with leftover adrenaline splash.

Vaguely wondering if she had subconsciously picked up some horror movie preview, she dropped the phone, glad that she hadn't dialed an emergency operator in her sleep. Joy rubbed her patch. She'd had one too many emergencies lately, thanks.

She shook out her hands and checked the clock: 2:29. Joy shivered and wondered what Dad was doing out so late. She grabbed the pizza plate—something for her hands to do—and went to dump it in the sink.

Froze.

There were shards of broken glass in the four corners of the window, like jagged photo holders.

One pane left.

The plate shattered against the floor as Joy grabbed the phone and called her dad's cell.

TWO

JOY GAVE THE SAME STATEMENT FOR THE THIRD TIME, BUNDLED in a sweatshirt and her tea growing cold. She kept forgetting to drink it. She held the mug in her hands, letting the warmth seep in. She said she'd seen a "monster face" at the window and had thrown the flashlight at it, but decided not to mention the words written in light. She remembered hearing stories of her great-grandmother seeing things, and they'd ended up putting her in an asylum. The idea of being crazy had haunted Joy throughout her childhood.

"Could've been a prank," the officer said. "Someone wearing a Halloween mask. Having any problems at school, Joy?"

"No."

"Anyone bothering you on the bus? On your way home?"

Joy rotated the #1 Dad mug in her hands. "No," she said and took a lukewarm sip.

"What happened to your eye?"

Her father glanced up at the question, too.

She set the mug down, not liking to link the two things together. "I got a scratched cornea at the Carousel—a splinter, I think. I was looking up when something fell." Joy pointed at the patch. "I have to wear this thing for two more days."

The officer glanced at her, then Dad, forehead crinkled in

a what-can-you-do ripple. He dug into his pocket and held out a business card. "Well, we didn't find anything out of the ordinary outside. We've got your statement. If you remember anything else you want to add, my number's on the card. Feel free to give me a call." He handed the card to Joy's father, who nodded.

"Thank you, Officer Castrodad," he said with a firm handshake. "I appreciate you coming out."

The policeman nodded. "Just doing my job." He cast a last look at Joy, who hid her face behind the cheap ceramic cup. "Mr. Malone. Joy." The officer let himself out.

Her father flipped the card onto the table and took a stroll around the room.

"Well, that was some excitement," he said, setting his hands on his hips. "You certainly got my attention."

Joy frowned. "You think I made this up?" She felt more angry than scared, but he was obviously angry, too.

"I don't know, Joy, did you?" he snapped. "You weren't particularly truthful with the man when he asked you about school."

"Dad—"

"No. Don't 'Dad' me," he said. "Grades slipping, quitting gymnastics and ignoring calls from your mother may be par for the course after something like this...." Mothers leaving their families for younger men in California was apparently considered a *something like this*. "All the damn books say acting out is normal, and, yes, getting suspended last year for knocking over chairs is a little rough for a zero tolerance–policy school, okay, but lying, Joy? The E.R.? Police? That's not like you. And you were lying tonight."

"I wasn't lying!" she insisted. Joy hated when he threw the

suspension in her face. That was forever ago. Just like Mom leaving, or quitting gymnastics and giving up her Olympic dreams, not to mention her entire social life.

Dad threw his keys hard into the couch. "Oh, really? Where's Monica, Joy?"

Joy gaped. "*She* ditched *me!*" she said, but knew the facts were stacked against her. "That wasn't my fault! I didn't know she was going to back out last-minute to go dance with some guy!" She squeezed her eyes shut, refusing to cry. It was so unfair! She was half inclined to tell him what had really happened yesterday, but he already thought she was a psychopathic liar.

"When I called the Reids to tell them I was on my way, I *woke them up*, Joy! Monica was asleep in bed *after* telling her parents that she'd been here all night."

Joy groaned. "So Monica's a liar and *I* get the blame?"

"Were you covering for her?"

"No!"

"Did you make this all up?"

"*No*."

He crossed his arms. "Joy, I won't be any madder than I am right now—"

"*No!*"

Dad softened a little; he was still mad, but he wanted to believe her. She could tell. They had to trust one another—they were all they had left. It was like he was thinking the same thing. He deflated over his belly.

"I get that you're angry, Joy. We're all angry. But there's defiant, and then there's reckless. The constant moping and lashing out..." He rubbed a hand over his face. "Did you break the window, Joy?" he asked softly.

"No, Dad." Joy punctuated her words with a fist on the table. Frustration shivered through her body. Why wouldn't he believe her? Her voice broke like glass. "I didn't! The outside pane's broken and we're two floors up! There was someone at the window and I was all alone *and I was so scared!*"

He wrapped her in his arms, rubbing her shoulders through the sleeves as if she were cold. Tears trapped under gauze were suddenly dripping off her chin. She sniffled as he rocked her slowly. Everything felt twisted and wrong.

"I'm sorry, Dad," she whispered, but she couldn't say what she was sorry for.

"I'm sorry, too," he said with a squeeze. "Tomorrow I'm getting an alarm. We'll both sleep better then."

She gave his forearms a last bit of hug.

"Did I ruin your date?" she asked. Joy felt her dad pause.

"Do you want me to answer that?"

She thought about it. "Not tonight."

Her dad sighed and stroked her hair. "Deal."

Monica trailed behind Joy in the hall.

"Sorry," she said. "Sorry! Sorry! Sorry!"

Joy trusted her hair to provide some cover for her anger and the frayed, peeling patch. It looked hideous, like an old wound, gummy and gross.

"You're sorry," Joy muttered. "Dad's nearly got me under house arrest." She picked at her patch in irritation, then stopped. Dad had caught her trying to remove it this morning and threatened a serious grounding. Joy hated the way she kept bumping into things and misjudging distance. Plus the nausea. And the stares in the hall. She hadn't felt this awkward since she'd dropped out of training. "I've gone from being invisible to Public Enemy Number One!"

"Sorry to infinity," Monica begged. "Sorry to infinity plus one!"

Joy thumped her head against her locker.

"Stop it," she said, working the combination. "Just tell me it was worth it."

"It was worth it," Monica said dutifully.

"Really?"

"No," Monica said. "Not if it got you into trouble." But a smile crept into her voice and over her lips. "Otherwise, yes. It was *totally* worth it!"

"Small comfort," Joy said, but added, "I'm happy for you."

"Thanks." Monica relaxed against the bank of lockers and poked at the plastic fob on Joy's key ring. "So, what's up with this?"

Joy stacked books in her arms. "Dad had a security system installed. Either he doesn't believe me and he's locking me in, or he believes me and he's locking everyone else out." Neither option sounded too appealing.

"Did you find out who it was?" Monica asked. "At the window?"

Joy felt guilty feeding Monica her cover story, but the truth was just too crazy. "No," Joy said, but something else slipped out. "It was a message."

Monica raised her eyebrows. "Mmm-hmm? Somebody whacks your window with a baseball bat and you *might* take that as some sort of message," she said. "Before we came to Glendale, my daddy was from Arkansas and he talked about growing up with all kinds of 'messages' left burning on the lawn."

"That's not what I meant," Joy said as the locker door squeaked shut.

"What? The burglar left a Post-it?"

Joy shook her head behind her hair. She was momentarily glad she had the excuse not to look at Monica; she felt as if she'd somehow said too much. Joy didn't know what *48 deer run midnight* meant, and she didn't know how to *tell ink*, but Joy could still see the glowing words and the giant tongue pressed flat against the glass. She hugged her books to her chest and scrolled through her text messages for a distraction.

Alice June Moorehead, 1550 Hewey, Apt 10C, Strwbry

4 INK: RAZORBILLS SOUTH 40 OVERPASS, 4PM—SEVER STRAIGHT & DON'T BE LATE! THX

Joy had the crazy instinct to smash her phone against the wall. She eyed the mob of students chatting and banging locker doors under a chorus of squeaky shoes and six hundred ringtones. A flash of bright orange in the crowd made Joy's head turn, but she couldn't see the source. She curled against her locker and cupped her hand over her phone's screen. She checked the numbers: both unlisted. She wished she'd programmed Officer Castrodad into her contact list.

How did these people get my number?

Monica glanced at the cell in Joy's hand. "Mom again?"

"No," Joy said. She'd been storing the rest of her mother's messages. Not playing them. Not deleting them. Not even thinking about them. Not yet. "Have you given anyone my number?"

"What? No."

"Gordon or anybody?" Joy fished. "Did he borrow your phone?"

Monica's happy face dropped several degrees, her tone dipped into low centigrade. "When I say no, I mean no. Nobody got your number from me." She frowned. "Is somebody cyber-bothering you?"

Joy killed her screen. "No. Just being paranoid." She started walking. Fast.

Monica jogged to keep up. "Somebody comes and breaks your window, that's not paranoid. That's legitimately scared. And now someone's texting you?" She sounded worried.

"Wrong number," Joy lied. "They might not be related."

"Yeah, but they might," Monica said. "Seriously, I don't want to see your name on the news and feel bad that I didn't say something." She tapped Joy's shoulder. "You tell your dad about this? About what really happened at the Carousel?"

"No," Joy muttered. "You know he'd freak."

Monica shrugged as they made for the doors. "Let him freak. It's okay to freak. Especially if things are freaky." She shook her head, jangling the gold hoops in her ears as she took the stairs. "Just tell him. Okay?"

"Yeah, okay," Joy said with a wave, but she knew she wouldn't. Dad was just coming out of that zombie state of post-marital shock and they finally had a delicate peace. Then he'd been out at 2:00 a.m. and called her a liar. She'd told Dad about the thing at the window and look what had happened! Joy wasn't about to do that again any time soon.

Joy stayed in the stairwell and clicked into Maps. There were highway 40s in Pennsylvania, Oklahoma, New York and Florida. A quick search of Alice Mooreheads turned up hits in Maine, Connecticut, Kentucky.... There were too many to be sure. Something snapped into place as she looked at the White Pages listings. A number plus a street equaled an address!

She hesitated, popping back into Maps, and typed 48 Deer Run with her thumbs. Three hits. One in Glendale, North Carolina.

Joy enlarged the image and smiled at the map. She didn't even need directions. She could practically walk there from here.

She took the stairs two at a time, determined that no one was going to mess up her life and leave her behind to pick up the pieces. This time, she was going to do something about it first.

She didn't walk, she ran. It felt good, even with too-heavy clothes and an underwire bra. Joy's feet hit the pavement with an even, steady *thud thud thud*. Her skin tingled with heat and sweat, cooled by a breeze that smelled of dry leaves. It didn't feel as good as training, but it felt better than sitting still.

She'd tied her hair back with a rubber band, missing half her bangs, and her taped-over eye made her awkwardly blind on one side, but it felt good to move, to be doing *something*. Joy grinned and added some speed.

Her feet took the corner, pounding the sidewalk squares and squashing the tiny sprigs that had dried in the cracks. She barely realized when she'd turned onto Deer Run Avenue. She slowed to a walk and placed her hands on her hips, inhaling through her nose and exhaling through her mouth, digging a knuckle into her patch as she read mailbox numbers.

Number forty-eight was a gray clapboard house tucked

into a wooded lot. Its roof was littered in pine needles and the shutters were painted dark red. Joy hesitated at the mouth of the gravel drive. Now that she was here, she didn't know what to do. Whatever might or might not have happened would have happened last night. Midnight. But everything here looked normal. Joy wiped her face with her hands. What had she expected to find?

Walking up the driveway, Joy was all too conscious of the sound of her footsteps crunching loudly on loose gravel, reminding her of shattered glass. As she approached the porch steps, she saw the first hints that something was wrong. There was a mess of overturned planters and downed hanging baskets, trampled, half-buried flowers littered the porch, and smears of what looked like mud dripped down the steps. Joy looked up at the door, also splashed with mud. The windows were intact, but there was something about them.... She didn't want to climb the stairs. She didn't want to touch the mud or the flowers or the broken pottery. Some instinct told her to back away, and she did. Joy knew that there were answers here, but if there was more to see, it was around the back of the house.

Joy had never considered trespassing before.

She hesitated, then walked quickly around the side of the garage, blood pulsing in her ears. Her steps crushed bits of stone and crispy, dead leaves. Joy kept glancing anxiously toward her blind side, afraid of getting caught.

She stopped. It was as if this was what she'd expected to see.

The back deck was destroyed. Smashed planks, broken fence posts, and wide pieces of fiberglass lay scattered in the grass. Chunks of raw wood had been gouged out of the wall with what looked like a hand rake with four tines. Joy squeezed the straps of her backpack and whirled around. Whatever it was that had been at her window had come here, too.

With one hand on the railing and the other outstretched, Joy sidestepped the splinters and pieces of glass. Easing herself around the corner, she peered into what had been the kitchen. It was demolished; the sink, counter and opposite wall were completely blown through. The floor was nothing but shattered tile and crumbly powder. Even the light fixtures were husks of busted glass, their tiny hanging wires trembling in the wind.

That's what made her look up.

The ceiling was a thick canopy of green—an enormous mandala of leaves, shoots and thorns spreading out from a decorative center medallion. Climbing ivy hugged the plaster with millipede roots, and clusters of red berries shone ripe in the dark. It was unlike anything Joy had ever seen, beautiful and eerie. It made a picture, almost like writing. She craned her head sideways, trying to make it out.

There was a blur on her blind side.

Joy spun around. The backyard was empty. A cloud moved, casting shadows and bringing a sudden scent of rain. Branches flickered. Twigs creaked. A shower of sound rustled as the wind overturned leaves.

There was a whisper of something....

A crack of wood turned her stomach cold.

Her curiosity vanished. She'd seen enough—she wanted out of here! Joy crept down the stairs, being careful where she placed her feet, and stepped off the path onto the grass.

"Excuse me?"

An old man stood on the edge of the yard wearing a soft felt hat and a long wool coat, clutching a ragged umbrella. His mismatched clothes were all the colors of brown and his face was a raisin of smiles. He hadn't been there before.

"Excuse me," he continued. "Did you see the Kodama?"

Joy swallowed her first response. While she wasn't certain what he meant, it was pretty clear the answer he expected.

"Yes," she said.

"Ah, good," he said, visibly relaxing. "It *is* you." He shuffled forward, and Joy watched him shake his head. "Bad business," he clucked and gestured offhandedly to a Japanese maple that had been recently cut down; its smell permeated the air and a large twist of rope lay coiled around the stump. "He tried to warn them, you know—tried asking for help—but do they listen? Hardly ever. Pity that." He smiled up at Joy. The man was a good deal shorter than her. His eyes were soft and his hair was the color of bone. "If you would be so kind..."

He offered her a wrinkled envelope. It looked as if it had been sat on, left in slush and dried overnight. Joy looked at the envelope and him, not knowing what to do. This didn't seem like a drug deal, but that was the only thing she could think of that made sense. Maybe this "Ink" was a dealer? Maybe she was under surveillance? Maybe this guy was an undercover cop? She glanced around the yard with her one good eye. The old man waved his envelope with an imploring smile.

"I would've waited but, you know, he's so very busy," he said almost apologetically. "And with you being here, I thought, well, it never hurts to ask." Joy still hadn't moved to take the letter. The man paused and tugged at his many layers of clothes, growing awkward and confused. His eyes suddenly lit up.

"Ah! Of course..." He hooked his umbrella over one elbow and fumbled inside his coat pocket, then tried an inner coat pocket, his jacket pocket, a shirt pocket, a vest pocket and his pants pocket before he found something that made him grin. "Here." He placed a small white shell in her palm and folded the envelope gently atop it. "With my compliments," he added, beaming. "If you listen, you can hear the ocean." He winked and made encouraging gestures. Joy held the conical shell up to her ear. There was a cold tickle of air and a tiny *whooshing* sound. She flinched. With a satisfied bow, he turned to withdraw.

"Wait!" Joy was uncertain whether she intended to say that this was all a big mistake or demand some sort of explanation, but his next words cut her short.

"If you would be so kind as to deliver that missive to Ink, young lady, I'd very much appreciate it." Then he pointed to the shell in her hand and winked. "Don't spend that all in one place!"

"Ink..." Joy began. The man stopped and turned slowly, his eyebrows twitching with a sort of itchy suspicion. "...*is* really busy," she amended quickly. "I don't know when I'll see him next...to give him this." She held up the envelope, which quivered in the wind. "And I'd hate for you to have to wait." He looked at her and then at his envelope in her hand. Joy folded it carefully. "Is there anything you'd like me to tell him? In case he asks?"

The man's face shifted. "He lets you handle the business, then?"

Joy nodded. "Yes."

His face relaxed into a gentle smile. "Oh, well, *lehman*—I'm old. What do I know?" He shook his umbrella at the envelope. "It's all written down, of course. Always best to keep records. But then, this won't involve the Bailiwick, so that hardly matters, does it?" It didn't sound rhetorical and he looked expectantly up at Joy.

"No," she said.

"Fine, fine," he said happily. "I don't mind if you read it, then. Just be sure to let Ink know." He shuffled off, pausing to pet the tree stump with a gentle hand. "Pity," he muttered and gave a sad, parting smile. "Well, good day."

"Good day," Joy said and watched the little man amble off through the trees, picking his way through the neighbor's yard and poking at the ground with his umbrella as he continued out into the woods. Joy followed. She kept her eyes on him as she circled the house, one hand outstretched, touching the wall. She squinted across the neighboring property, but between one tree and the next, he disappeared.

She backed up a step and then inched forward. She turned around. There was no one there. Nothing.

That did it.

Joy sprinted across the driveway, half-blind with tape and fear, crossing the open expanse of lawn in a rush and dashing out into the street. Kept running. She ran herself to exhaustion, finally slowing halfway between home and school. Gasping, Joy tore open the envelope and read the shaky script:

Twelve roses on her bier, as promised.
Mary Anne Thomas-Wakely, Thursday, 5:15

Love marks her twice. Let it be done.
Thank you for the honor of your service,
Dennis Thomas

She folded the paper and placed it in her backpack. It didn't sound like a drug drop. It sounded like a sweet old man ordering flowers for a grave. Joy walked home, regaining her breath. But what did any of this have to do with a gutted house, a woodland monster, a bunch of strange messages and some guy named Ink?

The answer was as elusive as a pair of all-black eyes.

Joy fumbled with her keys as she punched in the new alarm code. The security system beeped clear. Instead of feeling safer, Joy felt caged. Something was out there and she was locked in here. Alone. Now Dad didn't even have to come home from late nights at work. He could just log on to the site and check in via remote. It was worse than being invisible—it was a high-tech way of being ignored.

Dropping her backpack, Joy went to get some ice water, gulping it down painfully cold. She ground her teeth against brain freeze and filled the glass again. The kitchen window was taped over, crisscross lines obscuring the view. Dad's note on the fridge said that a repairman was coming at five. She hurried out of the kitchen to avoid standing too near the glass.

Joy wrapped herself in the afghan. She didn't know what to think about what she'd seen at the house on Deer Run, or what she'd thought of the old man out in the woods, but whatever had happened there at midnight, she didn't want it happening here.

She picked up the rumpled envelope and Officer Castro-dad's card. From her corner of the couch, Joy considered both pieces of paper. She should call. She should file a report or make a claim or whatever. But she wasn't sure what she could say that didn't involve admitting that she'd both trespassed and withheld evidence that might have prevented a crime. Did that make her an accomplice? She didn't watch enough police dramas to know for sure and wasn't eager to find out. The last thing she needed was another reason to get in trouble with the police or, worse, Dad.

She read the two strange texts on her phone again. Maybe she could tell the police to warn everyone named Alice Moorehead or to keep watch over every South 40 overpass at 4:00 p.m. But that made her sound like a terrorist. How would she explain? She didn't even know what to say, because she didn't know anything herself and it would just link her to them—whoever "they" were—with no proof that she wasn't involved. Would the police even believe her? Would anyone?

Joy sat debating what to do when the doorbell rang. As if on cue, her stomach rumbled. Monday. Dad's late day. Frozen dinner in the fridge. She'd forgotten about the repairman.

The bell rang again.

She got up, wincing around an old injury of two broken toes, and dropped the afghan on the way to the door. For the first time ever, Joy looked through the peephole, attempting to see into the hallway with her untaped eye. Colors slid up the sides of the lens, bowing out of focus and bending out of shape. Frustrated, she called through the door.

"Hello?"

She felt the second knock by her ear. Joy flipped on the lights and opened the door.

Five frail women glowed in the hall.

They were identical in that they all had long golden hair, warm, honeyed tans and the same high-cheekboned faces with tiny, button chins. They wore plain sleeveless dresses that hung down to their knees, and all five were barefoot. Their toenails were far too long.

"Ink," they said together.

Joy shook her head. Their mouths had moved, but the sound hadn't come from them. The word hadn't even sounded like a voice, but more like feedback from hidden speakers. It buzzed in her teeth.

"Um..." She felt her fingers on the doorknob. She couldn't remember how her hands worked.

"Ink," they repeated.

The world slowed, unfocusing into a fuzzy, muzzy mess. Joy tried to think of what you were supposed to do when something like this happened. Glowing, honey-colored girls appearing on the doorstep did not compute with her version of *something like this.*

"I think you have the wrong apartment," she said thickly.

"You bear his mark," they said. "We have a message for Ink."

Joy's hand still wasn't working. Everything felt slippery.

"We require a witness at Grandview Park by the head of the foot trail at 3:16 post-meridian, tomorrow." There was a pause. "Can you remember that?"

Could she? Why should she? She couldn't quite recall. Breath oozed in and out of her lungs, shaping words.

"I think so," Joy said.

"Tell him," they chimed.

"Wait," Joy managed. "Who is Ink?"

While they might be identical, they each had a unique expression of disdain.

"Don't be coy, *lehman*."

And the door swung closed under her hand.

They were gone when she opened the door a second later.

The fuzzy feeling wore off as she stomped down the hall, slammed the bathroom door and yanked off the patch.

Glue stuck in gobby smears across her cheek and above her eyebrow. Light speared a quick flash into her brain. Shaking the prescription bottle, Joy tipped back her head and dripped several cold drops onto her eyeball, runoff spilling into her ear. She blinked into the mirror, monofilament light splicing her vision. It happened every time she opened her left eye: *Flash! Flash!*

She scrubbed her face with a washcloth. Her skin burned angry pink.

Swaying on her feet, she grabbed the edge of the sink, trying to focus on her own face. There was an afterimage of something superimposed over her left eye. She blinked, trying to see it clearly—*Flash! Flash!*—no good. The rush in her ears grew louder and wilder. She felt faint.

This wasn't happening. It wasn't. She wouldn't let it.

Joy slapped off the lights as she stormed into the kitchen. She scooped up the card with Officer Castrodad's number and snagged one of the handheld phones, dialing on the way back to her room, letting her feet fuel her anger. The phone rang as she paced.

"Castrodad speaking."

"Hello. This is Joy Malone."

"Hello, Joy. How can I help you?"

She stopped suddenly, trying to catch her breath. "I don't know if you remember me. I'm the one with the broken window at one-forty Wilkes Road...." She trailed off, wondering where to begin.

"I remember," he said. "Is there something you wanted to tell me?"

"Forty-eight Deer Run," Joy said.

"I'm sorry?"

"It was written on the window. Forty-eight Deer Run. Midnight. Tell Ink." She improvised innocence. "I think it's an address for someone named Ink." The spear of light flinched in her eye: *Flash! Flash!* She thought she saw something move. A shadow danced. She shut her bedroom door with a slam. "And today, there were two weird texts on my phone." Joy crossed the room, hugging herself with one arm. "And a funny envelope and another message just now—something about a meeting at the foot trail of Grandview Park, tomorrow at 3:16."

She could hear him scribbling. "Who told you this?" he asked.

"I don't know," she said. "I don't know any of them!" Joy realized, dimly, that she was pacing again. "They just...show up."

"Would you recognize these people if you saw them again?"

Joy snorted. Like she'd forget? "Yeah."

Officer Castrodad kept writing and talking. "When did this happen?"

"Right now!" She sounded a little hysterical. Maybe because she was. Joy lowered her voice and locked her door. "Like, a minute ago," she added. "Maybe two."

"Are you alone in the house?"

Joy nodded, which was stupid since she was on the phone. "My dad works till ten." Then it clicked why he was asking. "Wait! Don't come out here! Please? I don't want him to..." She knew she should say *worry* but what she thought was *find out.* "I just thought you should know."

"No one's going to be upset with you, Joy," Officer Castro-dad said. "We just want to be sure you're safe. I'll send a car around to check out the neighborhood. Stay in a room with locks and a phone. If anything else happens, I want you to dial 911. Got it?"

Joy rubbed her arm. "Yeah, okay."

"Good. Call again if you need to—for any reason. I know this is scary, but we're on it." Officer Castrodad's voice shifted from official to empathetic. "You've done a brave thing, Joy. Don't worry. Have you got anything to keep your mind occupied?"

"I've got a history test," she muttered.

"Okay. Go study," he said. "And good luck on your test."

Joy sat on her bed, blinking. *Flash! Flash!* "Yeah...right."

She hung up and flumped against her bed. Studying was out of the question. Fear quivered under her skin—that jumpy fright-flight adrenaline dump she knew like an old friend, the rush before a competition. It made her want to run laps or do back handsprings, hard and fast, and instead here she sat, trapped in her room, with it percolating in her blood-stream, threatening to explode.

She couldn't stand it. She couldn't stand sitting still. She couldn't stand the quiet. It sounded too much like the Dark

Days of Dad's depression when she'd haunt the house on egg-shells and hide in her room. The only laughter had been Stef's. She missed him! His inside-out shirts and dorky glasses and snarky sense of humor. How could he leave her alone like this? How could she be so homesick when she was the one at home?

Joy auto-dialed Stef's dorm room, hugging her knees to her chest, stretching her legs one at a time, widening slowly into a split. She felt the burn where her muscles strained against denim. Joy bounced her feet impatiently as the phone rang, one yellow sock with smiley faces and one green sock with shamrocks. Joy needed to hear his voice. She needed to know that he was okay. She needed distraction and a little encouragement, like at State when her brother would say, "You can do this," and she'd say, "I know I can," as if saying it aloud made it true.

The phone picked up after the fourth ring.

"Hey." It was Stefan. Relief washed through her.

"Hey, Stef," she said gratefully.

"Hello?" He sounded uncertain. Joy's smile froze.

"Stef?"

"Hello? Hello?" Now Stef sounded anxious. Joy sat up, heart pounding. Had something happened?

"Stef!"

He laughed. "Ah, well, I guess I can't hear you because I'm not home right now. Please leave a message after the beep."

At the beep, Joy screamed, "Stef! That wasn't funny! I was calling you to talk about...something important...." Although now Joy couldn't decide what was most important: the creepy stalker stuff, getting stabbed at the Carousel or having just called the police. "Gimme a call when you get this, or text me before midnight. I'll be up." She eyed the window and closed the curtains. "I miss you." She hung up and drummed her feet against the sideboard.

She needed to run.

She needed to scream.

She needed to totally let loose.

Instead, Joy sat in her room, twitchy and alone.

She didn't answer the door when the repairman came; she heard the callback card slide across the tile as she watched the room grow dark. Shadows crept over the ceiling, reminding her of the plant thing spread over the ceiling at Deer Run. She didn't turn on the light. She didn't turn on her music. She wanted to keep an eye and ear out for anything. Everything. Just in case.

Flash! Flash!

What was going on? Who was Ink? And what were these... *people*...doing leaving messages, coming to her home? How was she supposed to find out anything when she didn't *know* anything?

She lay in the dark with the phone on her chest, scared to death, listening.

THREE

"YOU LOOK LIKE CRAP," MONICA SAID.

"Thank you," Joy grumbled as she spun the dial on her locker. She'd waited half the night for the police to come knocking or Officer Castrodad to call back or, better yet, Stef. But no one had called. Not even monsters. She shook her head against the fog in her brain. "Couldn't sleep."

"Aww. Well, at least you have *both* eyes half-open," Monica said. "That's an improvement."

Joy glared at the lock. *Flash! Flash!* She sighed.

"There's something wrong with my eye," she said. "I keep seeing these bits of light. It's annoying." Joy resumed twisting her combination. "I told Dad about it this morning and he said if it doesn't clear up by the end of the week, he'll take me to the ophthalmologist."

Joy opened her locker and noticed the photo of her and Stefan taped on the inside of the door. He'd written, *Keep strong!* in silver marker, which Joy once thought had been an attempt at brotherly wisdom before realizing that he'd probably known about Mom's affair roughly six months before she did. She frowned. Why hadn't he told her then?

Why hadn't he called back?

That's when she noticed a slip of paper tucked beneath the magnetic photo frame.

Joy pulled it out. The paper was thin, almost transparent, with pale brown handwriting. Her fingers left oil spots where she touched it. Folded inside the message was a perfectly pressed four-leaf clover.

Bairn Madigan, Phineas Dorne. Bantry, West Cork
Mark't un ryghte mit spare pointe, reg. Umber #4
Curse o' the Isles be on it.

Monica leaned in. "What's that?"

"Nothing." Joy stuffed the note and clover into her pocket. The icy-hot shiver down her spine might have been anger or fear. This was going too far. How had these people found her locker? How had they gotten the note inside? This was evidence. Harassment. Maybe there'd be fingerprints?

A dull pulse throbbed behind her nose and heat flushed her face. No. She was *not* going to cry!

Joy slammed her books around, catching her sweater on the notebook spiral and banging the door shut.

"You sure you're okay?" Monica asked.

"Nothing twelve hours of sleep couldn't cure," Joy lied.

"O-kay," Monica said as they started walking. "So ask me about last night."

"How was last night?" Joy asked dutifully.

"Gordon-ocious!"

Joy smirked despite herself. "You've been waiting all morning to say that, haven't you?"

"I practiced in the car."

"For real?"

"For real."

"Is this love?" Joy asked.

"Maybe," Monica said slyly. "And a little bit lower."

Even distracted, Joy could appreciate Monica's delight in smarm. "Well, I'm glad you and your hormones are happy."

Monica stood up straighter and adjusted an earring. "I am happy," she said, sounding surprised. "Who'd've thunk it? Gordon Weitzenhoffer makes me happy!"

"Weitzenhoffer?" Joy snorted.

Monica tried to look unruffled. "It's German."

"It's hideous," Joy said. "Monica Weitzenhoffer?"

"*He's* gorgeous."

"Gordon-ocious, so I'm told."

"It completely makes up for the miserable last name."

"Good thing, too," Joy said, pointing left. "Off to precalc."

"Later, lady."

They parted and Joy sighed, chest tight. Monica had found an actual *boyfriend* the night she'd been stabbed in the eye. How fair was that? And what had she gotten? Monsters at the window, glowing girls at the door, a flash in her eye and a note in her pocket. Joy took out the piece of paper and smoothed it against the wall, then snapped a picture with her phone for insurance. She'd forgotten to ask Officer Castrodad for a text address. She'd have to send the pic when she got home.

Somebody thought she knew something. Obviously they hadn't heard that she was always the last to know anything. Joy stomped up the stairs with all the unknown questions and half answers fluttering uncomfortably under her stomach.

And even with a four-leaf clover, she totally blew the history test.

* * *

Joy slammed the front door.

Fixated on her impending F, Joy completely forgot about the alarm system until the moment before sirens blasted both her ears. She punched in the code while swearing loudly. In the ringing after-silence, her skin crawled and her eye twitched: *Flash! Flash!* Dad's increased security was doing nothing for her nerves.

The phone rang. She gave the operator her name and code number, apologized and said everything was okay.

But everything was *not* okay.

Joy could all but feel the thin note crinkle in her pocket as she clicked through the call history. Joy hit redial. It connected on the second ring.

"Officer Willis speaking. May I help you?"

Joy hesitated at the pleasant-sounding female voice. "Um...I think I have the wrong extension."

"Were you calling the police station?"

"Yeah, but I was looking for Officer Castrodad," Joy said, rooting for the business card on the side table. "Officer Gabriel Castrodad?"

"Officer Castrodad isn't here today. My name is Officer Willis. Can I help you?"

"I don't know," Joy said. She knew what to say to Officer Castrodad, but now she was improvising. "He was looking into something for me and I thought he was going to call me back."

"Oh." Officer Willis sounded a little flustered herself. "Well, he's out on leave, actually. If you can give me some of the details, I can look up your file. What's your name?"

Joy ignored the question. "He's on leave? Like on vacation?" she said. "What? Now?"

"No, he's not on vacation," Officer Willis said. "He's taken a leave of absence. I don't know when he might be back, so I'm handling—"

"When he *might* be back?" Joy interrupted.

"—so I'm handling his caseload," Officer Willis said stubbornly. "May I have your name, please?"

Joy's insides seized up with an odd prickle of premonition. "No, thank you," she whispered and quickly hung up. She wasn't sure if it was a good idea to hang up on the police, but she felt eerily guilty. Something was wrong.

Joy opened her computer, typed his name and hit Search. The answer popped up in a brief news blurb:

Officers were dispatched to Grandview Park at approximately 3:30 p.m. Wednesday afternoon to apprehend local policeman Officer Gabriel Castrodad, 42, who was arrested for brandishing his weapon without cause. The park was quickly evacuated and Castrodad was taken into custody without resisting arrest.

Officer Castrodad's sister, Emilia Castrodad, was called into the precinct to translate for the twice-decorated officer, who refused to give testimony in either Spanish or English. Ms. Castrodad explained that her brother had been speaking Rarámuri, the native language of the Tarahumara, Castrodad's first language, which he'd learned from his grandmother, a native of Cerocahui, Chihuahua.

"But I have never heard him speak a word of it since he was very small," she told reporters on Thursday.

Officer Castrodad was immediately relieved of duty pending a psychiatric evaluation and indefinite leave of absence due to traumatic stress.

Joy read the words twice, a vague horror creeping up her spine. She was the one who had sent him to Grandview Park. Whatever had happened, it was because of *her*—she'd caused it. It was her fault. That could have been her—or Dad—because she'd answered the door! Because of those women. Because of this Ink.

Digging in her pocket, she found the tiny brown note and, separating it from the clover, tore it to shreds. Wiping the cascade of confetti into her wastebasket, she debated using matches. Joy did the same with the crumpled envelope, tearing it into smaller and smaller pieces. She took out her phone and deleted the pic. Then the weird messages. All of it. Delete. Delete. Done.

She started scanning online for more about what had happened at Grandview Park or Officer Gabriel Castrodad or any connection to anybody named Ink. She lost herself in searching—there *had* to be more! Her eyes watered from staring at the screen. Nothing. Nothing but wrong leads and dead ends. She IM'ed Stef. Nothing. Called again. Left a message. Checked her cell. Her email. Her chat boxes. Nothing. Nothing. Nothing. Nothing.

She opened her cache and trashed the entire history.

"Joy?" Her father's voice spooked her out of her trance. The clock read 6:26.

"Crap." She jumped up from the chair. "Sorry...!"

"It was your turn to cook," he said as his keys hit the table.

"Sorry sorry sorry," she said as she clicked windows closed and shut off her screen. "I was online."

"For three hours?" Her dad appeared in the hallway, still wearing his coat. He didn't look pleased.

"Um...yeah."

"I think I should listen to the talk shows and yank that thing out of your room."

"I have to do my homework," Joy said.

He crossed his arms and leaned in the doorway. "Were you doing your homework?"

"Um, no," she admitted.

"That tears a small hole in your argument."

"Dad..."

"Never mind." He sighed. "I hate to reward negligence, but I'm starving. Grab your shoes and let's eat out."

"Saigon?" Joy asked hopefully.

"You wish," he said. "Subway or KFC?"

Joy pulled on her coat. "No fried foods," she reminded him.

"Subway it is."

In the car, Joy watched her father as he drove, noticing the deep wrinkles by his eyes: smile lines and worry. She debated telling him about last night and the glowing visitors at the door. Maybe tell him there'd been strange texts on her cell, a note in her locker, a man in the woods, that she'd called Officer Castrodad, trespassed on a crime scene, and confess that it had been a black-eyed boy and not a splinter that had sent her to the emergency room. That she was scared. That she was lonely. That she was going to fail history this semester. But she knotted her fingers in her lap and sat quietly in the passenger seat, unable to find the words, afraid to rock their fragile boat. Joy settled on feeling oddly proud that she had inadvertently forced Dad to eat something healthy for once.

He had never talked about her eating habits while she'd been training for competitions, so she wasn't about to start lecturing him now. Besides, she could have said something a year ago. Six months ago. Looking at him forty pounds later, it was clearly too little, too late. Like quitting gymnastics or dropping her blog or Joy's mother leaving—when some things went unsaid long enough, they got way too big to talk about now.

They ordered dinner and sat down, chewing and slurping soda noisily through too much ice and not enough syrup. Joy debated life's tiny cruelties as she stabbed her straw to the bottom of the cup.

"So Monica has a new boyfriend?" her dad said into the quiet.

"Fresh out of the box," Joy said. "Name's Gordon."

"Sounds old," he muttered.

"He's our age," Joy said while thinking that she didn't really know his age, and that he had looked older in the half-light. It had been an Under 18 Night, but of course, everybody knew that some older guys came to hook up with younger girls. She'd have to remember to ask Monica about it. They hadn't talked that much lately.

"How about you?" he said, interrupting her thoughts.

"How about me?"

Her father took a huge bite and had to chew and swallow first. "Do you have a boyfriend?"

"Dad!" Joy cried.

"What? Can't a father ask?"

She sucked noisily at the last drops of her drink. "I think there might be some law against it." It was easier to hide behind banter armed with a straw. She fumbled it around the ice some more.

"So, no guy?"

"No guy," she quipped. "Not even one stashed under the bed."

Dad groaned. "That's not funny."

Joy wrinkled her nose. "It's a little funny."

"That's a little funny like being a little grounded."

"Hey!" Joy said. "Seriously, Dad, no guy. I've got no guy, I have no beau, I have no boyfriend—there, I said it. Happy?"

"Okay, okay," he said, wiping his mouth with a napkin. "I wanted you to know that if there was a guy, I'd want to meet him," he added. "I'm your father and if some boy wants to date my daughter, I would have to meet him...if there was a guy."

Joy popped her cup down on the laminate. "What's all this about guys?"

"Nothing," he said testily. "Just making conversation."

"Because you're hardly one to talk seeing as we're both dateless wonders...." Joy's voice trailed off as she saw her father's face: a mix of hope and guilt. "No," she whispered, the truth finally dawning. "You have a date? Last Saturday—the late night—you had a *date?*"

"I had a date," he confessed.

"I thought you were out playing poker with guys from work!"

Dad scoffed. "When was the last time I played poker with the guys?"

"Is she...?" Joy tried to make the word fit her mouth. "Your *girlfriend?*"

He raised a hand to whoa. "Now, hang on—no one said anything about 'girlfriend'—just friends. Friends who went out on a date to...find out if there was something more."

Joy watched her own fingers play with a balled-up napkin, recycled brown paper twisting over her knuckles.

"So this was just a friends thing?" she asked. "Not a date-

date?" Her father looked as rattled as she felt. She twisted the napkin tighter, a matching feeling in her chest. It had been an innocent question! They never talked about stuff like this. Why here? Why now? She didn't want to be having this conversation. In this restaurant. At this table. They were in *public,* for Pete's sake! Other people were watching, listening, like the old guy behind the Plexiglas sneeze guard wearing the white paper hat—he knew as much about her father's love life as she did!

"Is this the real reason for your late nights at work?" Joy asked.

"No, no. No more office romances for me," he said. The words hit her like a slap. Joy knew her mom and dad had met at the office. She stirred her straw around the hurt. "Just trying to get ahead at work. You know what they say, 'If you can't be a yes-man...'"

"'...be indispensable,'" Joy muttered. It was cruel to use one of her mother's old sayings right then. "So what's her name?" she asked hollowly.

"Shelley."

"Shelley?" Joy repeated. "As in Michelle, or is her name really Shelley?"

"I don't know," her dad admitted, chewing. "I didn't ask."

"How could you not ask?" Joy said. Had they been talking on this date, or doing something else? She scrubbed that mental image. *Ew.*

"Well, are you going to ask?" she said.

"Is it important?"

"Yes. No," Joy snapped. "I mean, are you going to see her again?"

"Well, not just to ask about her name..."

"Dad!"

"Yes," he said, finally, with a strange look on his face. "Yes, Joy. I want to see her again. But I want you to meet her when I do."

Her stomach fell, a punched hole through her seat. A circle of her insides and recycled molded plastic should have been lying on the floor.

"Is it serious?" Joy asked.

"Not yet," her dad said. "Maybe not ever." He folded his napkin carefully into fourths. It crinkled softly, muffled under his hands. "But you're my family and I wanted you to know."

Joy examined the lines of her paper cup even though she couldn't really see them. Her eyes were open, but nothing registered. Ice sloshed around like kaleidoscope beads.

"Does Stef know?" she asked.

"Not yet."

That was something. Petty, but something. This time, whatever it was, she knew it first.

The need to talk to Stef burned in her throat.

Joy looked at her father, the worry creasing his hands and the corners of his mouth. This was too hard. She wanted to give him a break. But it hurt more than she'd thought it would.

"So..." she said, "this wasn't really about you meeting my theoretical guy as much as me meeting your actual girl?"

"Something like that," he admitted. "So what do you think?"

What did she think? Her thoughts were a jumble.

Mom. Dad. Doug. Shelley. Gordon. Monica. What did she think? *What about me?*

She gazed out the window, seeing the spark zip by each time she blinked. Shots of color winked orange and purple, silver and white, echoes of shadows and carousels and all-black eyes. Her mind whirled.

What did she think?

"I think I have to go to the doctor."

Dad frowned. "You feel sick?"

"No, just that bit of light whenever I blink," she said. "It's annoying."

There was a long pause. The only sound was the rumble of ice cubes inside her paper cup.

"I'll make an appointment," he said softly and stuffed their trash into the bag. Standing up, Joy instantly wished that she could take it back, rewind and record over, but then, she wished that about a lot of things.

They got in the car and, just like that, everything went back to being unsaid.

FOUR

JOY DRIFTED THROUGH THE SCHOOL DAY. SHE BARELY LISTENED as Monica chattered endlessly about Gordon Weitzenhoffer, age seventeen and a half. No word from Stef. No email, no text, no IM, nothing. He had a new answering message recorded during a loud party. It sounded like he was having fun. Her brother hadn't been half this popular when he'd lived at home. Instead of feeling happy for him, Joy wanted to smack him with her phone.

She'd been stabbed with a knife, weirdos were stalking her and Dad was dating some unknown person named Shelley. Joy knew Stefan would somehow understand, but if he was busy with some new girlfriend, it might be weeks before he remembered to call. And if Dad hooked up with this Shelley person, then *he'd* be busy, and Monica would marry Mr. Gordon-ocious, and Joy would end up living alone in an attic apartment with too many cats.

Returning home, Joy punched in her code and found a plate of cookies on the kitchen counter, proof that last night's father–daughter bonding over Subway sandwiches had met with Dad's approval. She snagged two, stuffing one in her mouth as she vaulted the couch. She welcomed the slightly sick, stuffed feeling of eating unhealthily on purpose, and promised herself she'd have something low-calorie for dinner. Sugar never tasted as good as gymnastics felt. She ate the second cookie just to smother the guilt.

Joy cracked open her homework. It started to rain. Around six-thirty, she made a frozen Lean Cuisine and ate while reading about the French Revolution. She wiped a spot of marinara off the textbook page and tried to ignore the sound of frightened squirrels on the roof.

There was a skittering of tiny nails, a nervous tickle across the ceiling. She followed the sound with her eyes. Being on the second floor meant that she was used to the local wildlife using the roof as a communal playground and convenient highway between trees. The *pok-pok* of acorns and drumming rain against the shingles often forced her to wear earphones to bed.

The noises made her twitchy. She couldn't concentrate. Pushing back from the table, Joy washed her knife and fork in the sink. Wind and rain pelted the new window, copious steam obscuring the glass. Scrubbing, Joy wondered what was on TV, but as soon as she shut off the water, she heard the squirrel sound again.

But it wasn't on the roof. It was inside the building.

Something scrabbled past the front door and faded down the hall. Every hair on her arms rose and all her senses cringed. She didn't believe for a moment that it was a squirrel. But instead of fear, she felt a hot flare of rage.

Joy slammed down her dish. She'd had it! If this was another one of those creepy things with a message for Ink, she was going to tell it to leave her alone! If it was small, maybe she could scare it. Maybe it would just go away.

She grabbed the broom just in case.

The hallway was nearly dark, lit only by a failing fluorescent light. She stepped out onto the old, flat carpet beaten down by years of feet. The moldy smell normally hidden under air fresheners was newly kicked up by the storm. There was no noise now save the applauding gush of rain. Joy cautiously leaned farther into the hall and glanced both ways.

The small window at the end of the hall was propped open. The baseboard dripped rainwater and there was a puddle on the floor.

"You."

Joy ducked, already knowing that it was too late. She was only half surprised to be pushed into the wall by something vaguely resembling a human-size bat. Nostril slits puckered between its enormous yellow-green eyes and a wide mouth split its football-shaped head as it spoke.

"You are the Scribe's." Its voice was gravelly, menacing. "*Lehman* to Ink."

Impossibly long fingers wrapped clear around her throat, cutting off her voice. The horrible face glared at her with its wet, bulbous eyes.

The broom clattered against the floor.

She choked out, "I...don't..."

"Tell him—tell your master that Briarhook is waiting. Mustn't be kept waiting," the thing emphasized with a brain-rattling shake. "Hear?"

Joy nodded, fingers scratching against his knuckles, pulling for air.

"Yes," she croaked with tears in her eyes. "Yes!"

The creature released her with a shove, banging her head against the wall. Colors sparked and wobbled. Her tears were more fear than fight. She stared after it as her vision cleared.

Skeletal arms hung from its bony, gray shoulders, with pink scar tissue blooming over its back and ribs. The wide head sneered as he turned. "Don't dally like you did for the *guilderdamen*. Won't stand for it," he warned. And with a sniff, he clambered up on the windowsill and leapt silently over the edge.

Joy propped herself against the wall as if it were the only solid thing in the world. Her legs were boneless beneath her, her breathing quick and shallow. A tingling swept over her limbs, all pins and needles, and there was a sudden taste of nausea in her mouth. Joy swallowed, took a deep breath and lunged through the door, slamming it closed, flipping locks and punching the alarm's safety code with shaking, spastic fingers.

Joy slid to the floor. She started crying and, as soon as she realized it, stopped. Her face felt hot. Her eyes hurt. Her neck stung with what felt like a million tiny paper cuts. She rubbed her throat and coughed.

This wasn't real. It couldn't be real....

She'd been thinking that a lot lately.

Stumbling to the bathroom, Joy switched on the lights and craned her chin back to look at her neck. Tiny cuts wound across her throat, nips in her flesh like thin tire tracks. She scrubbed at them, first with her fingers, then with a washcloth. They looked angry and red.

She threw the washcloth into the sink. Balling her fists, she screamed. Shaking, wet, horrified, she screamed again. She yanked out her hair tie, tears pouring out of her eyes as she trembled and kicked the cabinet in helpless rage.

Joy ran to the kitchen. The new sheet of glass reflected the pelting darkness. She threw out her arms.

"STOP IT!" she screamed. *"LEAVE ME ALONE!"* Joy shrieked her throat raw. "I don't know *what* you're talking about! I don't know *who* you're talking about! I don't know anyone named *Ink* and I have *no idea what the HELL is going on!"*

"That was an aether sprite," said a voice behind her. Joy spun around to stare into a pair of all-black eyes. The boy gave a bored shrug from just inside the front door. "And he was looking for me."

"You!" she shouted. It was the psycho from the dance floor. In her house. Joy blinked in half-remembered pain. "You're Ink?"

"I am Indelible Ink," he said. "My sister is Invisible Inq." He pronounced her name with a clipped "q" as he pushed off the doorframe. "Personally, I call her Impossible Inq." He gave a humorless smile. Joy didn't know what to do. Panic lodged in her throat.

Ink stepped forward.

"Don't," she said.

He stopped.

"What would you do?" he asked. "Kill me?" Joy stared at him—at his whiteless eyes—without saying a word. She weighed her options and snatched the phone from its stand.

"Get out," she said. "Get out or I'll call the police!"

Flash! Flash!

Ink was gone in the blink of light.

"Yes, well, what good would that do?" he asked from behind her, frighteningly close. Joy choked and stumbled sideways as she turned around. Tilting his head, Ink calmly took a seat at the kitchen table. Joy watched him move, sinuous and serious. His boyish face looked harsh in the overhead light. "No one can see me," he said. "No one but you."

Impossible. It was all impossible.

"I came to talk," he said.

"About what?" she asked cautiously. Joy held the phone in her hand but didn't want to make any sudden, telling moves.

"About that night at the Carousel."

She glared at him. "You mean the night when you stabbed me in the eye?"

"About what has been happening *since* that night," he amended.

"The messages?" She swallowed, wetting her voice. "Those were for you?"

His voice was as expressionless as his eyes. "Yes, but they should never have come to you. That was a mistake. *My* mistake," he said bitterly. "One of many mistakes."

Joy gave a little laugh and gestured with the phone.

"Aren't you going to say you're sorry?"

Ink leaned into the back of the chair. "My only regret is that I did not take your eyes. Blind of the Sight, you might have been spared all this."

Joy gaped, mind blank. This stranger had just admitted that he'd tried to blind her with a knife! And he'd said it so casually. As if he could do it anytime.

"You're being perfectly awful, you know that?" a new voice said from the bedroom hall. His Goth sister walked quietly into the kitchen. She hadn't come through the door. Her eyes and long lashes were as black as Ink's, but her smile held a kindness. "Look," she said. "You're scaring her."

Light moved strangely around Inq. Slithering calligraphy swarmed over her skin. Strange designs moved like living watermarks, like pale worms, writhing. It made Joy queasy to watch.

Inq smiled wider, crinkling her wide, fathomless eyes. "Sorry. This is his own fault—and he knows it—so it's making him surly."

"Stop," Ink warned her.

"You see?" Inq said. "Surly."

Inq stared at Joy, running her fingers over the edge of the counter as if caressing Joy's arm. "Still, now that we're stuck with each other, I suggest we make the most of it."

Joy slammed the phone onto the counter and quit considering the steak knives as potential weapons. It sounded like the sister could be reasoned with. And, besides, now the odds were two to one.

"Will one of you tell me what the hell is going on?" Joy asked as she ticked off her fingers. "Who are you? What are you doing here? And what do you want with me?"

"It isn't really about you," Inq started to say.

"Oh, but it is!" her brother interrupted. He turned his accusation to Joy. "You saw us at the Carousel."

"I didn't see anything—"

"He means you saw *us*," Inq explained.

Joy frowned. "What? I'm not allowed to look at you?"

"Wrong question." Inq scooped Joy's phone off the kitchen counter and flipped it playfully. Before Joy could protest, Inq held it up and gave Joy an impish grin.

"If it makes you feel any better..." Inq flashed a huge smile and snapped a picture of herself. Glancing at the phone, she handed it back to Joy. "Here. See for yourself." Joy did. There was nothing on the screen but the auto-flash bouncing off the wall, catching the corner of a picture frame directly behind where Inq stood.

"Is this some sort of trick?" Joy asked. "And that somehow gives you permission to cut out my eye?"

"Technically, yes and no," Inq admitted, leaning against the breakfast bar. She had the same spiky hair and liquid eyes as her twin, but she wore a corset of gunmetal gray and layers and layers of black, lacy clothes. She looked like an upscale street kid or somebody terribly, tragically hip. "There's no trick. Simply put, very few people like you can see people like us, and there's an old rule that says if someone like us ever comes across someone like you, we should remove your Sight, one way or another." Inq shrugged. "True Sight is rare, but often runs in families, sometimes skipping a generation or two. Sound familiar?" Joy's stomach lurched. Great-Grandma Caroline might have actually seen things that were all too real. And she'd been locked away for life. "My brother might have gone to extremes, but he's right—you might have thanked him in the long run."

"Thanked him?" Joy shouted. "Screw him! And screw you!" Terror had a taste in the back of her throat. "Get out of my house!"

"You cannot banish us," Ink said softly. "The fact that you are even able to see us puts all of us, including you, at risk. Removing the Sight might have let you live a normal life."

"Minus eyes!" Joy spat.

Ink tilted his head. "A more normal life," he amended. "More normal than the one you will have now."

"That's all in the past," Inq said. "*No mas.* Capice? Ink didn't blind you—he missed. Instead of taking your eyes, he accidentally marked you." She lifted her small hand up to one midnight eye. Her hands were perfect and perfectly smooth. No knuckles. No fingernails. Like a doll's. She gazed at Joy through the space between her fingers. "You wear it on your face."

Joy touched her cheek. A trick of light caught her eye. *Flash! Flash!* Was that what she'd seen in the mirror?

"You've been touched by a Scribe," Inq continued, "and since no one ordered that you be marked, you've been imprinted as his. As belonging to Ink." She turned and regarded her brother sitting at the kitchen table. "He's had to claim it was on purpose, that he chose you as his own, so that no one learned of the mistake." Her voice grew quiet. "We are not permitted mistakes." Inq switched her infinite eyes to Joy. "So we must find a way to work together. It would go poorly for everyone otherwise."

Joy didn't understand half of what Inq was saying, and she didn't like the sound of the other half. "Look, I'm sorry," she said, not feeling very sorry, "but I think everybody has me confused with someone else." She looked desperately from Inq to Ink. "I have no idea what you're talking about. I've never seen anything weird until last Friday night and—no offense—but I didn't mean to see you and, frankly, don't want to see either of you ever again. So, if you don't mind, can we just forget this ever happened and will you please *leave?*"

She'd meant it as an order, but it came out more like a plea. She knew she should call the police or hit the red emergency button or simply scream for help, but Joy clung to the insane hope that these two might go away quietly if she said or did the right things. Besides, there was an unspoken threat that she couldn't stop them if Ink and Inq decided to get ugly.

Ink spread his hands on the table. They were smooth and unearthly against the polished wood.

"Let me explain," he said. "We are Scribes. Our job is to draw *signaturae*."

"*Signaturae?*" Joy echoed.

"Special marks. Symbols worn upon the skin," Inq explained.

Joy frowned. "Why?"

"To keep track of who is who," Inq said archly, "and, more importantly, whose is whose." She reached her arms over her head in a lazy stretch. "Once upon a time, our people and yours shared this world. We were tied to certain territories and a few chosen bloodlines, bound together to safeguard the world's magic from corruption and decay. Nowadays, with so little unspoiled land left, we require far more people to anchor the magic and maintain the balance." She drew something on the counter with her finger. "We use *signaturae* to mark those who are ours the way the land was once ours, those who share a little bit of magic, identifying who is connected, who can be claimed and who is strictly off-limits."

Ink held up a hand. "We take orders and place a *signatura* upon a person," he said, choosing his next words carefully. "A human, according to ancient laws." Joy shivered. They weren't human—that much was obvious, but Ink saying it aloud put it out there for real. "But a *signatura* must be given willingly and only to those who qualify. Our work safeguards our people from corruption and signifies that the chosen human is protected, formally claimed by one of the Folk. It is a message to others—touch this human, and you risk offending their patron and upsetting the balance. A *signatura* gives fair warning of whom you might cross."

Joy turned his words over like a snow globe in her head,

her thoughts scattered and shaken. "But no one asked you to mark me?"

Ink looked away. "No."

"Anyone can order a mark." Inq played with a bead of water. "At least, anyone who takes an interest and makes a legitimate claim and pays the fee," she said. "But that's not important. What *is* important is that there are very few who can place others' *signaturae* onto living flesh. As Scribes, our job is to take orders from the Folk and make a mark in their stead. We are their instruments by proxy. *Per procurationem.* In absentia. *In loco deus.*" She flicked the bead of moisture, sending a spray over the laminate. "You understand now why we can never make mistakes."

Joy pointed to her eye. "But this was a mistake."

"Not if Ink claims that he has chosen you for himself," Inq said. "It doesn't happen often, but any of the Folk can claim a special little someone for themselves."

"By stabbing them in the eye?" Joy said. "How romantic."

Inq cast a catty glance at her brother. "His heart clearly wasn't in it."

Ink frowned and kept his eyes on the table.

Joy crossed her arms. "But why mark me at all?"

"Humans are dangerous," Ink said darkly. "And one with the Sight is the most dangerous of all."

"The Folk are few," Inq added. "Detection makes them skittish. We exist as a buffer between our worlds." Her eyes flicked over Joy. "We protect our people from taking unnecessary risks."

"By *stabbing people with knives?*"

Inq laughed. "Not always," she said. "In fact, I don't need

anything but these." She spread her hands before her; images swirled and the air bowed like warped glass.

Joy glared at Ink. "And you?"

For an answer, Ink drew out a long leather wallet attached to his belt by a silver chain. Unfolding it, he revealed a number of strange implements: a scalpel, a straight razor, a silver quill, a glassy black arrowhead, a sleek metal wand and a wooden handle ending in a single fat spike.

"She is Invisible Inq," he said. "Her marks are not meant to be seen—they exist below the skin. I am Indelible Ink and my marks are meant to be obvious, permanent, there for everyone to see." He glared at her. Joy felt it in her scratched cornea. She tried very hard to ignore the sharp objects spread out on her kitchen table and the intense way he stared deep into her eyes.

"You marked me," she whispered.

"Not intentionally."

"No," she said, finding her voice. "You *intentionally* tried to blind me!"

"Yes. And I failed. Now you wear my *signatura,* and everyone can see it." Each sentence was clipped, hard, almost an accent in its precision. His anger might have been with himself or her. Ink waved a hand as if to dissipate something between them. "I had not realized that some might see this as an opportunity to circumvent the Bailiwick. That is why they have been coming to you with messages, requests—there are those who believe they will find special favor through you because they believe that you are mine."

Joy flung her arms out and shouted, "That's because you *told* them I was yours!"

Ink's eyes grew impossibly darker. "I never thought..."

he started, then sighed. "I would have come sooner if I had known."

"It had to be done," Inq said. "If anyone knew that there had been a mistake, that a *signatura* had been given in error, all our work would be put into question." She gestured off-handedly to Joy. "You would be killed as a matter of course, to save face—a human with the Sight is especially dangerous, after all—and my brother and I might be judged obsolete and destroyed. You wouldn't want that, would you?" She pouted dramatically. "Come now. This way you have status, a place in our world and considerable protection, and Ink keeps his reputation. Everybody wins." Her voice pitched lower. "Know that this thing has never happened, not in all these years—instead of an error, it would merely be seen as about time Ink chose a *lehman* for himself." Inq didn't hide her smirk. Her brother did not share it.

"*Lehman?*" Joy said. The word sounded familiar. "What does that mean?"

Inq shrugged as she considered the overhead lights. "A human who has been chosen by one of our kind. Confidante, contact, significant..."

"Slave," Ink said dully.

"What?" Joy snapped.

"Or lover," Inq added. "It loses something in translation."

"No," Joy said. "No way!" Pretending to be his...whatever... was *so* not happening! Joy glanced desperately at Ink. "Just take it back, all right? Fix it." She pointed at her left eye, which flashed as she talked. "Can't you undo this?"

"Not even to take out your eye," Ink said as he folded his wallet back into thirds. "That option is now closed. Since you are mine, I would have to explain why I would maim you so soon after claiming you, unless for my own amusement." He smoothed the leather flat. "It is not unknown to happen, but I am without precedent and not known for malice." His attention turned to Inq. "Evidently, I have a reputation to think of."

Inq circled around the counter, approaching Joy with tentative steps.

"It's merely a ruse, a title to spare your life. You see now that this is the best way?" Inq asked. "We did not mean to do you harm."

"He tried to cut out my eye!" Joy yelled, pointing at Ink.

"Sometimes, we must choose immediately unpleasant things in order to prevent greater unpleasantness," he said flatly. Joy bristled. Ink barely noticed. "It is nothing personal," he added. It sounded as if he regretted the situation far more than Joy.

"See?" Inq said, smiling. "One big happy. We can work together, right?"

Joy dropped her eyes, massaging her palm with her thumb. Pretend to be a pseudo–sex slave for a supernatural freak or end up either blind or dead. Was this a choice? Her maimed eye split the light—*Flash! Flash!* She sighed.

"So what do I have to do?"

Inq patted her arm. Joy tried not to shrink from her touch. "We're not certain yet," Inq said. "While we figure it out, Ink will bring you along with him sometimes so that you can be seen in his company. Try to appear...together." Joy couldn't help glancing at Ink. He stared pointedly at the fridge. "It's just for a little while," Inq soothed. "Keep quiet, act natural and, after a time, the novelty will fade and no one will question why you are no longer with us."

An unsettling chill crept up Joy's spine. She didn't like the way Inq said that last part. Was that a threat? And, if it was, what could she do about it?

A parental voice whispered in the back of her mind, *If you can't be a yes-man, be indispensable!*

"I'm sure I could do something useful," Joy said quickly. "I could help. I could learn."

"You cannot even take a message," Ink muttered.

"That's unfair," Inq said, stepping closer to Joy. "She had no idea what the messages were, nor for whom. She was frightened, poor girl." Inq petted Joy's hair. Joy stood very, very still. Inq played with a curl. "Something unfortunate might have happened," she cooed.

"Is that what happened to the policeman?" Joy asked, sliding from under Inq's hand.

Ink sighed. "Who?"

"Officer Castrodad," Joy said. "Gabriel Castrodad? He went to Grandview Park after the glowing girls left."

Ink glanced at Inq. "'Glowing girls'?"

His sister coughed, attempting to smother giggles, but soon erupted in rich belly laughter. "The *guilderdamen!*" she crowed. "Glowing girls—*hahaha!*" Inq clapped her hands together, delighted. "Oh, this will be fun! I'm tempted to steal you away from my brother just for that!" Inq laughed harder. Joy cringed. Ink grinned without humor.

"Ah, the witness," Ink said. "There was a man who was meant to see the Rising. I was supposed to mark him as theirs, a witness to their majesty." He cocked his head, a gesture similar to Inq's. "But since I was not present to mark him at the manifestation of the *guilderdamen*, I suspect he went mad." Ink spoke with a hint of accusation. "They are an awesome and fearsome thing to behold, naked in their glory."

Joy shook her head, guilt and fear constricting her throat. "But...he wouldn't have *been* there if I hadn't told him where it was happening!" she insisted. "They couldn't have chosen him *before* he even knew about it. That doesn't make sense."

"Perhaps so, perhaps not," Inq said. "Fate's a fickle thing."

"It wasn't fate," Joy said hotly. "It was you!"

Inq pouted. "Don't shoot the messenger."

Joy shuddered very slightly, containing her temper. "None of this makes any sense," she whispered. She shook her head and tried to think. "Look, there was a note in my locker, an envelope from some guy and two texts," she said to Ink. "They were for you."

"Do you still have them?" he asked.

"No," she admitted. "But...there may be more on my computer. I can go check. In my room." The idea of getting to her bedroom held the promise of shutting and locking the door and never coming out.

"Do you remember what the notes said?" Ink asked, sounding exasperated.

"Some of it," Joy said while inching her way past the counter. "Hang on."

Snippets of an escape plan flashed through her head. Joy eased her way between Ink and Inq, glancing at the foyer and considering sprinting for the door. If she could turn the knob fast enough, open the door and scream...

The alarm beeped. The locks unlocked. And the doorknob twisted with a familiar rattle of keys.

Joy whipped around. The microwave clock glowed 9:51. The kitchen was empty. Ink and Inq had disappeared.

Her father wandered in looking ragged and worn.

"Hey," he said, sighing.

Joy slammed into his arms.

"Dad," she breathed gratefully into his coat.

He chuckled, caught off guard. "Well, hello to you, too." Her dad gave her a quick squeeze and patted her arm. "Mind telling me why our broom is in the hall?"

FIVE

Joy couldn't tell Dad or Stefan or Monica. She didn't want any of them thinking that she was crazy, and she *really* didn't want any of them ending up like Officer Gabriel Castrodad. She had to keep quiet. Act natural. Keep everyone safe. She was almost grateful that everyone else was too preoccupied with their own lives to notice anything wrong with hers.

Almost.

She felt eyes on her during the bus ride to school—kids turning to look at her just as she was looking at them. She glanced away quickly. Joy wondered if people always did that? She'd never noticed it before. Then again, it hadn't creeped her out before.

Could they see that her world had changed? Could they read it in her eyes?

Flash! Flash!

Joy hunched down in her seat and willed herself smaller.

Ink's people, whoever they were, knew where she went to school, where she lived, her locker, her phone number... What else? She was grateful that she'd listened to Monica and been extra careful with her online profile, but who knew where or when the next note would appear? She'd buried her phone in the bottom of her book bag and stuffed it beneath her seat. Pushing her hands in her pockets, she kept her back to the window and concentrated on the floor.

Joy tried thinking about ways that she could make herself indispensable and yet stay as far away from the Scribes as possible. She figured any information she got she would hand over to Ink and then walk away, job done. Stay silent. Not one word. If they could keep things just business for a little while, then, Inq had said, the scrutiny would eventually go away. It grated on her that she had become some sort of secretary for the weird, but she could do that if it kept her family and friends safe. Be indispensable from a distance. She could do that.

But she walked into school with a head full of worry about Stef and Dad and news blurbs and glowing girls and inky, all-black eyes.

"Hey."

Joy jumped. Her shoulder bounced off her locker door. Monica frowned.

"Try decaf," Monica suggested as Joy dug inside her locker. "What happened to your neck?"

Joy touched the redness at her throat and gave the same answer she'd given Dad: "Fashion accident." She shut the metal door.

"Touchy," her friend said.

"Sorry," Joy apologized. "Really bad night."

"It's more than that," Monica said.

Joy nodded, having a preplanned explanation handy. "Dad started dating somebody," she said as they began walking. At least it wasn't a lie.

"Really?" Monica said, but—like a good friend—bit back the

chirpy *That's great!* which Joy appreciated. Instead she asked, "Know her name?"

"Yes. Shelley."

"As in Shelley or Michelle?"

"I don't know," Joy grumbled. "*He* doesn't even know!"

"Pfft. That's criminal."

"I *know!*"

Monica glanced at the hall crawlers as Joy regained some composure. Her hands felt hot. Her fingers twisted in her shirt. She suddenly missed the feel of powdered chalk, soothing and smooth on her skin. She wanted to take a running jump down the hall, kick over and fly, but instead hugged a textbook hard against her chest. Monica patted Joy's shoulder in sympathy.

"We'll talk later, 'kay?" she promised. They shared a quick shoulder squeeze before splitting at Hall B. Joy watched her go. Monica was the best, and Joy resolved that she would do whatever she had to do to keep her friend safe. She checked her lucky tartan and black-and-white checkerboard socks as she headed off to precalc.

She had almost forgotten about the weirdness until her calculator started speaking in tongues.

Cubic runes danced across the tiny gray screen. They weren't numbers or English letters or any language that she knew, but it was clearly a message. Grabbing her pencil, Joy copied the shapes as best she could. It looked like some old language written in liquid crystal lines. Joy gripped the pencil, turning her fingernails white.

"Joy Malone," a voice barked. She flipped her notebook over.

"Sorry, Mr. Grossman."

"Something more interesting than proofs, Miss Malone?"

She turned to the next blank page. "Um, no."

Her teacher smiled. "Somehow, I find that hard to believe." The rest of the class gave halfhearted chuckles. "All right, people, back to question ten..."

Joy smoothed her hands over the lined paper, promising herself that when the time came, she would simply hand the message over to Ink and be done with it. No muss, no fuss. She could do this. For Monica. For Dad. For a little while, anyway. Then things could go back to normal.

Hooray.

"Anything for me?"

Joy glanced over her monitor at Ink, then spun around to check that everyone else in study hall was busy clicking mice and keys.

"What are you doing?" Joy hiss-whispered, forgetting the silent treatment. "Go away!"

"No one can see me. Or hear me," Ink said. "You have a message?"

Glaring, Joy yanked out her notebook and tore off the page. The rip of paper rent the quiet, but no one looked up. She held it out, but Ink shook his head.

"Not here."

Joy grated through clenched teeth, "I'm in class..."

"It will only take a second," he said and disappeared.

Joy sighed and stuffed the note into her pocket, then reluctantly asked the senior proctor if she could use the bathroom. Grabbing the bright pink hall pass, she slipped quietly out the door. Ink was waiting for her by the fire extinguisher.

She dug out the paper and handed it over.

Ink took it and read it quickly, then handed it back.

"Easily done," he said. "Ready to go?"

"What? No!" Joy whispered angrily. "Can't you see I'm busy?"

Ink glanced around in mock surprise. "No."

"Well, I am," Joy insisted. "This is school. I can't go anywhere right now."

Ink opened his wallet and drew out a thin knife.

"That is where you are mistaken," he said. Joy stepped back. Was he going to gut her right there in Hall C? Somehow she didn't think so, and the more she watched him, the more she thought that he didn't look menacing—he looked like he was being clever. Ink twirled his blade with a hint of mischief. Joy hesitated, wondering what he was up to.

Ink slashed, acting as if he didn't care whether she was impressed, but obviously pleased that she was as he peeled back a layer of nothing. A thin membrane of space hung loosely in midair.

He'd cut away a flap of the world.

Joy stared at it and him and the school and what once was.

Ink offered his hand, smooth as glass.

"Come with me," he said.

"I—I can't," Joy said, but found that she'd somehow already stepped forward. It was all too impossible as he slit the door wider and they walked together into nothing at all.

The breach disappeared with a sharp scent, like limes.

In that instant, Joy was aware of Ink beside her—a soft smell of rain clung to his clothes, his shoulder hard against hers. She held on to his shirtsleeve and tried to adjust to the new light.

Flash! Flash!

She blinked and let go as Ink stepped into a softly lit room. The bedroom had that blanket quiet Joy recognized from years of babysitting: a mix of moon-shaped night-lights, pastel colors and talcum powder. Ink leaned over a wooden crib, a blue-footied baby curled inside like a tiny cat. The plug-in monitor whirred and clicked, registering Joy's footfalls in the thick, plush carpet.

Ink opened his wallet and selected an instrument, holding the long, thin razor up to the wan light. Joy froze, danger tingling down her spine. She wasn't sure what Ink was about to do, but she didn't like where this was going.

"What are you...?"

Ink silenced her whisper with a wave and a finger to his lips, then to hers. The touch was impersonal and strong. His hand was stone solid, as if he could easily nudge forward and break her front teeth. Joy shushed but looked worriedly down at the baby, swallowing protests. He saw her anxiety.

"I will not hurt him," Ink said.

Joy twisted her fingers, uncertain. "Really?"

Ink frowned slightly. "I cannot lie," he said as he lifted the blade. "Watch." The monitor did not so much as click at his voice.

Joy watched Ink place the long knife between two of the baby's shrimpy fingers. She held her breath, not sure whether to scream or keep from screaming.

At the touch, a tiny pattern of black script burst across the bitty palm. Joy stared, surprised at the unexpected tattoo fireworks as they faded and disappeared. The baby didn't even change its deep breathing. Spellbound, Joy leaned farther over the crib's edge to watch Ink do it again.

Switching to the left hand, Ink repeated the procedure.

Like a drop of dye in water, the pictographs expanded and curled in invisible eddies, fading quickly. She caught a few images that danced in the design: something like fat blueberries and a bird with a crown. Then those, too, disappeared and the baby slept on.

Ink withdrew the blade and blew on it, then folded it back into its sheath with no wasted motion. He stepped away from the crib.

"That's all?" Joy said.

"Shh," he chided, but smiled, pleased. It made his boyish face even more so. She was shocked that he had dimples.

"That is all," Ink confirmed.

"Huh," she whispered. "That wasn't so bad."

"Still, it is good that you came along," he said. "It is important that you be seen with me."

Joy frowned, glancing around without moving her head. "There's nobody here."

"Shh." Ink hushed her again and stepped back, pointing to the telltale monitor. The cow-over-the-moon night-light outlined his features, catching all the impish hollows. He shrugged with open hands, as plainly as if he'd said, *One never knows who is watching.*

Joy nodded, eyeing the shadows. They were supposed to act "together." She slipped her hand into his and gave a soft squeeze. Ink stiffened, staring down at their hands. Turning them over, he inspected the configuration of their fingers from all sides. Joy wondered if he'd ever held hands before. His staring at their entwined fingers felt stranger by the moment.

Finally he said, "Time to go."

"Okay," Joy whispered, the weirdness tossing her mind

in strange directions. Ink sliced a new doorway and Joy decided she wouldn't be half surprised if she saw a giant caterpillar with a hookah or a Mad Hatter sipping tea. She was more surprised to find neither of these.

Joy stepped gingerly into Hall C, nearly bumping her nose against the red emergency case. She blinked at the fire extinguisher. She was in the exact spot where she'd last been in school. Ink waited calmly at her side.

She exhaled. Slowly. Somewhere in between, she'd let go of his hand. His gaze stayed on her fingers a fraction longer, then it was gone.

"If there are no other messages, I should go," Ink said, running his finger absently along the chain at his side. "Should you need to contact me, close your eyes and speak my name."

"Ink?"

He smiled. "Exactly." He turned to go.

"Wait." Joy tried to get her bearings. She glanced back at the classroom door. She held up her hall pass. She'd forgotten she'd had it the whole time. "What was that all about?"

"It is a covenant," Ink said. "The boy is a descendent of high priests. A promise made, a promise born."

Joy frowned. "That means he'll be a priest?"

"No. He is the son of holy men. He *is* a priest."

"That's what the symbols meant?" Joy wondered.

"Symbols?" Ink sounded surprised.

Joy nodded. "The letters, the birds, the fruit...?"

"Ah. The images are embedded in the *signatura* of those who ordered the mark," he said and shrugged. "They release when I inscribe the mark. I hardly notice them anymore."

"Oh." Joy peeked through the glass, trying to catch sight of the clock. "How long have we been gone?"

"As I said, it only takes a second," Ink said. "If that." He gave a strange sort of bow and waved his arm in a swirling, downward stroke. This time Joy noticed the razor tucked inside the palm of his hand, slicing the breach. He sidestepped to the left and disappeared.

Joy stared at the spot, trying to see something that was no longer there. She lifted her hand, raising her fingers as if she could touch the edge of an invisible door, nearly leaping out of her skin as the class bell rang.

It was impossible to sit, impossible to concentrate, let alone take notes. Her daydreams were a jumble of colors and questions. She had stepped through space and time! U.S. history paled in comparison. She bit her fingernails and wandered through the rest of the day in a haze, feeling that itchy, excited terror that she hadn't felt since competing for State.

And, being an adrenline junkie, she *really* wanted to do it again.

Joy begged Monica to take her to the next best thing.

"You know, *normal* people go to a dance club or something," Monica said as she drove out to the abandoned soccer field after school. "It doesn't have to be the Carousel—there are a few good places midweek."

"I need space," Joy said as she shimmied into a pair of yoga pants. "It's not like dancing. I need to *move*."

"You need to move like I need a manicure." Monica turned up the side street past Abbot Park's welcome sign. The well-kept field stretched before them, framed by an ironwood fence and short, brown grass. While the old soccer field had long since retired, John Abbot tended his family's donation to the town as a matter of personal pride. He faithfully brought his own lawn tractor and seed based on *The Old Farmer's Almanac*. The field was flat and even, stray rocks and shoots carefully plucked and discarded, and the earth beneath it springy yet firm. Joy knew every inch of Abbot's Field by hand and by foot. It was her secret personal training ground ever since she was six.

The gravel crunched under tires with the sound of country roads. Monica sighed as she pulled into the empty lot, grimacing at the woods and weeds.

"This place has Lyme disease written all over it."

"You don't have to stick around," Joy said.

"I am *not* leaving you alone while you're currently a crazy stalker magnet," she said. "Let it not be said that Monica Reid is a fair-weather friend. Nor is she to be found unprepared."

Joy rotated her ankles. "You going to do homework?"

Monica blew a raspberry. "Get real. I've got video calling on my phone."

Joy laughed and got out of the car. "Tell Gordon I say hi."

"Will do, sunshine. Now go burn off some steam."

Joy beamed, bouncing on her heels, feeling the stretch in her ankles and calves and massaging her wrists over and back. She shook out her fingers and took off for the fence, top speed, the first chords of "Alegría" ringing in her head. Her palms hit the worn wood as she cleared it, landing smack against the ground, her feet remembering the feel of the terrain. She'd braced for it in her knees. She knew it without thinking.

She didn't want to think. She felt better already!

Joy ran, building speed, preparing herself for the cold, hard earth. She swung into a roundoff, launching into a back tuck, the world singing sideways, the sting of grass on her hands. She punched the landing and took off hard. The building chorus in her head egged her on, the blend of synthesized organs and drums and a high voice imploring longingly in French.

Joy flung herself into a series of back handsprings, end over end over end like the beating of her heart, like her feet at Deer Run, like the feeling of flight—a wheeling momentum that carried her far from her self. She twisted, landing smoothly, and performed a split leap, touching down lightly. She wound from the shoulders, leading with her chin, diving in quick succession: one leap, two, three. Spinning, she launched into another roundoff, pushing from her toes, hips twisting sharply midbend and snapping her feet to the ground. It surprised her how easily this all came back. Part of her wondered why she'd ever left.

Mom.

Joy tucked and bolted, leaving that thought far behind.

She wanted to do a bigger tumbling pass, knowing she couldn't really do it out here, but a wild recklessness ran through her, as if she didn't care what happened as long as she didn't have to stop. Joy pumped her arms hard and threw herself into it: roundoff, back handspring, double back tuck, one-eighty. Joy stuck the landing and gazed around, dazed. Had anybody seen that? There was no one around but Monica chatting on her phone. Joy tingled like snowflakes, her own eye blinking: *Flash! Flash!* She bounced on her toes, testing the ground. There was no way she could have done that without a sprung floor.

She stared at her own hands speckled with earth.

Curious, breathing deeply, she ran, gaining speed through the stamped-on grass, jumping into the roundoff, hitting the handspring, flipping into the stratosphere of a three-sixty, soaring over: *Bam!* She hit it. Not even her toes complained. She tilted her face up, fingers splayed, beaming out of habit for an imaginary audience. She felt incredible; her body sang.

It was impossible, but she'd experienced a lot of "impossible" lately.

She spun, dramatic, knee counting the beat. Thinking, *artistry* and *expression*, daring a judge to not notice her eyes. Joy twisted into two turning leaps, graceful and full, the wind in her teeth, her arms stretched like wings. She scissored into a tour jeté, half twist, and stuck: supple arms drifting down, completing the haunting Cirque chord.

Final pass. Roundoff, back handspring, quick and flowing. Joy committed herself to the Arabian even before she left the ground, turning midair to somersault forward, sailing clear and clean, her feet kicking out to complete their arc like a gentleman's bow. She sank her weight into her knees and locked the pose, slowly becoming aware of her own body's sudden stillness. She lifted her lashes like waking from a dream.

Joy looked up into all-black eyes.

Ink flinched, surprised.

He'd been staring at her while leaning against a fence post, startled at being caught. And he *had* been staring at her—again—just as he had that night at the Carousel. But this time his face wore an odd expression of awe and pride and disbelief. Joy could feel herself blushing. For a long moment, they stayed that way, Ink hovering by the fence post and Joy posed in the grass. It was as if an entire conversation was happening between them without words, him asking, "Who is Joy

Malone?" and her wanting to know more about the mysterious Indelible Ink.

"Are you done?" Monica called from the car. Joy's head snapped around so fast, she felt a crick in her neck. She glanced back. He was still there. Dimples framed his smile. Monica couldn't see him and Ink kept looking at Joy as if he were about to say something, but no words came. He just stood there, watching, smiling at her.

"Yeah," Joy said, keeping Ink on the edge of her sight. "Yeah, I'm good."

Joy felt his eyes on her as she marched past him, launching herself over the rail in a showy front hand tuck. Her feet landed together with a satisfying crunch. Behind her, three words followed with crisp clarity:

"Yes. You are."

Joy smiled to herself, but didn't turn around.

Monica switched off her phone as Joy hopped into the car, sweaty and spent. She grinned, exhausted, as she pulled on her seat belt. She no longer saw Ink in the side mirror, but then again, he might still be there.

"Girl," Monica drawled. "We have *got* to get you a boyfriend."

Joy worried her dad would guess that something was up, and if he did, she was totally doomed. She popped with unspent energy. She couldn't sit still. She squirmed through their late dinner, trying to stay quiet through the scrape and clink of silverware and polite requests like "Pass the salt?" Joy was overly conscious about making too much noise. Their house had succumbed to a sort of mausoleum hush over the past year as the dinner table grew smaller and smaller. But now she wanted to shout and laugh and scream—she hadn't felt that way for months and it was incredibly awkward tamping it down now.

Placing the leftovers in the fridge, her dad groaned. "We're out of milk."

"I'll get it!" Joy said, jumping to her feet.

"Never mind. I'll get it tomorrow."

"No, really," she said. "I could use the walk."

Her father closed the fridge and frowned. She'd pushed too hard, sounded too eager. When had she ever volunteered to buy late-night groceries?

"Oh? Care to tell me anything?" he asked.

Nnnnnno. She switched to the old fail-safe.

"Just that time of the month," she said. "Biochemical warfare and all that. I'd like to get some chocolate at the C&P while I'm there."

Dad hesitated, then fished out a ten. The mention of anything "womanly" made him fidget. "Fine," he said. "Remember—milk and chocolate, not just milk chocolate, understand?"

"Yes," she said and gratefully snatched the bill and her keys in one hand while she shrugged on her jacket. "Be right back," she called over her shoulder and bolted down the stairs, flying across the courtyard and out into the cool night air.

The walk to the convenience mart wasn't exactly convenient, but it was well lit and paved and gave Joy some precious room to breathe. She knew she had been expecting creatures at the window, scrapings at the door, mysterious notes under her pillow or in her locker or in her shoes, but it hadn't happened since she'd gone out with Ink and being outdoors after Abbot's Field, she felt better and less vulnerable than she had in a long while. She skipped down the sidewalk. Freedom felt good!

Pushing open the door at the C&P, the electronic bell buzzed its two-tone hello. No one was there save the store manager, a man of unknown ethnicity and uncertain age, who was busy shelving cigarettes.

"Hello, Joy."

"Hi, Mr. Vinh."

Joy grabbed a gallon of milk out of the refrigerated compartment, two chocolate bars and some sugarless gum. She plunked them on the counter and watched him stack the menthols as she dug out the ten.

"No smoking, right?" he asked.

Joy shook her head. "Bad habit."

"Underage," he said as he rang up her total and began to count change. "I noticed the gum. Not many kids chew gum nowadays unless they quit smoking. Chocolate, yes, candy, yes." He smiled. "Not so much gum."

"It's a nervous habit," Joy said.

"Too many habits," he chided. "You're young. Relax."

Joy pocketed the candy bars and change and hefted the milk. "Not many kids relax nowadays, either," she said with a wry smile. "Have a nice night."

"You, too, busy kid. You, too."

Shouldering open the door with its two-tone goodbye, Joy backed out into the night. The air was cool and the sidewalk looked surreal in low-glow orange, flecks of mica winking like stars in the concrete. It looked almost magical. Joy stepped on the constellations, lost in thought. It was tough to know what to think of a world that held black-eyed time travelers and $3.19 milk.

A rising prickle on the back of her neck should have been from a cold breeze, but the air was eerily still. Her eye snagged something white wafting by. *Flash! Flash!* She watched the wisp of motion. A silvery sort of light danced on the edge of her already-altered vision, slipping like steam off a storm drain, playing a sinister tag with her nerves. Joy swallowed and kept walking, trying not to quicken her step. Acting afraid only made you look weak. Girls' Self-Defense 101: walk confidently, head held high. And carry your keys. Joy fitted hers between the first two knuckles of her right hand and tightened her grip on the jug of milk.

A distant roar, like angry whispers down a long tunnel, echoed in her ears. She turned to look. Her footsteps faltered, a misstep on the edge of the pavement. The milk's weight sloshed, pulling her off-balance. The vapor circled her, like a shark on TV. Girls' Self-Defense 102: trust your gut.

Her gut said, *Run!*

The milk was heavy. Should she drop it?

She shouldn't have hesitated.

The shriek was feral and high-pitched. Joy spun as the colorless film rushed toward her wearing a woman's face, hair snaking out in a veil and fingers outstretched for Joy's throat.

Joy ducked, covering her head with one hand, scratching her own cheek with her keys as the thing swooped by. A strange numbness spread over her shoulders as it passed with an odd tingle like Novacain.

She bolted down the sidewalk, hands tight with milk and keys, unable to let go of anything in sheer terror, trying to stay in the streetlight's sickly orange path. The phantom face swam through the air, a lazy kite trailing a tail of tattered dress. It watched her with dead eyes, matching her in effortless pursuit.

Joy ran.

Panting, eyes stinging, Joy crouched beneath a lamppost and whirled her arm around, whipping her keys sideways. The misty specter slipped through her body, heedless of her blows, and the dentist-office sensation seeped further into her veins. Joy's knees buckled, her bones filled with heavy, pins-and-needles lead.

The ghost-woman's eyes contracted like twin mouths, emitting another unearthly shriek, flattening Joy against the ground. The weight of it pressed her into the earth, grinding her down. Her forehead scraped painfully against the edge of the concrete. Covering her ears, Joy whimpered against the feeling that her eardrums might burst.

She couldn't think. She couldn't get up. Joy held her keys over her head, squeezing her eyes shut, and screamed.

Something bloomed in the back of her brain, changing her scream to a single word: *"INK!"*

Her voice rose, as did the phantom wail. A crackle and electric pop, and the orange streetlights exploded, one by one, spitting a hail of glass that bounced against the walk. The numbing buzz in her body wound deeper, filling her lungs, slowly creeping up her throat, smothering her heart. It was getting harder to breathe. Joy wheezed and felt the world tilt.

A metallic *shing* split the air. The terrible cry ceased.

Joy felt something cover her, heavy and dark, a comforting weight against the pale, numbing light. Joy clung to it blindly, dimly recognizing the slippery shimmer of silk and the cool smell of rain. Joy felt his voice vibrate in his chest flat across her back.

"Stop," he said.

She could hear the wraith reeling closer. Ink switched his grip on the blade in his hand. The cleaving sound struck again, clanging and clean. The howling retreated.

"She did not get your message," Ink said, his arm held high. Joy cowered beneath him. "We will heed it," he promised. "Presently. Now."

Joy chanced a look. The wraith woman, her eyes wide holes of fury, exhaled a high, modulating cry before spinning into the darkness like a dandelion puff.

Silence returned.

Joy relaxed in small increments, joint by joint. Ink pressed against her numb shoulders and the ground sank with their combined weight in the grass. Joy lay curled protectively under Ink, dizzy and trembling.

Ink stood swiftly, gazing out into the pinpricked sky.

"That was a *bain sidhe*," he said. "A banshee. The curse of the Isles. Evidently, a message has gone unanswered for too long."

Curse of the Isles. Joy remembered the note in her locker. She groaned. "Crap."

Ink turned and stared at Joy for a long moment before offering one of his glovelike hands. "Now, *lehman*, you must come with me. We have an obligation, you and I—understand?"

Joy nodded and stood up, her palm sliding off his like oil. "I thought..." she began, swallowing her icy jitters. "I thought you said you couldn't lie."

"I did not lie," Ink said as he folded his knife into his wallet and tucked it away. "I said you did not 'get' the message, not that you did not 'receive' it. I intended 'get' as 'understand.'

And I was correct that you did not understand the message," he said archly. "Did you?"

"No," she admitted and bent to get her keys.

Ink watched her with that shy, intense curiosity she'd seen when he'd inspected their joined hands.

"I felt you," he said quietly. Joy hesitated. "Even before you called for me." His eyes met hers. "Inq never said it would be like that."

Joy didn't know what to say. Her arms felt heavy, full of wet sand. She debated leaving the milk on the ground.

"Pick it up," Ink said, as if reading her thoughts. Obediently, she did. Through a woozy sort of haze, Joy hadn't the will to refuse. Ink followed her movements with those penetrating eyes. He took a deep breath and let it out slowly. "Do you want to see a trick?"

His words surprised her. And she wasn't really up for any more surprises, but the way he'd said it made her wonder if this was an offering of some kind.

"Sure," she said. "But can I sit down?"

"No. It requires your participation and speed." At her groan, he added, "It will help—the *bain sidhe* effects fade quicker if you keep moving. It reminds your body that you are still alive."

Joy rubbed her hand against her jeans. Tingles pricked like electric sparks.

"Great. Okay," she said. "What do I do?"

Ink extracted one of the deadly blades from his wallet and gestured with it. A dimple teased in one cheek, threatening a smile. "When I tell you to," he said, "drop the milk, then jump."

Joy frowned. Was he kidding? Was this a test?

"Jump?"

"I am certain that you can," he said. "You jump very well."

It shocked her like a dare. How long *had* he been watching her at Abbot's Field? Joy bit back a retort and sank into her knees, ignoring the numb, prickling sensation, ready to spring.

"Okay."

"On my mark," he said.

There was a familiar swoop of motion, a tear in the world, and Ink peeled back a flap of nothingness.

"Drop it," he said. "Jump!"

She tossed the jug high and jumped through.

Her feet landed on green fields so bright they shone. Joy's first, crazy thought was that she'd stepped into Oz, but that illusion disappeared with the smell. Wet, woolly sheep with dirty coats dotted the hillsides, their spray-painted butts reeking of poop and the smoky scent of peat. Joy squinted up at the open sky, robin's-egg blue with an early, silver-gold sun. The nearby narrow road was lined with low walls of uneven gray stone. A rock cottage squatted on the hillside, its bright red door ajar.

She gawked in a trance of delight and awe. Ink stood by her side.

"Where are we?" Joy asked.

"Ireland," said Ink, and he marched through the open door in blatant disregard for personal property. Joy hurried after him, wondering how anyone could live with a door open to the world, where anybody off the street could walk in like this. She tiptoed gingerly into the house.

A boy of nine or ten lay dozing in a chair. A heavy plate littered with the remains of ham and eggs sat on a table beside a cold mug of strong-smelling coffee. He slept in a button-down shirt, loose pants and thick boots, with a floppy hat pulled down over half his face. Only the very end of his nose and his chin peeked out; both were heavily freckled. Joy thought the boy might be more freckle than not.

He didn't stir as Ink plunked his wallet onto the table and selected the leaf-tipped wand. Joy leaned on the edge of the thick, wooden table, watching Ink unbutton the boy's sleeve and tug it up over his elbow. No one should have been able to sleep through such treatment, but somehow, the kid didn't wake. Joy wondered if that was some magic of Ink's or the young boy's impressive commitment to sleep.

"Can you move?" Ink asked Joy, pointing the wand. "You are blocking the light."

"Oh," she said. "Sorry."

The sleeping boy stirred. Joy froze. Ink's eyebrows crinkled a stern warning. Joy nodded and silently crept around the table, touching nothing. While Ink might go unnoticed, obviously she did not. Joy stood very still and watched from over his shoulder.

Ink tilted his head and considered the skin: a line dividing the freckled, pale part from a deep farmer's tan. Ink shifted the boy's elbow, attempting to drape the rest of the arm awkwardly over the sunken chest, but the loose weight kept dragging the arm down. After three tries, Ink scowled and turned black eyes to Joy.

"You want to be helpful?" he asked finally. Joy nodded. "Stand there." Ink indicated a spot behind the wooden chair. Joy picked her way over. Ink held up the boy's speckled right hand.

"Hold this," he directed, slapping the hand on the boy's

shoulder. Joy gingerly pressed down on the knuckles to keep it in place. Satisfied, Ink reexamined the spot near the elbow and poised the blade like a paintbrush.

Joy watched the serrated leaf outline a slow curve, its touch bursting black fireworks, strange tattoo symbols dancing on skin. Celtic knots slithered into two woven patterns. She saw a dove, an eagle and something like wheat. Ink drew the line steadily, ignoring the play of pictures, until he'd drawn a small, bean-shaped mark. It glowed fiery pink—the color of fingers on flashlights.

"The banshee was sent to complete this transaction," he said as he worked. "A gentle reminder that there are promises to keep." Ink spared a glance at Joy. "The Madigans have been under *Luighsaech* protection for ages. Every generation develops the mark of the clan."

He traced the bright line into its final shape. The design expanded and collapsed, forming a fresh, brown kidney mole—a dark bean upon pale, freckled skin. Not a whisper of anything unusual remained.

Satisfied, Ink inspected the leaf and blew it clean. Placing the wand back into its sheath, he folded the wallet into thirds and stood. Joy, remembering her hand pressed on the boy's knuckles, let go. The arm slumped forward. Ink tugged the sleeve down and buttoned it into place.

"Time to go," he said.

Obediently, Joy backed out of the room, the floor creaking thickly under her feet. She could still hear the fat bleating of sheep outside. There was a flitter of motion by the boy's boots and Joy knew she hadn't imagined the tiny blue face smiling there. Joy hurried outdoors.

Ink was waiting patiently under the eaves, taking in the

panoramic view. The scenery was picture-postcard perfect, but smelled sharply of manure. That one imperfection was what made it believable. Still, Joy kept expecting someone to pinch her so that she would wake up.

Ink switched the blade to his left hand, spreading the fingers of his right.

"Now, keep your eyes on this hand," he said. "And when I say go, go quickly."

Her heart pounded. Joy didn't know what to expect, but she felt herself grinning.

"You call it," she said.

Ink crouched, knees bent, ready to spring. It was excellent form. Joy recognized it instantly: he'd copied it from her. Ink drew a wide curve, eyes intent. He nodded to Joy.

"Ready?" he said. "Go!"

She jumped, plunging into darkness and skidding on the landing. She tried to keep her eyes on Ink's hand but could only manage to follow the flicker of his arm. She resisted blinking as sidewalk solidified underfoot. Reality clicked into place the instant Ink caught the milk.

He held it up proudly.

"Only takes a second," Ink said casually. "If that."

Joy stared at the plastic jug swinging in his right hand and laughed. "That was amazing!"

He glanced aside through lowered lids. "You are easily impressed," he said and handed her the milk. Joy examined it as they started walking, her shoes scraping through broken streetlamp glass.

There was a comfortable silence while Joy struggled to sort the questions and exclamations and impressions in her head.

Everything suddenly felt bigger, brighter somehow, but she managed to find her priorities.

"Thank you," she said. "For rescuing me."

There was the shortest pause before he answered. "You are my *lehman*," Ink said. "My charge and my troth. Perhaps now you will not forget to give me a message in the future?" His rebuke didn't sound half as harsh as it had in her kitchen. It was warmer, closer to teasing, but tentative, unsure.

"Don't worry," she said. "I won't forget!"

Ink gave the slightest nod, the slightest smile. "Good."

She struggled in that moment. Ink was almost...friendly. Not menacing or threatening. It still shocked her when she felt his unfamiliar touch, taking her hand and carefully threading their fingers together, one by one. Remembering her role and the possibility that unknown eyes were watching, she didn't pull away, but was keenly aware every time their forearms touched. They walked that way for a while in silence, a growing electricity traveling up her arm. Flustered, Joy attempted casual conversation.

"So...how does this work—marking people?"

Ink faced forward, unreadable in profile. "I take the order and make the mark," he said, finally. "I do what I do because I was made to do it. Inq and myself. We mark people with *signaturae* to keep the Folk safe. Otherwise, they would be at risk of exposing the Twixt and themselves and upset the balance. Our job is to be the pen and knife." He gestured with his free hand to the trees beyond the walk. "The Folk have been pushed to the edges of the world, all but forgotten. Without the old territories, our kind are desperate to have magic remain part of the world. We must preserve the balance or be lost."

"And so you and Inq can mark people, but ordinary Folk can't," Joy said. "And that keeps everyone in line?"

"In theory," Ink said. "Anyone can lay claim to a human inside their purview, setting their own *signatura* upon their skin. If one of the water Folk claims a river and a human swims there, they would be well within their rights to mark that human as theirs." He gave a little bow. "But it is considered far more...civilized if *signaturae* are assigned through proper channels. It makes things easier for the Council and puts fewer of our people at risk."

Joy searched his face. "What about you?"

Ink frowned slightly, his dimples drawing down. "The risk is mine," he said. "It is what I do." But something in his voice went flat. She caught his eye. He shrugged. "Inq says that the Folk are an endangered species," Ink said. "We preserve our world by minimizing their exposure to danger."

"Is marking people so dangerous?"

Ink looked her straight in the eye. "It is always dangerous, dealing with humans."

"Ah." Joy dropped her gaze and swung their hands. "Case in point."

He half smiled. One dimple. "Yes. If you want to know more about dealing with humans, perhaps you should ask Inq," he said. "She has far more experience than I."

"Really? Is it the same when she marks people?" Joy asked, thinking about the swirling calligraphy on her pale skin. "I'd love to see that."

Ink smiled fully. It changed his whole face. "It is...different," he said. "Inq marks those who have undergone profound, life-altering experiences that affect them deeply, internally—invisible, yet there. I mark those who have survived such experiences who wear proof of it on their skin. I have fewer clients, mostly inherited protections and badges of honor." Ink glanced at Joy. "Mine is a less graceful art. Maybe next time, we will visit Inq. You could watch her work—she would welcome it. She likes you." He smirked. "And she appreciates an audience."

"Really?" Joy said.

"She is quite the exhibitionist, which is a shame when you are invisible."

Joy laughed. Ink looked up, surprised.

"That was funny," she said. "I didn't know you could be funny."

Ink glanced sideways at her. "No one has ever said so before."

"Trust me," Joy said. "You're a laugh riot."

They slowed by the front gate. Joy withdrew her hand and hugged the milk. She knew that she should say something. Or he should say something. It was awkward and growing more so, because there was no reason to be awkward. Who was she kidding? The whole night was awkward—impossible and frightening and beautiful and strange. The moment sputtered and sparked with unsaid things.

"That was a neat trick you did with the milk," Joy said too quickly.

The dimple reappeared. "It is something I developed over the years."

Joy leaned against the gate and looked at his face, smooth as a sculpture, ageless as the moon. "How long have you been doing this?"

He matched her stance against the gate. "Many, many years."

"Care to give a number?"

Ink spread his hands. "When you can slice through time, what do years matter?"

"Point taken," Joy said. "So how old are you?"

Ink crossed his arms over his smoky shirt, impossibly pristine after battling a banshee, catching a jug of milk in midair and taking a round trip to the Emerald Isle. Joy watched the silk ripple as he traced a finger over the mortar between bricks.

"How old are *you*?" he asked.

"Sixteen," Joy said. "I'll be seventeen in May."

"And how do you know that?"

Joy rolled her eyes. "Um, 'cuz sixteen years ago, I came out of my mom on May twenty-third."

"Exactly," Ink said. "I have no mother. I was not born. I just am," he said, leaning forward from the waist. "How old am I?" Oddly, it sounded as if he really wanted an answer. It was an impossible question, asking for something that Joy couldn't give.

She shook her head. "I don't know."

"Exactly," Ink said. "No one does."

Silence enveloped them. Joy rocked on her heels. Lingering at the gate, she found that she didn't want to go back to being normal. Not just yet. As if sensing her hesitation, Ink stepped forward. She felt his shadow on her skin and smelled the scent of rain. It twitched something inside her.

"No mother," Joy said adjusting the milk jug in her arms. She found it hard to meet his eyes. "That's sad."

"Is it?" Ink said, curious. "You have a mother."

A sudden tightness welled in her throat. "Sort of."

He was very close now, his voice crisp as apples. "Does having a mother make you less sad?"

Joy couldn't swallow. It was too much. Much too much. She had the crazy impulse to tell him how it felt, to say aloud what it was like to be alone and abandoned and lose everything in the world that made sense, but she couldn't. She couldn't.

She shook her head. "No."

Joy stepped back. Ink did, too. The moment wasn't broken, but it was bruised. He stared at the tears caught in the corners where her lashes met. She saw him staring, guileless and open. He waited like a question. It wasn't one she could answer.

"Well," Joy said, touching the hinges and forcing a smile. "I'd better get going. Dad's waiting for me." She lifted the milk jug. "And this. He'll be worried."

"It only took a second," Ink reminded her.

"Right," Joy said, punching in the key code. "If that."

"Yes," he said softly. "If that."

The gate opened and Joy pushed past, pausing to wave, remembering to keep things looking friendly, feeling awkward and sad and happy all at once. "See you," she called back, which seemed a stupid thing to say. She jogged for the door.

"Wait." Ink's voice sliced across the courtyard. Joy turned around.

"What?"

"You were helpful today," Ink said.

Joy laughed, walking backward. "Gee, thanks!" Pausing, Joy dared one last question. "So, if I'm going to be your *lehman* or whatever, why don't you try using my name?"

Ink stared through the gate. He looked hopeful. Intense.

"I do not know your name," he confessed.

"Oh." She smiled, feeling silly. "It's Joy," she said, bumping unexpectedly against the doorknob. "Joy Malone."

"Joy," he said, unblinking eyes wide. "Good night, Joy Malone."

She fumbled with the door and mumbled, "Good night."

Joy ran up the stairs and went straight to bed with two uneaten candy bars, a pack of gum and a smile.

SIX

THE SCENT OF RAIN HAUNTED HER THROUGHOUT THE NEXT DAY, something not even hot lunch or bleached locker-room smell could erase. Joy could hardly believe she was walking through the halls of her school—she'd gone to Ireland! And not even a stamp on her passport to prove it.

Sheep and shattered glass and ice-cold milk seemed far more real than chemistry or *The Crucible* today. Even though the banshee had frightened her, Joy secretly admired something so set on fulfilling a pledge that it flew across the ocean and half a continent to get it done. That was real loyalty. It was something that could not—and would not—be ignored. This shepherd kid, whoever he was, was from a family that had not been forgotten, even after hundreds of years. Someone remembered. Somebody cared. Somebody watched over him, even if he didn't know it.

Joy envied that. But then again, Ink had come when she called.

Flash! Flash!

That splice of light was a reminder that all of this was real. She felt less invisible, less sad, having that spark in her eye. It made her important to someone, somehow. That's what Inq had said. Joy wasn't sure she felt important, but she felt looked after. Safe. When had she stopped feeling like that? When had she started feeling so alone?

Monica flung herself at Joy in the hall.

"Gordon," she said happily.

Joy grinned. "Tell me."

"I will," Monica said. "We were up until almost two in the morning texting back and forth—I swear, I'll have to put him on the plan before my folks get the bill and nix my phone. Mom's threatened it before."

"What did you talk about?" Joy asked, rising to the best-friend cue.

"Nothing. Everything. You know how it is."

And for the first time, Joy thought that she might.

Monica gasped dramatically.

"What?" asked Joy.

"You're blushing," she said.

"I'm not...."

"You're blushing!" Monica insisted. "It's all over your face. It's a guy. There's a guy! Who is it? Tell!"

Joy felt her face radiate heat. If she wasn't blushing before, she sure was now. She stumbled over the word "Nobody."

She was furious at herself. How completely mental to be blushing over some guy. Especially a not-really-real sort of guy. A guy, by the way, who'd tried to *stab her in the eye*. Whether he had really wanted to or not shouldn't be the issue. He was dangerous. She was obviously insane. Psychologically unstable. Joy adjusted her book bag and started walking quickly down the hall. Monica matched her step for step.

"Well, Mr. Nobody has left quite an impression, I see,"

Monica drawled. Her voice dropped. "It's not someone you met online, right?"

"No."

"'Cuz you know those always turn out to be some old pervert or a crank with a rusted pickup and a shovel," Monica said. "You aren't going stupid on me, right?"

"No," Joy said, feeling stupid. "No Stupid."

But somehow, Joy felt that she might be trying to convince herself more than Monica as she scribbled black eyes in her notebook margins all during class.

Finding the wax-sealed envelope felt like winning the lottery.

Ink was written across the heavy paper in beautiful script, the black lettering elegant and liquid thick. Joy whispered his name as she closed her locker door, heart thudding as she walked into the cold outdoors, welcoming the sparkly, breathy excitement as she saw him standing by the Glendale Oak.

The giant oak tree loomed on the corner of school campus, heavily tattooed over the years by couples carving a bit of infamy for themselves and their high school sweethearts. Ignoring the bus line, Joy consciously kept her feet from running and her face from looking too eager as she approached.

"Your school day is over," Ink said. Light played through last season's stubborn leaves, skipping shadows over his face and silk shirt. He wasn't wearing a coat but didn't seem to mind the cold. Joy glanced around so she wouldn't seem to be talking to herself.

"Yeah. I was about to catch the bus home," she said. "But then I found this." Joy handed him the thick, folded paper,

strangely conscious that their fingers were only an envelope's width apart.

Ink popped the seal, unfolded the paper and read it to
himself. Joy found her hands empty with nothing to do. She
hadn't realized her hands had ever needed something to do—
they always just *did* things—and now that she'd started thinking about them, she couldn't stop. What the heck had she
ever done with her hands? Joy tucked them under her arms
then, worried that she might look angry, rested them on her
hips, hooking her thumbs through belt loops. It grounded
her, tying herself to denim.

"We have a social engagement," he said. Joy's heart beat
faster. She wasn't sure if she should smile. He folded the
paper and tucked it away. "There is someone who wants to
meet you and someone whom you should meet."

Joy joked, "Is it the same person?"

Ink flashed that oddly impish grin. "More or less," he said
and sliced open a door right through the Glendale Oak, cutting a clean line through chopped-out hearts and penknifed
initials to someplace beyond. It was just as unreal as the first
time. Just as magical.

Casting a glance over her shoulder, Joy hurried through.

They arrived at the base of stone steps leading up to an
old brownstone, its bricks covered in ivy and surrounded by
a squat wrought-iron fence. The door was painted in black
lacquer and flanked by neat evergreens in Chinese urns. Ink
began climbing the stairs. Joy hung back.

"Why didn't we appear inside?" she asked.

Ink glanced over his shoulder. "It is considered polite to
be let in."

Without further explanation, she followed him up the

stairs. The stone was worn smooth beneath her feet and the sound of the old iron knocker hitting the brass plate was a pleasant change from electronic buzzers or rings. Joy noticed that there wasn't any button for a doorbell, something that struck her as strange. The only thing odder was when an honest-to-goodness butler answered the door. Joy covertly wiped her feet.

The butler stepped aside, looking professionally capable of deep courtesy or deep trouble. Joy pictured butlers as old and British, but this guy looked fresh from an underground street-fighting ring—if he flexed his muscles, he'd probably burst through his sleeves. Joy kept herself small and made no sudden moves as she followed Ink inside.

They were ushered into a dark-paneled antechamber of baroque paintings and ivory lamps. Two upholstered wingback chairs sat in stately feng shui around a marble-topped table bearing a silver tray, a cut-crystal bowl and an elegant orchid arrangement. Ink reached inside his left back pocket, as opposed to the wallet on his right, and placed a crisp business card on the silver tray before settling himself into one of the chairs. Joy sat down in the opposite chair. Wordlessly, the butler picked up the tray and marched down the hall, rapping smartly on a set of double doors. After a moment's pause, the manservant quietly let himself in. The doors closed behind him with a heavy sound.

Joy turned to Ink. "Where are we?"

"In a receiving room."

Joy rolled her eyes. "I got that," she said and switched tactics. "Why do you need business cards?"

Ink cracked a small grin. "We do well to observe the niceties and use proper etiquette here. The Bailiwick enjoys his little games." He touched the upholstery with his inhumanly smooth hand. "We are in his receiving room and are waiting to be received. The dance is old, but so is he, and we are his guests." He tapped the trim with two fingers. "He is also the one we must convince of our ruse."

"So...humor him?" Joy guessed.

Ink's lightness fell. "Humor me. Respect him. Always."

Approaching footsteps silenced further conversation. Joy twisted her fingers in her lap. Her stupid hands had nothing to do! She debated sitting on them, but that hardly seemed ladylike. She folded them over one knee.

The butler locked eyes with Ink and gave a short bow, his Adam's apple bobbing behind his stiff mandarin collar.

Joy glanced at Ink for a clue of what to do.

"Stay here," Ink instructed, but paused where he stood. Fishing out his long wallet and unhooking the chain, he looped its lengthy weight into her lap. "Hold this." Ink said formally, "I entrust it to you." Then he turned and followed the butler down the sconce-lit hall.

At the sound of heavy doors closing, Joy exhaled a tiny sigh. She had no idea how long this might take and there wasn't so much as a magazine or book to be found. The oil paintings weren't much to look at, so she eyed the ceiling medallions and elaborate crown molding for as long as she could. There were loose frosted grapes in the bowl and Joy moved to take one. The globes were deep purple, almost black, and it turned out that the white dusting on their surface wasn't cold, but actual dust. She left fingerprints where she'd touched one and it jiggled when she let go.

She decided she wasn't hungry.

Joy finally inspected the wallet in her hands. The leather

was thick and shiny, worn and glossy with age. Shifting the chain, Joy opened the trifold compartments, noticing how the leather had molded to each instrument's shape over time. The tools of Ink's trade winked in the buttery half-light.

Joy examined the scalpel, the most ordinary-looking thing in the case. She was careful not to touch the blade, suspecting her fingerprints might leave telltale marks. Instead, she put it back and marveled at the narrow black arrowhead next. She carefully lifted the stubby weapon out by its wooden handle.

At first, she thought it was some stone-age thing, but up close, it looked cut by precision lasers, each notch more sliced than struck, every edge sharp as broken glass. Joy realized that it probably *was* glass—obsidian or something like it— microscopically sharp. She carefully placed it back into its sheath and removed the next of Ink's tools by the hilt.

The leaf wand was the most unusual, its serrated shape mimicking an ivy leaf or a rose. Veins had been carved in long grooves, capillary-size funnels that looked made for drawing ink or blood. Unlike the others, this piece looked handmade and old. It *felt* different. She spun it around in her fingertips, watching the light climb along its edge like stepping stairs. Joy tilted her head as it rotated in her hand. It looked like a homicidal fairy wand.

She touched her finger to the flat surface; a tingly chill prickled up her fingers, cold and clean like peppermint. Startled, she tucked it quickly back into its place, wiping the surface with the hem of her shirt, and folded the wallet back up just in time.

The door opened and something huge stepped out.

The thing that lumbered down the hallway took up most of its berth. Joy first thought of a giant amphibian with scoliosis. Its spine curved up and over in a hunch, its low-slung head moving slightly back and forth as it shuffled forward wearing tailored clothes.

It wore a smoking jacket made of dark Chinese silk, white cuffs turned crisply over each of four hands that ended in long, manicured claws. The rippling skin was mottled olive and gray with a low protruding brow shading surprisingly blue eyes. Its fleshy lips pursed in what Joy guessed was a thoughtful expression—that or something more sinister— it was tough to tell. Its eyes shone like chips of pale mirror under a thick postorbital ridge. It was hairless and wrinkled and when it opened its mouth, it had lots of pointy teeth.

Joy sat very still as the thing squeezed into the foyer. It looked even larger up close. Ink stood in the hall at a polite distance. Both gazed down at Joy. The monster's head hung nearly level with her own, although it must have stood eight feet at the shoulder. She tried to look calm as its nostrils flared. She could feel the whiff of air as it sniffed.

"Innocence." The thing's voice was scraping stone. "Delicious." Another deep sniff, and its ice-blue eyes slipped closed. "Fear," it said with a grin like a shark's. "Divine."

Joy stared helplessly at Ink, who was devoid of expression. She glanced back at the monster, who extended two of his four arms.

"Welcome, *lehman* to Ink," it intoned formally. "Miss Malone. Come."

Ink slid to one side as their host shouldered past, the hardwood creaking under its elephantine feet. She was amazed to discover that the monster wore spats. Joy decided it was hard to be too frightened of something that wore spats.

Everything in the hall was expensive in that subtle-yet-obvious way: hand-carved chair rails, glittering sconces and elaborate corbels mounted along the length of the hall. Paintings and gilded mirrors reflected Joy's face in portraits of antique silver and glass as they passed.

Joy felt maybe she should have worn a skirt. With hose.

The private office had built-in shelves, a wide wooden desk and a very modern computer, sleek and slick as one of Ink's razors—the only thing that looked as though it belonged in this century. A deep stone basin filled with water stood in a corner with fat lotus flowers blooming through waxy, heart-shaped lily pads. The four-armed, blue-eyed toad monster settled into an incredibly large chair. Joy suspected that it might have originally been a throne. He gestured for them to sit.

"I understand that you now serve our associate, Master Ink."

Joy kept her eyes on the monster and her hands on the wallet, feeling the strange things shift inside. She could almost hear Ink whispering, *"Respect him."*

"Yes," she replied.

"Very good," their host approved. "I am Graus Claude, Bailiwick of the Twixt, comptroller of the edge between worlds." He introduced himself with one clawed hand as another lay flat on the desk, while the two remaining hands poured a swan-necked carafe and filled lowball glasses with ice. Joy was mesmerized by the horrific ballet of limbs.

"The Twixt comprises all the places where magic still exists—the fringe of what remains after the post–Industrial Age. Your home, the Glen, is part of the Twixt, and perhaps is the reason for your extraordinary Sight." He adjusted himself in his seat. "We are ruled by the Council, which has decreed that one amongst us must assume the role of intercessor between humanity and ourselves. I hold that honor and distinction. There is no need for you to know my history or that of my title, only that I am an associate of the Scribe, Master Ink," Graus Claude said politely. "An intermediary, if you will, between his many clients and himself. Requests and claims for his services filter through me."

Joy tried to catch Ink's eye, which turned out to be harder than she'd expected. It was impossible to tell where he was looking except obviously not at her. She glanced back to Graus Claude, who placed two glasses of amber liquid on their side of the desk while simultaneously pouring himself a third. Ink did not move to accept, so she refrained, recalling the grapes. Graus Claude pretended not to notice.

"When it came to my attention that certain parties had been circumventing the normal order of our established protocols, I felt pressed to investigate." He inclined his stout head. "Apologies for any impropriety, but in the case of humans, it fares best to be discreet." Graus Claude sighed mightily through the slits of his nose. "Without the due courtesy of a formal introduction, I thought it important that we meet to have a little chat..." Graus Claude sipped at his drink, which looked impossibly tiny perched at the end of his wide lips "...in the hope that we might come to some satisfactory arrangement."

Joy was afraid if she started nodding, she wouldn't be able to stop. The palsy quiver of the Bailiwick's head was making her more nervous than the sight of his teeth. Ink gave no hint or clue of what to do. She'd have to wing it.

"Of course," Joy said. That seemed to please Graus Claude.

The monstrous gentleman grumbled deep in his chest

and drummed sharp claws in two sets against the polished wooden surface. "I am sorry to have learned that some have attempted to curry favor while others have treated you, shall we say, less than favorably?"

Joy thought of the clover, the kitchen window, the old man's shell and the aether sprite's hand on her neck. She touched her throat. "You might say that."

Graus Claude grinned. It wasn't pretty.

"Yes, I thought I might," he agreed, enunciating the *T*s. The throne groaned richly as he shifted his bulk. "I wanted you to know that I do understand. Being the one who most often deals with such persons, it is no easy task." He said it sincerely as he gestured to his mahogany office. "Once upon a time, we each ruled a domain and would claim those who fell under our auspice by placing our sigils upon them, forging bonds and alliances for generations in good faith. And while some continue to do so, it is considered somewhat improper nowadays. It is why I attempted to organize a system that ensured a level of decorum. The Scribes have willingly shouldered this burden of distributing others' marks and perform the task admirably. Our Master Indelible is truly one of a kind, and Miss Invisible is a class unto herself. Their services are of the essence, their delivery, impeccable." Graus Claude set his tumbler down. "This recent ripple notwithstanding."

Joy inhaled. She was a "ripple"? That didn't sound good. She squashed the temptation to defend herself; this didn't seem like the time for back talk. Joy shifted in her seat and kept silent as the Bailiwick's gaze swept over her and paused to settle on Ink.

"We require a flawless record so that we may maintain order," he said.

Ink barely nodded. Joy barely breathed.

The Bailiwick sat back in his chair. "I realize this is not your doing, my dear. You have been enveloped by a much larger world because of your charms." The four-armed toad sighed. "I empathize with what can only be described as a complete upheaval of your former life and for that, I apologize. Had I but known..." Graus Claude cast his white-blue stare at Ink. "The young sometimes forget their obligations when the heart's folly blinds them."

Joy remembered then that she and Ink were supposed to be lovers. She felt a heat flush her face and quickly placed a hand on Ink's sleeve. He glanced at it curiously as if wondering why it was there. Joy tapped his chair leg with her toe and prayed he'd get a clue. He placed a hand over hers. The Bailiwick's eyes flicked between them.

Joy stammered to take the lead. "I'm..."

"The fault was mine," Ink said swiftly.

Wood creaked as Graus Claude leaned forward and laughed—a bellowing laugh that echoed in his cavernous maw. Joy could see halfway down his crimson throat.

"Ah," the Bailiwick said, sighing. "Delightful!" Graus Claude simultaneously opened a drawer, dipped a fountain pen, smoothed a bit of paper and reached inside the drawer. "You had to but mention her to me and I would have vouchsafed her family and her dwelling sooner." Graus Claude wagged the fountain pen like a finger at Ink. "I will bring it to the Council, and no more need be said. She will be under the Edict's protection while you attend to your duties. Mind you, remember that you have obligations that lie outside your lady's eyes." The Bailiwick shook his head and chuckled to himself as he wrote.

"Here." Graus Claude directed his words to Joy. "This is a number where you can leave a message," he said, scattering a pinch of ash to set the ink. "Should you have any further disturbance, do not hesitate to make it known to me and I will do my utmost to intervene on your behalf." He handed the crisp cardstock forward, but withdrew it momentarily.

"And I would appreciate it if you could remind any of those who attempt to contact you personally to go through proper channels. In other words—me," he said, his voice thrumming low. "Are we understood?"

"Definitely. And gladly," Joy said with real warmth. Her family would be safe. These people would stop bothering her. She was happily willing to let the well-dressed toad deal with all the crazy as long as she wouldn't have to worry about that anymore.

"You are most kind," Ink added.

The Bailiwick shut the drawer. "Kindness may oft be considered a business expense and, thus, a wise investment," Graus Claude added as he wrote himself a note in a leatherbound ledger. "In this case, it is also an honor and a pleasure." He scattered more ash upon the page and blew the script dry before heaving himself to his feet. Graus Claude bowed with his neck and eyelids.

"Do treat the young lady kindly, Master Ink. She is both your business *and* your pleasure. Others will take note of it."

Joy tightened her hold on Ink's arm and tried a smile.

The butler swung open the doors behind them. It was a polite but clear dismissal.

Ink bowed. "Yes, Graus Claude. Bailiwick. I shall."

"Of course you shall," Graus Claude said. His eyes flicked to Joy. "A pleasure to meet you, Joy Malone." He offered one of his hands and she gently took it. His skin was thick and pliant, the claws filed smooth, and his lips—when they touched her skin—were surprisingly gentle.

"Thank you, Graus Claude," Joy said formally.

He gave her the tiniest squeeze and a fatherly word. "You do not have cause to thank me yet," he said. "Pray you never do."

As the butler escorted them out of the foyer, Ink held his hand out between them.

"My belongings," Ink whispered, voice tight. "Please."

Joy reluctantly handed him the wallet. It had been the only thing keeping her fingers from shaking, and her hands felt strangely empty without it.

Joy walked up the condominium stairs, followed by something between a boyfriend and a ghost. Ink's feet didn't make a sound and there was no telltale swish of denim or the soft shush of arms brushing back and forth as he walked. In fact, Joy didn't even hear the rattle of the chain she knew hung at his side as they made their way down the hall.

It was eerie and cool.

She gagged the alarm with her four-digit code. Dropping her keys and her backpack, she walked into the kitchen.

"Want some water?" she asked. "Do you drink water?"

Ink watched her. "Do you?"

"Yes, I do." Joy punched herself some cold water from the dispenser on the fridge. She took a large gulp and shivered as the liquid slid into her stomach. It gave her a good excuse for shaking. Joy glanced across the counter at Ink.

"You don't drink?" she guessed.

"No, but I can." He said it almost defensively, taking a glass from the shelf, pouring some water and sipping it smoothly through his lips. He swallowed defiantly. "I watch and learn."

Joy crossed her arms and looked at him—really looked at him. "You and Inq study humans," she said. "You observe them in order to look more human."

"Yes," he said. The admission might have made him uncomfortable, but he didn't sip more water like a nervous person would, avoiding the need to speak. He hadn't learned that.

"Why?" she asked.

He put down the glass. "It was something to do. Someone to be." Ink paused. "Inq and I decided that we would fashion ourselves like this."

"Like this?" Joy said.

"Or some close approximation." Ink grinned. "Styles change over time."

Joy crossed her ankles. "So what do you really look like?"

"Like this," Ink said. "For now."

"Well, what did you look like originally?"

"There were no mirrors."

"Ha-ha," Joy said. "So you look like this and act like this and talk like this all because of what you've observed. The field study of *Homo sapiens*."

"Of what?"

"Humans," she clarified. "Which makes you...?"

Ink cocked his head. "Observant?"

"No," Joy said. "Other than human."

"Of course."

"Which would make you...?" She trailed off, growing more uncomfortable.

Ink frowned. "What?"

"I mean, what are you, exactly?" Joy asked.

He glanced at his glass. "Thirsty?"

"No."

"Is this a riddle?"

"No," Joy said, exasperated. "Listen—if you're not human, what are you? What is Graus Claude? Or those *guilder-whatsits?* Are you a spirit? A vampire? An elf? A demon?" She didn't mean for her voice to drop to a whisper, but it did. "A god?"

"No. None of those things. Although we've been called all of them before." Ink placed his hand on the counter, having watched her do the same. She recognized the gesture. "We call ourselves 'Folk' much as you call yourselves 'people' or 'human.' But I am not one of them, exactly, either. Inq and I were made, not born."

Joy shook her head slightly. "So, do you even know...?" Joy couldn't decide whether to say *what you are* or *who you are*, and when Ink met her gaze, she wondered which was the real question. His face was open, lost, his fathomless eyes searching. There was a sudden thinness to him, as if he'd become a shadowy outline of himself, doubting his existence.

But he hadn't seemed that way back in the Carousel. Since the first moment Joy saw him, he had been all too real. Even now, leaning against the kitchen counter, he looked exactly like any guy in a rare moment of self-reflection, contemplating big questions, asking the unanswerable whys. How long had Ink struggled wondering the same things that humans did?

"Inq has had many *lehman*," he said. "She says it helps her understand, that it helps her do her job, but I do not understand how."

"You want to understand," Joy said. She did not specify whether she meant human beings or *lehman* or what or who he was, and there was a sense that it was all the same.

Ink hung his head as if ashamed.

"Yes. I want to understand," he said softly. "I want to do good work." He straddled a kitchen chair and leaned against its back. "I am only an idea, a requirement breathed to life—" he flipped his wallet onto the table "—an instrument. A tool." The word fell flat and slapped like leather. "I accepted that for many years, but now I want...more." He did not look up at Joy as he paused, but she felt his eyes nonetheless. "Inq had hoped—I had hoped—that eventually I would learn something from humans, learn to feel things, to adapt, to understand why we do what we do, and gain purpose from it. But I have never understood it." Ink slid the heavy chain against the table. "It is an empty, hollow life."

Ink ran his smooth hands over the wallet's surface. Joy watched his every move. "Inq has wanted me to choose a *lehman* for a long time, but I ignored her," he said. "A *lehman* is a distraction. It is not part of our work. How can we improve ourselves by being frivolous? And if nothing else, my sister is frivolous." Ink straightened in his chair. "But she is also correct. She reminds me that we may be the Scribes, but we are merely a means to an end, and by no means the only means."

Ink's fingers curled into determined fists. "So I must work flawlessly in order to preserve the Twixt and to justify our existence, both for Inq and myself. But I do not want to be merely a 'job well done.' I do not want to do as I have always done until the day that I fail and am deemed obsolete." He picked up the wallet with his impossible hand. "All I have is this. And, without this, I wonder what I am." Joy remembered how he had sounded when he'd given her the wallet and the strain in his voice when he'd asked for it back. His voice, as crisp and clear as ever, sounded distant. "I have traveled the world, and time has no meaning, but I often stop and wonder, I am ever truly *here?*"

Joy took her glass and sat next to him at the kitchen table. She didn't know what to say. She didn't want to understand him, this weird guy with the knives—but a part of her did. That feeling of being lost, feeling not-quite-here and not-quite-whole—*that* she understood. She studied his face in profile as he stroked the edge of the leather.

"You think Inq's onto something, being more human?"

Ink said nothing. His quiet was a silent shrug.

Joy turned more fully toward him, wondering why she felt like reaching out, why she was even about to suggest this. "You could learn to be human," she said. "You could learn it from me."

Ink's eyes, deep and fathomless, sought hers. His voice was sharp and low. "How?"

"Well..." Joy found herself staring at his profile, and something elusive slipped into place.

"Your ears," Joy said.

Ink frowned, confused. "My what?"

Joy leaned closer. "Your ears. They're smooth." She pointed. Ink's ears, slightly hidden by long spikes of hair, were more like tiny cups with a hole, no whorls or hollows and hardly any lobe. "Like your hands," Joy said, and lifted hers up to show him. Ink's hands were just as doll-like as Inq's, featureless and flawless, completely unreal.

Joy tucked her hair behind one ear and tilted her head to the side. "See?" She slid her finger along the cartilage. "Ears curve around so sound travels in. There's a lot of extra space for sound waves and then there's this fatty bit here." She pinched herself at the piercing. Ink moved to take a closer look. Joy felt more than saw his face near hers. She stared at the living room, distracting herself.

"There's something genetic about whether the lobe attaches or not," Joy continued, tugging on her earlobe. "Mine don't, but Mom's..." Joy stopped and switched topics. "Anyway, I noticed your ears look more like a rough idea of ears than real ears."

"Does it matter? Ears?" Ink sounded confused but at the same time intrigued.

Joy laughed. "Probably not. But you talk about trying to understand humans by looking like humans when all you've had to go on is glimpsing people a few moments at a time. Maybe Inq's onto something by having humans around more often. Maybe she's learned something by studying us more." Joy glanced at him out of the corner of her eye, holding still as he considered her. She tilted her head. "You said you wanted to know."

"About ears?" he said with a touch of humor.

"Sure." Joy shrugged. "Why not?"

Ink drew his chair closer. "May I?"

Joy hesitated. What was she offering?

Be indispensable.

"Sure."

She rested her head in her hand, her elbow on the kitchen table, as Ink scraped his chair nearer, inspecting her skin. She smiled a little, self-conscious and feeling silly as the black-eyed boy inspected her ear. Eventually, she closed her eyes rather than stare at the blank wall like an idiot.

Big mistake. Joy was suddenly hyperaware of everything. With her eyes closed, her other senses ramped into high focus against her will—the tiniest breeze of his breath, the shush of his movements, the sea-smell of his skin. She'd preferred it when he'd been at a comfortable distance, silent and surreal. Having him so close made her feel shy and confused. There was nowhere to look away, nowhere to hide, nowhere to pretend that something else was going on other than his eyes intent on her.

It was only her ear, but she imagined his gaze wandering. Where would he look next? What was he looking at now? Should she open her eyes and check? Would he stop if she did? Did she want him to stop? Joy's smile quivered and she tried not to move. She sensed that he was very close, but she couldn't be sure of more than that.

The first touch surprised her and she turned her head quickly, eyes closed.

His voice was soft, like music. "I was only..."

"No, it's okay." Joy unhooked her earring and placed it on the table. She readied herself for the touch of his fingers.

And waited.

A gentle hush of expectation filled the room—she could hear him, sense everything about him, he was so close. A touch at the tip of her ear drew a long, smooth line along the outer ridge, down to the soft edge of her lobe. Achingly slow, curious, his fingertip slipped unexpectedly off the skin, bumping the soft flesh of her neck, and quickly withdrew.

They paused.

She felt his question, and hers, a moment of consent approved before the pad of his finger lifted her earlobe, his thumb brushing the soft down of her skin. Joy could hear the whispered touch in her ear. A trickle of goose bumps slid down her back.

That's not what this meant.

Joy tried to ignore it. She tried to hold still.

But it felt real.

He was just looking. Learning. She'd said it was okay.

She felt his fingertips cup her ear, pillowing the silence in the room. Not silence, exactly. Tension. Joy told herself it couldn't possibly be all hers. His fingers traced, captivated, intimate and intricate. He was studying her so completely, she could feel it in his hands. Mesmerized. She knew he could see her swallow, the skin fluttering as a vein jumped in her throat. Joy didn't want to open her eyes, turn her head and see him—watch him watching her. He was too close. She couldn't seem to speak. Maybe if she'd said something earlier, kept talking, it could have been different, but now with the silence stretching longer with each second, it became more impossible to say anything to laugh it off, keep things casual. She couldn't think of what she *could* say.

This was anything but casual.

Ink touched the curious bump protecting the cave of her ear, following the seashell whorl as if memorizing its design. Joy felt it. Heard it. Could almost see his rapt staring behind her eyes. His fingers left for only a moment before settling gently at the top of her cheek, the juncture between her ear and her cheekbone. It took everything for her not to turn her face to meet that touch.

They were both fascinated: Ink touching her, Joy feeling him, his fingers exploring the slope of her face, guided by the slight dip at her temple. His fingertips tickled the edge of her hair, brushing the last tiny darts of her eyebrow, sliding against them as if smoothing each one into place. She tipped her chin back.

He was reading her like Braille.

Joy turned her face following the touch of his hand. His fingers caught a few strands of hair and lifted them, letting them fall, one by one. She felt a brush outside her eye and along the side of her nose. She opened her mouth slightly. She couldn't quite catch her breath. She couldn't think. She couldn't look. Joy was frozen in the moment, eyes closed.

The lightest touch on her quivering eyelid felt like butterfly wings, hardly anything at all. Her lashes fluttered against his thumb. She could feel the closeness of his palm, her head full of his scent. He feathered the tips of her eyelashes and followed their edge to the bridge of her nose—tracing a long line down and resting a hush on her lips.

Like a kiss.

Her eyes opened. She stared straight into Ink.

He dropped his hand.

Both stared at one another, speechless.

"Thank you."

They were both surprised when he said it.

Ink stood up, backing away cautiously—Joy kept her eyes on him as he moved, step by step. It looked as if he might do something, as if he wanted to maybe say something more, but he waved a hand and stepped forward into the breach, disappearing as he'd come.

Joy stared at the space where he'd been, doing everything in her power not to touch the side of her face.

SEVEN

"What happened to you?" Monica accused over a tray of leafy greens.

"What?" Joy said. "Nothing."

"Well, that nothing has you eating your salad with a spoon."

Embarrassed, Joy switched utensils, tucking her hair behind her ear and letting her fingers linger there. She grinned again.

"I'm just thinking," she said, poking the lettuce, "about stuff."

"Thinking stuff." Monica nodded and chewed. "Sounds dangerous."

"Not yet," Joy chirped.

Monica slapped both hands on her tray, "Okay, that's it—spill."

"What?"

"What 'what?' Don't give me 'what' and expect me not to ask 'what?'" Monica pointed her fork at Joy's nose. "You've been a total nut job ever since that night at the Carousel, and what with breaking windows and random notes and skipping off after school, you think I don't know there's a 'what?'"

Monica sounded angry, which was her protective-sisterhood thing. Joy tried not to laugh.

"Is it drugs?" Monica hissed over her salad. "Because if it's drugs, so help me, I will beat your sorry pale pink butt from here to next Thursday. I will call your dad, I will call the cops and I will even call Gordon and cancel our date!"

"Whoa." Joy waved a napkin in surrender. "It's not drugs. No drugs. I swear. Remember? No Stupid," Joy said, but had to add, "But there is a someone."

"A someone?"

"A someone."

"A guy?"

Joy rolled her eyes. "Yes, a guy. There's a guy. I like guys."

Monica pursed her lips. "There's a guy and you like guys and you met a guy, this Someone-A-Guy?"

Joy prodded her lunch, picking at the crust of her sandwich. "There's a guy and I don't know what I think about him. I'm just...thinking about him. A lot."

"Mmm," Monica said noncommittally. "So does this guy have a name?"

Joy considered the question. "Yes."

"Yes?" Monica prompted with a wave of speared iceberg lettuce. "And?"

"And there's not much to talk about." Joy shrugged and took a wide bite of sandwich, filling her mouth. She couldn't decide whether Indelible was his first name or Ink, but neither sounded particularly normal. As opposed to Gordon Wiener-Schnitzel. Still, it was a subject best avoided.

"Uh-huh." Monica joined Joy in a long bout of chewing. They exchanged glances and evasions like fencing partners until Monica swallowed. "Okay," she said. "So, this myste-

rious Someone-A-Guy that you can't stop thinking about—
would I, as your best friend, theoretically speaking, give him
a thumbs-up or a thumbs-down?"

*Two thumbs down, definitely, for mystery-guy-who-stabbed-
me-in-the-eye.* Joy swallowed. "He's not your type," she said
diplomatically.

"But he's *your* type?" Monica said. "And, what is *your* type,
exactly?"

"He's..." Joy stumbled, trying to find the words. "Exciting.
Intellectual. A little sad, which can be sweet." The flash in her
eye inspired her. "He's an artist."

"An artist?" Monica sneered around cukes. "Please do not
tell me that you're going to go all emo on me. That's worse
than drugs."

Joy grinned, thinking of her first impression of Ink and
Inq. "Observe—no black." She gestured to her pink zip-up
hoodie, cupcake T-shirt and mismatched pastel socks. "No
silver, no heavy makeup, nothing dreary on the playlist. You
can consider me clean."

"Artists!" Monica grumbled. "At least tell me he's cool
enough to make graffiti or tats."

Joy brightened. "He does, in fact."

"Really? Well, then you go, girl," Monica said, finishing
her meal. "We'll try to ignore the mushroom cloud over your
house when Daddy finds out."

Joy lingered at her locker—waiting, hoping—slightly disappointed that Ink hadn't shown up yet. She bounced in her
shoes and rearranged her books, buying time for a theoretical something to happen. She picked at bits of foil wrapper

and old, crumpled scraps and dug an odd dried leaf out of the metal corners along with random bits of fluff.

Ink never said he'd meet her after school, or even every day, or every other day, or ever again. She could call his name, but that would be cheating. Or, at least be sad and desperate. She drummed her foot against the locker. It was stupid to keep waiting around. The fact that he might appear any moment didn't make her feel any less pathetic.

Joy crumpled the handful of trash in her palm. She was being an idiot. And she was going to miss the bus.

She slammed her locker, shouldered her backpack and sprinted down the hall, checking the clock on her phone and swearing. Maybe she could still catch the bus if she cut through the cafeteria? Pelting down the stairs and jumping the corners, Joy burst out of the school into the cold, the wind whipping her hair with gusts of dry chill, threatening snow.

Joy squinted at the grubby orange school buses, passengers huddling against ghosted windows for warmth. Taillights glowed red as bus number four inched in Reverse, warning siren beeping. She wasn't going to make it. She stopped running. She felt stupid that she'd waited. Stupid and cold.

Digging her hands into her pockets, she tucked her chin into her scarf and debated calling Dad. She could kill an hour easy in the library, if she had to. As long as they didn't start vacuuming. The ancient machine the janitor used smelled of burning motor oil and sounded like a robotic catfight.

She shivered in the breeze of indecision, then noticed someone lounging naked by the Glendale Oak.

A long-limbed, dark-skinned woman sat propped against the trunk, her arms crossed over her knees and her head held imperiously high above her shoulders. Her skin and eyes were matching shades of nutty-brown, riddled with thin, dark veins like rings of age, and her face shone like glossy, polished wood. The shape of her eyes was faintly Eurasian, tilted up at the tips. She wore a lazy smile and nothing else.

"So you're the *lehman?*" she said. "The first to bear his mark?" Joy didn't answer. There were too many people milling about and about a hundred cars full of witnesses. The woman's eyes roamed frankly over Joy. "I don't believe it."

The withering look she gave Joy was intense and unnerving—things Joy was beginning to associate with members of the Twixt. The chill of the outdoors seeped into her stomach. What could she say? She couldn't deny it and blow their cover story. Inq's semi-threat still rang in her ears, and Ink was counting on her. For the first time, Joy got that her life—and his—depended on keeping up the lie. She shrugged her book bag higher on her shoulder and blinked hard, flashing the *signatura* in her eye.

The dryad was not impressed. "Look at you. You're hardly a stripling," the dark woman said dismissively. "But then, you *do* have the Sight. You can see me, can't you?" She pivoted her head slowly as if it took effort. "Such pretty eyes," she simpered. "I could pluck them out and feed them to the birds."

Joy squeezed her shoulder strap. Was this really a threat? It felt more like a test. After the aether sprite, this tree nymph seemed almost civil. Still, there was something predatory about her that crawled along Joy's skin. Perhaps it was the fact that her eyes were missing pupils, the striped orbs spinning in their sockets as they followed Joy.

Fishing her phone out of her pocket, Joy pretended to check the screen.

"Any messages?" she said aloud. The ploy seemed to amuse the woman, whose smile was the only thing that moved.

"I suspect something is amiss, little miss."

Joy held the phone to her ear. "Sorry, I think you have the wrong number," she said, looking straight at her. "Who may I ask is calling?"

The dryad smiled again, wide and serene. "I'll be watching you, little stripling. Both of you," she said. "And then we shall see."

Shaken, Joy turned her back on the stick figure and walked toward the school. She could still feel those eyes following her. Joy refused to turn around and broke into a jog. Only one thing was on her mind....

"Ink," she whispered as she headed for the stairs. Turning blindly around the corner, she nearly ran into his chest.

"Yes?" He smiled, unperturbed by the wind.

Joy spun around. The Glendale Oak across the lawn was empty; no one was there, naked or otherwise.

"There was someone—" she pointed vaguely over her shoulder "—over by the Oak who just volunteered to be our personal stalker." Ink glanced over her shoulder. "She's not there now," Joy said. "But she didn't sound too thrilled with the idea that I was your *lehman*." Joy tried what she hoped was a joking smile. "Any jealous exes I should know about?" Ink frowned in confusion. Joy waved it off. "Yeah. Never mind."

"Inq mentioned that we could expect something like this." Joy marveled at the expanding definition of *something like this*. "Ours is an enigmatic circumstance, and the Folk are nothing if not curious." He looked at her ear and she blushed. He smiled shyly, caught. "Do not let it worry you," he said. "I am here now."

Joy almost said that she hadn't thought he was going to show up and then didn't want to sound as if she'd been waiting to see if he would. She glanced once more at the Glendale Oak, shaking off the last snowflakes of fear before checking to see if anyone else had noticed the guy with all-black eyes wearing a silk shirt in February. No one was paying attention to anything but the cold.

"She said I was your first," Joy said and then felt herself blush a beacon of heat against the chill. "I mean, she said that I was the first to bear your mark."

"Thousands of humans bear my mark," he said. "I delivered their patrons' *signaturae*. I am the one who marked them. Therefore they retain a copy of my mark, as well." Joy felt oddly disappointed, which was stupid. She twisted her fingers in the lining of her pockets. She looked away as he reached out and touched a tendril of her hair. "But I have never *given* my *signatura* to anyone before," he admitted softly. "You are the first."

Joy felt a warmth spread over her body as he stared at her. She ducked shyly into her scarf and sidled past him, her brain chanting giddy nonsense to the rhythm of her heart, whose beat had changed from angry/scared into something else. She was sure that Ink could hear it thumping through three layers of clothing. Joy pushed her way into the foyer. Ink followed.

Students were hanging out by the doors, staring forlornly through the frosted windows, waiting for their rides. Joy marched into the empty stairwell and flicked on her phone.

"I missed my bus," she said, pretending to talk into the receiver.

"On purpose?" Ink teased. "I am not your taxi, Joy Malone."

He was smiling, easy, familiar—acknowledging that something *had* happened back at her kitchen table, but that neither of them had to say, yet, what it was. She liked it. Like a secret surprise.

"So?" she whispered. "Why are you here then?"

Ink pushed off the wall and circled her playfully.

"Once upon a time," he began, "there was a young girl..."

"Not so young," Joy shot back.

"Once upon a time, there was a not-so-young girl," he amended, "who was invited to go on a magical trip."

"With a prince?"

Ink grimaced. "Hardly."

"A magician?" she guessed.

He shook his head. "A myth."

Joy poked him purposefully with one finger. "You feel real to me."

Ink glanced at her finger and where it had touched his chest.

"Come with me."

"Are you asking?"

"I am asking," Ink said, offering his hand.

It was the best thing she'd heard all day.

"Okay." She shut off her cell. "Let's go."

They entered a dark place that looked like a dungeon and stank like a sewer. It was hardly what she'd envisioned as their next magical date. Ink walked easily into the blackness, unfolding his wallet as he went. Joy picked her way over the straw-strewn cement as her eyes and nose adjusted. The walls wept oily water that clung to her boots.

Ink settled himself into a corner, thin light from a high

window playing zebra shadows over his face. The windows were barred, as was the door. This had to be a prison far away somewhere. Joy couldn't imagine this being anywhere in the United States.

Ink rolled something over that made a wet sound in the muck. An arm flopped into the light. Its skin was smeared and scabby in places. Joy clamped her lips together to keep from making a sound.

Ink selected the fat spiked needle and, after rewrapping his instruments, settled himself down in the dank. Propping the limp arm up on his lap, he ignored the rest of the body hidden in shadows, a mass of matted hair and rags. The size of the hand made Joy think it was a man, but there was no other hint of who or what else he might be.

Wiping a little spot clean of dirt, Ink took a few experimental stabs. Joy clenched her teeth, wincing in sympathy. The body didn't even twitch.

Ink jabbed the man's arm as if it was a voodoo doll. Each pinprick exploded in tiny fireworks of black calligraphy, compressing quickly into a bloodred dot. Ink poked dozens of them in seemingly haphazard patterns.

"This will take some time," Ink said. "Sit. Talk to me."

Joy debated sitting and decided against it. She breathed through her mouth and wrapped her fists in her pockets.

"I'll stand for now," she said. "Won't he wake up?"

"Eventually, but not soon," Ink said as he continued to stab needlepoint scars. "He is a prisoner and not accustomed to sleep or food and he has recently had both. Plus, the food was drugged. He will be questioned within the hour."

"He's a prisoner?" Joy said, as though this wasn't obvious.

They were in a cell with bars on the windows—a prison, ergo: a prisoner. "Can we help him?"

"Help him?" Ink asked.

"Yes. Help him." Joy imitated Ink's grand, swooping gesture. "Help him escape?"

Ink smiled a little at her imitation and inspected his progress. "I am helping him by placing the *signatura* on his skin, showing that he has survived," he said. "This experience will give him a place of honor in all manner of auspices—prisoners of war, survivors, visionaries, true believers. He has earned this and I would not take it from him." He tilted the stylus to point with its hilt. "Watch the patterns. You will see what I mean."

Joy crept closer, trying to skirt the brown gunk and the round shadows that scuttled out of her path. She crouched down—careful not to sit—and watched where he next pricked with his pen.

A blur. A dart of motion. There was no blood, but confetti swirls scattered on impact. Black crescent moons and crossed cutlasses, claws and six-pointed stars, vines of what looked like razor wire and flowers made of eyes popped and disappeared, leaving behind the tiniest of bloodred pocks. The result was a constellation of burst capillaries close to the surface of the prisoner's skin.

"What do they mean?"

"I have come to recognize a great number of them over the years." Ink brushed the smooth end of the handle against the soiled skin. "In there was Scythe and Whisper, the Tale Maker and Flight-of-Crows. Your world has different names for them, but their auspices remain the same." Ink inspected the skin as he spoke. "Scythe watches over warriors that have not yet fallen, and Flight-of-Crows watches over those imprisoned for loyalty to a greater cause. There are still more here that I do not know, but every one of the Folk has an auspice and all are proud to claim those worthy of their mark." Ink shrugged. "Many have claimed him. He will be looked after the rest of his days."

She didn't know how to feel about that. That this man should suffer but not have it be meaningless was something. Still, to have to suffer at all...

"Will the marks heal?" Joy asked.

"They are not wounds," Ink said. "These are permanent. Scars. *Signatura* etched upon his skin." Ink paused and glanced over the man curiously. "Whatever happened, it happened for a reason and it has changed him. I merely bring it to the surface. The *signatura* marks him among my people and yours as one of an exclusive few, a soldier among fawns, respected and untouchable. It is my work, my honor and my auspice, having marked him. It is difficult to explain." Ink rested his hand on his knee as if struck with a thought. "Do you want to try?"

"Me?" Joy asked. "Why?"

Ink shrugged. "You do not have an auspice. I thought that maybe this could be a way for you to understand. I thought, perhaps, to find something that you could do...to contribute." His voice dipped as he started jabbing again. "You said that you were willing to learn."

He sounded disappointed—worse, hurt. He busied himself as if what he'd offered Joy was no big deal, underlining the fact that it *was* a big deal. To him, anyway. She weighed Inq's threat and Ink's offer against the floppy, dirty arm in his lap.

Be indispensable.

"I'll try," she said, surprising them both.

Ink handed over the instrument and shifted so that Joy could sit. She rolled the needle in her hand, feeling more and more that she should hand it back and tell him to forget it. She stared at the wicked tip. What if it didn't work? What if she stabbed a stranger? What if he woke up? What if he screamed? What would happen next?

What if it changed her and she could never change back?

"Gently," he advised, sounding unsure himself. Joy tried to hold the needle steady as Ink guided her. His hand on hers, his chest against her back, his face by her ear, he hovered as if debating how to put into words something he'd done for aeons without thought. She felt it quiver along her skin like an itch, his words by her earlobe. "A slight touch will suffice."

Joy nodded, trying to ignore the smell of rain on his skin.

"How do I make the mark?" she asked, trying to keep her voice calm. Curling her fingers around the needle's handle, she gripped it like a pencil during a test.

"Touch the point to the skin," he said. "And press down. The mark has been ordered. The *signatura* should appear." He didn't sound certain, either, but there was something comforting in the fact that neither of them knew what might happen but were willing to try it together.

Joy took a tight breath. Her knuckles strained. The tip quivered. This was something she had to try. She had to prove that she was willing to be a part of this. To him. To Inq. To herself.

She couldn't do it.

"He'll wake up," she whispered, buying more time.

"He will not."

"Yes, he will," she insisted. Her fingers cramped. "I'm not you. I'm *real* here." She shook her head. "It won't work. It can't!"

Ink stiffened. "Perhaps. Are you frightened?"

She recoiled from the smell, the filth, the wet, slack skin.

"Yes!" she hissed.

"Then we will find something else."

...no one will question why you are no longer with us...

Joy stabbed. There was no shower of black squiggles. No claws or moons or eyes. Nothing. Ink brought his face close to the man's arm.

"Where did you mark him?"

Joy confessed, "I didn't look."

Ink swiveled the slack arm back and forth. "Can you try again?" he asked, curious, pointing to a spot higher on the biceps. "Here?"

Joy held her breath and poked. Not a thing. Not even a drop of blood.

Ink pointed lower. "Again. Here."

She tried again, thinking *pincushion*. Ink checked again.

"Wait." He ran his fingers over the skin as if searching for something tactile. He opened his hand and Joy handed him the needle. Ink stippled the skin with rapid-fire jabs, burying its surface in black hieroglyphs and capillary-red dots. Ink handed the needle back to Joy.

"Try again," he said. "Anywhere in here." He pointed to the freshly speckled spot. Joy tapped a few times. Both she and Ink saw it happen—a tiny patch of clear skin grew in the red.

"You've *erased* them," Ink said, giving Joy a look. She felt strangely embarrassed. He laughed, an unexpectedly loud sound in the cell. "Give me that back before you undo all my hard work!" Joy blushed and hurriedly handed back the needle, secretly glad to be rid of it.

"Well," Ink said, returning to his task, relieved. "It was worth a try."

Joy bounced on her knees with leftover nerves. Digging her fingernails into her palms, she could hear a distant, turbinelike roaring and the rush of wind. Circulation returned to her legs and cramped feet in tingling waves.

"Is that what normally happens when someone else uses your stuff?" she asked.

Ink kept his eyes lowered as he filled the gaps with a sure hand. "I have never let anyone else touch them," he said quietly. "Let alone use one before."

Joy stopped fidgeting. She didn't say anything else, but watched him work with a growing and humbling awe, remembering the comfortable feel of the worn leather wallet, the knapped edge of the arrowhead, the peppermint spice of the wand. When he filed his tools away, she placed a gentle hand on his shoulder. Ink stilled, but didn't look up.

"Thank you," she said.

He hesitated, speaking into shadows.

"No one is watching," he said. "You do not have to pretend."

Joy left her hand where it was and squeezed.

Ink stood, turning smoothly, only a few inches between them. Her fingers slid off his shoulder but lingered on his sleeve. She stared at him, caught in a moment she hadn't intended or expected, but now that it was here, she wanted it. Ink searched her face and touched the edge of her ear. She watched his lips move.

"One more stop," he said quietly. Then stepped back and drew his blade.

Joy sighed, both grateful and sorry as he tore an exit free.

* * *

Joy hadn't dressed for the beach.

The sun beat down warm and lazy, casting long four-o'clock shadows on the sand. The air smelled of baked salt and coconut oil, and Joy kicked up furrows stippled with seashells. She wasn't sure if she was invisible to the tanning tourists strewn over beach chairs and towels, so she tried looking nonchalant in her long-sleeved coat and jeans. She squinted as they approached Inq lounging in a fabric chair, sporting a pair of expensive sunglasses, a skimpy swimsuit and a wide-brimmed hat. She dropped her magazine as they approached.

"I thought you'd never get here," Inq said. "Hi, Joy!"

"Hi," Joy said, feeling totally out of place.

"How was your last assignment?" Inq asked.

Joy looked at Ink. His eyes lingered as he said, "It was unexpectedly enlightening."

"Welcome to the world." Inq got up from her folding chair and brushed off imaginary sand. "So you came to see me in action?"

"Joy mentioned to me that she would like that," Ink said. Inq beamed.

"Perfect! That's my girl, over there." Inq pointed to a knot of college students talking/laughing/tanning in the late-day sun. Their skins shone with oil. It made Joy sweat in envy. It had to be ninety degrees.

"Which one?" asked Ink.

"Blue bikini," Inq said. "I've been waiting forever for her to flip over."

Ink and Inq made their way easily through the throng of vacationers, eroded sand castles and tittering gulls. Joy noticed that she left footprints behind, kicking up little sprays of sand that flung onto blankets and newspapers. There was no way people weren't going to notice that she was dressed for February weather. She expected to be called out at any moment.

Inq knelt down next to the young woman stretched out on a blue beach towel, sunglasses reflecting the bright, sunny sky. She was oblivious to everything, asleep on the beach, her friends gabbing happily not three feet away.

"Isn't she pretty?" Inq said. Ink stood back, indulgent.

One of the girls glanced up at Joy. She froze, a deer in headlights.

Inq coached her smoothly, "Ask her for the time."

"Excuse me," Joy stammered. "Do you have the time?"

"Sure." The girl glanced at her watch. "It's 4:18."

Inq settled herself on the beach towel. "Now look around and say, 'Where *are* they?'" Inq pouted dramatically, miming hands on hips.

"Thanks," Joy said and scanned the beach. "Where *are* they...?"

The girl lost interest. Inq looked smug.

"Piece of cake," she said and spread her unlined hands wide. "Now watch this."

Joy swallowed a gasp as Inq laid her tiny palms against the bikini girl's belly, Inq's skin a startling cream against the caramel-colored tan. Pale lines, the inverse of Ink's dark script, burst over the young woman's body. Inq's fingers dove deeper, disappearing into flesh, slipping inside and just underneath the girl's skin. It was an intimacy even more shocking than the touch itself. Joy could hear her own heartbeat thick in her ears.

The design was beautiful, an intricate snowflake unfolding over the girl's abdomen—a glimpse at something wonderful and impossible etched in near-white. Ribbons wove feathered wings, wreaths of long-lashed eyes, and drooping, flowered vines that stretched and wound over themselves, making a reverse reflection lower down. The image sharpened and collapsed, fading as Inq withdrew, her fingertips sucking the last vestiges of *signatura* from the sun-warmed skin.

Joy didn't say anything. She'd forgotten to breathe.

"Very nice," Ink approved.

"Thanks," Inq said and stage-whispered to Joy, "She lost her virginity!"

Joy gasped, horrified. "You...mark that? All the time?"

"Sorry?" one of the tanning girls said.

"Nothing. Sorry," Joy apologized, embarrassed, and walked away quickly, her boots slogging through sand. Ink fell into step beside her and Inq skipped on her left. Joy didn't speak again until they were past the lifeguard post.

"Isn't that...private?" she hissed. When Joy lost her virginity, she didn't want Inq to know it.

"Well, perhaps," Inq admitted. "But this is a special case. Miss Emily Elizabeth Dawson-Brown comes from a long line of particularly gifted women as long as they remain pure. It's an important guardianship, honoring a sacred pact that dates back to the Early Age." She said it with reverence before adding, "Of course, now her natural power can mature free of constraints and should become *much* more interesting from here on in!" She laughed and pumped her fist in the air. "Let's hear it for modern women!"

Joy crossed her arms and rubbed her shoulders as if suddenly cold in the sweltering heat. "You enjoy your work a little too much. You know that, don't you?"

Inq smirked. "Indeed I do."

Ink smiled with full-on dimples, patting Inq's back much like a real brother teasing his sis. They had no mother, so Joy knew that they weren't technically siblings—they weren't even human—so what did that make them, really? The thought made her more uncomfortable than she wanted to admit.

The three headed to the parking lot while Ink fished for his blade. Joy pointed back behind them as she shook off her boots.

"Aren't you forgetting your magazine on your chair?" she asked.

Inq glanced back, surprised. "Oh. That wasn't my magazine," she said with a laugh. "This isn't even my hat!" And she flung it off into the wind with a whoop. Ink shook his head and Joy followed the tumbling brim with her eyes. Would anyone wonder about it? Or the magazine? Or the chair?

"So? What did you think?" Inq asked Joy, breathless.

"It's...amazing," Joy admitted, finding the easiest word to use. "Really beautiful."

Inq turned to her brother. "See? I told you she would work out. Everything's going to be fine!" She grabbed Joy's face in those iron-and-steel hands whose strength, like Ink's, could be felt in their core. "You're beautiful, too!" she said and squealed. "Eskimo kisses!" Inq rubbed her nose against Joy's. Joy stumbled back. Her mother had called them that: Eskimo kisses. She touched the memory tentatively, like sunburn or a bruise.

"Okay then," Joy stammered, rubbing the tip of her nose, "thanks for the field trip."

Inq winked. "You're welcome anytime!" She glanced at Ink and her manner shifted. "That goes for you, too."

"I know," he said and rested his forehead against Inq's, sharing a quiet moment, eyes closed.

Joy stared at a tree for no reason at all.

"Come," Ink said to Joy. "Time to go home."

Joy took a last look at the beach vacation burning brightly off rainbow umbrellas and dark bodies and blue water.

"Okay," she said. "If I have to."

"It'd be awfully hard to explain tan lines when you got home." Inq laughed.

Joy shrugged. "I'm tempted to find an excuse."

Ink drew his long, sloping line and peeled the universe free.

"Maybe next time," he said and gestured through the door. Joy checked to see that no one was looking in their direction and leapt through, leaving Inq waving cheerily behind.

Joy shook out her boots, peppering the shower floor with fine sand. Ink had left her at her front gate and disappeared with hardly more than a shy glance. *Ask me*, it had said. But Joy had let him go.

She welcomed the gush of hot water, imagining herself back on the tropical shore. Where had they been? Florida? Fiji? The Bahamas? Her mind reeled. She wondered—if it really took no time at all, could she convince Ink to take her on a holiday now and again? She'd even let him examine her other ear.

Changing into comfy pj's, she launched herself at the computer, buying time away from mundane things like homework or the fact that Dad was still not home. She was about to ping Monica, but saw Stefan online. She pounced.

joy2thewurld: hey stranger!

Stefan_malone: hi yrself

joy2thewurld: what gives? havent heard from u in ages!!

Stefan_malone: college = busy
havent u heard?

joy2thewurld: nobdy works that much

Stefan_malone: didnt say I was wrking

joy2thewurld: HA! so who is it?

Stefan_malone: lol
nobdy u know

Joy actually laughed out loud and clapped her hands in glee, forgetting for the moment that she was mad at him and all the stuff she'd planned to say.

joy2thewurld: IT'S A GIRL!!!! xoxoxoxoxoxo
whats her name?

Seconds ticked. Joy wondered why it took boys so long to type.

Stefan_malone: james

Joy stared at the monitor, her infectious smile fading. She read the last line again. Then the ones before. She read through the entire, brief conversation thinking, *I've watched this happen a million times on TV.* But here, now, on her own computer, wearing flannel pajamas and a damp towel on her head, the whole thing seemed somehow unbelievable. Even more unbelievable than invisible tattoos on a tropical shore. Was this real? Is this how it worked? Was he kidding? Was he coming out? Maybe it was a nickname? A misspelling? Maybe?

She'd stared for too long.

Stefan_malone has logged off.

"No..." Joy frantically typed a few impotent *Hellos?* and *Stefs?* No response. She dug through her backpack and speed-dialed him, cursing herself and him and modern technology. He didn't pick up. She didn't leave a message. She didn't even know what to say. All the things she should have said in that moment sat in her stomach and squirmed.

She ought to write back. Send a text. Send an email. She picked up the phone. She ought to say *something.*

Joy clicked a new email and stared at the white page. Her fingers twitched. She didn't know what to do. The letters didn't make sense. The words wouldn't come. She pushed away from her desk and fell onto her bed and stared up at the ceiling, bunching the wet blue towel in her hands. It was cold.

She felt like crying.

It had been an innocent question! But lately innocent questions had had unexpected answers and caused all sorts of trouble.

Joy buried her head under the cool side of her pillow.

That's what I get for asking.

When she'd been in level-nine gymnastics, Joy's friends had all been from the mats, joined together by blood and sweat, hugs and sprains, victories and defeats, before school and after, six days a week. Obsessively watching Olympic videos together, counting calories, comparing injuries and split kicks. School was just a thing that happened in between training, students and teachers were nothing more than backdrop shapes, extras in chairs. Joy's life had been her coach, a tenth of a point and Mom sitting in the bleachers. After Mom had given up and left, Joy had given up the rest, creating a giant vacuum hole in her life right next to the Mom-shaped one. Her world funneled into that black hole and disappeared.

Monica was the one person who had never been a part of that world. They'd been friends from Monica's transfer in fourth grade and had picked up right where they'd left off without missing a beat, despite the years in between.

And today, she really needed a friend.

Joy dropped into her usual study spot between Nonfiction and the library Reference Desk. Monica stopped texting Gordon and watched her wordlessly with cat-wide eyes.

"So? Spill."

Joy swallowed a deep breath and said, "Stef's gay."

"Stef's gay?"

"Stef's gay."

Monica blinked and sent her text, dropping the phone in her purse to give Joy her full attention. "Huh," she said. "What do you think of that?"

Joy picked her nails. "I hate it."

Monica shifted in sympathy. "What about it, exactly?"

"I don't know," Joy said, having trouble with words. It was like she woke up this morning and realized that she didn't know anybody, really, and—as usual—she'd been the last one to figure it out. No one had bothered to tell her that they'd already changed. Mom, Dad, Stef, Monica. It was like she was the only one not in the know. She blinked hard. "I guess it's the fact that he didn't tell me—that he knew and didn't tell me." Her heart added, *again*.

"We're talking about Stef, right? This isn't about your mom," Monica asked with piercing accuracy. Joy felt shameful heat flash like the light in her eye. "You never knew for sure if Stef knew about Doug," Monica pressed. Joy didn't say anything. It was true. She didn't know *for sure*. She'd never asked Stef directly if he'd known about their mom's affair. They didn't talk about that stuff in her house, but mostly, she didn't want to know. One betrayal had been enough. "*And* you don't know if he knew about *this* beforehand, either. Maybe he just found out and you're the second one to know."

Joy tore a cuticle and frowned. "Third," she muttered. "His name's James."

"Nice name," Monica said. Joy glared at her. Her friend shrugged, bangled wrists jangling. "So, what do I know? I'm dating a guy named Gordon Weitzenhoffer." Joy didn't want to smile, but it tugged at her lips. She flipped open her notebook. It was full of black eyes in the margins. She closed it quickly. Monica sighed against the wall of Joy's anger.

"This isn't a whole 'going to hell' thing, right? 'Cuz you know how much I love my uncles Marty and Mike and I'd hate to have to smack you right here in a quiet library."

"No," Joy said. "It isn't that. I mean, I don't like the idea of Stef being...looked at differently or anything. But it won't be by me. At least, I don't think so. I don't know," she added honestly. "I couldn't even think of what to IM."

"He came out on the *computer*?" Monica gasped. She sat up and shook her head. "Miss Manners does *not* approve."

"This may be outside Miss Manners's jurisdiction," Joy said. "I just don't know what to *do* about it."

"Is there something you're supposed to do?"

"Yes," Joy insisted. "What was I supposed to say? 'Congratulations'? 'Are you sure'? 'Thanks for telling me'? 'Does Dad know'?"

"*Does* your dad know?" Monica asked.

"I don't know," Joy said again. "Stef was always..." She trailed off, not wanting to admit aloud that her brother had always been closer to Mom. That's why Joy was sure he'd known about the affair—that Mom had told him that she was leaving, but hadn't told her. Had he kept this secret from her, too? And for how long? Did her *mother* know about Stef? That would be the ultimate betrayal. *"Keep strong." HA!* How many secrets did people keep from each other? Or was it just from her? Why was she *always* the last to know everything?

Joy rubbed her eyes, on the edge of tears. Rule Number One: no crying at school. Weeping was an unforgivable offense ripe for the rumor mill. She couldn't afford any more drama right now. She knuckled her flashing eye.

"I've been texting and emailing and calling ever since. I stayed up late in case he wrote back. Even if I don't know what to say...I want to say something." Joy lifted her eyes, blinking back watery traitors. "Don't tell anyone, okay?"

"Who would I tell?" Monica asked.

There was no one to tell. Nobody noticed. No one cared.

"Just don't," Joy said.

"Okay," Monica said. "But what about your dad?"

Joy shrugged. "What about him?" The way she said it sounded petulant and dumb.

"Hi, there!"

Joy turned and almost fell out of her chair. Inq waggled her fingers hello. Joy glanced at Monica, who had looked to see what had spooked Joy. Naturally, she didn't see anything. Or anyone. Joy sat, stuck in horrified shock.

"Can we talk a little girl-talk?" Inq asked as if nothing was out of the ordinary. Monica couldn't see or hear her, but Joy sure could. Fresh panic felt like snow against her skin. Joy didn't know how to answer without sounding crazy in front of Monica or rude in front of Inq, who was still armed with unspoken threats about making Joy disappear.

Joy gripped her chair. Monica raised her eyebrows.

"What?" her friend said.

"I just..." Joy stalled. Her brain was a total wash. *What had she been saying?*

"You have to go to the bathroom," Inq suggested, slipping her arms around Joy's shoulders. "Isn't it fortunate that humans have to pee a lot?"

"I just can't think about Dad right now," Joy blurted, scratching her shoulder, effectively shooing Inq away while simultaneously ignoring her—a small win for sanity. Joy sat up a little straighter. "I have to talk to Stef first."

Monica relaxed. "Fair enough."

Inq grinned and whispered, *"Pssssssssshhhhh!"*

Joy flinched and pushed her away.

"Joy?" Monica sounded alarmed.

"Let's go!" Inq insisted, incredibly close to Joy's ear. It tickled.

"What is the *matter* with you?" Monica nearly shouted.

Joy stood up quickly. "I think something landed on me!" she said. Inq giggled. Joy swatted her sleeves and neck and seat. "Ugh! Creepy!" she spat the veiled accusation. Inq laughed aloud, but no one else heard. Monica stared at Joy like crazy was contagious.

Inq sauntered nearer to Monica. Just seeing Inq within a few feet of her best friend sent prickles down Joy's back, but she dared not move. She didn't want to think about what Inq might do.

"Say it," Inq cooed.

Joy gave in. "I gotta pee," she muttered and fumbled with her bag. She wanted to get Inq as far away from Monica as possible before the impish Scribe got creative. The more distance, the better.

"I'll see you later, okay?" Joy said. "Thanks, Mon."

"Sure. No problem." Monica waved stiffly and went back to texting Gordon. "Ping me if you need me back on planet Earth."

"Later," Joy said as she headed toward the girls' bathroom.

"Much later!" Inq called back. Joy prayed there was an otherworldly mute on Inq's volume control. Was her invisibility voluntary? Could she cause a scene and then disappear, leaving Joy to deal with the fallout? Joy hurried a little faster, just in case.

Joy pushed in the door and did a quick foot-sweep of the stalls before turning on Inq.

"What the *hell* were you doing?!" Joy hissed. "I've already had more than enough therapy to last a lifetime, thank you very much!"

"You're not crazy," Inq said simply. "You're just stressed out. That's why I'm throwing you a party."

Joy stopped. "A party?" she said suspiciously. "For me?"

"You're the guest of honor," Inq said. "Wouldn't be much of a party without you. Besides, it's not like you were doing anything important." Her dark eyes brightened with mischief. "I have come to rescue you from tedium!"

"Tedium?"

"Boredom," Inq said. "You looked bored. And this—" she gestured around the bathroom "—is boring."

Joy dug in her bag and started fixing her makeup. She desperately needed some recovery time and wasn't getting any.

"This is school," she said, glossing her lips. "It's supposed to be boring."

"Life's short," Inq said. "Well, yours is, anyway." Another chill prickled over Joy's limbs. She hated how Inq made everything sound like a mortal threat. The Scribe laughed and one-arm hugged her. "Lighten up, Joy—you're only human, after all. I got everybody together just for you."

"What, now?"

"Yes, now. Why? Have something better to do?"

Did she? Joy glared at herself in the mirror. Everyone else in her life had changed and moved on to bigger and better things. Why hadn't she?

Did she have something better to do?

"Nope," Joy said, dropping her gloss in the bag. "Lead the way."

Inq smiled and offered Joy her small, smooth hand. Joy took it, trying not to think about how similar it was to Ink's. The quiver she felt had nothing to do with him, but rather a defiant excitement plus a good dose of fear. Inq seemed to sense that, too, and smiled wider. Joy hesitated.

Why was she doing this?

But then it was too late.

Spreading her right hand, Inq gathered power invisibly, like a storm. Joy felt electricity crackling her hair, tasted the ionic tang on her lips. The air under Inq's fingertips rippled like heat waves and wind.

"This way," Inq said as she pulled Joy gently through a fissure of light.

"Happy Lehman's Day!" Inq crowed, throwing her arms open. Joy might have thought it was to show off the private pool, sunny skies and emerald seas that kissed the low horizon, but it was evidently to greet the six half-naked men who waved back. A few rushed over to give Inq hugs and kisses in the European fashion. One did it in the French fashion—all tongue. Joy accepted a couple of pecks on each cheek and a glass of something fruity as an excuse to look away.

They were ushered into lounge chairs flanked by a patio table and bright white umbrellas. There were balloons and tinsel and silver streamers. The water sparkled a million shades of turquoise and green.

"This is Luiz," Inq said, indicating the dark man with long hair who filled her glass with ice. He smiled at Joy. She felt a twang somewhere deep inside her and sipped her tropical slushie to hide it. Luiz did not pour any beverage into Inq's glass. Instead, Inq slipped a cube into her palm and trailed it along the inside of her wrist. Slithering, pale calligraphy followed the melting water. Inq glanced coyly up at Luiz and he ran his lips over the droplet. She mussed his hair playfully and gestured with the dripping ice.

"That's Tuan and Antony in the pool, goofing off. Ilhami is by the bar, and Enrique, the one with gray hair, is wear-

ing sunglasses in the shade...and here comes my Nikolai!"
She held her arm out to a gorgeous, muscular man who took
it and kissed her knuckles as if she were a queen. "He's my
newest *lehman*," Inq said proudly. "He speaks six languages,
has visited every continent and has excellent taste in, oh, just
about everything!" She laughed. He did, too. Joy wasn't certain, but she thought she recognized Nikolai from a magazine ad. The hot Russian possible-underwear-model offered
her a paper napkin, which she accepted with a quiet thank-
you as she dabbed her lips.

"Happy Lehman's Day, Joy," he said with a grin. His accent
was like marzipan, rich and sweet.

Joy wiped the glass's condensation—or was it sweat?—off
her hands. She desperately wanted to take out her phone and
snap some photos, but didn't dare. Monica would kill for eye
candy like this—Gordon or no.

"Is there really such a thing as Lehman's Day?" she asked
Inq.

"Well, there should be," Inq said. "In fact, yes there is. I
just made it up! What day is it?"

Luiz said, "February tenth."

"There you go," Inq said. "Lehman's Day."

Joy grinned and sucked red slush off a strawberry. "That's
awfully close to Valentine's Day."

"Saint Valentine?" Inq said primly. "Never heard of him."

They laughed. Joy kicked off her shoes and leaned back in
her cushioned beach chair. "And this party is for me?" Joy
said. "Where's *my* Cabana Boy?"

Luiz laughed. "You *are* a Cabana Boy! Welcome to the club!"

As if on cue, tight-and-tan Ilhami cranked up the sound
system and the two guys in the pool started spike-splashing

each other. Enrique ignored them and raised a toast from across the pool. Many voices followed suit: "To Joy!"

Embarrassed, she saluted with her own glass and took another sip. She wasn't sure if she should be relieved or insulted that it was a virgin daiquiri. Joy didn't need alcohol to make her head swim—the scenery was more than enough to boggle her mind. Her fellow *lehman* splashed in the sunshine, music played, balloons danced and Inq languished in adoration. It was a taste of finer things, an exclusive club that she'd just joined.

It wasn't bad!

Joy tore off her socks and rolled her jeans up as far as they would go, declining the skimpy swimsuit in the Água de Coco bag by her feet. The deck warmed her toes, her eyes adjusted to the piercing gold sunlight and she drank sips of fruity, ice-cold slush as exotic men frolicked like little kids in the pool. Luiz returned to refill her glass and offer her a slice of cake. It had her name on it in frosting.

"A little overwhelmed?" he asked, handing her a fork.

"Just a bit," she said.

"You get used to it," Luiz said, laughing. "Actually, I lie. You never get used to it, but you get used to their whims." Joy thought Ink's whims were hardly anything like Inq's, but the possibilities were dizzying. Five-star restaurants instead of dungeons. Pool parties instead of stinky sheep.

"Hand me your phone," he said. He snapped a photo of himself flashing his butter-melt smile and entered his phone number with quick-typing thumbs. "If you need anything, call. That goes for all of us. Consider it one of the perks of membership." He winked toward Inq, who cuddled in Enrique's lap. "And that's not even one of the better ones!"

Joy accepted her phone back. "Thanks."

Inq circled, spending a little time with each of her *lehman*, allowing Joy to enjoy some time to herself. Joy's thoughts were like her hands—unsure of what to do. Everywhere she looked there were impossible colors, bright, hot smiles and water dripping down six-pack abs. Nowhere was safe. She even got splashed.

Finally, Inq plopped down next to Joy.

"You like?"

"It's awesome," Joy admitted. "And they can see you, too. So all of us have the Sight?"

"Oh, no," Inq said quickly. "You're pretty rare. I had to purchase a tincture at great personal cost." She wrinkled her nose as she squinched in her chair. "But so totally worth it, right?"

Joy considered the beautiful men milling under the streamers and shiny balloons. She set aside her empty cake plate. "Yeah, well, thanks for thinking of me."

"Oh, I think about you a lot," Inq said. "Ink does, too. He just doesn't know what to do about it yet."

Joy's heartbeat picked up speed. The idea that he thought of her—even a little tiny bit—was undeniably exciting. Inq watched Joy as if reading her mind.

"You think about him, too," she said.

Joy gave a little nod.

Inq shifted her attention out into the pool yard where young men dove underwater and older men conversed in the shade. Inq slid an ice cube down her throat, pale pictographs flowing like music at her touch.

"You'd be the first, you know. His first kiss." Joy started, because of either the subject or the information. Inq smirked in a way that reminded Joy much too much of Ink. "Remember, Joy, he's never had a *lehman*. He doesn't know a kiss from a thimble. Don't get upset with him and don't expect him to call the shots," Inq said sagely. "It wouldn't be fair—to either of you."

Joy placed her empty glass down. "You sound like his older sister."

"Well, he's like my younger brother in many ways, and I have far more experience being human than he does. Ink, like my *lehman*, is my responsibility," Inq said and shrugged. "But Ink doesn't know what it is to be human—to be *with* humans—and I do." She waved Nikolai over. He hadn't strayed far. He settled down next to Inq. The deck chair groaned.

"You see, there is this debate regarding your world and mine," Inq said while she twined her and Nikolai's fingers together. "On the one hand—" she smirked at the pun "—there are those who believe we are meant to live together, in balance, that one world cannot exist without the other." She examined their light-and-dark fingers and placed a kiss on each of his fingertips. A tiny spark of scrollwork and vines faded like fireworks after the pop. "Others argue that there are cycles—eras—and that when the Age of Man fades, our glory will return and vice versa. Always waxing and waning, polar opposites, each allotted their time in the sun." She playfully swung her and Nikolai's hands back and forth. "But the most radical argue that humans hamper our rise and that they must be abolished so that we may 'rule supreme.'" Inq simpered at the full-lipped Russian, who nipped at her nose. She pouted playfully before turning her black eyes to Joy. "Nonsense. Where would we be without humans, I ask you? Our lives, like our worlds, are intertwined and I, for one, welcome it." She seemed to relish the words in her mouth. "Ink, however, has kept himself apart, forever on the outside, only briefly looking in." She shook her head. "He does not yet understand how people think, how they feel." She teased the joined hands closer to her face. "What they *like*."

Inq kissed the back of Nikolai's hand in an explosion of eggs-within-eggs-within-eggs-hatching-birds. The details were one or two shades lighter than the color of his skin, like henna in reverse.

"Ink doesn't know chalk dust from chocolate," Inq said, her lips caressing Nikolai's skin. "He doesn't know the difference between a nip and a bite." She playfully nipped his forefinger. Nikolai gasped as a river of patterns raced down the thick of his wrist. "If he likes his first taste, he might gobble you up. Swallow you whole." Inq gave her a sidelong glance. "And you might like it."

Joy kept her eyes on her glass, stabbing the straw as she stirred. She knew what a kiss was, and what it was like to be kissed, but she'd always been the one being kissed, not the one who kissed first. And how did Inq know if Ink wanted to kiss her, anyhow? Did Ink even want to be kissed? By anyone? By Joy?

"This is all new to him and he doesn't know what to do with it—doesn't know what to do with you, specifically," Inq continued. "I wanted you to realize that before this goes any further." Her voice dipped low. "Because it will all be for nothing if you get caught. His work will be in question and your life will be at risk. I'm here to make sure that never, ever happens." Inq disentangled herself from Nikolai and sat up. "You think you've seen weirdness? You haven't seen anything yet. These monsters? They are just the first experimental prods checking you out. The Twixt wants to see what you're made of, where you stand and whether Ink will stand by you."

"Will you?" Joy asked before thinking. But Inq laughed and clapped Joy good-naturedly on the leg.

"You bet! This was my idea, after all. I'd never live it down if one of my own plans failed." Inq smiled convincingly, but Joy hardly felt convinced. At least Inq was being honest. Not like Stef or Mom. It was brusque, but oddly refreshing to be having a frank conversation for once.

Joy's phone made the rounds, each *lehman* taking photos of himself and entering emails, phone numbers, names. She was one of them now. *Cabana Boys.* Joy tried on how that felt.

"I like you, Joy, really," Inq said. "But you've got to lighten up." She scooped up a truffle from an iced silver dish and popped it into her mouth.

"Can you tell the difference between chalk dust and chocolate?" Joy teased.

"Oh, yes!" Inq gushed. "It takes some maneuvering, but I've learned to concentrate and create touch and taste and smell—I can move my senses around like billiard balls." She gestured to Enrique, who had been smoking a cigar, and he obligingly brought out an embossed gold lighter. With a practiced flip, he lit the flame and Inq stuck her finger into the fire, holding it there for far longer than she should. Enrique snapped the lighter lid closed. Inq stuck her finger in her mouth as if it were a Popsicle and gave him a wink.

"Show-off," he scolded her and ran strong fingers through her feathery hair. She leaned her skull back and groaned in her throat.

Inq popped her finger out of her mouth and grinned at

Joy. "It doesn't hurt if I don't want it to," she said. "I can taste what I want and smell the flowers or feel the cold." She held up her arm, which sprouted a shiver of tiny goose bumps. "I don't *have* to, but I *want* to. Ink has never bothered, and so he is learning as he goes. Watching you." She spoke gently. "Remember that he will be learning about everything, watching you."

Joy crossed her ankles, feeling the sun on her bare feet. "No pressure," she muttered, taking a truffle.

Inq laughed and poked her playfully. "You can handle it."

Joy blinked. *Flash! Flash!*

"I know I can," Joy said and bit through the chocolate shell.

EIGHT

JOY SAT AT THE DINNER TABLE, SNEAKING PEEKS OVER THE instant mashed potatoes to see if Dad suspected anything. About Stef. About Ink. About her. But he ate calmly and quietly, sprinkling pepper on his meat loaf as if nothing were any different. She dunked forkfuls in ketchup, trying to make certain, checking the landscape of his face for hints. Did he know? He couldn't know. Joy rubbed her flashing eye. Either her father had developed a perfect covert-ops mask of indifference, or he really didn't have a clue.

She hadn't seen Ink all day. She wasn't sure when she'd started expecting him to be waiting for her, but not having him show up made her twitchy and anxious, as if bees were humming under her skin. She took her last bite and picked up her plate.

"I'm turning in," she announced.

"Really?" Dad checked the microwave clock. "It's seven-thirty."

"I've got homework and a headache and I'm beat." At least two of those things were a lie, but it might as well have been all three. Joy couldn't concentrate. Her mind was a whirlwind of blue skies, half-naked male models and a cell phone full of new pics from halfway around the world.

"Okay," he said. "I'll try to keep the party down to a low roar."

Joy grinned, secretly thinking of chocolate truffles and Mylar balloons. "Thanks. I appreciate it."

On the way to her room, in her head she replayed the pool party, the beach landing, squatting in the dungeon, the jab of a needle, the splash of pool water and the taste of frozen strawberries. She was already a jumble of mixed emotions when she opened her door and saw the large greeting card on her bed.

The handwriting reached into her chest and squeezed. The sight of her own name and address was enough to give her shivers and a tight twist in her side. She hadn't received an actual letter from her mother in months—just phone calls and texts that Joy mostly ignored. They were too painful. They were too *this*.

Joy sat down heavily, aware of every ache and pain, from the tiniest twinge of sunburn to the echo of her two broken toes from that missed aerial three years ago. Her mother had taken her to the hospital, wrapping her tightly in her arms and a thin blue blanket—sacrificing her hand to Joy's squeezing when they'd snapped the bones back into place—and then had taken her out for ice cream to feel better.

It felt like a million years ago. It felt like yesterday.

She opened the envelope without thinking, already registering the generic Get Well message and every blank space filled with Mom's handwriting.

Honey, I know you're still angry with me, but I wanted to make sure you were all right. When your father told me you'd

gone to the E.R., I was so worried! I tried to call you, but
there was no answer. I couldn't help thinking about the time—

Joy snapped the card closed. Her father had put this in
her room and hadn't said anything. He'd known the whole
time, and she was the one who hadn't had a clue. *Fine*, she
thought, feeling sick, betrayed. *Fine*. Now they all had secrets
and separate lives. The difference was Mom's could be kept
at a comfortable distance, available on folded, recycled cardstock with a Forever stamp.

Joy opened her top drawer and dropped the peach-colored
card onto the stack of envelopes with the same L.A. address.
Most of them were unopened and postmarked last year. Dad
had asked her to stop writing Return to Sender and mailing
them back as a petty way to hurt her mother that she "might
regret later," but Joy never opened them. Her father hadn't
mentioned them since.

Joy shut the drawer with the flat of her hands and wiped
them against her jeans. She debated going back into the
kitchen to yell at Dad, to scream at him, to cry with him, to
lay everything out on the table until it pushed the dishes off
the edges and crashed into pieces on the floor. She slammed
the drawer again. That was how *this* felt!

Exhausted, palms stinging, Joy flumped onto her bed and
plugged herself into angry guitar wails.

She must have fallen asleep. She must have forgotten to
turn on the lights. She must have also forgotten to lock her
window and take off the earbuds, because while the sudden
breeze woke her, she never heard a thing.

Her shins scraped the bedpost as she was hauled backward

by her throat, surprise and pressure squeezing her mute. Being airborne ended abruptly as she slammed against the wall with a bone-rattling shake. She was face-to-face with the bulbous yellow eyes of an angry aether sprite.

"Remember me?" it drawled and lifted her higher. Joy's legs kicked at nothing, her fingers scrabbled at her neck. She curled, wrapping both legs around the thing's bony arm, squeezing her thighs and wrenching to one side. Something popped. It switched hands. Her hair whipped across her face as it flung her toward the opposite wall. Was Dad home? Had he gone out? If she could scream... A hooked finger pointed a claw in her face.

"Don't speak," it warned. "Your silence is what brought us here, yes? Why start speaking now?" It cackled. "'Won't stand for it,' I said," the sprite's scratchy voice lilted. "You should have listened, little one. Words have power, and you have forfeited yours."

She swallowed and inhaled to scream, but a talon poked deep into her trachea, the tip sinking sharply into her skin.

"*Lehman* to Ink," it said. "Did not heed." It tsked and wagged its claw back and forth. "Did not listen. *Tchoo tchoo.*" Fingers coiled about her throat, joint by joint, like a bicycle chain. "Now you go to Briarhook."

She closed her eyes. All she needed was enough air to say Ink's name. She moved her lips. She couldn't swallow. Her tongue lodged between her teeth. Air wheezed through her nose. The aether sprite tossed her casually over one bony shoulder, slamming her against his back, which felt as if she'd hit brick. His head was a rock; his ribs, iron bars. What little breath she had popped out her mouth. She gagged.

"Do not speak," it hissed. "Try to speak, I crush your throat."

The ropy fingers slithered closer by a fraction, and her vision tunneled.

"Good. You understand. Don't fight—you do not want me to drop you."

It clambered back to the window, slipped the screen wider and jumped.

Even in free fall, Joy couldn't manage a scream.

They never hit ground. She felt the sprite hook onto something, her stomach dropping and bouncing against her closed throat. They bobbed, swinging forward and gliding swiftly over the yard. Her hair and pajama pants flattened in the wind. The chill scurried over her bare breasts as her shirt billowed around her. She shivered, blinking back tears and bright flashes that sparked in both eyes, winking on the edge of consciousness, in terror and with growing speed. They were moving fast, every second carrying her farther from home.

The creature stopped with a clatter of claws. Joy craned her head to the side and looked down. They were high above the ground, zip-lining over the cable wires, carabining overhead along the telephone poles. Cars passed beneath them with a whoosh of slush. Joy stiffened. It was a long way down.

Look up, she prayed in her head. *Please, somebody, see me!*

But if anyone did, she couldn't tell. It was dark, it was late and she was thirty feet up. No Officer Castrodads would be there to save her. Nobody knew where she was. And no one was likely to report a girl in pajamas blowing like a flag in the dark. Part of her really hoped to pass out, but the cold kept her vividly awake. Her teeth chattered. Her nose ran. Her cheeks stung with salt as she cried.

Another launch onto the neighboring pole and Joy was able to better position her legs. Pinning her heels against her captor's hips, she arched her spine in an easy backbend. It wasn't comfortable, but it was better than banging against the brick-hard body, hanging tethered by her throat. Her knees absorbed the jostling and her shoulders anchored her head. The aether sprite jumped again. They swung like silent apes through a power-grid jungle.

Then: nothing—an unspooled ribbon of free fall.

Smack! Joy whiplashed against his skull and saw stars. Her mouth felt funny. She might have bitten her tongue. The thought of blood made her nauseated and she half swallowed. Her ears popped. Her eyes watered. She needed to breathe!

Her feet stumbled against the earth as the ground tilted. They were clambering down a ravine bank, her bare feet kicking up dirt tinged in frost. It got warmer as they descended. She could feel moist heat on her face and saw gray tendrils of steam misting the air. A car passed overhead in a spray of asphalt-heated slush. Drops of wet snow slapped her face as the sprite dragged her down.

There was a massive drainpipe built into an archway below the street. The concrete blocks hung with heavy ivy and moss still clinging to life in the cast-off heat. Steam rose off the surface of puddles and surrounded the grate where Joy's feet dangled, the elongated hand still noosed at her throat.

"Briarhook," the aether sprite called out like a summons. "I brought the girl."

Joy hit the ground hard. She spat out some bits of bark and

leaf that clung to her face and covered the ravine floor. The aether sprite pushed her flat against the mulch. She struggled, stopping when a large portion of the undergrowth detached from the wall.

Huge and filthy, it gave off an overwhelming smell of mold and rotting leaves. When it moved, it kicked up puffs of brown pollen that hung in the air, scratching the back of her throat and making her sneeze. Her eyes watered; the left side of her face stung.

Briarhook's eyes were piggy pinholes in its fat, fleshy face, all but hidden under massive quills, its striped porcupine hair pockmarked in leaves. Its cheeks sagged and its clothes hung in mealy rags. It might have looked pitiful if not for the cruel curl of its lip and the rusty meat cleaver it clutched in one hand.

Hooked feet clawed through the earth and debris, dragging a sluggish tail behind it. Its voice was thick and scratchy as it folded over its belly.

"*Lehman?*" Briarhook asked the sprite, sounding suspicious. Joy gagged and her eyes ran. His breath smelled of fetid meat.

"Yes." Her captor smashed her face in the dirt for emphasis. The aether sprite sounded far away—one of her ears had plugged with water. "*Lehman* to Ink."

Briarhook shuffled forward, quills rattling, and she instinctively shrank back. His terrible face hung over hers, the floppy ends of his cheeks brushing her forehead as he spoke his broken, putrid English.

"You. Take message. My message. No?" Briarhook said. "Make message. You take." He gave a satisfactory grunt. "Make message. You."

Joy scrambled against the ground, all thoughts on the cleaver. It amused the sprite and Briarhook both. She ground her teeth and kept flailing in her cold, soaked pajamas. Girls' Self-Defense 103: Never give up! Her teeth chattered. Strange sounds eked from the back of her throat.

"Hold," Briarhook ordered, and its moleish toes clenched over her right wrist, pinning it. Something poked her in the shoulder. "Here."

No! She couldn't speak. She was beyond terror.

The aether sprite wrenched her arm, inverting her elbow and locking her spine. She craned backward. Soggy things clung to her skin. A leaf stem poked her eye. She'd scraped her chin. She tasted mud.

The cleaver thunked an inch from her nose, the tip buried two inches into soft earth.

She'd peed herself warm, then cold.

"Think use this?" Briarhook chortled. "No. That Ink. Job Ink. My job, this." He grasped one of his quills and with a grunt ripped it from his own skull. The quill came loose with a flap of skin. Briarhook picked it off and twisted the pointed end with deft fingers, forcing it into a shape. Joy watched, horrified, as Briarhook flattened the end with a bang against the wall.

Satisfied, he snapped his fat fingers. His palm burst burning-hot red, turning near white in the center. The glow lit his features. She struggled to move. She quivered, whimpering in her nose. He pressed the flat end of the quill to his hand, like a branding iron. It began to smolder. A thin plume of smoke slithered up, gray and sharp smelling.

Briarhook huddled closer. The aether sprite laughed. Joy tried to do anything. *Anything!* Tried. Struggled. Failed.

"This, job mine," Briarhook hissed. "Now you? Job yours."

He held the glowing thing in front of Joy's eyes—she could feel the heat curl her lashes. Briarhook withdrew and she saw a flash of orange on the edge of her vision. Someone else was there in the dark. She tried to turn and see who it was, tried to beg for help, but Briarhook pushed the quill deep into her arm and the world went white.

She screamed a thin, animal noise, tasting the burning of her own skin in the smoke. Her mind went nova, nerves raking, clawing, scrabbling. Denial. Disbelief. She couldn't think. Couldn't think. *Couldn't!*

She barely grunted when he yanked the brand free, blood and melted poly-fibers caking the end of the quill. The world was somewhere beyond a haze of red pain. Joy twitched with hot spasms, sparklers of shock.

Briarhook slapped a fistful of slush onto the wound. She whimpered, hoarse from screaming. There was a crackle of branches. A small hum of approval. Hasp hissed in the dark. Briarhook tossed her loose arm aside.

"Put back," Briarhook grumbled, sticking the brand in the snow. The quill sizzled as it died. "Message for Ink."

The aether sprite picked her up and slung her over its back. Joy stumbled backward in her head and everything snuffed out.

Joy hit her bed and felt the snap of cold in her room. A shadow moved and disappeared. She was left wet and shivering. Alone.

Her arm! She wanted to cut it off and throw it away. The pain spread sweat over her whole body. Every hair hurt. She shied away from thinking too much about why. She said the first word she could think through the agony: "Mom...?"

Her voice whispered through a raw, frightened throat. Joy's fingers shook, barely touching her shoulder, feeling the crispy, sharp edges of either her nightshirt or her skin. She woke up a little more, remembering who she was, where she was, and who was no longer with her where she was. She hadn't the strength to cry.

"Dad...?"

It wasn't a dream. Wasn't a nightmare. This was real. She didn't want to look. She couldn't look. Jagged images flashed red and black, orange and white.

Blinking back the roaring tightness in her head, she closed her eyes and hissed the last name like a prayer.

"Ink!"

Although it came out in a shudder.

"I-I-I-I-I-nk!"

She rolled onto her left side, the constant flashing in her marked eye a strobe keeping her awake. Joy moaned softly, curling as tight as she could, trying not to touch anything while she smeared her runny nose against her pillow. Smothering her face in the familiar scent of fabric softener, Joy tried to escape the sickening smell of her own charred, blackened skin.

She became aware of him when he brushed her hair out of her eyes and she focused on his face, piercing and intent. She opened her eyes, glaring hate and hurt and blame through the tears.

"I-I-I-I-I-nk!" she chattered again and started shaking uncontrollably.

"Joy," he said and scooped her up in his arms. She whimpered and strained her neck against the awful wrenching pull along her skin. He lifted her easily. "I have you."

She didn't see how they went, didn't feel the change happen, but he lowered her into the wingback chair and the musty smell told her where they'd gone.

The butler stormed into the foyer holding a gun.

"Kurt," Ink said and placed a hand at the back of Joy's neck. "Graus Claude, please. Now."

Without a word, the butler U-turned and ran down the hall.

"He will help," Ink said quietly, his voice hard as steel. "May I see?"

Joy shut her eyes as Ink touched her elbow, right below the heart of the pain. She pushed her forehead against the upholstery and sucked air through her teeth. A thousand smaller pains scattered like bits of hail. She didn't know where it wouldn't hurt. She concentrated on not throwing up.

"Briarhook," Ink said flatly. "Briarhook did this?" Joy didn't answer. She didn't have to. "He'd sent a message to you before? One you did not give to me? It was likely written in the veins of a leaf...."

"I DIDN'T KNOW!" she screamed.

Ink nodded, unperturbed. A violent stillness filled the room.

"I understand. This was done for me, not you." His voice was slicing, deadly calm. "I will not tolerate it. Joy, I..." Ink stopped, his hand snaking along his silver chain. "But that does not help you now," he said quietly. "It hurts."

"Yes!" she cried. "It hurts!"

Ink sank to his knees next to her chair, his hand cautiously placed on the armrest near her knees. Graus Claude and his armed butler had appeared in the foyer and hovered in the entrance.

"Joy, do you want me to stay with you?" Ink asked, his voice dropping low. "Or do you want me to bring Briarhook an answer he will not forget?"

Joy glared as hot as her skin.

"Get him!" she hissed.

"Consider it done," Ink said and stood, addressing Graus Claude, who hulked resplendent in blue silk pajamas and robe. "Please tend her for me."

"Consider it done," the Bailiwick said and inclined his head.

Ink nodded, flicked his razor and sliced the world free. With barely a step, he was gone.

"Vicious," Graus Claude rumbled, nostrils flaring. "I approve. Now let us see if we can't clean you up."

Graus Claude gestured to his butler, who silently lifted her up. She screamed again.

"Gently, Kurt," the great toad cautioned as he led the way down the amber-lit hall.

Joy's vision throbbed. Dirt and blood caked her crispy clothes. Her body shivered violently and her face radiated heat and sweat. She rested her head against the butler's shirt and felt guilty about the stain. She couldn't help it. She could barely keep her head up. She could barely...

They entered a wide room of cool, pale pinstripe wallpaper, brass fixtures and ivory porcelain, dominated by a claw-foot tub. Kurt placed her on a satin fainting couch, which she thought appropriate considering she felt like blacking out. He swiftly opened an inlaid chest, removing tinkling glass-stopper bottles, metal aid kits and a tray. Graus Claude settled himself onto a fringed ottoman and bent his great head to hers. He sniffed the wound like a delicate hound.

"Briarhook, indeed," he said. "Sent his message loud and clear, the vagrant. While marks are given voluntarily, I am afraid that they are not always received that way. If he'd gone through proper channels... Ah, well, no need to hear all that again." The Bailiwick lifted one of his four hands to raise Joy's chin, inspecting her neck. Two of his other hands braced on his knees. "You've a new necklace. Looks like a fine choker of jellyfish pearls. Aether sprite, correct? That would be Hasp, most likely. Stings, does it? Beastly creature." He let her chin droop. "Hasp answers to Briarhook over kin and clan. Can't buy loyalty like that, no—that comes with leverage. Promises. Threats."

Kurt looked up from his silver tray of bandages, ointments and oddments, and gave only a twist of his lip as commentary.

Graus Claude chuckled deep in his gut. "Yes, well," he acknowledged and glanced at Joy. "Not all such indentures are dishonorable. If it was merely a matter of loyalty, Kurt would speak his mind, but his alliance is deeper. Yet deeper still is Hasp's devotion to Briarhook, but we know not why. He cannot be held by his name—his name is useless now." Graus Claude gestured with his four hands. "We are all beholden to someone, somehow. Being a *lehman* is perhaps more pleasant than most." He cocked his head sympathetically. "Most of the time."

Kurt snipped the seam of her sleeve with a pair of long-handled scissors and dropped them in a tall glass of rubbing alcohol. The smell made Joy wince.

"Any medical conditions?" Graus Claude asked casually.

"I'm...h-hypoglycemic." Joy stuttered.

"I am unfamiliar with the term."

"Low blood sugar," she said. "I have to eat...a lot."

"Fascinating," Graus Claude said while placing her hand on the carved edge of the settee. "Here, hold on to this."

At the first touch of antiseptic, Joy catapulted off the couch. Graus Claude himself held her in place with his four arms—something that struck her as an honor of sorts, as he didn't seem one to normally get himself dirty. His stern strength gently but firmly gave her permission to weep. She couldn't follow the things that happened to her, no longer caring whether the instruments looked old or if the syringe was sterile. Monica's communicable disease and drug warnings rang deaf in her head. Sometimes the giant toad would instruct, "Swallow these," and she did, or "This will undoubtedly hurt." And it did.

Kurt worked silently and efficiently, although Joy finally became aware of his hand gently cupping her cheek as he slathered a sharp-smelling balm on her neck with a long cotton swab. It felt careful and somehow motherly, not at all like his burly muscleman exterior. Kurt washed her face with a cool cloth and Joy blinked up at him, focusing on the long scar at his throat. The high mandarin collar nearly hid it from sight.

"You *can't* talk," she whispered.

Kurt met her eyes and looked away.

The world felt more lucid under a blanket of painkillers and clean gauze. There was something oddly calming about the smell of antibiotic cleansers and the flowery, sweet scents of crushed marigold and calendula. Joy admired the Edison sconces with a carefree interest buoyed on drugs.

Graus Claude coughed politely and Joy swam to focus on him. Even his mottled gray-green skin was strangely gentlemanly in the muted gold light of the salmon-pink room.

"I can advance the healing, but I cannot undo it. You have been branded. Do you understand this, Miss Malone?"

"Sure," she said.

"Very well then," he answered uncomfortably. "Kurt, please apply this over Miss Malone's injury and secure the bandage so the new skin may breathe." There was the faint clinking of glass stoppers and thick pipettes. A smell of mint or pine, clean and spiky, filled the room. It felt good—soothing and cool.

"It will take approximately one or two days to callous. If the skin grows red or swells with pus, leave a message for me. You retain my number, I trust?"

Joy nodded. Even nodding felt good. "Yep."

Kurt cleaned up the mess, gathering everything onto the silver tray. She didn't like how much of the white cloth was stained red or black. He carried it out of the room. Joy watched him go, wondering what had happened to his throat.

Graus Claude pushed back on his haunches, his low-slung head bobbing in approval. "It is masterfully done in some ways. It may please you to know this and bring you small comfort."

Joy frowned, feeling the skin of her forehead pinch.

"What?" She struggled against the tide of sluggish fuzz.

"Briarhook's brand," Graus Claude said deeply. "A rose fletched in thorns—his insignia, his *signatura*. It suits you. A wildflower with bite."

Joy tried to look at her upper arm and grimaced.

"Screw you."

The Bailiwick chuckled. "I may have forgotten to mention that the medicines I gave you might lower your otherwise polite and cautious inhibitions. Be careful what you choose to say aloud, Miss Malone. Knowing this, I will grant you a certain leniency in your current state."

"Oh, yeah?" Joy said. "Well, I thought you said I'd be protected, that I couldn't get hurt."

"Rightful claims cannot be covered by the Edict," Graus Claude said without apology. "Briarhook's auspice is finding those lost in the woods, and indeed, that is what you were. Hasp brought you to an unfamiliar grotto, following Briarhook's instructions in order to let him lay claim. It was a legitimate action by illegitimate means." He pursed his lips. "The same will hold true for Ink regarding whatever he is doing to Briarhook at this moment. The devil put himself in Ink's path by crossing you."

"Well, good," Joy said as her eyes slid over the mini-chandelier. "What is it with this bathroom? You'd never fit in that tub in a million years."

Graus Claude smiled, a shark's grin, as his four arms spread wide in an elaborate shrug.

"Who claimed that this is where I make my toilette?" he asked. "My apartments are upstairs. This suite is for guests."

Joy gave a goofy grin and touched the pink satin chaise longue.

"Your *female* guests."

"Indeed." The Bailiwick inclined his head as if pleased that they understood one another. "I do not garner much company outside of my home and I entertain only select individuals who do not have trouble with teeth." He clicked his jaws together as if to emphasize the point. Joy laughed a little, but it hurt her ribs.

"Ow," she said and swallowed painfully. "My throat?"

Graus Claude waved off the question imperiously. "Hasp's scales only pricked you. The skin will heal clean. I'd be surprised if it is still noticeable by morning, given the balm. But do try not to cross him. Aether sprites aren't particularly fond of humans."

Joy frowned. "I guessed that much on my own."

"Oh, it's not you personally. Aether sprites have suffered under human industrialism more so than most. It's the pollutants, you see," Graus Claude said, settling back. "There are many who believe that our rightful place and time is being hampered by human domination, that when the Age of Man passes, ours will rise. Yet there are equally as many who believe that without humans we would cease to exist. Aether sprites tend to favor the former philosophy, that humanity is a scourge." He sighed. "It is a perilous line, treading on the politics of entitlement, but the Council believes that balance is essential, which is why I've placed myself at its axis." Two of his hands meticulously arranged brushes, combs and cosmetic pots as he spoke. "Not many choose to barter between your world and ours, but it must be done." Graus Claude grinned. "And many years ago, I determined that it should be done by me."

"And the pay's not bad," Joy added.

The Bailiwick laughed his barrel-chest laughter.

"Indeed. That is also true."

Joy fingered the tiny threads of color in the upholstery—rose and gold, orange and cream.

"There was someone else," she said. "Someone besides Briarhook and Hasp in that ravine."

Graus Claude wiped a finger along the gilt mirror frame. "Oh?"

"Yeah," she said. "Someone orange."

There was a knock, and both Joy and Graus Claude turned. Kurt stood in the open door, allowing Ink to pass. Ink's eyes were flat as plastic chits, his arms soaked with blood up to the elbows, his silken shirt spattered and dotted in spray.

"May I use your sink?" Ink asked.

"Of course," Graus Claude said. Joy stared. Ink walked to the basin and turned the ivory-handled knobs, leaving crimson smears on the porcelain. Graus Claude raised a single hand to halt Kurt's motion to protest or clean. Everyone waited, watching the water run red.

"You may want to remove your shirt," Graus Claude suggested. "Better yet, find a new one."

Ink wordlessly pulled his shirt over his head. It peeled wet and sticky off his arms. He tossed it into the bathtub and stuck his hands back under the water. Kurt gathered the ruined material and draped a towel pointedly on the brass hook nearest Ink. The Scribe continued scrubbing his arms with pink-frothed soap.

Joy watched the play of muscles on Ink's back and limbs. She knew Inq had shaped him, and he, her. It was strange to think of it—their flawless hands on one another. But they weren't really siblings. They weren't really...anything. Joy wondered what that must have felt like, shaping their flesh soft as clay or hard as marble. That's what Ink looked like: a statue in motion. She watched his neck and shoulders move.

Something caught the light, slithering just under his

skin. A faint shape moved clockwise over his back. When he shifted, it winked like a galaxy of stars drawn over his shoulders, circling half the length of his spine. She thought maybe it was the drugs, but its shape became clearer when she looked out of the corner of her eye—*Flash! Flash!*—it was a curling whorl of scales and a vaguely oblong head. It rotated, slowly, like a paddlewheel on his skin.

"What's that?" Joy asked.

"Payback," Ink said into the blank mirror.

Graus Claude raised his brow.

"No," she said. "On your back. That."

Ink glanced over his shoulder. His hands stilled in the sink. "What do you see?" he asked.

Graus Claude looked at her, too, curious.

"Swirls," Joy said, "like an Olympic circle. With a head."

Ink smiled slightly and turned back to the sink. "It is my *signatura*. An ouroboros. A dragon swallowing its tail."

"Immortal," Graus Claude acknowledged. "Infinite."

"Indelible Ink," Joy said thickly.

Ink nodded, eyes on his hands.

"I cannot see this thing," Graus Claude complained.

Ink dried his hands on the towel and wiped off the sink. "No one can." He turned to Joy, clean and open. "Or so I thought." He dried the surface of his chest and stomach. She stared longer than she should have.

"There is more to you than meets the eye, Joy Malone," the Bailiwick murmured as he struggled to his feet. Ink dropped the towel over the back of a chair and leaned close to Joy.

The smell of rain filled her head.

"I can take you home now," Ink said softly, like a question.

Joy nodded. "Please."

When he lifted her this time, it was through a cloud of unfeeling, a furry notion of where her body went from one moment to the next. Joy thought she might slip through his hands and puddle on the floor, which would be fine. The bath mat looked comfy. The tile looked comfy. Graus Claude looked comfy.

She placed a hand against Ink. He was perfect, lean and supple, but something was off. She squinted through mental fog, trying to figure it out. Her head wobbled on her bandaged neck. She touched his chest lightly, her fingers sliding on the surface of his skin. No nipples. Joy laughed— she couldn't help it. It hurt. The sound slid perilously close to weeping.

"My thanks to you, Bailiwick," Ink said, holding her close. "I am in your debt."

"I believe there are no debts between us and you have brought me more than one riddle tonight," Graus Claude demured. "There is so little that excites the mind nowadays, and Sudoku bores me." His voice held only the lightest tinge of sarcasm. "Be well, Miss Malone."

"Thank'll..." she slurred.

When Ink swung aside, they appeared in her room, dark with night and cold and the familiar smell of home. Ink settled her onto her bed and shut the window. Joy saw him traced in blue against the black-and-purple dim.

No belly button, either.

Of course—he'd never been born.

Joy's head sloshed against the pillow, loose and wobbly. Ink pulled back her covers, taking care not to set them near her bare and bandaged arm. Joy realized her pj's were ruined. Maybe she could cut off both sleeves? Would Dad believe it was a new fashion statement? Did pajamas have fashion statements? Where was Dad, anyhow? Shouldn't an attentive parent be aware of stuff like this? She'd been kidnapped. And burned. And there was a guy in her room.

As if he read her thoughts, Ink placed a hand against her lips.

"Shh," he cautioned. "Quiet, now. Your father is asleep. Take these." He placed a plastic bottle by her clock. "Graus Claude said that they will help you through the night."

"I don't want to—"

"Joy, please."

In the dark, he sounded vulnerable, undoing her completely.

"I'm scared," Joy said and saying it made it real. She started to cry and Ink held her, solid and warm.

"It is over," Ink said. "No more harm will come to you. No one will hurt you again."

She shook her head against a bat-wing flurry of thoughts, against his naïveté or her own. "I didn't know what was happening or what to do," she said, feeling that she somehow had to explain. "I couldn't breathe. I couldn't say anything. I—I couldn't say your name." She stuttered, wringing her sheets in both hands.

"Ink," she said urgently, squeezing her eyes and chanting loudly: "Ink. Ink. Ink."

"Shh." He placed his hand gently on hers. "Joy, I am here."

She opened her eyes and nodded. "Yes. You are here. You are very, very here." She looked at their hands next to each other, blinking back tears, muzzy and scattered. "You have no knuckles," she said. "Or fingernails. Or belly buttons. Belly button. Singular." Joy fumbled and lifted her nightshirt, showing the flat of her stomach. "Like this." She smoothed a hand over her innie and shook her head sadly. "You don't have one. That's just wrong."

Ink gave a tired twist of a smile. "Is it?" He looked tender, relieved.

"Oh, yes. Belly buttons. Very important," she said. "And you should speak with contractions," Joy added. "You sound like a robot."

Ink straightened the blankets, both solemn and amused. "Do I?"

"Don't make fun," she said. "Graus Claude warned me that I'm not supposed to say anything, because I could say anything. I have to be careful because it just slips out. Like the fact that you're stunning, like a statue or a photograph, or a photograph of a statue. A naked, old one. Like the Greeks. Not that I think of you naked, because I don't, but if I did, I shouldn't." She took a breath. "It's not real and it's not fair. You're freaky and dangerous and I can't stop thinking about you."

His hand stopped moving and rested against her pillow. His voice was overly casual.

"Is that right?" he said.

"I know—it's ridiculous. You've been horrible to me and kind to me and all sorts of weirdness is now in my life, but I can't imagine going back to the way it was before," she said in a rush. "It has to be this way and it has to be with you, but I can't seem to concentrate on anything else. And now that you've been in my room, I think it will be hard to think of you being anywhere else," Joy confessed. "Nowhere is safe." She blinked as her words slowed, growing quiet and mopey. "I'm gonna totally fail school."

Ink stared at her with those fathomless eyes, saying nothing for a long time—long enough for Joy to wonder what, exactly, she'd just said. She couldn't quite remember, but was too exhausted to ask. It couldn't have been too bad, whatever it was, because the way he kept looking at her felt okay. Joy studied him in the half-light for a clue. She gasped.

"Your ears!" she said, raising her hand to touch one. Ink froze under her fingertips. Joy ignored his distress. "They're perfect! They look so *real*." She marveled at the change. His ear gave and bent like cartilage and skin. She giggled. "I mean, they are real, right? They work like ears. They look..." Then it hit her. "They look like mine!"

"They are like yours," Ink said. "I studied them. Remember?"

She shuddered, not unpleasantly. "Yes. I remember."

There was a question. Permission. Would he touch her again? Did she want him to? Did he want to? She trembled. Where? How? Her heartbeat jumped at her throat. Could he see that? Could he hear it, being so close? Her vision swam on delicate fins through warm water. Ink leaned over her, naked to the waist.

"Was I wrong to do that?" he asked.

"What?" Joy asked. "No."

"Do you wish me to leave?"

Joy quivered. "No."

He saw something in her eyes that made him wonder. "What is it then?"

Her fingers twisted the edge of the sheet.

"I'm afraid."

"Of me?" He almost stood.

"Yes," she admitted. "But it's more than that. Stay."

Ink paused. "Are you asking?"

"No. Telling," Joy said. "You owe me. Stay."

He settled back, almost reluctantly.

"A message may come," he cautioned.

"Then tell them to wait," she said. "Your *lehman* is injured. You have to stay. I'm your responsibility."

Ink's face formed a question, but he quietly rose from the bed and rolled the desk chair near her nightstand. He sat, crossed his arms and gazed down at her, his silver chain spilling off the edge of the chair.

"I suppose you are," he said.

"Yes." She nodded against the pillow. "Remember, you have a reputation to maintain."

"So I am told."

"Have to keep up appearances."

"Yes," he said. "That, too."

They almost smiled. They almost said something more. She wanted to keep talking, but the words were fading on her tongue. She wanted to sleep, but she couldn't close her eyes while he was there watching her. She wanted to match him, second for second. She wanted to stay awake. She wanted to sleep. She was pinned by his stare. She was anything but invisible.

The way he tucked his hands close to himself, no part of him near her, made it all the more obvious that he wanted to touch her. She wanted him to want to. His chest rose and fell, but Joy wasn't entirely certain that he needed to breathe. He was watching her breathing. She needed to breathe. She needed to know.

"What is it?" she asked finally.

Ink's glance fell on the armrest instead of her eyes.

"When I saw that you were hurt, I felt it—" he tapped his chest "—here." Ink's voice trembled like a plucked string. "I still do." His fingers cupped like hooks. "I dislike this feeling. I want to dig it out."

Joy tried to sit up, but winced. She propped herself up on her good arm, her elbow tucked under her head. "It hurts," she guessed. "It hurt you when you saw that I was hurt."

Ink nodded. "It hurt. Yes," he said. "I want to make it stop."

"Where does it hurt?" Joy asked.

"Here." He placed a hand over his breastbone. "And here." His fingers traced along his stomach. "And here." He touched the corners of his eyes that did not tear. "How do I stop it?"

Joy smiled sadly, feeling warmer. "It doesn't work that way."

Ink frowned. "Why not?"

"Because when we care about people, their hurt is our hurt. We want to take it away, to make them feel better." Joy's eyes slid to her computer screen, her phone, her dresser drawer. "And we feel badly if we were the ones that caused them pain."

"It was my fault," Ink said. "But punishing Briarhook did not make you feel better. It made *me* feel better." He looked to the window and back at Joy. "Bringing you to Graus Claude was the better thing to do."

"Yes," Joy whispered. "And he said I'll get better soon."

"Yes, Joy, get better soon."

"I'll try," she said, her eyes slipping closed. She heard the lightest scuttle of the chair wheels on the floor.

"Then I will stay," Ink said, and she trusted that he would.

NINE

HER ALARM BUZZED. THE AUTOMATIC SMACK OF HER HAND produced a wounded cry. Her body was all at once burning and bruised—not half so much as the day before, but it was still a hell of a way to wake up.

"Joy," Ink said quietly, making her remember.

He was there—right there—his face filling her world.

"Joy?" her father called from the hall. "You okay in there?"

"Fine," she croaked. "Ow." She sat up. Every movement was agony. Strings of hot wire tugged from her neck down her spine, drawing taut over her shoulders and down her right arm. She sat gingerly on the edge of her mattress, her feet flat on the floor as she steadied herself. Joy let the clock radio play, masking her voice and the sounds in her throat. Ink crouched next to her.

"You are not finished healing," he said, his voice slicing through the music.

"No kidding?" Joy was all too aware of her wounds, her bruises, her torn pajamas, her bad breath, her bad hair, and him sitting there. She barely moved her lips and kept her chin tilted down. Her head pulsed. Her arm throbbed. "I'm never going to get my bra on."

"Need help?" Ink offered.

"You wish," Joy said, but it was obvious that she was going to have trouble getting dressed and the only one home was Dad. Even the idea of putting on her sweatshirt over her burnt and bloodied jammies was unthinkable. She wanted a shower, but pressurized water promised sheer torture. Joy didn't want to move. She picked a pair of jeans off the floor and tried pulling them on using only her left hand. She groaned. Tears wet her eyes. She looked skyward. "Holy..."

There was a knock on the door. "You sure you're up?" her father asked.

"Yes," Joy groaned through her teeth. "Just didn't sleep well."

His voice came through the pressboard. "Well, get a move on. You're going to be late."

"You should stay home," Ink said.

She shook her head. "He'd want to know why." Joy wiped away a layer of sweat. Her face felt clammy. This didn't look good. She glanced at Ink. His expression was so open, so plain, Joy was surprised at how much her hurting hurt him. He'd never looked anything like this before. He looked almost human. He was learning, watching her.

"It hurts," he said.

"It does," she admitted.

"Wait here." He sounded resolute as he stood up. "I will only be a moment."

Joy grinned thinly. "If that?"

A quick flick of the wrist and his odd sweeping motion, and Ink vanished. Joy held her breath and pushed herself to a standing position, moving everything but her right arm. The bandage was tight and stiff and smelled funny. How was she going to put on deodorant? Joy stood in the middle of her room, equidistant from all her clothing in drawers and shelves and hangers, feeling pathetic. How would she open drawers? Button up? Zip? Maybe she could come up with a plausible reason to stay home...?

Before she could concoct some believable excuse, Inq strode into her room through a ripple of air.

"Need a little help?" Inq asked and held out her hands. Joy nodded and allowed Inq to help strip off her top while standing on the bed, holding the armholes extra-wide so Joy could slip through. Inq busied herself rifling through the closet, giving Joy a bit of privacy with her underwear and pants.

"The less formfitting, the better, but it's cold outside," Inq said.

"I thought the cold didn't bother you," Joy muttered, slipping on black yoga pants.

"It doesn't. But I'm not blind," Inq said. "Everyone's bundled up like Christmas ornaments out there. And there's snow on the ground. It doesn't take a genius. Here, turn around."

Inq quickly and efficiently hooked Joy's bra.

"Thanks," Joy said.

"No problem. Now, this looks roomy." Inq held up an XL hoodie from U Penn. "Let's get this on and I'll help you with your socks and boots."

"You're a goddess," Joy muttered gratefully.

Inq crinkled her nose and laughed. "It's been said before."

Joy dry-swallowed a couple of painkillers on the bus, and the sour taste rang in her mouth all through first period. She moved stiffly and clenched her teeth as she accepted back her English paper. Raising her arm above the elbow was nearly impossible.

Fortunately, Graus Claude had been right about the cuts on her neck—not a whisper of them had remained when she'd exchanged the bandages for a scarf. Inq had been right, too; it was freezing outside with a windchill of twenty-two. She'd nearly cried when she'd put on her coat, the sleeve like a blood pressure cuff over her arm. Give it one or two days, he'd said. She could make it that long. She'd have to. One or two days. She could do that.

Still, swimming in her giant sweatshirt wasn't easy and Joy had to carry her book bag, her binders and her lunch tray all on the wrong side. By noon, her neck ached every time she turned her head. She swallowed another two painkillers with her chicken noodle soup, which was unsurprisingly tasteless but surprisingly hot.

Monica slapped down her tray and eyed Joy's ensemble. "Why in the world are you wearing your Bloat Pants to school?" she asked. "Might as well stand up on the table and announce you're packin' Tampax."

"I'm not menstrual," Joy said.

"Could've fooled me with how moody you've been," Monica said. "What has gotten into you? You totally freaked me out in the library and you never answered your cell. What were you doing in the bathroom? Pitching a tent?" She plucked Joy's sleeve to emphasize the point.

Joy snatched her sleeve back. "I just lost track of time," she said in defense. How long ago was that? So much had happened since then.

"'Lost track of time'?" Monica said. "Were you too busy reading all the witty remarks written on the walls, or were you...?" Her friend's eyes widened and then narrowed menacingly. Monica's voice dropped ice cubes, each word a *thunk*.

"Joy, Lord help me...."

Joy snorted. "What?"

"Dressing like a garbage bag and camping out in the bathroom do not a pretty picture make," Monica declared. "Ever since you got involved with Mr. Somebody-A-Guy, you've been acting totally mental."

"Says Mrs. Gordon-ocious."

"Don't sass me," Monica warned. "And now this stuff with Stef?" She waved herself to silence as if erasing the air between them. "Are you pregnant?"

"What? No!"

"Give me your hand."

Joy frowned. "'Scuse me?"

"I said, 'Give me your hand,'" Monica snarled. "Now!"

Joy held out her left hand. Monica glanced at the back of it and waved *gimme* for the other. Joy moved delicately, but passed inspection.

"No scabs on the knuckles, so you're not poking your finger down your throat," Monica declared. "And you need food too much to go without." She gestured to the soup, dinner roll and bowl of grapes. "Did you gag yourself with a pencil?"

"What? Gross! No," Joy winced.

"Laxatives?"

Joy sighed. "Monica, you seriously read too many pamphlets."

"Then what is it?" Monica asked earnestly, giving Joy's hand a squeeze. Joy tried not to wince, but Monica caught it.

"What's this?" Monica pulled. Joy sucked in her breath

against the scream and yanked her hand away. Monica let go as if stung. A weird comprehension lit her dark eyes.

"Dear Jesus, did this guy hit you?"

Joy almost laughed. Almost. "No."

"He. Hit. You." Monica's voice was deadly calm.

"No!" Joy said louder, then dipped her own voice. "It's nothing like that. Honest!"

She searched Joy's face.

"Okay, so what is it like then? Did you...?" Monica trailed off when a surprised glint of mischief lit her smile. Joy was more stunned by that than the accusation. "Did he *mark* you?"

Fear stabbed her gut. "What?!"

"Did he draw on you? Mr. Artist?" Monica asked. "Did you get a tattoo?"

The idea clicked together like Lego blocks. "Yeah, sorta," Joy said. "It's on my upper arm."

Monica squeed in her seat and hopped up and down. "I can't believe it! You let this guy *draw* on you? Something permanent?" Joy nearly laughed. The level of irony was ridiculous. "Damn, Joy! Can I see it?"

"It's not done," Joy said hastily. "It's healing. It's not... I just got it done."

"And your dad...?"

"Doesn't know."

Monica scraped her fingers *no-no*. "You are being naughty, naughty, naughty. He'll have a cow. I nearly calved! Why didn't you text me? What is it?"

"A rose," Joy said. "I think."

"You think?"

"It hurt a lot," Joy confessed, warming to the lie. "And I think I had a kind of...reaction. It was sort of hard to tell."

"Mmm, I've heard that can happen," Monica said wisely. "Did you ask to see the autoclave?"

"What are you? A walking PSA?" Joy sat back and rubbed just over her shoulder, pain cascading down her arm in pintable waves. She picked up her spoon.

"Well, I'm glad it's nothing psycho-stupid," Monica said. "Just a little bit stupid."

"Right," Joy said dryly. "So much for No Stupid.'"

"Well, nobody's perfect," Monica said, taking a bite of her Granny Smith apple. "Just please tell me he's being good to you."

Joy nodded and traced her ear, thinking he was the first thing she'd seen this morning and the last person watching over her at night, keeping her safe. She smiled.

"He's being very good to me."

"Then there you go," Monica said. "That's good enough for me."

Joy hadn't realized she'd healed until the pain was already gone. It must have happened sometime between the bus ride and home. The biting cold had kept her mind off her arm. She'd dropped her book bag and hung up her coat and suddenly realized that she could—she'd moved both arms freely out of habit. Joy stood there, feeling as if she'd misplaced something, and it took her a moment to realize that it was the pain.

Racing to the bathroom, she yanked her hoodie over her head, leaning her arm, thick with bandages, over the sink. Even though she hadn't turned up the thermostat, she was suddenly sweating. Joy realized she needed to eat, but she needed this more.

Joy unwound the wide pillow of gauze in hasty circles, gathering the wadded material into a medicinal-smelling heap. The bandages gradually began to darken to yellow, then amber, then umber, then a strange-smelling mixture of brown and black. She felt a tug as the layers pulled free and she wondered just what she'd find under there, drawn on her skin. Although she'd told Monica that it was a rose, she'd had only Graus Claude's opinion of it and, let's face it— the guy was a toad.

She ran warm water and soaped up her left hand, slipping it under the last layer of sticky, crackling gauze. It didn't hurt. It felt slightly numb and bumpy, like the nerves were half-asleep and a little raw.

Wiping away the last bubbles of soap, she stared at the perfect pink scar. Drops of lather trickled down her arm and pooled over the back of her hand.

A briar rose. Graus Claude might be a toad, but he was a toad with good taste. And he had treated her very well. She'd remember that in the future.

For all the horror, the brand *was* beautiful. A single line drew layers of sharp petals and etched one jaded leaf. Joy twisted her shoulder and traced the brand with her finger, feeling the dead skin ridge, the tightness of sunburn without the sting. She touched it tentatively and then with a grow-ing confidence. She'd gone through something horrible and emerged with this. Through every insane, upsetting and em-barrassing thing she'd been through—her mother, her father, her brother, Ink, Hasp, Briarhook, the police—all of it had built up inside her, but nothing ever showed. Nothing ever *looked* different despite the fact that it *was* different, she *felt* different, and all the therapist talk was about going back to being the same even though she knew she would never be the same again. How could she? Some things were permanent—indelible—and could not be changed back.

This change was permanent; it showed inside and out.

She buried her fingers in the soiled bandages and brought her hand to her nose. It smelled of so many things, blood and flowers and fresh cotton and mint. She wondered if she should keep it for some reason, some sort of pharmaceutical analysis. It could pay for college—or a new house—but Joy suspected that would be more than a breach of trust. It was probably some otherworldly arrestable offense. She wanted no more police, human or otherwise, in her life. She grabbed a spare plastic bag and chucked everything inside, tying it tight.

After dumping both it and her sweatshirt in the back of her closet, Joy grabbed a sleeveless T and pulled it on, weighing how she looked with a rose brand and a Happy Bunny shirt. She looked kind of manga badass. She twisted her hair into two floppy pigtails for effect.

There was a low, stretching sound like someone lifting a heavy wicker basket in the hall. Joy peeked around the closet mirror.

"Dad?"

She hadn't heard him come in, but she didn't feel alone. The dry, twiggy sound came again, reminding her of the kitchen window and something just beyond her sight. The hairs on her arms prickled alert.

"Joy?"

She whirled. Ink stood a hand's breadth behind her.

"Are you all right?" he asked.

"Hi," she said, hugging her bare arms and trying to regain

her dignity. She didn't understand why she felt awkward, given what they'd been through. She gulped a few breaths and rubbed her shoulders. It was really cold in the house, she'd just noticed. "Actually, I'm fine. Really. Thanks." She turned her shoulder inward. "It's healing—see?"

He pivoted toward the light. "May I?"

Joy shrugged. "Sure."

Ink touched the scar. Joy felt something akin to pressure, but no sensation of his fingers there. He traced the unbroken line of the brand. When his fingertips brushed the very edge of the leaf, they slid against her warm skin. She felt that. She felt every bit of that.

"It's healing well," Ink said diplomatically.

"It is."

"I am sorry," Ink said.

She cupped the scar under her palm. "Don't." It hadn't been his fault, even though she'd been angry with him at the time. Ink dropped his hand and set his thumbs on his hips. She felt oddly guilty, embarrassed for having been captured, for becoming Briarhook's victim, for being so helpless. But she didn't *feel* helpless—she was strong. She was stronger than this. The rose brand reminded her: a wildflower with bite.

Ink's quickmetal shirt slithered over his chest as he sighed.

"Graus Claude was correct," he said. "It is beautiful."

The way he said it sounded like *So are you.*

Joy turned away and faced the mirror, a reflection of herself sans Ink.

"You were very brave," Ink said. "Throughout all of it and after. And now here you are, smiling."

"Am I smiling?" Joy said, almost in disbelief. Then she realized that she was. She was smiling at him.

Ink placed a hand on her shoulder; she felt it all over. "Are you willing to be brave again so soon?"

Joy turned to him, no longer smiling. "What do you mean?"

"There have been rumors, many rumors, since last night," he confessed. "There are those who believe that you have been killed. By Briarhook, by Hasp, by Kilties or Caps. Others claim that you went mad and took your own life. A few, sensing the blood on my hands, suspect me and cry murder."

He drew his blade. It slipped through nothingness as he spoke. "The eyes that are watching are now beyond count. It would be good to have you with me, if only to prove that you are well."

She watched the knife. He watched her eyes.

"What they are saying...about the blood on your hands."

"I have never killed anyone," he said.

Joy swallowed. "Until now..."

"Briarhook lives."

"What?" Joy said. "Really?"

Ink grimaced. "When I felt it, that pain—" he pressed two fingers to his chest, below the sternum "—here, I went to Briarhook and told him that I had received his message and had come to give him my reply." His fingers hooked into a small claw. "And since I could not dig that part out of myself, I attempted to share the experience with him." Ink poked the silk that rippled and bore as he twisted his fingertips. "I dug it out of him."

"Dug what out?"

"His heart."

Joy felt dizzy, about to pitch backward into the dark part of her mind. She'd all but told him to do it. Did he realize what he'd done? If he didn't know chalk dust from chocolate, did he understand mortality? Life and death? Or was he as innocent and arrogant as Inq claimed? The implications chilled her.

"Ink," she tried to explain, "without his heart...you've killed him."

"No," Ink said. "I put it in a box for safekeeping."

"In a box?"

"You are no longer smiling," Ink observed.

She shook her head, pressing her palms to her temples. "You ripped out his heart and put it in a box?"

"If he were wise, he would have kept it hidden," Ink said. "Now Graus Claude has it and Briarhook is beholden to me, as witnessed by the Bailiwick of the Twixt." Ink did not hide his pride. "His heart of stone lies in a box of iron and he will have to earn it back, piece by piece."

Joy fumbled over the sense of it. "So...Briarhook isn't dead?"

"No," Ink said. "He is mine. And he cannot harm you ever again."

"Oh," she whispered. Her mind reeled with the sharp realization that the Twixt was not her world and it did not abide by human rules. "Well, that's good, I guess."

"And now you need to come with me," Ink said. "To show that I have not taken *your* heart."

She stopped, her veins warming, her pulse thumping.

"What if you have?"

Ink drew a fine line of fire in the air and spoke softly over his shoulder.

"Well, then, fair is fair."

Joy sat idly by the feet of a giant blond man who had beaten seven others in an ugly bar fight. He'd pushed himself drunkenly out a small bathroom window, landed in the glass-strewn alleyway and collapsed atop a pile of flattened cardboard boxes by a recycling bin. Now that the guy was unconscious, Ink could begin his work. Joy munched on a handful of peanuts and handed him instruments in a steady stream.

"Seven by seven," Ink said as he traced a small line of erupting black birds. "Reminds me of one of the old marks—the seventh son of a seventh son." He exchanged the razor for the wand. "Not much call for that anymore."

"Why not?" Joy asked.

"Birth control," Ink answered and blew the leaf wand dry. "The whole system of *signatura* began with the pacts sworn between Folk and humankind, back when they were united in safeguarding the places and people who kept magic alive." He gestured to the hulking man splayed across the alley. "But then the Folk became greedy and the humans became clever and the Council chose to shape True Names into sigils so that none of the Folk would ever again be tethered by humans against their will. Scalpel, please."

"Yes, doctor!" Joy quipped and passed it over.

"You jest, but it was not I who healed you," Ink said as he cut a new design. "I knew Graus Claude would know what to do."

"More like his butler, Kurt," Joy said, placing the wand back in its compartment. "Do you know anything about him?"

"We are acquainted." Ink's words fell like lead weights.

"O-kay," Joy said. "Well, do you know what happened to his throat? Why can't he talk?"

Ink's mouth was a thin line as he worked around a shard of glass. "Kurt came to Graus Claude as a casualty of war—a victim of some plague let loose upon your world." Joy moved one of the size-fifteen shoes. "It brought fever and sweating and swelled throats closed with growths the size of fists. Kurt's mother knew the Old Ways, summoned the Bailiwick, and begged for his life. Graus Claude took her offer and her son and removed the glands, which saved him. He lives in service to the Bailiwick, but it is done with equal parts debt, gratitude and pride. No one knows if Kurt took a vow of silence, or if his voice was forfeit in the exchange, or whether Graus Claude's actions consciously or accidentally made him mute. It is one mystery of many surrounding the Bailiwick's manservant."

Joy widened her eyes and shook her head to clear it. "Wow," she said.

Ink smirked as he completed the line. "Wow, indeed."

"Hoy," a voice behind them snapped like the wind. "How did he do, then?"

A young woman stood tall and proud in the alley. Joy didn't need Ink to tell her that she belonged to the Twixt. Her blond hair was braided and knotted together in a complicated nest at the back of her neck. Thin blue lines ran vertically from eyebrow to eyelash, and she had a blue dot centered just under her lower lip. She wore a heavy, hard corselet of worn, beaten bronze. A short cape fell behind her shoulders. A ram's horn hung at her hip.

"What was he supposed to be doing?" Ink asked.

"Fighting," she said.

"Then, yes," Ink allowed. "If he was meant to be fighting, he did that very well. However, if he was meant to stay upright, then I am afraid that he failed miserably."

Joy gaped. Had Ink made a joke?

The blonde warrior-girl laughed right from her gut, and a delicate rattling echoed behind her.

"Indelible, indomitable, irrepressible Ink!"

Ink smirked as he looked up from his work. "I think you have me confused with my sister."

"Oh, no! I think I should know the difference. But you," she said admiringly. "You look no worse for wear. Those blithering hags at the Halls have it all wrong, am I right?"

"You are right," Ink said. "As always."

"As always!" She smacked her breastplate. "Of course!"

Joy smiled at the woman's easy bluster and charm. Leather-and-steel vambraces shone on her arms, and a horse-head pendant hung at her throat. She cast her sea-blue eyes to Joy.

"And you must be the *lehman*. Let's have a look at you!"

Joy stood up timidly. The tiny chitter of wood chimes followed the tattooed woman as she slapped Joy's arms.

"Good," she said. "Strong. I can see it." She poked Joy unceremoniously in the chin, just under her lip, like pressing a button. Joy staggered back and licked the spot. The young woman tossed her head in delight. "What's this?" She gripped Joy's biceps hard as she twisted the arm over, inspecting the scar. She could have easily flipped Joy heels over head.

"Briarhook," the young woman said. "He learned his lesson, did he?"

"More like 'earned his lesson,'" Ink muttered. "It was eagerly taught."

She laughed again. "Vicious! Just as the Bailiwick said."

"You have been listening," Ink noted.

The blonde fighter jerked her chin, unapologetic. "It's not difficult. There is a lot being said," she shot back. "Still, it is good to see what is true and what is not with my own eyes."

She nudged Joy. "Speaking of which, keep your eyes on this one. He is our prize stag!" She laughed uproariously as Joy blushed. Those sea-blue eyes seemed to peer straight to the back of her head. "Virgin!" she howled triumphantly. Joy could've died.

"Feel free to tell the others what is true and what is not," Ink said, "but some details are private." He gestured to his work. "Come, I am nearly finished."

The woman bent over the fallen man, already bruising in his sleep. "He's one of the *Einherjar*, you know," she said. "His name is Gunner. Strong name. A good name, but they spelled it wrong." Joy noticed that when the blonde woman leaned over, her cape had fallen forward. It was made entirely of finger bones. When she moved, Joy heard the tiny things clatter.

"What is your name?" she asked Joy.

"She is unfamiliar with..." Ink started.

"Joy," she said, then realized maybe she shouldn't have spoken by the way Ink looked at her. She finished, albeit quieter. "Joy Malone."

There was a short silence punctuated by an approaching ambulance whine.

"Sweet natured and strong," the tattooed woman said. "A good name! Names have power. May it serve you well." As strange as her words were, they sounded sincere. She slapped Joy roughly on her back. "Remember, should the EverBattle come—ring a bell and call for me! I am ever-vigilant!"

"And what's *your* name?" Joy asked.

"Filly."

"*Filly?*" Joy almost laughed. Almost. Then she remembered the bones.

"Of course we will," Ink added smoothly. "Good quarter to you."

Filly raised a fist in salute. "Victory!"

Ink saluted with his blade. "Victory!"

A crash of light and she was gone.

Joy rocked back at the suddenness of Filly's grand exit. There was a hollow patch of quiet where she'd been standing larger than life a moment ago.

"Okay—who was that?" Joy blurted.

"What we've been waiting for," Ink said, standing up. Joy handed him his wallet, which he folded and pocketed in one smooth motion. "She is young, comparatively speaking, and more than a little brash," Ink explained. "But she will boast the right words into the right ears. Filly was merely the first to step forward—not surprising, considering I invited her to do so—so now we have the tale telling somewhat under control." Ink smiled proudly, dimples creasing both cheeks.

Joy stared at him. "This was a setup?" she said. "You planned all this?"

"Not entirely," Ink said. "He was already drunk and loud and all too eager to impress a certain pretty, blonde woman who was egging him on to fight."

Joy looked uselessly over her shoulder at the open window behind them. "*Filly* was in there? She was at the bar?"

"It was a convenient culmination of circumstance that resulted in providing a necessary scene that could be passed along to interested parties." The dimples betrayed his nonchalance. "Besides, she owed me a favor."

Casting a last glance at the blond man, bruised and bleeding, Joy gave an overexaggerated shiver. "Remind me not to owe you any favors."

Ink laughed. Really laughed. It transformed him for an instant into a person. Joy smiled.

"I cannot blame him," Ink added, looping his chain around his finger. "She is very pretty."

Joy stopped smiling.

"You think she's pretty?" she asked.

Ink shrugged, slicing their exit. "And I said that you were beautiful."

Joy's mouth was open and she tasted the strange, cool rain of him as they walked through the breach. It infused her sinuses like wine and lemon, a vapor of Ink soaking into her brain.

"No, you didn't!" Joy said. Her words came out mist. A February chill filled her room—the electricity must have gone out. She rubbed her arms, pushing past Ink to grab a fleece out of her closet. His eyes followed her as he struggled to puzzle out her words.

"What did I not do?"

"You never said..." she started as she pushed her hands through the sleeves, her breath ghosting in the room. "You said that about...my arm. About the brand. Not me."

Ink cocked his head. He stepped closer. Joy shyly tucked her hair behind her ear.

"That may have been what you heard," he said softly. "But that was not what I said."

The words hung like mistletoe.

Joy stumbled beneath them, trembling slightly.

"I saw your face when I said it," he whispered. "You did not understand. I see that now." Ink struggled with something internal. Joy watched, transfixed.

It was his innocence that allowed it. His hand slid inside

her unzipped fleece, pushing the sleeve aside, heedless of anything other than the most direct path to touching her skin. Joy shrugged her shoulder free as Ink cupped his hand over the rose, smoothing his palm against its rippled surface. He ran a thumb over it lightly.

"You are strong, Joy Malone," he said, acknowledging, admiring. His eyes flicked to hers. "You are brave. And you are beautiful."

Even with the cold, her bare skin burned. The fresh-fallen rain scent rose between them in summer storm crackles. Lifting her face, she nearly brushed his cheek, looking from his eyes to his perfect Joy-alike ears. Ink stood tentative and still, unsure of what to do—one hand on Joy's arm, their chins almost touching, their eyes darting over details, yet to settle on any one place.

Joy's lips parted, but there were no words for what she felt. Ink tilted his head as if waiting to hear what she would say, what hadn't yet been said between them. Each tiny motion brought them closer. Each ticking moment asking a question. She tried to think of something to say, something to do, but she kept slipping further, unable to come up with one coherent, rational...

Joy felt his smooth face against the downy edge of her cheek. Lips hovering, barely touching, they were breathing one another's air. His hand squeezed her arm as if about to push or pull.

Joy touched the silky edge of his sleeve.

Pulled.

No one had ever just kissed her—just a kiss—and just *kissed*. There was no confidence or eagerness or have-to's or getting somewhere. No agenda. No next. Nothing else. There was only the kiss.

They kissed that first kiss for a very long time.

When it broke, they were breathless, their cloudy exhalations the only sound in the dark.

Ink spoke through quiet gasps, his hands kneading her skin.

"Again, please."

She did.

They both heard the door opening as her father came home. Their kisses subsided and the lingering began—they stayed within breaths of one another, ready to start again.

"Joy?" her father called out. "I'm home. Gah! It's *freezing* in here!"

"Tomorrow," Ink whispered. Joy felt the word puff on her skin. She nodded slightly. He made no move to leave or let go. She didn't want him to. *Stay,* she begged him silently. *Stay.*

"Joy?" her father called again.

"Tomorrow," Ink repeated, convincing himself more than her. He backed away. Joy moved to follow, but stopped at the door.

"Tomorrow," she said. And when she blinked, he was gone.

"Be out in a second!" she shouted, and looked back at the space where Ink had been, adding in a whisper, "If that."

TEN

IT WAS THERE LIKE A KISS GOOD-MORNING.

Meet me at the Carousel. Nine o'clock tonight.

Joy pressed the note to her chest. She laughed at herself and at him. Whoever heard of anyone actually writing the word *o'clock*? She adored that little detail and read it over and over again. She loved it. She loved him.

She loved Ink.

She carried the note, a tangible reminder of him, with her—tucking it into her binder or her pocket, using it as a bookmark, rereading it and reliving it through class after class. Joy memorized Ink's perfect penmanship and tried to imagine what he had planned.

The Carousel's Under 18 Night. Thursday night. Tonight. The trick was getting there, but that shouldn't be a problem. Monica *so* owed her. Joy readied herself in the lunch line. Negotiation was a delicate business, so armed with a lunch tray and an extra fudge brownie, she was in a good, strong position to start begging her friend for a ride. Joy approached their table with an opening bid on her lips.

Monica grinned. "Hey! Want to go dancing tonight?"

Joy's mental gearshifts did a full reverse. "Huh?"

"I told Gordon that I am not going out tonight unless you come with us," she said sternly. "And I didn't want you feeling like a third wheel, so I asked if he'd be willing to set you up with his hottie friend...." She hesitated. "Unless your mysterious Mr. Someone-A-Guy would be willing to reveal himself to witnesses?"

"You mean grilling?" Joy said as she took a seat.

"I mean *serious* grilling," Monica confirmed.

"Pass on the grilling and the hottie, but otherwise, count me in," Joy said, biting into her brownie.

"You sure?" Monica pressed. "Gordon's got this friend, Luke, who is seriously luscious."

"Pass," Joy said, thinking of Luiz and Nikolai and the other Cabana Boys. She doubted hottie Luke would even make the grade. "I just want to go to the Carousel and dance."

"The Carousel?" Monica said, shrugging. "Okay. You got it."

Joy played with her fork, congratulating herself on the win. It would be kind of like a double date, and not. Ink would be there, with her in public...but nobody else would know. A secret date. She nibbled frosting off her thumb.

"Hey, Mon," Joy said. "Can I borrow your mesh top?"

The air licked Joy's skin as she entered the club. Feeling nearly naked with the fine metal mesh tied over her chest, Joy tried locating Ink in the crowd. Her hip-hugger jeans drew the eye dangerously low and she knew that a lot of guys were looking. Neon-colored lights danced erratically over her broken-silver surface. She wore her hair up with long earrings dangling down. The borrowed clothing helped Joy feel beautiful and mysterious. She wanted Ink to be the one who was surprised tonight.

Monica had been shocked by the briar rose brand, but insisted that they "pump it up" with silver glitter gel. A breeze kissed the spot in delicious, cold tingles. Joy felt it all, like the eyes in the club. She smiled and didn't care if her teeth glowed purple.

"You look great," Gordon shouted over the grinding bass hum. He gave Monica a squeeze to show where his loyalties lay.

"Thanks," Joy said. "It's Monica's shirt."

Gordon cuddled his girlfriend closer. "I think I recognize it," he teased. "But it looked better on the floor!" Monica swatted his chest. He laughed and tickled her back. She squealed. Joy rolled her eyes and tried not to laugh.

Monica smoothed her hair to one side. "So are we here to chitchat, or are we gonna dance?" The three of them forced their way onto the rotating floor.

Forming a wedge, they were able to dance without having to fight for room. Monica and Gordon didn't mind being squashed together, but Joy widened her feet, defending her meager territory.

Joy waved her hands above her head, sparkling with glitter and sweat. She arched her spine, feeling the nostalgic burn in the back of her calves, welcoming the stretch like an old, familiar friend. Joy drew herself up slowly, keeping her knees bent and bouncing lightly to the beat, eyes always searching the slowly turning perimeter.

Swimming in the sound, Joy kept a lookout for Ink in a shock of black hair or a flash of shirt, each burst of excitement souring when she'd realize that it wasn't him. White fairy lights, black tattoos and bright afterimages flashed in her eyes, but no Ink. Where was he? What if he didn't show? What if something had happened? What if he left her waiting all night?

Joy stomped her feet to the driving rhythm. Dancing alone was never a problem until you were expecting someone else.

The tempo of the song grew faster, a soprano solo climbing the scales, inviting everyone on the floor to go wilder, higher. Joy tucked her chin and crossed her wrists and spun, feeding the rush, losing herself. She raised her eyes to the carousel ceiling and watched the mirrors spin, remembering not that long ago...the first time that she'd seen him, the first time that they'd met.

The painful lick of a silver blade—like his voice slicing through the din—*Flash-Flashed!* in her memory. But this was now and so much had changed.

She saw him. He saw her.

The music slowed, coaxing the crowd's energy like the tide. Ink rode the undulating waves as if walking through water, people parting for him though they were unaware that he was there.

The song was slow and sensual. Joy smiled, her eyes half-closed as Ink placed his hands along her waistline, his smooth skin sliding against hers. The silver mesh of her top winked pink-purple-black. It shone in his eyes, a thousand midnight sparkle stars. Ink followed her body's rhythm as he had traced the shape of her ear—wholly absorbed, fascinated, mesmerized with open wonder. Ink was caught in her currents, moving as she moved, his body gliding naturally along her ebbs and swells.

Joy danced with Ink's hands and his fingers and the touch of his lips, unseen, smack in the middle of a crowded room.

She felt the music change as the tracks combined, the first chords overlapping and pulling more couples to dance. The DJ pumped his fist and cranked the sound higher. The music kept thumping, thick as a pulse. The sound beat their bodies. Ink leaned his face close to hers.

"Joy," he breathed into her ear. The warmth of it made her shiver.

She closed her eyes and murmured into her neckline. "Ink."

"I am here," Ink whispered, clear as glass. His fingers trailed down her arms. "I am very, very here."

He leaned even closer, his face just touching hers. She felt a million tiny hairs on his skin rise.

"Can you feel me?" she whispered.

His voice was soft in awe. "Yes."

"Move the feeling," she said, kissing her fingertip, indenting her lip. She touched her finger to his lower lip and pressed lightly. "Here."

Ink smiled and closed his eyes, a flicker of his eyelids, concentrating. Her finger gave a little as his lips grew pliant, more tactile and supple. He drew his head sideways, feeling her finger slide over the newly sensitive skin. She watched his eyelids soften, his lashes flutter.

"Feel this," she whispered and kissed him.

He groaned and folded around her.

They were both so very, very there.

Joy floated into the house, somehow getting from the car to the gate to the hallway to the door of her room. She couldn't remember details. She'd said something to Monica and Gordon at the end of the night, but it didn't matter. Her body buzzed. Her lips tingled. She could smell Ink's rain-scent in her hair. Everything everywhere was a gorgeous midnight fog.

She was drunk on him. Ink.

Joy unhooked her earrings, scrubbing her fingers through her hair stiff with spray and sweat. She could call him just by saying his name. She knew she shouldn't—he'd left her with a caress before she'd ducked into Gordon's car—but she *could*. She knew that. And the temptation sang inside her.

Joy needed a shower, but she wanted to hold on to this feeling as long as she could. All of it. Down to the last flake of glitter stuck on her skin.

Her cell phone rang. Joy scooped it up, smiling.

"Hello?"

"Joy?"

Her heart slammed. She sat down.

"Stef?"

She burst into tears, which she knew was ridiculous, and they both were babbling, soothing one another as they had when they were kids scared by thunderstorms or their parents fighting, huddled together under Winnie-the-Pooh blankets.

The initial downpour finally settled down into a trickling silence. Joy sniffed.

"I got your calls," Stef said. "And your texts. And emails. I'm kind of surprised you didn't hire a skywriter."

"I'm sorry!" Joy said, cutting her brother off. "I should have said 'I love you' when you told me."

His silence was painful. "Yeah," Stef said. "You should've."

Joy swallowed and popped her ears. "But now you have. So, thanks."

They sat on the phone while Joy picked at her cuticles and Stef did the same bad habit several hundred miles away.

"When did you know?" she finally asked.

Stef chuckled in his tired, worn-out way. "You mean when did I know that I was in love or when did I know that I was gay?"

Joy shrugged, a gesture unseen. "Either. Both."

"Same day," he admitted, which sounded strange, but kind of awesome.

"How about you?" he asked back. "Is there a guy?"

"There is a guy," Joy confirmed.

"Okay, good." She could hear Stef's grin right over the phone. She drank it like hot cocoa. With marshmallows. "So? When did it happen?"

Before he yanked out Briarhook's heart. After he caught the milk jug. Before we walked on the beach. After he stabbed me in the eye. Tonight, most definitely.

"I don't know when, exactly," she said. "It sort of surprised me."

"Yeah." Stef laughed. "Me, too."

"So...do I get to meet him?"

"Someday," Stef hedged. She couldn't blame him. They hadn't even managed to figure out how to do things like Christmas without Mom.

"How about your guy?" Stef asked. "Do I get to meet him?"

"I don't know..." Joy began.

"Aw, c'mon," Stef said. "It's my sacred duty as your older brother to harass your boyfriends. It's practically my birthright!" Joy laughed as he carried on. "Can you at least send me a picture so I can have him followed?"

"Ah...no." Stef could never have a picture. No one could. And as for following Ink—fat chance! Joy smiled at the thought.

"Well, he'd better be nice to you," Stef warned.

"He is," Joy said. "Same goes for James."

"We take care of each other," Stef said. Then there was this long, long pause of nothing to say when there was everything to say. It poured into her veins and pressed on her chest.

"How did we get here?" she asked.

Stef considered the question. Joy heard doors opening and shutting, the background noise of U Penn.

"I don't know," he said. "Are you happy?"

Am I happy?

"I think I am," Joy said. "You?"

"I know I am. Yes."

"Then we're good?" she asked.

"Yeah. I think we're good." Stef cushioned his exit with a friendly pause. "Listen, I have to go, but I'll ping you with a time when we can talk over the weekend. I want to know everything that's going on. Everything. I mean it."

"Me, too," Joy said gratefully.

"And, Joy—does Dad know?"

"About you or the guy?" Joy asked. "Either way, the answer is no. Why?"

Stef hesitated. "He's not like Mom, Joy—he needs to know things. You've got to tell him."

"Oh, yeah?" she said. "What about you?"

"I've got to tell him, too."

Joy swallowed around the tightness in her throat. She couldn't picture how to handle either of those things.

"Well, then, good luck to both of us," she said.

"Remember," Stef said, "one conniption fit at a time."

"Great," she muttered. "You go first."

"How about I'll tell Mom about mine and you tell Dad about yours and then they can yell at each other about who's more at fault and that'll keep them off our backs for a while."

Joy laughed aloud. It felt good. "You're evil!"

"I try my best," Stef quipped. "Seriously, gotta go."

"Then go," Joy dared.

"Bye!"

"Bye!"

They both hung up and Joy grinned through tears. She hugged a pillow to her chest and laughed into the fluff, kicking her feet against the mattress in delight. Everything was going to be okay!

It was the absolute perfect ending to a perfect, perfect night.

Joy was busy ignoring Mr. Soares, writing a playlist to capture the feeling of right then, right now, when a weird pressure powdered over her eyes.

"Peekaboo!" Inq whispered in her slicing, clear chirp. Joy tried not to call attention to the fact that she had a visitor in class who no one else could see, casually ignoring Inq's smirk as she knelt next to Joy's chair.

"I think he liked it," Inq said, giggling as she marched her fingers across Joy's desk. "His. First. Kiss."

Joy exaggerated putting her pen to paper and wrote in large letters.

I think he did. I did, too.

"Enough for seconds?" Inq teased.

Joy blushed, making ticks in the margin. Two, five, ten, twenty...

Inq clapped her hands and laughed.

"Brava!" she said. "So how do we celebrate?"

Joy paused and wrote.

Celebrate?

"Well, I can't very well declare it Ink's First Kiss Day—he'd be awfully embarrassed. Although I've never seen him blush... It's tempting."

Joy tapped her next sentence with her pen cap.

Please no!

"Right, well, instead I had the idea to invite you out again—it's a unique opportunity, only this time, the party's over," she said. "But both Ink and I have to go. You'd surprise him! Interested?" Inq backed away, gliding up the aisle as if she had radar in the back of her head. Joy's classmates unknowingly shifted elbows and feet out of the way. She didn't bump into anyone once.

Inq fanned her fingers on either side of her mouth in a stage whisper and winked. "All your favorite people are going to be there!" she cooed.

Joy bit the well-munched end of her pen and considered

the screenful of dates she could easily look up on the internet. Inq teetered dramatically over Mr. Soares's desk, practically dropping her breasts on top of his open book. She glanced sideways at Joy and kicked up her heels.

"Say it," she lilted.

Joy raised her hand.

"Yes, Joy?"

"May I go to the bathroom?"

Mr. Soares sighed and waved absently at the hall pass, a garish hot-pink thumbs-up on a key ring. Joy scooped up the pass and soon she and Inq were bouncing giddily down the hall. Inq raised her hand as if pushing curtains aside.

"Keep your arms and legs in the fully upright position..."

They dropped right through the visible world and stepped into a living room piled with bodies. Joy stopped abruptly.

"...they apparently did," Inq finished.

Everyone was naked or in a state of half-dress. The hotel suite smelled of burnt candle wax and alcohol and sex.

"Ugh." Joy coughed on embarrassed laughter. "You brought me to an orgy?"

Inq picked her way delicately between two people curled on the floor.

"Don't be silly," Inq said. "The orgy's over. Even Viagra gives out eventually!"

"You are so gross," Joy said, staying clear of the tangle of limbs, sheets, and tissues, tripping over a vodka bottle on her way to the wall. She tried not to look at the landscape. Most of the faces were foreign and most of the girls were young. Every surface was covered in bottles, glasses, syringes or sandwich bags. Joy crossed her arms and blushed.

Ink zipped through a wall and stopped dead.

"Joy?" he said, dumbfounded.

She waved weakly. "Hi."

"Surprise!" Inq threw her arms over her head, exuberant. Ink glanced at his sister and something in his face flickered. A dimple appeared.

"You are impossible," he muttered good-naturedly. Inq shone with pride. He walked over to Joy. "I can take you back, if you want."

Inq clucked. "We just got here. Look, she has a pass!"

Joy rattled her laminated thumbs-up by its key ring. Ink smiled in sympathy. She wanted to be good at this. For him. With him.

"You do not need to be here," he said. "Inq gets bored sometimes."

"Bored? With this?" Inq lifted a hairy arm and waggled the sluggish hand. "We already missed the fun." Inq touched the tip of one finger, and shimmering calligraphy slid down the arm: pinwheels of eyes, herons, long-limbed tigers and spinning columns of characters popped like wax stamps.

Inq dropped the limb and turned to Ink. "You agreed that Joy should be seen in the field. I thought she might like to watch us working together," she said. "It doesn't happen all that often. You'd like to stay, wouldn't you, Joy?"

Joy didn't know what to say. She'd thought she was going with Inq to another cabana party. Ink's eyes held questions. Joy leaned against the wall.

"Sure," she said, matching Ink's gaze. "I'll stay."

He cocked his head, trying to piece together her clues. She saw him matching her words to their meanings, noting the subtle cues of her flesh. He'd been watching. He was learning. Which would he choose to believe?

"If you like," Ink said and stepped into the fleshy thicket. Pulling out his wallet, he picked up his silver quill and opened a girl's knees. Joy quickly looked at the clock.

"It's not always pretty," Inq said crisply. "Although many of these humans are." She lifted a young woman's face from a sofa cushion. "Look at those cheekbones!" Inq turned the unconscious face back and forth. "Do you think I'd look better with cheekbones like hers?"

"You look fine," Ink said dispassionately. Joy couldn't help but smile.

"How would you know?" Inq countered as she winked at Joy. "You like high-browed brunettes." Inq laid the sleeping girl back onto her pillow and traced her cheek gently as writhing filigree dropped a lace mask over the girl's eyes.

"So who ordered these marks?" Joy asked, trying to keep cool.

"Who knows?" Inq said. "After all this time, it's really more a matter of getting the job done. When large groups of humans come together—pardon the pun—it's usually an opportunity for several of the Folk to stake a claim." Inq smiled. "Everybody loves a good party!"

Joy crossed her arms. "I don't follow."

"Disease, conflagration, prophecy, pregnancy..." Ink rattled off words as he discarded another limb. "There used to be rituals attached to gatherings like these, but now only a memory of those rites remain. Still, there is a power to it and there are those who can claim it under their auspice." He looked up at Joy. "All part of being human, I suppose."

Joy snorted. "Not this human."

Inq laughed.

Joy watched as Ink took up his fat needle and drew a complex bead in the hollow above a man's buttocks. The black block calligraphy flowed like music—the man's back became a human cello under Ink's knee. She watched the intricate patterns dance and disappear.

"Can different symbols belong to the same person?" Joy asked.

"No. Each person's *signatura* is unique," Ink said simply. "But there are several claimants here. True Names mean only one thing, but the symbols comprising them have many interpretations."

"He means that the same embedded images can have multiple meanings, but the *signatura* itself is unique," Inq explained. "A hare, for instance, might mean longevity, luck, fertility, cowardice or death, depending on whose it is and how it is drawn." She hooked her two fingers and made bunny ears hop across the couch and vampire-bite a sleeping girl's neck.

Ink smiled as he looked at Joy. "The symbols flow automatically when we make our marks," he said. "I barely notice them anymore. You remind me there is beauty in this, too."

Inq winked. "Flatterer."

"So it's not unusual to have the same symbols show up again and again?" Joy asked, still confused.

Ink sat on the coffee table. "Some symbols have many meanings, but the same *signatura* occurs rarely," he said. "Inq and I have learned to recognize hundreds of them, but we have been doing this a very long time."

Joy frowned. "But I've seen the same symbol loads of times."

Inq looked down at the man's shoulder she was caressing into picturesque display. "What? These? It's classical Chinese." She sounded impressed. "Do they teach Chinese at your school?"

"No, not that," Joy said, pointing. "The spotted flower-thing. The pinwheel of eyes."

Ink turned and looked at the fading tattoo design.

"Pinwheel of eyes?" he asked.

Inq shrugged and looked at Joy. "You saw it before?"

"Sure," Joy said. "Lots of times."

Ink corkscrewed to look back at her. "You mean here in this room?"

"No, I mean everywhere," Joy said. "I've seen that same symbol nearly every time you've marked someone. I thought it was your mark or something."

"That is not my *signatura*," Ink said, regarding his sister. He addressed Joy again. "Are you certain?"

Was she? "I think so," Joy said.

He sounded curious, intrigued. "What did it look like?" he asked. "Can you draw it?" Ink pointed to a hotel notepad and a pen. Joy put down the hall pass and sketched eight petals in a circle, like a flower, with a dot in the center of each one. Ink inspected it and held the paper out to Inq.

"Recognize it?" he asked. Inq shrugged.

"Many symbols look the same," she said.

"Not to Joy. She has the Sight and she sees these things with fresh eyes." Ink held up the piece of paper. "We should ask Graus Claude."

"Why?" Inq asked, sounding exasperated. "We have work to do. No offense to your *lehman*, but she's new at this. Who cares whose it is? We can't keep running to the Bailiwick at the drop of a hat." She glanced meaningfully at Joy. "He already suspects something."

"I do not recall this being one of the ordered marks," Ink said gravely.

Inq sighed, annoyed. "Are you certain?"

"It is not familiar to me. And there is an easy way to find out," Ink said, standing next to Joy, cool and implacable. Inq frowned. Joy felt tension rising between them like an unscratchable itch.

"Maybe I was wrong," Joy said.

"See? She admits she's mistaken," Inq said. "Now can we get back to work?"

"By all means." Ink gestured with his blade.

Smooth and defiant, Inq yanked up a foot at random, drawing a line with her fingertip from big toe to heel. Light watermarks sluiced down the calf. Between soaring, skeletal cranes and a line of Chinese blocks, three eight-pointed stars tumbled like snowflakes, fading as they approached the knee and dissolved.

Inq dropped the foot like a brick. She splayed her fingers and gazed between them as if she were scouring the room with a magnifying glass.

"It's everywhere. On every one of them," she muttered quietly and lifted her eyes to Joy. "Even you."

Joy pressed back against the wall. Ink's hand was on her cheek, his thumb touching gently the corner of her eye. *Flash! Flash!* She looked at Ink with a strange panic blooming in her chest.

"Ink?"

"We go to Graus Claude," Ink said, taking Joy's hand. "Now."

"Of course," Inq said. "Let's go."

There was a fraction of a second between Ink escorting Joy by the elbow and their appearance at the base of the majestic stone steps. They vaulted the stairs quickly, footsteps light on the snow. Inq was the first to rap her knuckles on the door.

Kurt silently bade them enter, giving the tiniest bow to Joy. She smiled and mouthed the words *Thank you*. Kurt didn't smile, but his eyes did.

Ink placed his calling card on the silver tray, but Inq snatched it up before Kurt could carry it off.

"Got a pen?" she asked.

Kurt withdrew a fine, silver pen with gold clasp. It looked like it cost a small fortune. He held it out to Inq, who stared at it, then at him. There was meaning behind the exchange, but Joy couldn't grasp what. Inq took the pen and drew the eight-petaled flower carefully on the back of the cardstock, doodling a dot in the center of each eye. She flipped the card so the picture was faceup.

"There," Inq said, handing the pen back with a flourish. "That ought to get us some answers." But Kurt hadn't moved to accept the pen. He stared at the symbol, his face hard. Joy could feel a rage vibrating off him, something primal, pheromonal, urging her to run.

Kurt took the pen and the tray in one gloved hand and walked down the hall with tight, measured steps.

Joy stared after him. "What was that?"

Ink sat down. "What?"

"The way he acted…"

Inq shrugged. "Monkey recognized the mark."

Joy looked up. "Monkey?"

"No offense."

Joy flushed. Was that how Inq saw Kurt, or servants, or all human beings? As animals? Monkeys? Was that any different—or better—from *lehman*? Lovers? Slaves?

"His name is Kurt," Joy said, bristling. "And he saved my life."

Inq turned her drowning eyes to Joy with a look that was either scathing or curious.

"Really?" she drawled. "And therefore you think you share a special bond?"

Joy stood. "What is your problem?"

"Kurt was once her lover, Joy," Ink interrupted smoothly. "I think that may have more to do with it than any intended slight."

Joy frowned at Inq. "Kurt was your *lehman?*"

"No." Inq shot her brother a glare. "He's his own man. I was just having fun," she said, but something in her face betrayed an old hurt. A bit of Joy's anger melted, but only a little. The idea of Inq and Kurt together didn't fit in her head.

Inq glanced down the hall the way he'd gone. "Still, I wonder..." But she didn't get to finish her sentence before Kurt opened the great double doors, stepping aside so that they might follow. Ink stood, Joy joined him and Inq trailed behind, moving swiftly past her ex-lover without a backward glance.

Congregating in the office library, they gathered respectfully around the Bailiwick's desk. His two hands were typing as a third held the mouse and a fourth followed something on the monitor. Graus Claude peered through a rimless set of spectacles perched impossibly above his flaring nostrils. He clicked something closed and the mouse hand removed the glasses gently.

"Master Ink, Mistress Inq, Miss Malone—you are all looking well," he said. "I trust that you have enjoyed a speedy recovery?"

Joy didn't need a prompt. "Yes, thank you," she said, turning to include Kurt. "Thank you both very much."

Graus Claude nodded his low-slung head and rumbled, "Good." Three arms pivoted his massive bulk as he arranged himself before the black-eyed twins.

"You bring me more riddles," he said while flicking the card between his claws. "What is this about, eh?"

"We hoped that you might tell us," Ink said. "Do you know this *signatura*?"

Graus Claude gave an affirmative grunt. "Indeed, I do. But first tell me why I should tell it to you."

"It was in our order today amidst the claimant's mark," Ink said. "I did not recognize it. Nor did Inq."

"The *lehman* said she'd seen it before," Inq added.

"Joy," Ink corrected her.

"Joy," Inq said. "Of course."

Joy couldn't imagine why Inq had grown so frosty. Graus Claude turned his ice-blue eyes to her. "Is this true?"

She nodded. "I've seen that symbol a number of times, almost every time I've accompanied Ink." Joy didn't mention that Inq had seen it on her, too.

The great toad's eyes flicked to Kurt, who stood coiled like a rope twisting tighter. His gaze returned to Ink. "How many times has she accompanied you?"

"A handful," Ink said.

"And this—" a claw tapped on the cardstock "—was present at a number of assignments?" Graus Claude stared at Ink. "Did you notice it before?"

"I admit, I had not noticed," he said.

"And you, Miss Invisible?"

Inq bowed slightly, her hair stiff as a rooster's comb. "Once

Joy pointed it out, I thought perhaps I'd seen it before...." She trailed off, avoiding the storm cloud of Kurt behind her. "But I usually don't take note of the symbols embedded in specific *signaturae*, only that they are complete."

"And are they?" Graus Claude asked. "Complete?"

Inq's face flushed, cream-colored hieroglyphs flying over her features.

"Yes," she said. "Always."

The Bailiwick nodded. "Well, then." Graus Claude raised his sloping neck slightly to catch Kurt's eye. "Thank you, Kurt. You may go."

Joy felt more than heard the butler leaving, a click of the doors behind her and his crisp footfalls disappearing down the hall.

"I apologize," Graus Claude explained. "I am afraid my associate does not have the professional distance necessary for the remainder of this conversation." One of the four hands gestured. "Please sit."

They each chose a seat. Graus Claude towered over them. Joy thought he'd make an impressive school principal or Supreme Court judge. Heck, he was pretty impressive as a four-armed toad in a three-piece suit.

"This mark belongs to Aniseed," he said. "She is an alchemist and a powerful *segulah*." The Bailiwick's head swung to address Joy on the far right. "This means that she is a magician who works with natural elements. She is a member of the Council and one of the last of her kind." He brought his attention back to the twins. "She is a formidable opponent."

"Opponent?" Ink asked.

"Or ally, if you'd like," Graus Claude allowed. "Although many find the cost of her favors far outweigh the benefits."

Again, he sought Joy's attention. "As I may have mentioned, I have chosen to place myself at the crux between our worlds. Aniseed has positioned herself at its polar opposite—it is her belief that humans are a danger as a whole." His blue eyes sparkled. "One might sympathize knowing she bore witness to the slaughter of thousands of her people by human hands. Yet she has dedicated her craft to safeguard those who remain. She was the one to develop the practice of *signaturae* and created the need for Scribes."

Inq shrugged. "Then it shouldn't be unusual for hers to be among the marks."

Graus Claude pursed his lips. "Actually, it is most unusual," he admitted. "Aniseed prefers not to involve herself directly with humans, an understandable position given her personal experience. Even those legitimately under her auspice often go unvouched-for and are claimed by those with lesser ties. Aniseed is the voice of non-involvement and a proponent of separatism." Graus Claude smiled as one hand moved the mouse aside. "I'll admit that we are often at odds." He picked up the piece of paper with the flower of eyes. "While many have been aware of her personal leanings, she has never advocated open hostility, nor has there ever been cause for alarm. She is a stalwart supporter of preserving the Twixt and has a knack for finding and addressing its weaknesses, the adoption of *signaturae* instead of True Names being a prime example. Politically, she has always remained neutral. As you might expect, she makes a handsome ally, wooed by many in powerful debates."

Ink raised his chin in sharp profile. "I have no interest in politics."

"Well, they seem to have an interest in you, Master Ink,"

Graus Claude said with slight reprimand. "Although I cannot, at the moment, fathom why."

The long stretch of quiet prodded Joy to speak.

"And what about...?" She was about to say *me,* but a look from Ink changed her mind. "...Kurt?"

Did Graus Claude look surprised? Pleased? Or merely curious? Something in his expression hinted approval.

"I wished to spare him his anger. Few things can provoke him as this mark does, and he has worked hard to overcome it," he said. "Kurt's anger unleashed is a remarkable thing, but not one I'd care for you to witness, Joy Malone."

Inq smirked from her seat. "Some might call it passion."

"Some might," Graus Claude admitted. "But he would not."

The smirk vanished.

"That is all the information I can supply at this time. I will investigate the...unusual particulars of today's discovery," Graus Claude said with an ominous thrum.

"Could it simply be a dual claim?" Inq asked.

"Certainly possible," the grand toad allowed. "Many humans who are claimed by one often find favor by other Folk, as well. But I would have received the request and the fee." His great head shook. "The odds are more than odd, and I certainly would have noticed her *signatura* on the roster, I assure you. There have been too many strange happenings of late. 'Twice is coincidence, thrice is suspect.' It behooves us to be cautious."

"Why?" Joy spoke before thinking. "I mean, why worry over one *signatura*?"

His blue eyes sparked. "Because you do not know Aniseed as I do."

A hush filled the room with only the gurgling of the stone

fountains for comfort. Graus Claude grumbled and finally added, "A mark must be given voluntarily, Miss Malone. It is part of the contract in which we ply our trade. The symbol itself can be copied, but it holds no power unless it is bequeathed by its owner. It cannot be counterfeited, forged or stolen, which is why the inexplicable appearance of Aniseed's *signatura* is cause for concern...." His voice trailed off like distant thunder.

Inq glanced at Ink. Joy raised her eyebrows.

Ink stood. "Thank you, Bailiwick, for your attention to this matter."

Graus Claude inclined his head. "I will contact you when I have more answers," he said. "Master and mistress, be well and good fortunes. Miss Malone, I wish you continued good health."

"Thank you," Joy said, but she was the only one to respond. Dismissed, they walked out of the brownstone into the milder cold outdoors. On the stairs, Joy glanced back into the empty foyer.

Kurt had not reappeared to escort them out.

They sheared into the world outside the Glendale Oak, splicing through its bark riddled with initials and hearts. Joy shivered at the sudden drop in temperature. Her coat was still in her locker. She tucked her fingers under her armpits.

"Crap!" she exclaimed. "I forgot my hall pass."

"You don't need a hall pass," Inq said. "We're outside."

"I meant the one I had from Mr. Soares."

"Where did you leave it?" Ink asked.

Joy grimaced and hopped in place, thinking. "Probably

in the hotel room," she said. "I'm supposed to be in history class."

"You took her during class?" Ink accused Inq. "In a crowd?"

"Don't be silly," Inq said. "She excused herself—hence, the hall pass, or lack thereof."

Ink shook his head. "Impossible."

Inq beamed. "That would be me!"

"Excuse me," Joy said, pushing past. "It's freezing and I'm more than a little freaked out right now and I'm supposed to be in class."

Joy ran through the chunky snow. Ink called to her as she took the stairs, clutching her arms against the wind or fear or both.

"Do not worry," Ink said, his voice carrying. "The Bailiwick will take care of it."

Joy slipped through the doors, teeth chattering. "I'm not worried," she shouted back. The Scribes watched her from the snow, but Joy could still hear their slicing voices on the wind.

"You should be," whispered Inq.

ELEVEN

JOY NO LONGER QUITE BELIEVED IN THE WORLD. DAYS AT SCHOOL passed in a fog where even the sound of her shoes on the tiles seemed surreal. She didn't pay attention in class, instead spending the hours waiting and wondering who might come through a wall, unseen, and was constantly surprised to be addressed by name. Monica stopped asking if she was on drugs and was calling it "love"—something Joy didn't deny. It felt like love, all dreamy and mysterious. Joy almost didn't mind that Monica was too busy with Gordon to ask for details.

Almost.

She no longer got messages—Graus Claude saw to that—but Joy found herself looking for them in her locker, on her cell, in her pocket or her bag, as an easy excuse to call Ink. She had the four-leaf clover sandwiched between her ATM card and her school ID, and her text inbox boasted a single saved message from Ink himself, *I am here*, along with twenty or so unread ones from Mom, including two new ones. Joy clicked them into the Saved folder with a sigh. Would Mom ever give up? That part of their life was over. Joy wasn't that person anymore—she couldn't go back. Not now. Not ever. Too much had changed.

Her thumb quivered as she pressed Save. Joy had skipped breakfast and now had the weak, icy feeling of going too long without food. White dots sparkled on the edge of her vision. She hurried downstairs before the dizziness started.

The smell of the cafeteria made her swoon. Grabbing a tray, she joined Monica in line.

"You look white," Monica said.

"Caucasian, actually," Joy said, wiping her forehead. "Boy, you *have* been distracted. I blame Gordon-ocious."

Monica smacked her arm with the plastic tray. "No joke. Are you okay?"

Joy nodded, stomach clenching. She didn't want to keep talking. Her evasion was part safety, part jealousy and more than a couple parts selfish hurt. But she was so hungry she felt nauseous. She swallowed past words.

"Nothing a few hundred calories won't cure."

Her phone beeped. Joy checked the screen. There was a text from Stef: *Call ASAP!* "Crap." Joy eyed the lunch line and her phone, knowing it would be confiscated if she answered it here.

"Go call," Monica said. "I'll hold your spot."

"Thanks." She stepped out of the queue and pulled on her coat, hitting Call Back with shaky fingers as she stepped outside. She fished out a spoon and her emergency jar of soy butter, the permission slip from the nurse taped over its label. Joy scraped a dollop on her teeth as the phone connected.

"Hey," she said.

"Hey, yourself," Stefan answered. "You busy?"

"I should be at lunch, but you texted *ASAP*."

"Yeah," he said. "I did."

A long moment of silence let her sneak in a second bite.

"So?" she said around another spoonful.

"So have you told Dad?" Stef asked.

Joy licked the spoon. Fat and calories sang in her brain.

"About what?"

"About what?" Stef mocked. "About your boyfriend, Joy."

"Have *you* told Dad about *your* boyfriend?"

"I just told Mom," he said.

Joy swallowed. Stef had talked to Mom? Just now? Was that one of the messages on her phone? The thought made her ill—nervous and jealous and scared.

"What did she say?"

"Nothing much," Stef admitted. "Mostly that she loved me no matter what, that she wanted me to be happy and was this what I really wanted? You know..." He trailed off. "Mom."

Yeah, Joy knew. Still...Mom. Soy butter lodged in her throat.

"Joy?" Stef's voice brought her back from the edge.

"Yeah?" she said quickly. "Well, good for you."

"Now it's your turn."

A rush filled her ears, the familiar, hollow sound of held-back tears.

"Thanks, but I'll pass."

"C'mon, Joy!" Stef said sternly. "You can't go sneaking around Dad."

She force-fed herself another spoonful and spoke around the lumpy mass on her tongue.

"Watch me," she muttered.

Her older brother sighed loudly into the phone.

"Quit being a brat."

"I'm not being a brat!" she insisted. "It's just...complicated."

"Really? I can't imagine what that must be like."

"Trust me, this is different."

"So says the sixteen-year-old."

"Almost seventeen!" Joy said.

"Then start acting like it!" Stef shot back. "Mom's worried about you, but if you don't want to talk to her yet, fine. But Dad isn't like Mom. He's not all into the deep talking and heart-to-heart, but if you lie to his face, it'll kill him, Joy. You know it. Right now you're all he—"

"Don't!" Joy warned, her eyes gone wet. "Don't say it. And I'm not, okay? I'm *not* all he's got. Did you know Dad's dating someone? Did you know that? Huh? Some woman named Shelley."

The barest pause. "No, I didn't know that," Stef said. "Did he tell you or did you find out on your own?"

The answer squirmed inside her.

"He told me," she admitted.

"Well, then," he said, "don't you think you owe him the same thing?"

Joy rubbed her eyes, which started the one flashing angrily again. The cold stung her face. She wiped away tears. She didn't owe anyone anything. Mom, Dad, Stef, Monica. They'd all left *her!*

"I *can't*—I mean it, Stef. I want to, really I do...." And the weird thing was, she really did. Joy wanted to show off Ink, her boyfriend, to Dad and Monica and everyone else. To be seen as a couple. To be normal. She wanted *something* in her life to be normal. "But that's not going to happen," she said, more to herself than her brother. "It's just not possible."

The silence on the phone was harsh as the wind.

"Listen, Joy," Stef said. "I hate to put it this way, but if you don't tell Dad that you're dating some mystery guy, I will. When I tell him about me, I'll tell him about you."

Joy stomped her foot. "Stef, don't!"

"Trust him, Joy. He trusts you."

She railed impotently in the courtyard, kicking bricks with her shoe. He always knew how to get to her.

"I'll tell him," Joy said. "Okay? I'll tell him."

"You'll tell him," Stef repeated. "When?"

"I don't know," Joy said. "I didn't plan for this to happen!"

"Tell me about it."

"Hey, you took your time." Even Joy knew it was a low blow.

"I didn't lie to him, Joy. Or to you," Stef said quietly. "I'd been too busy lying to myself."

"Yeah, well, me too," Joy said, wiping her eyes. Why was she crying? "I didn't expect it... It just happened."

"Well, just make sure nothing else 'just happens,' okay? Remember—one conniption fit at a time, and the first two are mine." Her brother's voice softened. "But tell him soon, Joy. Dad doesn't need any more surprises."

"Uh-huh," Joy said with a sniff. "Okay. No more surprises." Scrubbing her face, she sighed. There was no kidding around this time, no teasing goodbyes. This conversation was grown-up and for real.

"Bye, Stef," she whispered.

"Bye, Joy. I love you." *Click.*

She thumbed the phone off and turned around.

Inq stood there smirking.

"Surprise!"

Joy marched quickly down the hall, leading Inq away from the lunchroom and other people.

"What are you *doing* here?" Joy asked under her breath. Salted soy butter stuck in her throat.

"Just visiting," Inq said. "I thought I'd bring you this." She held up the laminated thumbs-up sign, its key chain dangling off her palm: Mr. Soares's missing hall pass. Joy snatched it back. Inq grinned. "You're welcome."

"Thank you," she said. Checking the halls and the doors and the wall-mounted cameras, Joy retreated from the more congested parts of the school.

"Isn't there somewhere you need to be?" Joy whispered.

"*Need* is such a human word." Inq pouted. "Want and need are so subjective. I don't find them very useful." Joy turned a corner. Inq followed. "Where are you going?"

"My locker," Joy improvised, hoping that no one could see her talking to herself.

"Well, that *does* sound important."

Joy bit back her retort. Inq sounded bored, and she was in no mood for bored Inq, which promised to be both dangerous and highly annoying. Inq hadn't been too happy when they'd last been at Graus Claude's, and Joy was still feeling emotional after her conversation with Stef. Prolonged exposure did not bode well. Joy picked up the pace, skidding to a halt in front of her locker.

"What do you want?" she whispered over her shoulder.

Inq tipped her pixie face to the side as Joy dialed her combination.

"Well, I just thought..."

Joy pushed up the handle and darkness slammed down.

Stunned, Joy glanced around in the heartbeat that followed, the flash in her eye a weak firefly in sudden shadow. She squeezed the locker handle. It was solid and, presumably, real. She was in her school hallway, instantly transported into night. The world was coated in a thick film of heavy, brooding gray, but it wasn't nighttime. The few people between classes were stuck where they stood. A dropped pen hung in midair. The hall clock hands frozen at 11:47.

A thick, curving line held a concentrated darkness, as if a circle had been burned with gasoline on the floor. Joy was trapped inside a bubble—everything beyond it as still as a held breath.

Except Inq.

Inq struggled to her feet. She looked almost as shocked as Joy felt. Her dark, colorless eyes blinked rapidly as she frowned.

"Joy?" Inq called, her voice warped as if underwater, echoing weirdly although she was barely six inches away. "Are you okay?"

Joy waited for the sound of her words to fade before answering.

"Yes," she said. Her voice sounded normal to her. "I think so." She let go of the locker door, but nothing changed. The weight of the gray silence was like a deepwater dive. "What happened?"

"I don't know," Inq confessed. The sound seemed mismatched, penetrating the bubble a long second after her mouth moved. "It's a trap."

"A trap?" Joy stretched out to grab Inq through the veil, but hit something not quite solid that sparked. Joy hissed, clenching the feeling of electric ant bites from her fingers. Pain lit the fear inside her. She stared at Inq. "Get me out."

"I don't know..." Inq sounded upset, worried, for the first

time Joy had known her. And now was a bad time to start. "I don't think I can."

"Yes, you can!" Joy said. "Get me out! Try!" She held out her hand as if Inq might dare to take it, but the Goth girl shook her head and splayed her fingers as if she were waving good-bye. Joy's heart thudded wildly. "Ink..."

"Don't call him," Inq warned. "He'd appear inside with you, and we need to be sure we can get you both out first." She glanced over the fiery line, her mouth tight and grim. "Hang on."

Ripples swam from Inq's spread fingers. Concentric waves of scrollwork spun toward the bubble's wall, glyphs exploding where they touched the dark barrier, throwing fiery sparks. Joy covered her face and cringed. Inq held up both hands until the barrage of sigils and fireworks stopped. Quiet fell. Blue lightning coursed along the shadow like an angry electric fence.

"Joy?" Inq called.

"I'm okay," Joy said, checking herself slowly, then examining the unbroken line of charcoal light.

"There must be a trigger. Something that set off the trap." Inq pointed a smooth finger at the locker door. "Do you see anything?"

Joy leaned close to the metal, close enough to smell a whisper of paint. "Someone scratched a few numbers off:..." Realization skittered through Joy. "They knew my combination."

Inq groaned. "You invoked the ward by dialing it. I can't get in," Inq said. "You don't carry my *signatura*. I have no claim on you." She tried peering through the wall of shadow, her voice warbling. "Are you alone in there?"

The question brought a fresh set of fears. Joy glanced around.

"I think so." Now that she was listening, she wasn't so sure. Whispers teased and sparks crackled in the humming, buzzing stillness.

"I'll get Ink," Inq said. "Don't touch anything. I'll be right back."

Joy whispered a completely unnecessary "Hurry." Inq raised her hand and disappeared.

Joy sat on the floor and braced herself against her locker door. The metal was reassuringly real. She felt claustrophobic, the gray space pressing in on her, the tight, trapped feeling making her pulse race. She pushed back until the thin metal door behind her popped with a dull *thunk*. The slight glistening along the shadow wall crackled like the underbelly of a storm.

The sound, when it came, scratched with a finger of dread.

A long, drawn-out creak whickered just behind her ear. Joy turned her head quickly, but nothing was there. Nothing she could see, but she sensed something moving. Joy licked her lips to wet them enough to form words.

"Who's there?"

Another elongated creak, the groan of heavy wicker baskets. Something was circling, predatory, just on the edge of her Sight. The dance of static lightning swirled.

"Inq?" Joy couldn't see her. Just the frozen people beyond the bubble. Joy kept her eyes open and thought to herself, *Ink!*

Where was he? What was taking so long?

Flash! Flash! A freeze-frame spliced her vision—an interrupting image of a long hem and a vibrant rust-orange coat. Her sinuses swelled with the scent of old-fashioned candy and firewood. It made her dizzy, even sitting on the floor. She pulled herself tighter.

The phantom creaks became moans, a wail that ground into a series of small wooden pops. The sounds hushed to silence. It was probably standing right in front of her. She could feel its closeness. Malevolent. Invisible.

She was tempted to kick.

Ink zipped into existence just outside the barrier with a stony expression and sliced contemptuously through the dark. The barrier rippled and parted, folds wafting like wind-blown curtains. Ink stepped through, hauling Joy to her feet, as the breach behind him sealed itself closed.

"Something's in here," she breathed.

"I know," he said and held her to him in a marble grip. With his free hand, he withdrew the fat needle and braced it with the length of his forefinger, pointing it like an accusation. "This is my *lehman*," he said to the darkness, his eyes following the flicker that coursed along the wall. "She is my claim. Begone!"

They stood still for a long moment, but there was no answer. Nothing moved in the shadows except blue fissures of light.

Ink nudged her with his shoulder. "Show me the trigger," he said. "Quickly."

Joy carefully pressed her forefinger against the things that were once the numbers 18, 24 and 53, which now looked like crazy squiggles. Ink squatted down and blew his breath upon them as if he were whispering a secret. He pushed the point of the needle through the tiny glyphs—there was a puff of light as the sigils broke into powdery dust. The darkness around them dissolved.

People moved. A pen dropped. The second hand ticked.

Joy stood up slowly, stunned by the sudden normalcy. The bell rang. Hall A swarmed with students headed for class. Joy leaned heavily against her locker. Ink stood beside her, needle in hand, eyes searching the school, silently daring the invisible unknown. He'd placed one foot in front of her, shielding her from the throng. People slid around them, unconsciously moved.

"What was it?" Joy whispered under her breath.

"A warning," Ink said and took her hand without looking or asking, as natural as anything. "Come. I am taking you home."

Joy figured cutting class and teleporting home was better than being trapped in a lightning-walled bubble locked outside of time, but it still made her nervous. Ink grimly ran a circuit of the condo as she shut off the alarm.

"Are we safe here?" she asked.

"Yes," Ink said. "And I intend to keep it that way. These people are not the only ones who can make or break wards." He took the black arrowhead and knelt by the door, carving a small symbol deep into the tile, kicking up bits of ceramic powder and dust. Before Joy could ask, he blew a long breath, erasing it from view. Running her fingers over the spot, Joy was amazed that she couldn't feel any difference. Ink walked through the house, carving symbols into the window ledges, the doorways and the vents, making little piles of wood and metal shavings and yarn fibers that he dispersed with a breath.

Returning to Joy, he gestured outdoors. "I am going to secure the grounds." He spun the scalpel in his hand in a kind of a salute. "Wait here."

"Okay." Joy twisted her hands in her shirt. "Be careful."

Ink hesitated, grinning ominously, then zipped into the air.

She fiddled with her sleeves and sat down on the edge of a chair. It felt as if everything was spinning out of control. She felt the walls pushing in closer than ever. The room felt small. She sorted the mail for something to do.

There was a FedEx package addressed to her on the kitchen counter. She flipped it over, not recognizing the business address, and cautiously ripped the seal: a plane ticket fell out.

She stared at the ticket. First class. From Mom. Joy pressed a hand to her mouth and sat down again, furious and embarrassed, knowing that Dad had to have brought it in. Did he know what was inside? Had Mom told him? Did he think Joy knew? That she had asked to visit? That she'd made plans behind his back? That she wanted to leave? She wasn't even *talking* to Mom! Could he think Joy had forgiven her? That she would betray him like that?

Joy bunched up the cardboard envelope and shoved it into the trash. The ticket remained on the counter, untouched, like a rebuke. What was Mom *doing* sending Joy plane tickets? It was completely presumptive and obnoxious, forcing her hand—making Joy out to be the spiteful teenage daughter, petty and selfish, if she didn't accept such a generous gift. She hadn't even *asked* Joy if she wanted to come! But then again, maybe she had. Maybe that's what all the phone calls were about.

Joy slapped the ticket down on the table, caught between throwing it out or throwing it in the drawer—hiding it or sending it back or tearing it into shreds. She didn't know what she wanted to do with it, except she didn't want Dad to see it. She didn't even want to *think* about it. There'd been a lot of that going on lately.

Furious and frazzled on a near-empty stomach, Joy had only one clear solution: brownies. Lots of them.

Fifty-five minutes later, the brownies came out gooey in the middle with a crispy black crust. Maybe adding extra chocolate chips hadn't been a good idea. Joy was quick-stabbing her way around the nine-by-thirteen pan when the door opened. She glanced up, surprised, as her father walked in...with Shelley.

Shelley had a long face that seemed out of place on her plumper body. Her lips were poppy-red, which matched her hair, and her earrings were far too large for her head. Joy tried to quell her first impression of "not like Mom," which, if she thought about it, was probably the point.

"Thought we'd come home for lunch," her dad said awkwardly. Her father's eyes were dangerously bright. "What's this?"

Joy opened her mouth.

Ink sliced through the wall.

There was a moment when her heart stopped. Her skin felt too tight. Her palms damp with sweat. The mix of unexpected company and two completely different lives converging made her head spin. Luckily, she was already stabbing: a good nervous activity. Joy stopped when she began to enjoy it too much.

Ink surveyed the scene. Joy shook her head slightly.

"Hi, Dad. Um..."

Shelley smiled as Joy's father took her coat. "Hi," she said, offering her hand. "I'm Shelley Auerbach. And you must be Joy."

Joy switched hands, thankful Shelley wasn't offering a hug. "Hi. Yes. I'm Joy. That's me."

Her father looked at the pan. "And what are you making?"

"Brownies, sort of," Joy said and gestured vaguely with the knife. "It's kind of an experiment."

"Perfect," Shelley said with a smile. "I'm always up for experimental cooking."

Joy grinned despite herself. "Um... It's a really 'interesting' experiment." She gently elbowed Ink while she edged the pan over the plane ticket. Dad looked as though he wanted to ask what other "interesting" things had happened today, for instance, why she was home and not at school. His eyes promised, *We'll discuss this later.* Ink followed his steely gaze.

"He is protective of you," Ink said. "I approve."

Joy shifted the pan and muttered, "Great."

"Hmm. Got any ice cream?" Shelley asked. "I find that always helps."

Dad's bad mood melted at the words *ice cream*. "We have chocolate and vanilla mint chip."

"Perfect," Shelley said, giving Joy a conspiratorial wink. "Let's get some bowls and test the theory."

Shelley and Dad bustled into the kitchen. Unseen, Ink touched Joy's face with gentle fingers.

"You will be safe here," Ink said. "Nothing can enter by door or window." His voice, unheard by Dad or Shelley, tickled her ear. "I am going to the Bailiwick. We will speak again soon." She nodded, unable to reply as Shelley counted out spoons. Ink retreated two steps, swung his knife and disappeared, leaving Joy to survive her first meeting with Shelley, not with politeness or preparation, but over burnt brownies à la mode.

Joy was reading in bed when Dad knocked on her door.

"Come in," Joy said around a fluttery stomach that she blamed on the weird afternoon rather than the half-baked brownies.

Dad sat heavily on the edge of her bed, jostling her as if she was six years old and about to hear a bedtime story. In that moment, Joy felt sad and way too big. Her father struggled for a long moment, stretching for words that wouldn't come. Joy twisted her highlighter cap, waiting, knowing that this wasn't going to be easy.

"I forgot to ask how your eye was feeling," he said lamely. "You still want to go to the doctor?"

"Uh..." If he was going to ignore the whole skipping school thing, she was perfectly willing to do that. In exchange, she was willing to forget about Shelley's secret noontime visit. Joy blinked purposefully: *Flash! Flash!* She wondered if that was the only way she would be able to see invisible stalkers who creaked as they moved.

"No," she said, finally. "I'm fine."

"Fine," Dad said and nodded. He took a deep breath and held his hands in his lap. "I...wanted to say thank-you for being good about Shelley—we hadn't planned on stopping back here," he said. "We met for coffee and spent so long talking, I didn't want to miss out on lunch. I was the one who suggested grabbing something from the fridge." His eyes dropped to the floor.

Joy shifted her pillows around the awkwardness and the uncertainty; it was a vulnerability they didn't often share. She and her dad didn't talk about stuff like this. It stayed where it belonged: behind closed doors and private. A squirmy, uncomfortable empathy itched beneath her ribs.

She knew *exactly* how he felt—unsure whether two separate parts of life could coexist in the same space or if they would explode, destroying or irreparably damaging one or both. Being forced to choose and not wanting to, afraid to try and dare to have it all... When had her dad become a regular person?

Joy dropped her book on her chest.

"She's nice," Joy said, which meant *I love you*.

Her dad nodded and leaned forward, giving her a hug and pushing a kiss into her hair. Joy kissed him back, unexpectedly choked up. They held each other for a while in a warm and comfortable quiet.

"You know you're grounded, right?" he said past her ear.

Joy sighed and squeezed him. "Yeah, I know."

He pulled away and considered her frankly. "Well, how about this—I don't know why you were cutting school, but you get a free pass, just this once, for being good about Shelley. You're starting to act more like the Joy I know. You think I haven't noticed, but I have. You're smiling. You're happy. I like that, and I want you to keep it up. But the acting-out stuff? I don't like that. So no more broken windows, no more skipping school, no more being stupid. Got it?"

"Got it," Joy agreed, crossing the book over her heart and smiling. "No more stupid."

Friday was full of sunshine offering the promise of spring and a warm-weather weekend. Joy sat in the cafeteria admiring her shiny red apple on its yellow plastic plate. All the colors looked a little brighter today.

"You look perky," Monica said.

"I am," she said. "Perky. Life is good."

"So everything's okay with Dad? With Stef?" Monica asked as Joy scooped yogurt into her mouth. Even the garish pink of her Super Strawberry looked more like Easter Sunday than toxic waste. Joy nodded and swallowed.

"Yep. All good."

Monica raised her eyebrows and stirred her own cup. "You tell him about your artiste yet?"

Joy wrinkled her nose. "I said all was good, not stupid. I have solemnly sworn, No Stupid."

Monica snorted, stirring morosely.

"You, however, are looking not so perky."

"Distinct lack of perk," Monica said. "Gordon's away for the weekend and I think I may pine."

"Pine?" Joy laughed. "As in 'pining'? You?"

Monica stuck out her generous lip and pouted. "Sad, but true."

"Hmm." Joy considered this as she magnanimously waved her spoon. "Then I believe I shall celebrate my escape from near-grounding by distracting you with bright, shiny objects on sale."

Monica sat up, alert. "Don't tease me, girl," she said. "I'm extremely vulnerable right now."

Joy looked smug. "I suggest we go Saturday. Evergreen Walk?"

Monica's eyes sparkled and Joy couldn't help but grin.

"*Shop-ping!*" they chorused and clinked their plastic

spoons. Joy grinned as Monica bounced in her seat. Sometimes, it took so little to make her happy.

So what made Ink happy?

Joy didn't know, but she decided that she was going to find
out. She felt the little note he'd left on her nightstand this
morning crinkle in her pocket.

Tonight, it said.

Joy smiled.

Tonight.

Ink sat at the kitchen table, carving his own fingers. It
wasn't exactly what Joy had had in mind, but she sat fascinated, mesmerized by his hands.

With an artist's concentration, he traced the edges of cuticles, tugging and tapping the skin into harder surfaces,
making nails. Switching instruments, he cut tiny lines into
his skin, tugging extra folds loose at the knuckles. He turned
his hands over to inspect the result.

"They are ugly," he said, flexing his fingers.

"They are not."

"Imperfections are ugly by nature."

Joy asked, "Then why do it?"

He grinned at her. "Sometimes I like ugly things."

"Hey!"

Joy pretended to swipe him and he caught her fingertips. "But mostly," he amended, "I like beautiful things." He
touched her cheek with a newly indented thumb. "Do you
like them?"

Joy took his hand in hers. His skin was still preternatu-
rally smooth, without ridges or creases or veins. She traced

his palm where lines ought to be, unblemished except where the knuckles bent.

"They're beautiful," she said.

He took back his hand and appraised it himself. "They are a work in progress," he said, which might have meant *"Like us."* The words warmed her inside.

He switched hands and began carving his right.

"Is that hard?" she asked.

Ink didn't look up as he teased some skin into place. "No. I am ambidextrous. I work equally well with both hands."

"That's not what I meant."

He picked up the leaf blade and cut a smooth, crescent thumbnail base. "Do you mean, 'Do I find it difficult to cut my own flesh?' The answer is no."

"Really?" Joy said. "Why not?"

"Because it is not really flesh," he said, "not like yours." He began expertly slicing squiggles into the nubs of knuckle as if he remembered precisely how the left had been done. "This form is...fluid. It's an embodiment more than a body. Shaping it, I find, makes it more my own." He paused as if considering the words he had just said aloud, then continued. "While the Bailiwick claims that the Folk are more than human, I believe we are—in many ways—less."

Joy slipped off her seat and leaned next to him at the table, resting her shoulder lightly against his. She watched him fashioning his hands for her, from her, creating himself more in her image because he wanted her to like them and he wanted to better understand humans...and her. She watched him mold calluses as if sculpting soft clay. It was true—the little details made him look far more human, but no amount of craftsmanship could erase his unnatural eyes. Or his smell—a delicate whisper of clouds and rain.

She whispered near his ear. "I like your embodiment."

Ink's face dimpled, secretive, pleased. "I like yours, too."

She watched the knife slide.

"Draw me a line," she said.

He stopped carving his middle finger, curious. "Where?"

She pointed, gliding her index finger gently against his palm, a half-moon from his wrist around the ball of his thumb. They both sank into a sudden, intense quiet.

He took up the razor and quietly obeyed. The silver edge separated his skin as elegantly as a skater on ice. They both sat hushed, admiring what they had done—what she had suggested and what he had made real. Drawn like a signature, her request on his skin. He looked up at her quizzically, intent.

"Again, please."

Joy moved closer, holding their hands up like mirrors, and delicately touched the valley of her palm. She repeated the motion in his. Ink concentrated, following her silent suggestion. The silver blade flashed under the kitchen light and her skin fairly hummed as she traced arches, loops and whorls, which he then copied onto his own.

They sat together, trembling on an edge.

Touching her own skin made it feel like his fingers. Watching him as he made his hands more like hers. She slid their palms together, feeling the rippling textures under her fingertips, the minute changes that were making him hers—her his—each of them one another's, theirs.

"Wait," Ink said and closed his eyes. Joy felt his hand grow warmer. His skin gave under hers. He squeezed her hand and spoke into her hair, each word a puff of breath.

"Again," he said. "More."

Joy drew her fingertips down into his palm—they became palpably warmer, sensitive, softer. Their fingers explored one another's hands: slow, curious interlacings of Joy and Ink.

She felt his cheek and the edge of his jaw on her chin. The flush of her skin echoed on his. The sweep of his eyelash brushing her face. She strained to feel the tips of his hair, the nonexistent scratch of his never-shaven face. All the while, she watched their fingers stretch along one another's wrists, afraid to look away and admit what was happening. What was touching. What they wanted.

It became too much. Joy squeezed his hand. Looked in his eyes.

It was as if he were surprised to see her.

"I can feel you," he whispered.

She nodded. "I know."

He tapped his chest. "Here."

Joy nodded again and said, "I know." Her lips were close. She could taste whispers of him and rain.

"We are here," she whispered, feeling the kiss before it happened. "We are both very, very here."

TWELVE

"I'M GOING," JOY CALLED OVER HER SHOULDER. MONICA WAS waiting in the driveway.

"Have fun," her father said. He and Shelley sat in the kitchen drinking coffee. She hadn't stayed the night, but it wouldn't be long before she did. They were trying out breakfast together. They'd asked Joy for recommendations and were off to Goldie's for pancakes.

"You, too," Joy said. "Bye, Shelley. Bye, Dad."

The inclusion made everyone smile. Joy couldn't help smiling today. She could still feel Ink's last kiss on her lips. It was a secret that beat in her chest like a pulse.

I love him. I love Ink.

She felt like she was thirteen again, giddy and silly and filled with music. She skipped down the stairs and across the courtyard. Monica honked the horn, poking her head out the driver's-side window.

"Get the lead out!"

"I'm coming, I'm coming," Joy said, opening the door and buckling herself in with a click. "Is your wallet burning a hole through your purse?"

"My purse, my jacket and possibly the floor. Hang on."

Monica shifted gears and roared them out of the driveway for extra emphasis.

"Oh, I've needed this like nobody's business!" Monica said, turning the wheel. "Baby needs Victoria's Secret."

Joy laughed. "That's no secret."

Monica winked. "And that's no lie!"

They flew down the road, chatting happily and singing along to a great indie playlist and scoring a prime parking space halfway down the plaza. Tasteful window displays gleamed under emerald-colored awnings. The sun shone warm and welcoming in all its butterscotch glory. Frost lined the edges of the grass. The stores were just opening. Everything felt new.

And they'd managed to park right in front of the lingerie shop.

"Sweet!" Monica giggled. Her mood was infectious. Joy grabbed her purse and they dove inside.

Monica immediately strung hangers over her arm—half bras and push-up bras and bits of nothing held together with string. Joy noticed that instead of her favorite bold colors, there was a lot of white and pink lace in her hands.

Joy held up a giant padded double-D in cherry-red satin. "Going all girly on me?" she teased.

Monica might have blushed. "Gordon brings out my softer side."

"TMI," Joy warned, replacing the bra on its hook.

"Maybe you should look for something," Monica said. "For Mr. Someone-A-Guy."

"I don't think so," Joy said, touching a display of polka-dot thongs.

"Why not?" Monica asked. "What's the matter? Are you...?"

They traded a look.

"Oh, no," Monica said flatly.

Joy pretended not to hear her. "What...?"

"No." Monica couldn't cross her arms because she was loaded with underthings, but her expression said it all. "You *aren't*. Why aren't you?" Monica shook her head in disgust. "I knew it. There was something about this guy. He's not telling you that he's 'waiting for you to be ready' or something, is he? Like *he's* the one who gets to say when *you're* ready to give it up so you, the independent woman, can rush to prove him wrong?"

Joy snorted. "No."

"Good. Because you don't deserve any reverse psychology, passive-aggressive crap," Monica muttered protectively. Joy tried not to smile. "You're too good to be living like a hermit or a nun, but guys can smell opportunity like steaks on the grill." She held up a cami for inspection. "He's not younger than you, is he?"

"No..."

"Because you are *not* dating-down."

Joy had to laugh. "I'm not!"

"Then he's older than you," Monica said, sounding suspicious. "Way older? How old?"

Joy was getting uncomfortable. She hadn't expected the Spanish Inquisition in a lingerie shop. Joy shuffled through a rack of thongs without seeing them.

"It's not like that," she said. "It's not about sex."

"Not about *sex*?" Monica ignored the fact that everyone and their mother could hear her. Joy cringed. "Girl, sometimes I seriously wonder about you." She peeled through the last season's sale items, scraping hangers against aluminum like fingernails on slate. "Okay, let's play this out," Monica said with a huff. "Let's say that you're right and that this mysterious guy isn't interested in sex. So who dates a pretty girl and isn't interested in sex? Hmm? Something would have to be seriously wrong with him. Ergo, weirdo. Dump him and move on. Or—" she held up a hand like a crossing guard's stop sign "—I am right and he is a normal, healthy member of the male species who *is* interested in sex with a fine young thing and somehow has gotten you to believe that he isn't." She drawled, counting fingers. "Head-case, manipulator, playa. Dump him and move on." Monica glared at Joy, who was caught somewhere between outrage and laughter.

"So which is it?" Monica asked.

"Neither!" Joy said. "It's *not* about sex."

Monica raised both eyebrows as Joy rifled through the thirty-percent-off undies.

"Mmm-hmm," Monica said. She held up a bunch of underwires like a peace offering. "Carry some in for me?"

Joy mutely took half Monica's haul and followed her into the changing rooms. Neither said anything as Joy unhooked and handed pair over pair under the door, hanging them back up when Monica had finished tucking, clasping and reboobing. They were still out together shopping, but now they were just going through the moves. Anger had smothered the mood with padded inserts. Joy quietly fumed outside the stall. This sucked.

"I can't reach—can you hook this?" Monica asked, opening the door while holding two tabs behind her back. Joy stood up and wordlessly fastened the straps. It reminded her of Inq.

"Thanks," Monica said quietly, giving a little tug. Both of

them paused before Monica raised her eyes to the mirror, catching Joy's reflection.

"Look," Monica said while admiring herself. "It's not my place to tell you who you should or shouldn't date." Joy bit back a snort. "But I'm worried about you, Joy. Really and truly. I haven't even met this boy of yours and I've never seen you so overboard. It makes me nervous." She turned and faced Joy's morose anger in adjustable straps. "I'm your best friend, right?"

Joy acquiesced, nodding. "Right."

"So if this guy is worth waiting for or something, good. Great. But if he's playing you a line, promise me you'll take a step back, or at least introduce me to him and I'll take him down a peg or two so he knows what's what," Monica said, trying a sympathy smile. "You know that I would. I just want to keep you safe."

That hit a nerve. Monica knew nothing about the world of the Twixt, but Joy knew *exactly* how she felt.

"I know," Joy said. "It's just...complicated."

Monica smirked. "Honey, it always is." She shimmied her shoulders, eyeing the result, and frowned. "Now help me figure my way out of this thing."

Monica ended up buying three bras and a bunch of panties, including two thongs. Joy shook her head as Monica waved her credit card dismissively. "You know these things all ride up your butt, anyway. Wedgies happen. Thongs tell it like it is!" Joy laughed and by the time they were ogling the cute sundresses across the street, they were back in the groove.

Flash! Flash!

A flicker of gray caught Joy's eye. There was a shadow hovering near the directory map that she couldn't quite shake. Instinctively, she steered Monica into the nearest store.

"Ice cream?" Monica asked.

"Sudden craving." Joy made a show of glancing at the selections, but kept an eye out the window. Something zipped along the edge of the plaza, near the tiny gazebo, frighteningly fast.

"See anything?" Monica interrupted Joy's worry. "I think I'm getting a toothache just by breathing in here."

"I guess not," Joy stammered. Exasperated, Monica pushed open the door. Joy hesitated.

"I gotta pee," she said.

The cashier behind the counter said, "For customers only."

"Forget it," Monica said. "You coming?"

Joy couldn't think up another excuse.

"Sure," she said. Outside, a quick blur raced across the rooftops, disappearing over a Crate & Barrel. Several more followed. Joy hooked her arm through Monica's and nearly bolted toward their parked car.

"Hey!" Monica said. "Pushy much?"

"Power walking," Joy muttered back, trying not to sound as panicked as she felt. "C'mon, let's skip!" Monica resisted, so they ended up awkwardly bouncing-slash-running when the first shouts started. Joy detoured quickly into the next open door.

"Hey, look!" Joy said and thrust something into Monica's hand.

Through the display window filled with candles and colored glass, Joy saw afterimages catapulting between people and trees, tossing leaves and hair and random garbage ahead of their path like a violent gust of wind. Whatever they were, they were closing fast.

"Beeswax owls?" Monica said uncertainly. "I don't get it."

Joy dragged on Monica's arm.

"Hey! Ow! What's the deal?" Monica snapped.

"Come on," Joy said and tugged her deeper into the store, placing rows of scented wax and wood shelving between them and the front window. The glass shivered with a prescient rattle.

"Look at these," Joy said, reaching for a distraction. "Organic candles!"

Maybe it was her imagination. Maybe it would go away. This might have nothing to do with her. Nothing at all. Joy twisted her fingers on the edge of her shirt.

"Oh, please," Monica said. "What's inorganic about *candles*? I swear, they are putting that word on everything...." Joy listened to her with half an ear, the other half cocked for screams. "Like, how can there be a 'natural dairy' section? What does that make everything else? Unnatural?"

"Plastic," Joy said vaguely. "With added hormones." She glimpsed a blur of oncoming shadows before...

"Duck!" she said, yanking Monica down.

Glass shattered. Women screamed. A shelving unit toppled and there was an avalanche of votives against the hardwood floor. People hugged the walls, the shelves and each other. Joy and Monica crouched beneath a heavy table full of pillar candles and spangled bags of potpourri.

A heavy thud careened off the wall and something rolled to a stop. Joy half expected it to be some sort of grenade and was oddly surprised to see that it was an ordinary rock. A good, fist-size rock. One of many that pelted through the broken windows. There were more crashes. More thuds. More shouts.

Joy had a flash memory of a large, ghoulish tongue. She grabbed Monica's coat to pull her closer.

"You okay?" she asked.

"Peachy," Monica spat back, dialing her cell one-handed. "You?"

Joy squinted through the table legs. Fleeting smudges of shadow threw a few more rocks, zoomed westward and disappeared in a flurry of wings. *Wings!* She wondered if anyone else could see them. There was a tense moment of nothingness before cell chatter and angry voices joined the tinkle of glass.

Joy picked up the rock and dropped it.

"Ow!" It was hot to the touch.

"Damn," Monica muttered. "Did you see them?"

"I saw something," Joy admitted. "That's why I grabbed you."

"Owe you one," Monica said.

Joy chanced some honesty. "Well, I want to keep you safe, too."

People uncurled, shaken, angry and confused. Monica and Joy stood up and brushed off bits of dried flowers and window glass.

"Everybody okay?" the guy behind the counter called out. "Please stay calm. The police are on their way. We'll be offering everyone some cider, on the house. Just relax, please. Is anyone hurt?"

"Hey, free cider," Joy said with forced cheer.

Monica dropped her shopping bags on the table and sighed as she hung up her phone. "I'm game."

They gave their names and phone numbers and signed the necessary paperwork along with everyone else, mutually agreeing to add this incident to one of a growing number of Things Not to Be Discussed With Parents as they headed back to the car. The mood was strangely optimistic, as though they were best friends again. There was nothing quite as bonding as surviving an unknown attack in a candle shop over instant hot cider.

"I can't believe this," Monica clucked over her watch. "We lost a good hour back there. My Mom's gonna…" Her voice trailed off. "No!" She hurried over to the car. The windshield had been smashed. She dropped her bags and gripped her keys. "No, no, no, no, no…." she wailed. "I don't *believe* this!"

Joy inspected the car with growing guilt. "It doesn't look like they took anything," she said.

"No, no, *no!*" Monica stormed.

Joy glanced down the row of vehicles. "It wasn't just you." The lot was full of cars whose windows were cracked, crackled or crashed. Police officers were already taking statements farther up the line. "Looks like it was random," she added. Joy really wished she could believe that.

"So much for keeping this quiet," Monica shook her head angrily as she fumbled with her wallet. "Thank Jesus for Triple-A." She began dialing the 800 number. "This is going to take forever," she groaned. "And I'm leading church youth group today at three."

Joy quietly flipped through her phone, staving off her guilty feelings, fearing that keeping too many secrets might show up on her face. Was this really a random incident? Or was Joy being followed? Or threatened? Had she put her best friend in danger just by being with her? She'd never get over it if something happened and she was to blame. Joy paused over the list of saved messages from Mom.

Then she remembered her several new entries.

"Hey," Joy said. "You want to call for a ride and deal with this later?"

Monica was listening to the automatic messaging system with one ear. "This isn't a convenient ploy to ruin your dad's date, is it?"

"Nuh-uh. The less Dad knows, the better," Joy said. "But there's someone who can maybe help us out."

Monica typed in her membership number and hit pound. "Yeah?" she asked. "Who?"

"Friend of a friend," Joy said while dialing. She was nervous as it rang, still more nervous when it connected.

"Hello?"

"Hey," she said, trying to sound casual. "It's Joy."

"Hey, Cabana Girl," Luiz drawled. "What's up?"

She switched hands as she talked. "My friend's car got its window smashed..." She trailed off.

"Call Triple-A."

"That's not the problem." Joy spoke a little lower. "The problem is how it got that way."

Luiz paused. "Ah," he said. "Gotcha. You both okay?"

"Yes. For now."

"What was it?"

"I don't know," she said. "But they move fast."

"They, as in more than one?"

"Yeah." Joy swallowed. "Any way we could get a lift?"

"Where are you?"

"Evergreen Walk in Glendale, North Carolina."

"Okay..." Luiz said. "Let me see what I can do. Hang tight

and don't look surprised when your ride gets there. Everything's cool."

"Okay, thanks." Joy hung up, wondering what she'd done. Her heart beat faster than it had in the shop. "I got us a ride."

"I'm still on hold," Monica said. "I don't think I'm going anywhere for a while." She waved at the officer who was already offering her a clipboard and pen. Joy scanned the plaza. They were too exposed, too out in the open. She felt invisible eyes surrounding her, armed with rocks and hummingbird wings. Monica was still filling out forms when a silver Lexus pulled to a smooth stop.

"Joy!"

She sprang off the bench, jogging up to the driver's-side window. Joy stopped, staring. She couldn't believe it.

"Nikolai?"

"Don't sound so surprised," he said in his husky English. "Quickly now—I am between shoots."

Joy glanced around the car. It had Carolina plates. "Is this your car?"

"Less talking, please," he said. "You want a rescue or no?"

Joy turned around quickly. "Monica," she called. "Our ride's here!"

"Just finishing up," Monica said as the police officer handed her a yellow carbon copy. "But the tow will take a while."

Nikolai frowned, still managing to be beautiful.

"Do it later," Joy suggested. "You want to make it to youth group or not?"

"Hang on!" Monica said irritably while she removed her MP3 player and emptied the glove compartment's contents into her Gap bag. Checking the trunk, she locked the car and hurried over. "Thank you, kind stranger!"

Nikolai nodded. "No problem." Joy got into the passenger's seat and Monica jumped in the back. He pulled gracefully past a half dozen cops as Joy kept her eyes forward, trying to act natural, as if she was used to hot Russian underwear models picking her up in expensive cars every day.

At the stop sign, Nikolai handed Monica a smartphone open to GPS. He smelled of rich, spicy cologne. "Tell it where you want to go," he said with a smile. "I can get lost in a paper bag."

"Just drop me off at First Anglican, thanks," Monica said, tapping the intersection and stuffing her Victoria's Secret purchase into the larger Gap bag and covering it up with a new red sweater. "So, how do you know Joy?"

Nikolai adjusted the rearview mirror and Joy twisted her hands in her pockets.

"We have friends in common," he said diplomatically.

"Really?" Monica said. "Who knows who?"

"Joy is dating my girlfriend's brother."

"Aha!" Monica cried and pointed a finger at Joy. "Gotcha!" Joy blushed. Nikolai laughed and turned left.

They dropped Monica off at the First Angelican Church. She said a quick thank-you and mouthed *Wow!* to Joy before she ran in. Nikolai chuckled and mumbled something in Russian as he pulled into traffic.

"So how does this work?" Joy asked, curious. "This rescue, I mean."

Nikolai shrugged in his tailored coat. "Luiz called. You were in luck—I was available. Inq brought me to your location and made some man conveniently forget to take his keys out of his car." He executed a slow, smooth turn onto Wilkes Road. "I wait for him to go into the shop, get in the car and pull around to pick you up. Now I drop you off, return the car and Inq takes me back to work in Pattaya."

"Sounds risky," Joy said.

"It is. But Luiz said you were in trouble."

"I think I am." Joy swiveled around in her seat. "Where's Inq?"

"Shopping, I think."

Joy rolled her eyes. "Of course."

He turned the wheel smoothly. "Do you know what happened to your friend's car?"

"No," Joy said. "I couldn't see more than a blur."

He pulled up to the condo on silent brakes, his window sliding down as she got out. "It will not always be this easy, but we do what we can." Nikolai kissed two gloved fingers and waved. "Goodbye, Joy. Be well."

Joy waved back as he went to return the stolen car. She ran upstairs, threw her things on the table and hung up her coat. The condo was empty, but she was inside the wards: safe. Dad was another matter. He was out there with Shelley. So was Monica. So was Stef. A stifling panic gripped her. If anything happened to them...

Her response was automatic: shutting her eyes, she called out desperately, "Ink."

He materialized behind her, a soft touch at her back and the clean smell of rain. Joy hugged him tightly. His arms came around her, awkward and new.

"What happened?" he asked.

"I don't know. I'm not sure. But it happened outside, with

Monica, and it was right out in the open. Tons of people were there." Joy spoke past his shoulder, hoping that he could understand her babbling. The words tumbled out the tighter she squeezed. "I knew they were coming and there was nothing I could do and all I could think about was someone getting hurt...."

"But not at all worried that that someone might be you?" Ink admonished gently.

"No," she said. "I wasn't thinking about me." And Joy realized she hadn't. She'd been thinking about Monica and feeling guilty about her car and getting her into trouble. The flying newspapers, the rattling glass, the heated rocks, the smashed-in windows—they were all show. Nothing was done to really *hurt* her, more like scare her. Whoever they were could have hurt her at any time. But they hadn't.

Joy wished that he'd stroke her hair or cuddle her or say something soothing, but he didn't. He didn't know how. Joy felt a flash of jealousy for Nikolai and Inq. Ink wasn't human. He'd never done this before.

She let go and looked at him fiercely. "What do they *want?*" she asked.

"I could guess," Ink said. "But I would rather know."

Joy sat in the Bailiwick's office with a cup of sweet chamomile tea, reciting all that had happened at Evergreen Walk. Ink sat in the opposite chair and Inq stood by the bookshelves as Graus Claude listened behind his polished mahogany desk. She had a momentary flash of déjà vu of her dad and Officer Castrodad listening to her at the kitchen table. She wished she was wearing a comfy sweater.

"You were supposed to alert me of anything untoward,

Miss Malone," Graus Claude chided. "You could have been seriously hurt."

"It just happened," she said.

"You do own a cell phone, I trust?" he said. Joy flushed. She didn't want to admit that she hadn't programmed his number into her phone. "No matter. The important thing is that you are safe and that the perpetrators did not cause undo harm."

Joy swallowed more tea. "Well, they broke a store window and damaged a lot of cars."

"Aether sprites could have easily leveled the building, Joy," Inq said.

"Aether sprites?" Joy asked, her veins chilling. "Like Hasp?" She almost touched her branding scar. Almost.

Graus Claude swiveled, his four hands clasping each other in twos. "Finding stones hot to the touch is fairly suspect. When aether sprites travel, anything they carry heats quickly—the friction of being pulled through the air at great speeds."

Joy fiddled with her memory. "But I wasn't..."

"Of course not," Inq said, leafing through a book in her hands. "If Hasp had taken you that way, you would have been delivered as cooked meat."

"Hasp is no longer capable of *loqcution*." Graus Claude's voice raised slightly, like a teacher getting annoyed at the class.

Ink leaned over and said, "Hasp was stripped of his *loqcus*, his ability to travel the winds, along with his True Name. The Bailiwick suspects that this is what made him league with Briarhook—that Briarhook somehow promised Hasp that he could rescind the Council's decree."

"A foolish promise or a bold claim," the Bailiwick acknowledged. "And something he should not have said aloud." The way Graus Claude's eyes widened made Joy wonder whether the Bailiwick was talking about Briarhook or Ink. She was starting to feel unwelcome and aware of Graus Claude's many teeth.

"Hasp was found guilty of criminal acts, an exile," Ink said. "Although his family and clan might still fly to their own. But why would they come after Joy?"

Graus Claude spoke soothingly, as if the air itself was ruffled. "If Hasp had simply wanted revenge, your *lehman* would have suffered it," he said. "This was a warning—an attempt at fright."

"It worked," Joy muttered, shivering without cold.

"But you did not run. Nor were you injured," Ink replied with some pride.

"No. But why throw rocks?" she asked. "If this was a warning, I don't know what for. And if I don't know what *not* to do, then it could happen again and next time it might be worse." She thought of Monica, Dad and Stef. "Someone else might get hurt."

"That is enough speculation," Graus Claude declared. "I would consider it an isolated incident."

"It wasn't isolated," Inq said, crossing the room. "There was a trap before this."

The Bailiwick blinked. "A trap?"

"At her school. I was there," Inq said. "It tripped so fast, it stopped time. And it was designed specifically for Joy."

"WHAT?!" Graus Claude roared.

The chairs rocked against the carpet and Kurt burst

through the door, hand in his jacket. Joy cringed. Neither Ink nor Inq flinched.

"That's *enough!*" Graus Claude bellowed, rising. "More than enough. You tell me nothing and then far too much! Kurt—" He motioned to his butler. "Escort Miss Malone into the foyer. Into the street might be safer, but we will try to maintain a semblance of decorum." His bright eyes burned and two separate hands pointed accusingly at Ink and Inq. "This trespass of discretion has gone far enough. You two will sit and explain yourselves, *now!*"

Kurt appeared at Joy's elbow. Joy stared at him and then Graus Claude.

"What?" she said. "You can't be serious." She couldn't believe it. He was kicking her out? Joy tried to appeal to the people in the room. "You can't sit here discussing things involving me behind my back! This is *my life* we're talking about—my friends, my family. I think I ought to know what's going on!" Joy shifted tactics. "Ink?"

"I believe she should stay," Ink said to Graus Claude. "She is my *lehman*."

"Yes, and as your *lehman*, she is a living compass needle that points directly to you." Graus Claude rested his four sets of knuckles on the hardwood and pushed himself to stand, looming over the three of them in order to emphasize his point. "She is a wandering target, as are all such things, and the aim is not to destroy *her*, but to destroy *you*." He swung his head to face Joy's. "This is nothing personal, Miss Malone. In fact, there is nothing more impersonal than being a *lehman* to one of the Twixt. While the benefits may reap fine rewards, the costs are high and the risks are great. You are just now learning this, and for that, I apologize, but when I request that you be dismissed, it is less a request than it is a command." Kurt knew a cue when he heard one, and Joy felt his hand close over her arm, pinching a nerve that instantly arced her spine. She whimpered in surprise. Graus Claude ignored it. "Now, Miss Malone."

Kurt hauled her up easily and she stumbled to keep stride.

"Unnecessary," Inq said in her slicing, wry voice as Kurt marched Joy down the hall.

"Stop it," Joy panted around the pain. "Stop it, Kurt. *Stopstopstop*."

They stepped into the foyer, his hand clamped like a vise above her biceps until he casually closed the doors behind them. He let her go without flourish or apology. Joy rubbed her arm and glared daggers.

"Ow," she muttered, close to tears.

Kurt said nothing, his face a mask.

"Seriously," Joy said. "You don't have to do everything he tells you to. Don't you have a mind of your own? Some choice? Some honor?" Kurt's head swiveled on the thick axis of his neck, and he gave Joy such a withering glare that she faltered and fell into the wingback chair.

"Fine," she said, sitting up. "Fine." Joy snatched a lukewarm grape from its bowl. "I'll just wait here for everyone else to live my life then. Why change now?" She popped it in her mouth and many things happened at once.

Her mouth flooded with a salty, thick *wrongness*. She gagged. Her salivary glands shriveled. The oily texture quickly congealed like brine jelly on her tongue. She couldn't spit it out. Couldn't breathe. It was as if her mouth had filled with seawater and quick-drying cement.

Joy stumbled, knocking something backward, vaguely

aware of Kurt reaching toward her. The doors burst open. Joy stumbled back. Black salt and bile eroded her teeth. Fumes lit her sinuses. She wanted to cry out, but couldn't open her chapped lips. Her cheeks flooded with saliva and tears.

And suddenly, Inq was there—hands tight on her face—kissing her.

Joy froze. Inq's lips pushed hard against hers, and Joy felt the girl's tongue probe past her teeth, forcing them open. Inq's mouth worked insistently even as Joy tried to pull away, jaws and lips moving hungrily. The salty weight lifted, funneling into Inq. Joy stopped fighting and tried to inhale.

It was thin, slow agony. The stuff separated like crude oil from pure water, siphoning through the filter of Inq's lips. Joy swallowed small gulps of air that echoed in Inq's mouth. She broke the kiss and fell backward.

Joy sucked air in deep, spasmed gasps. The taste of Inq, like dusty roses, lingered in her mouth. Joy stared up at the Scribe. Long black rivulets spooled from Inq's swollen lips, sliding over her jawline and disappearing down her throat. The tendrils had barbed, serrated edges that faded into tongues of misty-gray, then dirty-peach, and finally, the slightly lighter than flesh color of Inq as she took whatever it was into herself. Inq blinked at Joy and swallowed, licking her pink tongue over plump lips.

"I can see why he likes you," Inq said thickly.

Ink stepped forward. Hesitated.

"Joy?"

Joy stared at both of them. Then Graus Claude. Then Kurt. There was a rush as she fainted. Just like in the movies.

* * *

"...a tad less dramatic, by my preference."

"She couldn't've known. Or she would never have..."

"...might have ended tragically..."

"She is from the Glen. And has the Sight."

"Point taken." Graus Claude's voice rumbled as he swam into focus through a fog of ammonia and talcum. Joy blinked. "Ah, Miss Malone. So good of you to join us once again."

"He's sorry," Inq interrupted.

"Indeed, I am," he said. "Mistress Inq, if you would be so kind as to help her up now?"

Joy was hauled forward, her vision swirling. She blinked hard. *Flash! Flash!* Ink was there without her even having to speak his name.

"Joy," he breathed. She reached out and touched him, holding his near-to-human hand.

"What happened?" she said, her voice scratchy in her ears. She felt as if she'd been gargling iron filings.

"You swallowed..." Ink started.

Inq began, "You tried eating..."

"Roe," Graus Claude said primly. "Eggs."

"Eggs?" Joy gagged reflexively.

"They are not meant for human consumption," the Bailiwick said. "Point of fact, they are not intended for anyone's consumption. They are a precious commodity and dear to me. You were fortunate that Miss Invisible was able to so quickly discern the cause of distress." He considered the tumbler of half-melted ice and amber in one hand. "It was a mistake, perhaps, to have allowed you near them. I had forgotten that you were hypoglycemic and that eating is an unconscious mortal habit born of impatience and idle thoughts."

Joy frowned, massaging her throat. "What are they doing in a candy dish?!"

"Where better to hide a treasure than in the open? You have read 'The Purloined Letter,' I trust?" Joy stared at Graus Claude. He sighed, disappointed. "No one honors the classics," he grumbled.

"They're poison?" Joy said. Inq winked and licked her bottom lip. Joy spat into her hand. "What kind of prized eggs are poisonous?"

Inq shook her head. "You don't want to know," she warned.

Graus Claude grinned evilly.

"Mine."

Joy puked.

Afterward, embarrassed, Joy clung to Ink and avoided Graus Claude's eye despite his assurance that none of the eggs were fertilized and were kept in a dormant state. She didn't want to hear it. She didn't even want to *think* about it. Gulping cups of sweet tea, she sat in the bathroom, scrubbing her teeth with her finger near the sink. She rested her forehead against the cool porcelain and focused on Ink's words.

"We are going to enlist a tracker and follow the aether sprites' trail. Discover its source," he said. "We should find answers there."

"Get Kestrel," Inq suggested, handing a damp towel to Ink. "She's the best."

Ink knelt level to Joy. "Are you all right now?"

"In a minute," she said. The cycle of thinking about not thinking the thing that she shouldn't be thinking about brought her perilously close to heaving again. Inq tapped her brother and folded the wet washcloth into thirds. Taking his hand, she placed it in his palm and pressed both against the back of Joy's neck.

"Now brush back her hair," Inq whispered encouragingly. "It will help her feel better."

Joy felt the tug of his fingers lifting damp strands from her skin and softly combing her scalp. She was slightly annoyed that Inq was right: it did help her feel better. But it didn't help her feel less out of her depth, a human weakness to be exploited, a tool used to hurt Ink. She was done letting other people mess up her life. She was a wildflower with bite. She was stronger than this.

Joy removed the towel and squeezed his hand.

"I'm ready," she said quietly.

"Good. Let's go," Inq said.

Joy frowned. "All of us?"

"The three of us," Ink clarified. Kurt hardly moved.

"Is there a problem?" Inq said. "I just saved your life."

It was true. She had. Joy didn't want to think about the details.

"Right," Joy said weakly. "Thanks."

"You're welcome," Inq chirped as she helped Joy to stand. "Besides—" she winked bawdily "—if I tag along, I may get the chance to kiss you again!"

THIRTEEN

GRAUS CLAUDE HAD ORDERED A CAR TO TAKE THEM BACK TO Evergreen Walk. He considered it less obtrusive than their appearing out of nowhere, but Joy could not imagine anything more obtrusive than this. The classic Bentley looked like a candy bar, all rich chocolate-browns and caramels and white-rimmed tires. The driver even wore a matching uniform and a tidy black cap. Inq pushed off the cream-colored leather and brushed the side of his neck by his ear. Slithering calligraphy burst and sluiced down his skin, disappearing under his collar. Inq sat back and shrugged apologetically.

"Sorry," she said. "Habit."

Ink might have rolled his eyes, but it was impossible to tell. The car drove off smoothly, like milk chocolate on the road.

Ink placed one of his new hands on Joy's bouncing knee. "We are going to pick up our passenger and then take you to where it happened," he said. "It should only take a moment."

"In a Bentley?" Joy asked.

"Somewhat more than a moment," Ink admitted. "Still, the Bailiwick sent word ahead that we would be meeting our contact at a drop point that would otherwise be closed to us at such short notice."

Joy examined Ink's face. "You trust Graus Claude," she said.

"Absolutely."

Joy glanced at Inq. "You, too?"

Inq placed her hand flat against the window. "There is only one person I trust absolutely," she said to the sky.

Ink turned away leaving Joy and the driver sharing an awkward silence. She wondered if the man could hear the others in the car, or if he was simply too professional to ask Joy why she was talking to herself. She guessed it didn't matter, really. She was clearly crazy either way.

Joy dozed until the car suddenly turned into a national wildlife preserve, waking as the driver paid the five-dollar entry fee. Cruising into dappled sunlight, Joy squinted up into the bare-branch canopy and rooted around her memories to see if she recognized the place. Her folks were never really into the camping-nature-hike thing, but something about the woods hinted at a childhood feeling of freedom and exploration that she couldn't pinpoint but felt nostalgic just the same.

Ink lowered the window. It slid soundlessly down. The wind was a blast of cold, crisp air sprinkled with the wet of passing winter and the pollen promise of spring. There were even a few flashes of green rolling past the car in whispers.

Ink closed his eyes and lifted his chin like a dog, reveling in the wind in his face and hair. A smile lit his lips, simple and serene. He looked beautiful. Joy had never thought she'd be envious of air.

His eyes opened slowly; they did not squint in the breeze.

"There she is," Ink said and lifted his hand in greeting. Joy leaned forward to catch a glimpse.

At first, she didn't see anything and tried looking out Inq's side of the car, but Inq was looking in Ink's direction, so Joy switched back. The figure, when she saw it—"her"—was easy to miss, wearing a patchy cloak of grays and browns that blended easily into the background, her head completely cloaked in the hood, face unseen. As they drove closer, Joy was horrified to see that it was not the hood of the cape that hid the tracker's face, but an actual hood like a hunting bird's—cracked leather, worn and weathered, stitched together with brace cords pulled tight at the neck. A thick rope ran from beneath the cloak to a knot tied loosely around a trail marker.

The antique car rolled to a stop and Ink unlocked his door. Inq shifted to the opposite side of the seat. Neither Joy nor the driver moved.

Joy listened to the eerie exchange between Ink and the hooded figure, a sound like dragging a stick over fence posts, or the wooden, fish-shaped instrument she'd played in elementary school. It didn't sound like they were using words or voices. They spoke in choppy clicks and pops like dolphins.

"Agreed," Ink said in English. "After you."

The cracked leather headgear entered the car first. Joy pushed away, giving Kestrel plenty of room. The hood moved sharply, birdlike, pointing at the driver, then Inq, then Joy—Joy had no trouble believing that whatever it was could see them perfectly through the leather mask, sizing them up like a hawk.

A stork-thin leg stepped into the car, parting the cloak, and a bare foot dropped down, pockmarked with dirt and bits of dead leaf. Snow still clung to her toes. Joy stared at the foot to avoid looking at Kestrel's hood. The tracker settled into the seat, the fine leather upholstery sighing as the cloak settled around her like wings.

Ink shut the door with a surprisingly loud sound. He held the thick leash in his hand as the car pulled away.

"My *lehman* and associate," Ink said by way of introduction. "Joy. And you know Inq." There was no sound of confirmation from under the hood. Ink continued. "This is Kestrel," he said to them. "She has agreed to be our tracker."

Joy looked between Ink and the hood.

"Hi," she tried.

The hood nodded slightly. If the ride hadn't been so smooth, Joy would have sworn the motion had just been a bump in the road.

"Our quarry is aether sprites," Ink said. "Approximately four or five of them. *Loqcution* along an open expanse, cultivated lawn, sparse tree cover, developed land. Midday sun and minimal clouds. Decent wind. Is that correct, Joy?"

Joy shrugged, unable to keep her eyes off the strange person sitting next to her under the cloak. "Yeah," she said. "I guess so."

Ink wrapped the jesses around the back of his hand. "Having studied maps of the area, the Bailiwick designed our course as follows: we will exit the car behind where you first saw the attack. We will escort Kestrel quickly and directly across the courtyard while the car circles around. Inq will exit the car and transition us back into the vehicle. We will then leave the premises, review our report and Kestrel will receive payment once we return to her drop point."

The plan was clear and clipped and precise. Joy nervously picked at her cuticles. What would happen when she walked Kestrel across Evergreen Walk in the middle of a busy Saturday, returning to the scene of a crime? She couldn't guess. The idea was too ludicrous and frighteningly surreal.

They rode the rest of the way in silence. Inq idly traced invisible shapes on the window and Joy squeezed her fingers between her knees.

The Bentley turned onto Evergreen Walk and Joy's heart raced as she watched her two worlds collide. She tried to remind herself that it had already happened, that the aether sprites had been the ones to pierce the thin wall separating her carefully preserved everyday reality and her bizarre life in the Twixt, but this was different: this was the first time she would be actively walking out in public with a troop of inhuman creatures ferried in a very expensive car. There was no turning back, no possible excuse she could give if she got caught. Joy only hoped that no one would recognize her.

She breathed deeply. Her hands tingled. She noticed that Monica's car had been towed. A red sedan was parked in its place.

"Tell the driver where to pull over," Ink said quietly, the words piercing Joy's thoughts like a pin.

Joy pointed across the mall lawn, near the gazebo. "There."

Ink spoke to the driver. "Drop us off at two o'clock and circle. Pick up at seven. Keep the car running."

The driver nodded. Joy's shoulders twitched. Kestrel, sensing action, shook her shoulders like ruffled feathers. Anticipation lit the air. Joy watched dozens of shoppers crossing the sidewalks, chatting while pushing strollers, groups of kids sitting on benches and steps, parents carrying toddlers, security guards patrolling belly-first along the curb. This was *such* a bad idea....

"Here," Ink said, opening the door as the car pulled to a stop, the engine softly purring. "Up." He tugged the leash once. Kestrel slid out of the seat without further prompting.

Joy scootched over and forced her wobbly legs to stand. She didn't look up. She didn't want to be here.

"Good luck," Inq called from the backseat. "See you soon!" She pulled the door closed and the Bentley slid from the curb.

People watched the car, pointing and murmuring. A few glanced toward the three of them, but no one reacted. Joy hoped that she was the only one they could see. Scratch that—she hoped that she was invisible, too. She looked around for any telltale blurs of shadow, but everything was oppressively normal. She buried her hands in her pockets and kept her head down.

Ink touched her arm and Joy met his eyes.

"When I remove the hood, take Kestrel's cloak and drape it over your left arm. Hook your right arm through hers, guide her by the elbow and walk a straight line across the grass to Inq and the car. Move swiftly," he said. "I will be on her right, but you will be the one leading us. We will have one pass to do this cleanly. Any more, and the trail becomes more diffi-cult to decipher. The tracker is powerful and at the mercy of her senses. Do *not* let Kestrel take the lead. Once we get back into the car, we will see what we have learned. All right?"

Joy nodded, believing in him, at least. "All right."

"Very good," Ink said, handing her the leash and wrapping it over her palm twice. He closed her fingers firmly over the fat leather strap. "Hold on tight. Do not let go."

Joy was only able to register how the belt in her hand was scratchy and cracked before Ink removed the braces, loosen-ing and opening the back of the hood. He grabbed the top-knot of braided straps and tugged the ancient leather free.

It slid forward off a bald skull, long feathery antennae flowing out from beneath the hood, curling up and over Kestrel's scalp like banners in the breeze. Joy squeezed the hard strap in her hand for reassurance as she stared at Kestrel's face. She had long, hollow slits for a nose and her ears were cupped, like a fox's, swiveling independently, silky inner hairs quivering. Her eyes were wide and yellow with oval pupils, and stiff, impossibly long, clear eyelashes curved far away from her eggshell face. When she blinked, they gave a delicate sound like a sharpening knife. Her lips were full and pouty and eager, making her look more like a fish than a bird.

Kestrel bobbed her head up and down, sniffing. Her antennae trembled and her ears twitched.

Joy remembered to take off the cloak. The tracker was stick-thin from neck to ankles, a dewy shift barely hiding her nakedness. Long blond hairs like silken threads drifted off her body, tasting the wind. Joy gave a sympathetic shiver. She must be awfully cold. The lead in Joy's hand was attached to a ring that hung from a wide collar around Kestrel's neck. Elaborately dyed with strange symbols and runes, it looked less like a pet collar and more like exotic jewelry.

Ink spoke. Kestrel's ears and hairs turned toward him. "Go."

Joy pulled Kestrel's bony elbow to her side. Tugging the strap in her hand, she started walking.

Kestrel lunged, nearly yanking Joy off her feet, but Joy remembered to pull back hard on the limb and leash. Vying for control, Joy hugged Kestrel closer, digging her shoes into the earth to slow their pace. She looked nervously at people as they passed, spying her own reflection in shop windows and car windshields, trying to look normal as she stumbled over the walk.

The tracker made high-pitched sounds and woody *pic-pic*

noises that sounded almost like questions. Joy accidentally looked at Kestrel's face while she took a big whiff, and the deep red flesh of her open nasal cavities made Joy's stomach lurch. She kept her eyes on her shoes.

Kestrel trilled and trembled and tasted and tugged. Joy fumbled alongside her, Kestrel's pointy elbow clamped hard against her ribs. Ink kept apace, steadying the both of them. It was a jerky, uneven path full of sharp starts and stops. Nerves screaming panic and fearing discovery, Joy was already exhausted before they were halfway across the courtyard.

Kestrel blinked. The scrape of her lashes rang with a long, grazing *shing*. Joy could feel the harmonic ripples against her skin. She kept her eyes on the Bentley as it slid to a stop just opposite them. She focused on its doors and bowed her head, marching quickly and determinedly toward their goal. Her heart beat loud in her ears. Kestrel pulled again and Joy almost let go—it was like holding back a lion. Her hand throbbed where the leash dug deep. Joy made a small sound. Ink glanced over, nodding encouragement. She blinked back tears and held on tighter because it was the only thing to do.

Clenching her jaw, Joy kept walking. She could make it to the car. She would get through this. She had to. Thirty feet. Twenty. Ten.

"Excuse me." An authoritative voice brought Joy to a halt. The outdoor mall cop smiled, not quite kindly, down at Joy. Her arm buckled as Kestrel yanked, keening queries, jerking her head around, curious.

Joy blinked up at the security guard, her voice like a scratched CD.

"Y-yes?"

"Please don't walk on the grass," he said with the futility of having said the same words a million times a day.

"Oh," Joy said and tried not to look at her invisible companions. "Sorry."

"The signs are printed quite clearly," he continued. He pointed at one. "Don't Walk on the Grass."

Joy was desperate. She could barely think.

"Okay," she said and stepped onto the nearest sidewalk. Kestrel craned her long neck, confused at having left the trail. Ink struggled to hold the tracker back. Knowing his strength, Joy was afraid what might happen if she lost her grip. A long series of clicking began from deep in Kestrel's chest. Her antennae reached for the officer.

Joy batted them away and pretended to sneeze. Kestrel squawked in protest. Joy's shoulder wrenched at the joint.

"And please clean up after your pet before you leave the premises," the cop said tiredly, turning away. Joy wondered what he could possibly think was at the end of the leash. She glanced over at Ink, who kept one eye on the retreating cop's back. She struggled, holding Kestrel still, and nearly bumped into an elderly couple in matching knitted hats. Joy held her breath. Ink waited until the cop crossed the street.

"Now," he said.

They bolted across the lawn, Joy overly mindful of her feet on the grass. She kept her eyes on Inq, who waved them on with open arms, one foot inside the car and the other mounting the curb. Quickly, quietly, they bundled Kestrel like a starlet into her loose cloak and simultaneously slipped the hood over her head as they tucked her into the seat. Ink drew taut the straps and snapped the door closed. Inq flipped the lock. Joy fastened her seat belt. The car took off with a whisper of wheels.

"Give it here," Inq said, helping to unwind the leather from Joy's red-and-white hand.

"Thanks," Joy whispered, shaking in the aftermath.

"You did good," Inq said.

"She did well," Ink corrected. Inq stuck out her tongue and draped the leash in her hand. Joy massaged her bruised bones.

"Did we get what we needed?" Joy asked. Kestrel shivered and Ink adjusted the camouflaged cloak over her shoulders in a gentlemanly way. He thumbed up the heat, which blew up from the floor. The leather seats grew warm. Ink pursed his lips and gave a soft ticking sound. The hood lifted and swung sharply; a muffled trickle answered back.

"Kestrel is processing," Ink said. "But she said to turn east."

The driver obeyed wordlessly as they cruised onto the main road.

The tracker muttered in low hoots to herself.

"Open the window," Ink instructed. Inq thumbed down the glass. Kestrel responded almost immediately with another trilling sound.

"Turn north up ahead and look for a stone building—something near water," Ink said. Kestrel interrupted with her *pic-pic* sound. "Running water," Ink corrected.

"Dover Mill," Joy said, recognizing the road. Memory snapped like a bone into place. "Head to Dover Mill. It's an old fishing spot by the dam."

Joy gave directions and watched Kestrel's hood lean into the curves, crooning approval as they went. Ink nodded, satisfied, and Inq held the leash in a confident grip. Joy was glad that she could contribute something besides four aching fingers to the cause.

The car slowed in front of the aging mill. Joy squinted up at the stone edifice ringed by a suspended chain fence. The great wheel stood still, dormant and off its track, cemented into place by the town in an effort to preserve a local landmark. Joy realized that she'd never seen it turn. When a mill no longer milled, what was it? She studied its profile against the stark sky and thought, *Lonely.*

Wind poured past the walls and raced along the riverbank. The original glass of the windows sagged in its panes between wooden shutters that might have once been green, as the river might have once been blue. The water coursed down in a smooth gray sheet. Joy didn't think it was her imagination that everything was quieter here. She remembered hearing rumors that Dover Mill was haunted and dismissing them as silly superstition...but now she wasn't so sure.

Ink tapped Joy's knee.

"I need your Sight. If you are able to see the sprites *exloqcutious,* then you may also be able to see where they are now," Ink said and rubbed his pant leg in a sort of nervous gesture she'd never seen him use before. "It goes against protocol, but they were the ones who initiated the attack—I half expect it was an invitation."

"An invitation or a lure?" Inq muttered.

"Another trap?" Joy asked.

Inq smirked. "How many people have you offended, Joy Malone?"

Joy bristled, but considered it. "Would Briarhook want revenge?"

Ink smiled a not-nice smile. "He wants his heart," Ink said.

"And knows better than to irk me for it." Ink shook his head, another human habit he'd adopted. "No. I think it is something else."

He leaned forward, addressing Inq past Kestrel's hood. "Joy is with me. You have things well in hand?"

Inq smiled and waggled her fingers around the leash.

"No problem," she chirped. "If you need anything, remember—scream like a little girl!"

Ink ignored her. Joy did likewise.

The breeze felt good, a welcome change. Joy remembered the smell of the river even in the cold. People used to fish along the walk that ran the length of the mill, casting lines out over the edge of the man-made dam. Joy had learned to fish here. Now there were signs everywhere with bright red warnings. No one ate fish out of the river anymore. Joy watched a fast-food wrapper and a plastic cup make their way over the falls. It made her inexplicably sad.

"Stand behind me," Ink said. "Stay close. This is where the trail originates. Kestrel says the scent is too faint to be present, but with aether sprites, it is hard to tell. If you can really see them..."

"I can see them," Joy assured him.

"Well, they can certainly see you."

The idea of facing more than one thing like Hasp with the ability to teleport in bits and spurts made her blood freeze. It must have shown in her face.

"Are you all right?" Ink asked.

"Sure," Joy lied. "Peachy."

He'd learned too well. He wasn't fooled. "Perhaps you should not come with me," Ink said.

Joy shook her head. "You need me."

His face changed subtly. "I do, which is why I also wish that you would stay in the car," he said. "But you are right—I need your eyes." He looked up at the gray-green mill against the gray-green water framed in brown dead grass.

"That's been our theme," Joy said. She took his hand, threading their fingers together easily, and stepped onto the walk.

Together they crept alongside the building, passing its single door draped in long shadows and deep, weathered cracks. Joy could feel it shudder each time the wind snapped its reins. She brushed the hair from her face, pawing at a single strand that stuck to her lip gloss. All her senses prickled as they stepped over the chain.

"Feel it?" Ink asked. Joy nodded, a flood of memories bringing back a childhood fear of ghosts. It was like stepping into static. They glanced around the mill. Ink studied each window, each corner, each dark nook. His voice scythed the hollow wind. "We should get Inq."

"I can do this," Joy said.

"Can you?" he asked. "What do you see?"

Joy peeked out of the corner of her eye where things like Ink and Hasp and orange shadows dwelt. She turned her head slowly, trying to scan the area. Her eye muscles strained. She blinked hard. *Flash! Flash!*

"There," Joy said, afraid to point. There was an overhang of jutting wood, gnarled vines and uneven steps descending into darkness superimposed on an image of what wasn't there. "There's an arbor or something. With stairs going down." It was hard to convince herself that what she was seeing was real, because when she looked straight at the mill, there was nothing but mortared stone and a rickety tool shed with a rusted lock.

Wordlessly, Ink unsheathed his straight razor. The chain at his side swung heavy and loose. Joy followed, hand upraised, keys arranged between her fingers like an iron claw.

Three steps and it still looked like an old mill. Two steps and the wind smacked their chests, pushing them back. One step and Joy was certain she'd been mistaken, her strange Sight playing tricks with her head and her eyes. Ink pivoted his wrist, pushing the razor straight as a sword. They stepped forward. The tip of the blade popped the illusion like a balloon.

Wide, rough struts appeared through a roof of overgrown briars, bare and black. Thorns shivered down their lengths and grew so dense, it was hard to see where the tangle ended and the shadows began. Joy caught glimpses of smooth wood, the glint of glass and the first wide step going down. Each riser was made of one solid block of wood set into the ground and fringed in moss. This place had been hidden from the world for a very long time.

Ink let go of her hand and stepped down into the darkness. Joy followed, step for step.

The wind stopped with a vacuum-sealed sound. Joy's and Ink's footsteps clopped on soft wood and echoed off walls. Glass bottles of every size and color were stacked along mismatched shelves, each bottle labeled in strange runes and stoppered with wax. Joy was surprised to see a collection of plastic half-liter bottles, their runes written up their sides in black marker.

One slate wall stood exposed, chalk markings scribbled all over its surface. Archaic symbols fought one another for space—anorexic in some corners, a traffic jam in others, notations crisscrossed and reconnected by arrows. A large table in the center of the room was built out of an old door propped on cinder blocks, bowing slightly in the center and raining peeling paint. Papers and homemade journals littered its surface and a ratty quill stuck out of the rusty keyhole. Joy picked up a crumpled dry cleaner receipt scribbled with similar runes. The floor was speckled with bits of rock and leaf. Small shoots eked through the cracks in the stairs, straining toward the light.

Ink placed his blade on the table and opened the largest hand-stitched book. Its yellowed pages were filled with columns of arcane symbols. He flipped pages impassively as he skimmed. Joy compared the notes on the table to the markings on the wall and the labels of nearby bottles. Nothing seemed to match. And nowhere could she find the sinister eight-eyed flower. Or anything obviously linking to the aether sprites or Hasp.

But then she saw something she recognized and swallowed an ice cube of shock.

"Ink," she hissed, pointing at the stylized rose drawn in white chalk. Ink set down the book and examined the wall. His hand hovered above its surface, fingers moving slightly as if touching his thoughts. Ink considered the book on the table, the bottles on the shelves, the hidden staircase. His eyes sought Joy's.

"They led us here," he said simply.

"Who?"

Ink stood up. "The aether sprites."

Joy felt herself flinch. "It's a trap?"

"No," he said, resting his hand on a shelf. "The aether kin

knew about this—" he touched a bottle "—but could not tell us outright. We needed to discover this place on our own...or at least have it appear that way." He grabbed another book, talking as he read. "The aether sprites knew if they attacked you that I would track them down, so it would look like an accident that we found this place."

"They threw rocks at me to get your attention?" Joy said, annoyed.

"It worked," Ink said, closing the book and catching her eye. "Aether sprites are not particularly subtle and they do not like humans much." He glanced sternly at the room as if considering what to do with it.

"So what is this?" Joy asked, rubbing her brand through her sleeve. "What's this all about?"

"*Signaturae,*" Ink said. "True Names."

"Names?" Joy tapped the book. "This is...a registry?"

"No, an encyclopedia. An alchemical index. A catalog of *signaturae,*" he said. "A list of symbols, of True Names."

"Symbols like yours?" Joy asked.

Ink smirked. "Not mine," he said. "She does not have my *signatura.*" He patted the book's cover, his near-to-human hand rested there.

Joy edged closer. "'She' who?"

"Aniseed," Ink said. His voice burned. "This place is hers. She has been collecting True Names and is planning...something." Ink gestured to the wall filled with scribbles and script. Joy's eye snagged on a small set of concentric circles, like a bull's-eye, stashed in one corner. She glanced up as Ink knocked his new knuckles against the binding. "Folk have been bartering with Aniseed using their *signaturae,* which is illegal. It circumvents the Bailiwick and goes against the mandates of the Twixt."

Joy frowned. "I thought you said that the symbols are useless unless they are given willingly."

"Yes," Ink said. "But I believe these were given freely—they match the roster in the books." He ran a hand along one of the shelves. "Or, if not freely, then bought at an attractive price." He shook his head. "This is wrong. Selling your True Name is like selling your soul." Ink leaned closer to the chalked wall. "I wish there was a way to bring this to Graus Claude."

Joy pulled out her phone, aimed and snapped a picture. Hit Send.

"Done," she said.

Ink smiled. "Well, then let's go."

"You're not taking the book?"

"No," Ink said. "She will most likely realize that we have been here, but there is no need to confirm it. Or that we understood the significance of what we have found." Joy wasn't certain she understood its significance, but it was good to know that the aether sprites would not be bothering her again.

She took the stairs, picking her way up to the filtered daylight. Halfway up, she stopped and glanced at Ink.

"Did you just say, 'Let's go'?"

Ink touched the small of her back, urging her gently upward.

"I'm learning many things today."

The smell inside the Bentley was a spicy blend of animal and old leather. Inq held the leash slack as Ink reported what they'd found. Kestrel rustled under her cloak and hood. The driver drove on.

Joy watched the mill disappear in the distance. It didn't seem so familiar anymore.

"The connections are exponential," Ink was saying as they rode through the woods. "The map showed tiers of interlocking *signaturae*—one mark linked to a dozen others, each in turn connected to dozens more." He jerked his chin. "It was vast. Too complex. Too much like something the Bailiwick would have dreamed up."

"And you propose taking this straight to him," Inq said with disapproval.

"Who better?" Ink replied.

A tense silence followed.

"I don't understand what this has to do with names," Joy said, finally. She wanted to be part of this conversation. It was hard to be indispensable when she didn't know what was going on.

"Not just names. True Names," Ink said. "The essence of a thing is fixed once given a name. Names are powerful. *Signaturae* are True Names given form."

Inq leaned forward. "Think Rumpelstiltskin."

Joy gaped. "Rumpelstilskin is *real?*"

"No," Inq said. "'Rumpelstiltskin is a story. But stories hold old truths. And in the story, Rumpelstiltskin was outsmarted, controlled and banished by the use of his True Name. *Signaturae* were created to avoid being trapped by humans' speaking our True Names by transferring their power into a sigil, and we, the Scribes, were created to place *signaturae* on living beings in order to minimize the Folk's exposure and risk."

"So you can be controlled by your *signatura?*" Joy asked.

"Don't get any ideas," Inq said with a smirk. "It has that potential, but you are no warlock. You wouldn't know what to do with a True Name. They're used to create a bond between the Folk and those humans who are special, claimed by magic, even if they don't know it. And no *signatura* has power unless it's..."

"Given willingly," Joy finished. "I remember."

"*Signaturae* are our True Names, our selves, written down," Ink said. "A True Name is who and what we are." His voice grew oddly distant. "There are those who may regret their choices, their actions, but must still wear it in their name."

"Like Hasp?" Joy asked.

Ink nodded. "Yes. Like Hasp. There were two symbols in the book, slightly altered variations, for Hasp," he mused. "If Briarhook has convinced Hasp that he could somehow change his True Name, change his *signatura*, then the decree against Hasp would no longer be in effect. Hasp would no longer *be* Hasp in terms of the conditions laid upon him by the Council and he could potentially regain his *loqci* and clan." Ink sat back and mused. "Not a bad plan."

"A loophole," Joy said. "Could he do it? Change a True Name?"

"Not Briarhook," Ink said. "But a *segulah*, perhaps."

Joy got it. "Aniseed."

"She could sell such a service at any price if she could evade the Twixt's justice, perhaps changing her own True Name to escape it," Ink said. "I think Hasp's clan discovered the backdoor bargain and did not approve. Such a loophole would be a blot on their honor, defying their allegiance to the Council and its decree. I think the aether kin meant for us to find out, to hold Hasp and whoever was behind this accountable."

"You mean Aniseed?" Inq asked.

"Yes. Aniseed," Ink said. "This site could be one or one of dozens. But I don't believe this is simply a matter of changing names. She is connecting them somehow. Intertwining them. Linking them."

"But to what end?" Inq asked dismissively. "It doesn't make sense. Who cares how many *signaturae* a human has on its skin? Many of the Folk make multiple claims—it happens all the time. It makes no difference. It changes nothing."

"It does to me," Joy said. She knew she wore Ink's True Name, and now Briarhook's and, somehow, Aniseed's. She rubbed her forehead. It hurt to think. She'd gone through too much today. "I'd like to go home."

"After we deliver Kestrel," Ink said softly. The hood shot sideways with a hacking trill. "And after payment," he amended.

They left the tracker where they'd found her, in the deep woods tied to a post in the ground. Inq handed Kestrel a dead rabbit that she grasped blindly and massaged in strong fingers.

"Payment as promised," Inq said. "Delivery for the next two moons at the southern drop-off. Scent of cedar." Inq patted the cloaked shoulder, like a pet. "And good hunting."

Joy scootched over so Inq could slide into the backseat, turning away as Kestrel tucked the rabbit beneath her hood and pulled. Something pink and glistening tore through the fur. Joy flinched.

"Squeamish?" Inq taunted. "You eat meat." Joy didn't bother pointing out that her food came plastic wrapped and postmortem. It embarrassed her for some reason. She pressed next to Ink, who took her hand, lining up their fingers and threading them together.

"We will take you home now."

"Can't you just...?" She waved her hand in a familiar swooping gesture. He looked impressed and surprised that she knew it. She'd been watching, too.

"No," he said gently, "the car is far safer. Not just from Aniseed, but also for you." Ink considered their entwined fingers. He flexed the digits, sliding them gently against her skin. She could feel the warmth flicker, saw the change in his face that said he was *feeling* her now. All in a touch. If she thought about it, she could feel it, too—every hair, every ripple, every shift of skin on skin.

"When I take you with me, it feels like no time has passed," he said. "But it all moves forward. Always forward." Ink studied her fingers. "I am trying to be present in these moments. To be *here* with you." He turned his fathomless eyes to Joy. "I am aware now how swiftly it passes, and so I am left attempting to do the impossible—I am trying to hold on to time."

Joy hesitated. "It hasn't been very long," she said quietly.

"No," Ink said with weight in his words. He caressed her face slowly. "It is not long at all."

His lips touched her forehead—soft and precious and fragile as snow. He pressed her hand to his chest. Joy could almost feel his heart beating. She fell asleep to the sound of water and the smell of rain.

"We're here," Inq said.

Joy woke, embarrassed—she had nearly forgotten that Inq was there. Invisible.

Joy disentangled from Ink's embrace and struggled to say something.

"Thanks."

Inq grinned. "For kissing you or for saving your life?" Ink slapped his twin's knee. "What?" she said. "I am told that I'm a fabulous kisser."

The tension dissolved in a rush as Joy laughed. It felt good.

"I will check back soon," Ink said. "After I consult with Graus Claude."

"It was nice seeing you, Joy!" Inq called cheerfully. "Let's do it again soon!" Joy glanced at Ink. His face held a promise that lit a small candle inside her. She cradled it against the wind as she opened the gate. The Bentley slid away onto Wilkes Road.

Unlocking the door, she keyed the alarm off. *Beep-beep-beep-beep.* The red light flickered before it turned green. The house was quiet. There was a Post-it note by the microwave that said, *Gone out. Back by 5.* Next to the note was a cinnamon coffee cake.

Joy sighed and opened the silverware drawer, taking out a knife for her obligatory slice. She resolved to cut a big piece, since Shelley might have brought it over and she could use something to obliterate the lingering taste of Inq in her mouth.

She aimed for the best chunks of crumble topping and, in one smooth motion, cut. Knife hit plate.

Blackness came down like a hammer.

FOURTEEN

JOY FROZE, HAND ON KNIFE AND KNIFE IN CAKE. THE ROOM WAS all darkness and indigo shadows. It was eerie and cold. Sound had smothered dead.

This isn't happening, she thought. *This isn't possible. This is* home.

She gripped the handle of the knife as her eyes adjusted to the loss of light—midnight-blue shadows slid up the wall like beads of lava under glass, bending in weird directions, unnaturally slow. Was this still real? What had happened to Ink's wards? It looked like her kitchen, but not. She watched the clock tick forward. Time was still alive.

"Dad?" she said, not too loudly. She thought she saw movement, a black shape against blue. She wasn't alone.

Joy drew the knife out of the cake and held it in front of her, mimicking Ink and his blade against the bubble of shadow at school. She moved away from the counter, one step. Two. Sparks lit the tip of the knife. A pale, electric shimmer traced a curving path and disappeared. There was a shadowy barrier drawn in charcoal on the floor. Joy touched the knife blade—it was warm and strangely slick. A pale dust smeared her fingertips. She wiped it on her jeans and backed into the counter.

Squinting through the barrier, she thought she saw eyes. There were voices murmuring just on the edge of hearing; muttering, cooing, a couple of popcorn cackles popped…the low buzz of many voices growing closer. But she couldn't *see* anyone beyond the shadowy wall. Nothing moved, although she could feel them pressing closer, invisible predators in the false dark.

Joy retreated, the edge of the counter digging into her back. The growing swarm of sounds became screeches, incoherent babbling and wicked laughter throwing her imagination into overdrive. She sensed danger everywhere but everything in her kitchen looked just the same.

Blinking hard, she tried to see "between." She knew she could call Ink, but she hadn't yet. Would it trap him, too? She stood her ground, wondering. But what could she do alone?

The growing cacophony raged just outside the barrier. She squeezed the knife handle, which quivered in her hand. There was nowhere to run. Joy climbed onto the counter, braced one foot against the cabinet and slashed uselessly at nothing.

A voice pierced the hum of malevolent bees.

"Bring him." The voice oozed honeysuckle wine. "Bring him to me."

Joy shook her head and shouted, "No!"

"Bring him…" the voice curled like smoke "…or die."

The ceramic cookie jar on the counter exploded, pieces scattering like streetlamp glass. Joy tried to shield her eyes as tiny shards sliced her arm. The stinging made it all more real.

"No," she whispered without strength or conviction. There was a sudden rush and the violent sounds grew awesome, filling her head. One laugh rang above it all, delighted and chilling. Joy screamed against the pressure, adding her voice to the noise. Joy knew what they wanted, but it wouldn't come from her. She squeezed her temples and shook her head in her hands,

"I WON'T CALL HIM!"

The disembodied voice pressed down through the sound.

"You don't have to," it lilted. "Not with your voice. Blood calls to blood—" Joy watched a red rivulet run down her arm "—and, as they say, love conquers all."

The world zippered open and Ink stepped through.

"Joy." His voice punctured the din. He swept the bare razor underhanded, shielding them against unseen foes. He was inside the ward, which made her feel both guilty and glad. Her arm stung. Her head ached. He wiped away the small streak of blood from her wrist and looked pained.

"I'm fine!" Joy screamed. "What is it?"

"A trap. And a good one."

"Where are they?" Joy kept shouting, although Ink didn't need to raise his voice to be heard.

"More accurate to say 'Where are we?'" he said. "This is not your home."

Joy shook her head slightly, distrusting her covered ears.

"What?" she shouted.

"This is a replica, an illusion," Ink said again, shifting himself against her legs dangling off the counter's edge. She hooked him with her foot, pulling him closer. The knife in her hand shook. His razor did not. Waves of sound crashed over them. She could feel his voice buzz where they touched. "It was set on the edge of my wards," he said. "It smells coppery. A blood-key."

Joy gave an experimental sniff. She was comforted by the

cool-rain smell of Ink's hair. The pounding, malicious garble beyond the barrier grew thicker every moment.

"Can't we just go?" Joy shouted by his ear. His Joy-ish ear. "Can you get us out of here?"

Ink shifted his weight thoughtfully.

"Yes," he said. "Yes, I can. Easily."

She tried not rolling her eyes. "Then let's go!"

"No," Ink said. "I do not think so."

"WHAT?" she shrieked. "Why?"

He dropped his hand, and the razor hung limply in his fingers. He turned to face Joy.

"You are my *lehman*," he said, drawing her closer, staring into her left eye as if he could read himself there. "This trap was set for you. Why? Because you are my *lehman*, Joy. It was really set for me."

Joy hunched against the clamor and nodded, letting her own knife sink to the counter. "Yeah," she confirmed. "Someone out there wanted me to bring you here."

"And for me to get you out again," Ink said. "Easily." He drew the blade along the barest edge of the ward, seeing the lightning flash. A hot smell filled the room, the scent of blood. The voices rose. "Maybe not so easily for you," he concluded.

Joy grabbed his shirt to pull him nearer. "They want your *signatura!*" she shouted. "You draw it every time you cut through space! Maybe they keep calling you out, trying to force you to draw it, giving them the chance to see it—to steal it!" And she'd let them. She'd been part of it. Every trap. Bait.

He rested his forehead against hers briefly, a small surcease from the clamor. "It does not work that way," he said. "I would have to give it willingly. It cannot be stolen. Yet someone undoubtedly wants it and wanted us here." Ink scanned the darkness. "The trap is still set. And we still need to get out." He rested his fingertips on her collarbone. She breathed against his palm.

"I can smell you," he confessed. She blushed. "So can they. But they cannot see you yet." Ink jerked his head as if indicating over his shoulder, where nothing could be seen through the film of shadow. "Not until you cross the barrier, breaking the wards." Joy's pulse jumped. Her ears buzzed. She was both terrified and highly aware of his skin on hers.

He examined the small smear of red on his thumb. "Stay clear of the barrier. The wards are keyed to you." His voice sliced through the clamor. "If you attempt to break through, they will pounce. You are lucky you did not touch it. The blood would have alerted them. I assume you only used the knife?" Joy nodded. He smiled. "You are learning, too."

"Fair is fair," Joy quoted. "So what do we do?"

"Did you find a trigger? Like the combination lock...?"

Joy groaned, remembering. "The keypad!" Joy said, pointing to the front door across the kitchen in the foyer. "I didn't even look at the buttons. I should have checked for glyphs."

"Not your fault," he said. "I can get there to break them, but I am not certain whether the barrier will lift or shatter, and I will not surrender you by chance." He pressed three fingers to her chest, pushing strength into her core. "I can make it. But we must create a decoy." His eyes flickered. "One of blood."

Joy swallowed and looked around their sparse prison: there was the microwave, her knife, shards of plaster, a cup of pens and the cake. It only took a second to think of something. If that. She raised her voice over the din.

"Use the cake."

The onslaught of sound pressed them closer. Joy covered her ringing ears. Ink pinched a bit of crumb topping and rolled it between his fingers. He nodded.

"That can work," he said, then looked into Joy's eyes. "Do you trust me?"

She could still hear him, through flesh and noise.

"I love you!" she shouted.

It wasn't the answer he'd expected or the one she'd expected to give. It was the wrong time, the wrong thing to say, but her answer lit a fire in his eyes. Ink smiled grimly.

"When I cut your hand, place it on the cake," he instructed. "Let it soak for a count of ten. Count slowly." Ink took her hand gently from her ear, stroking her palm as if treasuring the feel of her unblemished skin. "Do not lift your hand until you are ready to throw." His thumb stopped in the center of her heart line. "Aim there, toward the fridge," he said. "If it hits, all the better. They are not to let you cross the wards and will swarm the decoy, believing it is you." His mouth rolled over the word and paused. His black eyes absorbed hers. "You must move quickly. Run the other way. Get behind something large and wait for me."

She nodded quickly. The heightened, wailing pitch made her ears ring. Ink pulled her closer, his jaw moving against her cheek, speaking cleanly into her ear.

"I will not fail you."

Joy screamed back, "I know."

Ink peeled her fingers back and placed his razor flat against her palm. He looked deep into her eyes and held her there. She forced herself to hold his gaze, ignoring the cold metal on her skin, shaking slightly in anticipation.

"I love you, too," he said simply and slashed her palm.

It was fast. Shocking. Light and lightness came before the pain, afterimages like flash cameras popping before her eyes. Ink pressed her hand against the cake, the sugar darkening around the wound. The dough grew slippery. The crumble, wet. Joy stared at her hand bleeding into cake.

Ink launched toward the foyer, a glint of silver smeared red against the purpled dark. Querulous sounds banked and barked, surging after him as he passed through the barrier, scything sharply to the left.

Joy counted aloud as she tested her feet on the linoleum, willing her hand to stay planted, her fingers smeared with red and cinnamon. The world chattered and screeched. A sudden spring of sweat made her light-headed. She couldn't faint. Not now! She had to count.

"...three...four...five..."

Her palm sank in the soft dessert. Joy couldn't help thinking that Shelley would never forgive her.

"...seven...eight...nine..."

Lifting the plate in one hand, Joy carried it to the edge of the barrier. It hissed static and light. She felt broken and floaty.

Her vision fuzzed. She lifted her eyes and stared hard at the fridge.

"Ten."

Lifted and threw.

There was a collective intake of breath as her hand peeled off the cake, kissing air. Joy tucked her palm under her armpit and moved on the moment of impact—cake, crumb, ceramic and red exploding against the side of the fridge. The monsters surged; a gross column of nameless things appeared and dove upon the bloody thing.

Joy ran. She sprang over the couch single-handed, tucking herself into an easy quarter-roll south of the pillows. She came up quickly, snagging the afghan and wrapping it tightly around her hand and arm. Blood had soaked her shirt and skin, the smell heightened in the dark. A rabid, snarling mass converged and fought, tangled on the opposite end of the kitchen near the fridge. Ink was at the keypad, busy breaking glyphs. She shrank behind the end table. The cake decoy wouldn't last long.

She couldn't stay here. Joy knew she should move, but she was stuck, weighed down by blood loss and the heavy crocheted blanket. Joy's hand started to burn and her knees locked. She couldn't even adjust her leg around the cell phone jabbing into her hip.

Then she heard them—monsters circling the counter, lumbering toward the den.

She needed help. Help! *Now!* Kurt or Officer Castrodad or the beefy, blond drunk at the bar... Someone big. Someone good in a fight. But she had no one to call.

Call!

Joy fumbled for her cell phone, digging it free with one hand and hitting autodial 1.

The kitchen phone rang, a thin trill of bells.

Joy inhaled and screamed: "FILLY!"

A crack of lightning, and she appeared: blue tattooed, braided, and caped in bones. Eyes flashing, the blonde warrior savored the scene, smiling at Joy like a lover.

"It's not the EverBattle," she said. "But it will do." She rotated her wrists in their vambraces. *"Victory!"* she thundered and grabbed the nearest hunk of hair and snarling teeth, breaking off a fistful in her hand. The shriek that followed died quickly when she plunged her arm into the creature's side and squeezed something vital. It choked, shuddered and fell, but Filly was already whirling.

She slammed a skull against the wall with a hollow, wet sound, cleaving through the next body in a wide arc that set her cape bones rattling as it swirled about her shoulders. Filly kicked viciously to one side and tore a snout sideways, broken. She laughed like a maniac. Joy crawled deeper into the afghan.

A cry rose along with a claw the size of gardening shears. Filly took the brunt of it on one armored arm and punched through the monster's trachea. It gagged with a gurgling cough. She spun quickly, landing two blows that fell from her arms like tethered weights. Something crunched and it lay still. A tail caught her face. Joy screamed, but Filly licked the blood from her lip and bellowed, launching herself viciously at her new opponent, pinning its long, ferretlike body over the counter's edge. Her leg muscles strained against the floor. She kept pushing, groaning—a battle of physics and will. Joy winced at the sound of bones snapping as it screamed.

A great, dripping mass peeked around the corner of the couch, its yellow eyes burning, its low-slung belly nearly brushing the floor. It crawled like a reptile and smelled like sewage. Joy inhaled sharply and flipped the end table over, creating a shield.

"Ink!" she cried.

"One moment..."

She grabbed the lamp in one hand. Her side hurt, the afghan slid under her armpit. The creature's back curled, rippling muscles and grime, shifting, preparing to pounce.

Joy tensed.

The second split.

Black underbelly filled her vision. No time to scream.

No!

False night lifted in a curtain of light.

Joy rolled backward on the floor and came up balanced on the balls of her feet. No impact. Nothing. Uncurling, she chanced a look: the creature was gone. The monsters were gone. The darkness was gone. The cake, the bodies and the sewer smells were gone. She rose still holding the lamp, trailing the electrical cord and the bloody afghan like a cape. Ink stood in the foyer. Filly, shocked and cursing, stamped near the sink.

"By the Halls!" Filly spat with rage.

"My apologies," Ink said, dusting off the keypad. "But I did not invoke you."

Filly spun on her heel, spying Joy. "You!" Joy cringed, her head pounding with relief and a pressing need to collapse. She focused on Filly's accusatory finger. "You called me to battle!"

"There *was* a battle!" Joy said. "You were in it!"

Filly snorted, horselike. "Too short." She threw a hank of something long-haired and bleeding into the sink and shoved it down the disposal, switching it on. It made a choppy, chunky sound. She snapped it off. "Call me when something interesting happens," she muttered.

"Victory!" Ink saluted her.

"Victory," she said halfheartedly and with obvious disappointment. There was a clap of thunder. Joy watched her disperse, static raising the hairs on her arms.

She blinked around her apartment, touching the couch with an experimental toe.

"This is...?" she said, almost unsure.

"Real," Ink confirmed. "Yes, Joy. This is real."

Something inside Joy began to relax, but not much.

"You did well," Ink said, coming to her side. "I would not have thought to ring a bell."

"Yeah, well, modern technology." Joy looked around, dazed. "This was Aniseed's doing?"

He touched the wall. "Yes."

"Because she wants your *signatura*," she said hollowly.

"Yes," he said. "I think that is why."

Joy nodded, clamping her bundled, bleeding hand under her armpit and staring stupidly into space. One thought bobbed to the surface. "Don't give it to her," Joy said. "Whatever happens, don't let her have it."

"I will not," he said. "But I will not risk you." Ink's face softened now that the fear had passed. He cupped the side of Joy's face and wiped wetness from her eyes.

"I can't leave you alone for a minute," he chastised her softly.

Joy chuckled in surprise. "You 'can't'?" she echoed. "You're using contractions more."

Ink rubbed his thumb against her cheek. "I blame you."

A key in the door rattled. Joy tensed and Ink stepped back as the front door swung open. Joy's father and Shelley walked into the house. Joy tried not to look at Ink as his black gaze followed them both.

"Dad," she said, adjusting the afghan around her. "Shelley. Hi."

"Hi," her father said. He took Shelley's coat and hung it in the closet. "How was shopping?"

Joy stared at him. Shopping? How long ago was that?

"Joy?" her dad prompted. "Did you buy something?"

She snapped out of it enough to look him in the eye.

"No," she said. "No. Nothing. Just window-shopping." Joy spoke a little more quickly than she thought must be normal. "Monica bought bras," she blurted out. "I mean she bought stuff and I just..." *watched? looked?* "...helped." The adults exchanged looks as if they might laugh. This conversation was officially veering out of control. Joy's brain replayed blood and cake and kissing Inq and demi-bras and Nikolai and monsters and Kestrel and sigils written in chalk. She'd lost track of time. Her head spun. She squeezed the afghan closer. Ink followed her dad curiously as he circled the counter. He was examining her father's clothes with interest.

"I'm going to my room," she announced loud enough for everyone to hear.

"Okay." Her father shrugged. "We'll be watching C-SPAN." He pointed to the counter. "Want a slice of cake? Shelley brought it."

Joy glanced at the pristine coffee cake in horror. "Um, no thanks," she said. "I'm...not hungry." She brushed past Ink, hooking his pants chain through a hole in the afghan, and tugged him quickly down the hall and into her room.

She shut the door with her butt and sucked air through her teeth. "Ow ow ow..." Joy sat on the edge of her bed, her body jostling on springs. Ink settled himself beside her as they unwrapped her hand. She shivered. The blood on her clothes and the blanket had to belong to someone else. It was everywhere. She couldn't quite feel it. She didn't understand how any of it could be real. She wanted Ink to stay with her and make it better, and also for him to go away and leave her alone.

He examined the clean cut under the blood with a look of regret.

"You need stitches," he said.

"No, I don't," Joy insisted.

"I am fairly certain that you do."

She shook her head. No more hospitals.

"Give me that," she said, pointing to his scalpel.

Ink hesitated, a question not quite formed on his lips, but he obeyed, placing the shining blade on her palm, handle first.

Joy took it and adjusted her grip, placing the sharp edge lightly against her own torn skin. The flesh had peeled back, exposing pink muscle and stringy things. The blood in the center of her palm pooled sluggish and dark.

Holding her breath, she drew the razor through the red—steady and clear—not a bit surprised that the wound sealed as she erased the mark Ink had cut. She slowly zipped the flayed skin together, ignoring the way her fingers shook. When she finished, she spat on her palm, wiped away the blood and blew on the blade. She handed the razor back to Ink.

"There," Joy said, voice quivering, daring him to say that what she'd done was impossible, deny that anything could happen right here, right now. She tested her fingers against her palm, tacky with blood. She felt remarkably whole and smug.

Ink looked unused to being surprised.

"Well done," he said, wiping his blade clean.

She became conscious of his eyes and her blood. Her stomach rolled. "Thanks."

"You are safe now."

"You said that when you placed the wards."

"That was in your house," he said, "your windows, your doors. You had crossed over into illusion before you even entered the room. Probably at the outer door, possibly at the gate." Ink bowed his head. "But you are right—no excuse is forgivable. I said that I would keep you safe, and I failed."

"Safe," Joy muttered. She tried wiping her hands on her stained hoodie, gave up and grabbed a fistful of tissues. Adding several squirts of hand sanitizer, she started scrubbing at the red. "I want to be safe, but I don't want...this. Illusion, monsters, blood keys? It's horrible." She opened her hands smeared with red and black. Pulling her sweatshirt angrily over her head, she rolled it and the afghan into a ball and tossed them to the floor. She examined her V-neck for stains.

"What do you want, Joy?"

The question struck her like a slap. Joy blinked back unexpected tears. What did she want? She shook her head violently, thinking of the tongue on the window, the brand on her arm, the drawer with its envelopes and a 323 phone number that she'd never had the guts to use.

Her breath trembled. *What do I want?* To leave. To stay. To change. To go back. To take it all back. Undo it. Move on.

Joy massaged her hand.

"Joy?" Ink brushed the hair from her eyes just as tenderly as Inq had taught him. "Please tell me what you want."

A tear slipped free. Joy tried to shrug.

"Why do you have such difficulty answering that question?" he asked.

"I guess..." Joy's voice shivered as she exhaled. "I'm scared."

"Scared?" Ink sounded surprised as he moved nearer. "Of what?"

Joy struggled to put it into words. "Of...asking...and not getting it," she said around the knot in her throat. "Of you saying no." She choked on the last confession. "And then leaving me."

"Joy..." Ink's voice warmed, a sound that was growing familiar. "Joy, I already chose you. It cannot be undone." He traced a line from the corner of her eye to the tip of her ear, tucking some stray hairs behind it. "Not even I can go back in time to erase that, nor would I want to." He turned her face to his. "I am not going away. It is an easy thing to accept once you choose to believe it." Ink smiled and touched her heart line in her unmarked palm. Joy leaned against his shoulder. He rested his cheek against her forehead and drew his finger along her wrist, following the vein that pulsed there.

He had no veins. No pulse. No blood. He wasn't human. He would never be human. He would never age or die. Somewhere in the silence, that truth surfaced like a mountain between them. Joy tried to ignore it, but she knew that if she chose this, nothing could ever be the same. Ink's whisper was crisp and clean and carried a world of sighs.

"Do not make things any harder than they must be."

Her father knocked on the door.

"Come in," she said.

He stood in the doorframe looking ragged. Joy was glad that she'd stowed all the evidence of the attack in her hamper, out of sight. The hall was strangely dark, the house completely quiet. It was an everyday sort of ominous, the kind that was horribly familiar. She checked his feet for telltale slippers, a sure sign that something was wrong.

Had he broken up with Shelley? Joy surprised herself that she hoped not.

"Hey, Dad," Joy said uncomfortably.

"I called Stefan," her father began, "to see how he was doing at school." He paused and Joy felt he could read the word *Oh* on her eyeballs. He knew that she knew and he nodded.

"So," he said.

"So," Joy repeated. Were they talking about Stefan or her? Was Dad upset about his son being gay or that his daughter was sneaking around with a guy he'd never met? Joy couldn't tell. Her father just stood in the doorway and she sat at her desk, a freeze-frame that should have cut to commercial, but didn't.

An entire conversation was taking place on another frequency. Inside her head, Joy could hear the words that they should be saying: *"When did you know?" "Did you know?" "Was I supposed to know or find out?" "How did this happen?" "These things just happen." "Should I have done something differently?" "No." "Yes." "What did I do wrong?" "Nothing." "Can you believe it?" "Honestly? It threw me, too." "Was it me?" "Was it Mom?" "Was it something Stef had to do?" "Have you heard about James?" "What? James who?"*

A whole heart-to-heart bubbled up between them, if only they could open their mouths—but that had been Mom's job, not theirs, to say these kinds of things—loudly, repeatedly, to absolutely anyone who would listen. Heart on her sleeve, volume cranked to ten, Mom always spoke enough words for everyone. But with only the two of them, they were left in a plucked-string silence.

Joy couldn't bear to think that Ink had sat in her room not two hours ago. That he'd wiped her tears and kissed her face and told her that the fear of losing love was foolish. He wouldn't stop loving her. She wouldn't stop loving Dad. And they wouldn't stop loving Stef.

Not like Mom.

But, Joy reminded herself, Mom *hadn't* stopped loving Stef. So that meant that she hadn't stopped loving Joy, either. The cards, the texts, the calls, the plane tickets... Her mother wouldn't stop loving her. No matter what.

"He's still Stef," Joy said into the heavy quiet.

Her father lifted his head without looking at her. "Oh?"

"Yeah." Joy nodded. "Just because you learn something new doesn't mean he isn't Stefan, right?"

A long, tense minute stretched on the rack. An echo pounded like a distant drum, *Right...? Right...?*

"Right, Dad?" Joy pressed.

He conceded. "Right."

Joy turned, squeaking in her desk chair.

"What did you say to him?"

He shook his head ever so slightly. "I didn't say anything," he admitted. "I just let him...talk." He caught her eye in a rare moment of intimacy, then stared back at the floor. "I didn't say anything. Then I said goodbye." She felt in his voice the weight of those words—the only thing worse than saying too much was not saying enough. She knew that from personal experience.

He placed his hand on the doorknob. Joy waited. Was he

going to ask about her? Did he know? Did Stef tell? Was he waiting for her to say something first? Was this a test? A trap? Maybe he knew. Maybe he was waiting for her. Maybe...

"Good night, Joy."

She'd waited too long. Again.

"Good night, Dad," she said, then added, "I love you."

He paused. "I love you, too." He placed a kiss on her forehead that made her feel guilty, fighting the urge to tell him everything. About Ink. About monsters. About marks and brands and falling in love...

But she couldn't. It was too dangerous. And sounded totally crazy.

She smiled as he left, her door clicking closed.

Joy opened her email, typing a quick one-liner to her brother, who was probably having his own conversation in Pennsylvania somewhere. Had he told Dad about Ink? Did it matter?

Not really. She wasn't going to leave him. No matter what.

Keep strong, she typed. I love you.

Joy hit Send with a satisfied smile.

FIFTEEN

Joy met Monica at Starbucks after church. Joy and her dad no longer went to services without Mom to harass them, but Joy felt vaguely guilty every time she saw Monica in her Sunday best.

"Are we going to talk about yesterday?" Monica asked, dipping her straw into her low-fat iced coffee. Stoppering the top with her fingertip, she shot the strawful into her mouth.

Joy stirred her caramel latte, feigning interest in the swirls. "Yesterday?"

"At the mall. Rocks smashing? Fragrant candles? Broken windshields? Russian hottie in a sweet ride? Any of this ringing a bell?" Monica's face grew stormy when Joy smirked at the phrase "ringing a bell." She'd been particularly proud of summoning Filly. Had that been only yesterday? It was hard to believe.

"Hey!" Monica snapped. Joy refocused. "Is this news to you? Because lately, you've been having more than your fair share of weirdness plus some, so if this is how it's going down nowadays, I have every right to know what's up and beat you with a reality stick, if necessary."

Joy sipped and sighed. "I was totally freaked out," she confessed. "I saw something coming fast and felt like we'd better get out of the way."

"That's it?" Monica said.

"That's it."

"No Spidey Senses tingling or anything like that?"

"No," Joy said with another sip. "Nothing like that. Just Murphy's Law."

"You have been Murphy's toy poodle as of late," Monica said. "Still, what's with the guy?"

"Which guy? You mean Nikolai?"

"He said you're dating his girlfriend's brother."

Joy nodded. "That's right," she said. "We're Significant Others-in-law."

Monica tapped herself another strawful of coffee, but let it sluice back into her cup. "Uh-huh." She looked both expectant and ticked.

"I don't ask you for intimate details about Gordon, do I?" Joy hedged.

"That's only because I tell you first," Monica said. "Did you know he tastes like pineapple?"

Joy stuck out her tongue. She could have made her own confessions about kisses and boys. That she had been kissed by a Goth girl who saved her life and that her boyfriend always smelled like rain. She and Monica could have bonded over it, laughing and sympathizing with tiny, appropriate noises, but it was just too strange, a hairbreadth from a world that was equal parts crazy, dangerous and awfully hard to explain. Joy kept quiet, placing her unsliced palm against the warm cup, and told herself it was better this way.

She watched Monica drip coffee out of the straw into her mug, the liquid bouncing on the surface, making perfect caffeine circles. Joy stared at the pattern. It reminded her of something...

She sat up straight, half expecting to see an identical ripple in the air. She remembered where she'd seen it before. If she could draw it as a picture, she knew exactly how it would look: three concentric circles like a bull's-eye in space. Or, drawn in chalk, on a giant slate wall.

Whipping out her phone, she shuffled through Contacts.

"Joy?"

She sped through the *L*'s, clicking madly.

"Joy?" Monica waved her straw, now emptied. "Hello! What's up?"

"Just remembered something," Joy mumbled and quick-typed a text to Luiz with her thumbs.

Tell inq i know what she did.

She hit Send.

"Trouble in paradise?" Monica asked nonchalantly. "Mr. Nikolai's girlfriend's brother? What's his name again?" she hinted heavily.

"No," Joy muttered. "It's his sister. I think she's done something stupid."

Monica squinched her face in sympathy. "Oooh. You should have let her in on our motto—No Stupid."

Coffee dripped off Joy's spoon. She watched the drops fall, the ripples rebounding off one another. Action, reaction, consequences. Aniseed, Briarhook, Hasp, Inq. They were all connected. It was there on the wall. Why hadn't anyone seen it before?

"I gotta go," Joy said, standing. "I'll catch you later." She shouldered her bag, feeling an urgent need to leave. Monica wasn't safe with her. No one was. The café was too crowded; there were innocent people everywhere.

"This sudden disappearing act is getting stale," Monica said. "You owe me an explanation and a windshield." She tapped her straw against the cup. "I'll take my payment in pizza."

"Name the date," Joy said. By then, she'd think up some cover story. Lying was way too hard. How had her mother managed it for so long? "I gotta go."

Joy rushed out the door, not trusting that Inq wouldn't simply appear in the coffee shop. She waved goodbye through the window and started walking quickly—anywhere, away—putting as much distance between herself and other people as she could. She felt more anxious with every pedestrian she passed and pushed herself to move faster. She had to get clear, for everybody's sake.

She sped through the old section of what used to be downtown before the malls moved the foot traffic north. The buildings were small with the dull patina of years of wind and rain scratched into their surfaces. The roofs had real shingles and some of the signs were brass placards. Joy passed a family-owned drugstore and a tiny tailor shop.

"What is with you?" Inq snapped, materializing out of a shimmer of air and falling into angry step alongside Joy. "Luiz is having a macho-snit-fit. He thinks that you just threatened me."

Having expected it, Joy didn't slow. Nor did she look at Inq, knowing that no one else could see.

"It wasn't a threat," Joy said, looking both ways before

crossing the street. "It was a message. For you. I figured it out. I know what you did."

Inq laughed as she touched a pedestrian walking past. Neither bothered to watch the calligraphic tattoo on the woman's hand rise and die. "I've done a lot of things over the years, Joy. Care to name my specific offense, or do I have to guess?"

"Names. Exactly," Joy hissed with a sudden heat. "True Names. *Signatura.* You gave yours to Aniseed and didn't tell anybody, not even Ink or Kurt or Graus Claude, and I want to know why."

Inq's voice lost its bounce, but not its crisp clarity. "Careful, *lehman.* You push," she warned, "someone might push back."

"Spare me," Joy said and ducked into an ancient phone booth, a leftover relic from a pre–cell phone era back when coins were worth something. Joy squeaked the folding door closed and held her cell phone to her ear, pretending that her private, one-way conversation was happening via satellite. She glared at Inq through the glass. "I saw your *signatura* in Aniseed's hidden workroom at Dover Mill—a circle of ripples—it was right there on the wall!" Inq stopped, startled. "*Signatura* can't be forged or stolen. You have to give them willingly." Joy's anger sparked. "So I want to know—whose side are you on?"

Inq muttered, "It's not what you think, Joy."

Joy laughed and banged her hand against the glass. "Seriously? That's the best you can do?" she said. "Yesterday was the *second* time I was used as bait. At first I thought it was just so that they could trick Ink into showing his mark, but then he said that that wouldn't work. He'd have to give it up. Willingly. Graus Claude said the same thing. So I'm guessing that Aniseed's after me because she wanted to see if Ink would come to my rescue so she could ransom me back in exchange for his True Name. Maybe she's even done it before."

"It's not like that," Inq protested.

"Well, *that's* good to hear—I'd hate to think that one of the Cabana Boys had been dangled over a cliff." Joy shouted past her phone. "So what was it? Money? Boys? A really tragic wardrobe?" Joy asked. "What did Aniseed promise you in return for your name?"

"Shut up!" Inq shouted and slammed her own hand against the glass. Joy flinched as the glass shuddered in warning ripples. "It wasn't like that. It wasn't like that at all—" Inq nearly shook with rage. "I had nothing to do with any of this!"

"Are you sure?" Joy asked. "How do you know that you had nothing to do with whatever's going on? I saw that wall—it's a huge web, Inq, a huge net of something. And it doesn't take a genius to guess that it's something bad." Joy tried glaring hard enough to make the ebon-eyed girl understand. "What if it's all a trap?" she asked. "You'd be caught in it, too, as well as everyone you've ever touched! How many people could she get through your *signatura*? Hundreds? Thousands? Millions? What if Aniseed got Ink's? How many more?" Joy said. "Aniseed has a huge plan for all those marks *including* yours. You can't pretend that you're not part of it!"

"My trade was made years ago," Inq said stubbornly. "Lifetimes before you were born, Joy. Long before your little melodrama with Ink." She tossed her hair and crossed her arms. "Believe it or not, *lehman*, not everything is about you. I welcomed you into this otherworld, and I can take you out." Inq cocked her head to the side. "And I *do* know something about humans—every one of you think that you are the star in some cosmic play where the universe is either for you or against you on some grand stage. 'Look at me!' 'Look at me!'" She waved her hands condescendingly. "It's a fallacy, Joy. No one is watching or paying attention to you." Inq shrugged. "You're just not that important."

"This is not about me!" Joy snapped back. "It's about Ink! And who knows how many millions of people? Isn't that important?"

"Of course he's important—he is *all important*—that's the only reason that I spared your life in the first place, you stupid little girl!" Inq said. "His mistake would have brought us into question." She gestured wildly. "We have to be flawless. We can't afford to make mistakes!"

"Why not?" Joy asked.

"Because then we'd *both* be replaced," Inq seethed. "You're human—you should be perfectly familiar with obsolescence. If it doesn't work instantly, perfectly, every time, you throw it away and get a new one."

Joy staggered. "So you made a deal with Aniseed in order to save your *jobs?*"

"NO!" Inq shouted and the ripples rose off her, warbling the glass and warping the metal frame. Joy stumbled against the hard black phone as the booth shook.

"This isn't a *job*," Inq raged. "This is *what we are!* We are Scribes! Our life *is* this—we weren't meant for anything more! We're supposed to be *glorified paintbrushes!*" Her hands fisted helplessly and beat at her chest. "But I knew that there was more to living than just this. I pushed for more, I watched, I studied for aeons, and I did it—I learned how to *live*. Ink's just discovering it now, but I've known it, I've earned it and I'm not going to give it up!" Her perfect mask crumpled in despair. "Don't you understand? Ink and I—we've only ever had each other. I have to protect him. We are indivisible!" Inq screamed. *"Because if he is expendable, then so am I!"*

They stared at each other through warped glass and a devastating silence. Joy dropped the pretense and her phone.

"Inq..."

Inq's shoulders slumped. "I love life too much to die."

"Everything dies," Joy said quietly.

Inq's eyes narrowed into black slits. "Not everything, monkey."

Joy twitched. "Is that a threat?"

"No," Inq said under her breath. "It's a message. And I'm going to deliver it, personally."

The air thickened and rippled under her fingers.

"Inq, wait..." Joy said, but the Scribe disappeared with a buzz of pressure in Joy's ears. She opened the phone booth with a rusty wail, the only sharp sound in the quiet Sunday afternoon. Inq was gone. And Joy hadn't had the chance to ask why Aniseed had Inq's mark in the first place. Inq wouldn't sell out her brother, but why would she sell out herself? It made no sense.

Exhausted and discouraged, Joy pointed her feet toward home more out of habit than a desire to be there. She stumbled up to the gate and paused on the steps. She wasn't sure what she would find at the top of the stairs, behind the door: Dad, Shelley, Ink, monsters...? Could be anything. She was tired. Joy stared at the gate's keypad, inspecting the buttons for strange glyphs, eyes in the shadows or magic wards on the ground. Screw it. Let there be grisly monsters or consenting adults in compromising positions—she was not about to let all this crap keep her from going to her own room! Outside felt too big all of a sudden. Joy wanted to go home.

Gate: fine. Door: fine. Hall: fine. Alarm: fine. As long as she was still in her reality, everything checked out okay. Joy hated that she hesitated before each step, half expecting some sort of attack. No Dad. No Shelley. No suspicious coffee cakes. Joy swallowed some of her paranoia along with a glass of Valencia orange juice and water. The wild theory that had popped out of her mouth while yelling at Inq didn't sound half-bad, but she didn't really know anything about the Twixt—or anything about anything, really. Things kept happening that you couldn't expect. She was a living case in point.

Joy walked into the bathroom and washed her hands in the sink. What she *did* know was that Ink wasn't going to give Aniseed his *signatura* and Inq had been surprised to hear that hers had been on the wall. Joy knew she'd probably have to apologize later and Inq would milk it for all it was worth. Like the kiss. But hopefully Graus Claude would figure everything out and life could return to, well, somewhat left of normal, but after today's wild accusation, she was willing to leave the investigation to the expert, four-armed toad.

The doorbell rang.

Joy felt a prickly panic, which made her angry. Why should she feel creeped out at the sound of her own doorbell? She wasn't a prisoner! This was her house! Joy marched toward the foyer, slowing as she saw her dad in the kitchen.

"Oh," Joy said, surprised. "I didn't hear you come in."

"Just got here," he said. "I took a long walk." There was something in the way he said it that made her slow down.

"Everything okay?" Joy asked.

"I needed to think."

Joy nodded. "Yeah. Me, too." She pointed awkwardly at the door. "Did you just ring the bell?"

"No, it rang as I closed the door. I looked, but I didn't see anyone there. Must've hit the button as I came in, I guess." Her father reached for the giant glass stein he only used for drinking imported beer. He didn't drink it very often, and usually only for special occasions. Joy was about to ask him about it when she froze. *Didn't see anyone...?* Joy turned toward the door, a rush of blood echoing in her ears.

She heard herself say, "I'll go check."

Joy moved as if in a dream, slow and tingly, somehow knowing what would happen, but needing to go through the motions anyway. She glanced through the peephole, seeing nothing, and cautiously opened the door.

Inq's body lay at her feet, open and gushing.

Swallowing a scream, Joy knelt over the body. Inq had been ripped sideways. There was blood everywhere—black fluid with slick, hot-pink hues shining like great puddles of oil. Beads of negative light sprayed the wall where the body had been dumped at their door.

Joy had to get her inside, out of the hall.

Dad was in the kitchen.

In full view of the door.

Joy scooped her arms under Inq's neck and knees.

"Hey, Dad," she called back into the condo. "Can you grab me a soda?"

"All right," she heard him say as he started digging into the back of the fridge and she pulled Inq's surprisingly heavy weight into her arms. She scuttled quickly into the foyer. Invisible Inq or no, Dad would be sure to notice Joy's posture if he turned around.

"You want ice?" her father asked as she backed up the hall.

"Sure!" Joy grunted as she hauled Inq into her room. She dropped Inq indelicately onto the bed and squeezed her eyes shut. "Ink! Ink! Ink!" she chanted in panic. Her clothes were soaked in black gore. Would Dad see it? What would he think? What could she say to explain? She yanked on her bathrobe over her clothes.

"Lots of ice," Joy called, shoving her arms through the worn terrycloth sleeves. "And lemon!" She needed to keep stalling. Her father rummaged in the kitchen. She heard the ice machine whir. Cubes clanging against glass. Footsteps on the floor.

"I'm going to call your brother," her father announced. "Do you want to say hello first?"

Joy was nearly weeping as she wrapped blankets over Inq. The Scribe's face registered no expression at all.

"Joy?" Her dad sounded annoyed. He was coming closer. "Did you hear me?"

She pushed the door closed with her foot.

"Hang on." She tried to keep the quaver out of her voice. "I'll talk to him later. You first."

There was a disappointed pause, and then the heavy tread of footsteps back down the hall. Joy trembled, trying to think of something, but her mind was a blank page of panic. Her fingers were spastic. Brushing her hair away from her eyes left smears of black blood on her cheek.

"Ink, come on—!" she whispered. "Ink, please!"

He appeared in an instant. Joy grabbed his sleeve.

"Take her," Joy nearly screamed with relief. "Take her to Graus Claude. She's torn in half."

Ink gazed down at his sister wrapped in blankets. He spoke like the dead.

"He cannot fix this," he said.

"What?" Joy said.

"Graus Claude cannot fix Scribes," Ink said, numb.

Joy could have torn her hair out. She clenched fingers slick with Inq.

"Fine," she hissed. "Give me a knife."

Ink glanced up, dazed. "What?"

"A knife! Now!"

He sounded hopeful. "Which one?"

"Any one!"

Joy steadied herself with the least sane part of her mind as Ink extracted the scalpel and she yanked back the covers. Inq lay blotted like a kindergarten card, a pale body in the center of a black Rorschach bloom.

Joy climbed onto her bed. There were no guts or bones, only a gaping hole of sludge that had ripped through Inq's corset and skin.

"Hold her closed," she said and Ink bent to comply, moving his sister's flesh in ways that humans don't move. Ink held Inq together as if willing her shut. The molded flesh kept slipping, eluding his fingers and leaking blood. Angrily, he dipped his hand inside her, tugging the edges closed, and pinched.

"Now."

Joy tried not to think about what she was doing, or attempting to do. She could fix this. Undo it. Erase it.

Hold on.

The blade dipped into the black and at her touch, the skin rippled and congealed. White embers of undoing burst through the dark fluid. The edge of the razor traced the tiny path of skin on skin. Ink's hands led the way as Joy sealed the wound. The seam grew steadily, the damage disappearing under Joy's scalpel, the seal exploding with sparks.

Joy shook with the strain. Doubt crept into her mind. There was no way she could do something like this and stay sane. There was no way she could stop or wonder why. Joy could do something—was doing something—that couldn't be done by anyone, not even Ink. *She* was doing this. For once, she was making something happen. It helped, but it didn't make sense.

And it worked.

She cut Inq closed.

Done. Joy dropped the scalpel. Ink breathed against the wound and into Inq's mouth, as if tasting her air for a sign of life. His black eyes shared the same color as the blood. Joy wondered if maybe they were nothing more than human-shaped shells filled with hot-black fluid? She turned the thought over like a snow globe in her mind.

"You did it," Ink said, wrapping Inq in the coverlet. He lifted the bundle of his sister in his arms, looking grim.

"Give me the scalpel," he said. Joy numbly obeyed. He reverse-gripped it in his hand. "She will live. But someone will die."

Her father's voice resonated down the hall.

"Joy?"

She stared at Ink. "Where will you take her?"

"Graus Claude's."

Joy grabbed Ink's arm. "Take me with you."

"Joy!" Her father sounded as though he expected an answer.

"I know what happened," she said. "I have to tell you—"

"Joy..."

"It will only take a moment!" she whispered.

"Joy...?" her father said, louder, closer.

"And that's *now*," Joy said. "Right now!"

Ink swiftly adjusted his sister and offered his hand. Joy took it.

He pulled Joy with him as they sliced urgently through.

SIXTEEN

INK APPEARED IN THE FOYER BUT DID NOT CROSS THE THRESHOLD. Joy hovered at his elbow and tried not to look at the stains.

Kurt appeared, opening his arms to accept Ink's burden. Joy watched the tense, silent exchange between the two men. Ink relented. Wordlessly, Kurt took Inq in his arms as if she weighed nothing, cradling her head in one hand, inspecting her face as he carried her off like a sleeping princess.

Ink's arms dropped like weights. Joy touched his shoulder. They, too, said nothing, but his fingers curled around hers and she threaded them together.

"Thank you," he whispered.

"Will she be okay?"

"She is whole, thanks to you," Ink replied. "But we do not heal the way you think of it, being made, not born. We can repair flesh well enough, but the rest has to be restored."

A deep bellow flung down the hall.

"Well, don't stand there, come along!"

Ink and Joy hastened into the office, where Graus Claude glowered in front of his computer, basking in twin lights from the monitor and an emerald desk lamp. His thin lip curled to reveal a snarl of pointy teeth. Two of his hands tapped the keyboard while a third held the mouse and a fourth lifted and discarded papers from open manila folders.

"Bailiwick," Ink said formally.

"Master Ink." Graus Claude glanced up and did a double take. "You're a mess," he observed dryly. "But I suspect Miss Invisible is worse."

Joy spoke up. "Will she live?"

"Under Kurt's hands? I doubt he'd let her go." The great gentleman-toad snorted. "He hasn't yet."

"Joy healed her," Ink said.

Graus Claude paused. "Is that a fact?" He looked as if this might pique his curiosity enough to stop his rummaging, but the moment fled and he buried himself back in his task. "Very good, then. I imagine that things will be well in hand." One claw pointed to Ink. "You will go to her shortly?"

"Yes."

"I'll tell Kurt to prepare," Graus Claude said, leaning toward a smooth intercom box.

"Wait," Joy interjected. Graus Claude stayed his hand. "I think Inq went to Aniseed and then I found her on my doorstep, slit in half!"

"On your doorstep?" Ink asked.

"She went to *Aniseed*?" Graus Claude's brow ridge jumped high. "Why?"

Joy struggled to put her wild theory into words. "She went to confront her. I think she felt...guilty," Joy said. "I told her that I saw her *signatura* on Aniseed's wall and knew she must have given it to her willingly."

Graus Claude snatched a photo printout from one of the folders. Joy recognized it as her cell phone pic. He pointed at the image. "Where?"

Joy tapped the tiny bull's-eye with her fingernail. Ink didn't bother to look. He looked impassive and cold.

"I thought she'd cut a deal with Aniseed," Joy admitted to Ink. "To trick you into giving your *signatura*."

"She would not do that," he said quietly.

"I know that now," Joy said. "But she admitted that she had traded her True Name to Aniseed years ago, and when you both said that the whole thing was interconnected, I thought, what if the whole network was like that? Triggered like one of Aniseed's traps? What if something happened to one and then it happened to everything else in the net?"

A slam of Graus Claude's three hands sent papers flying and toppled the lamp.

"She's done it," Graus Claude roared. "That witch has defied the Edict for the last time!"

He stabbed one claw directly into the heart of the remaining files. "I have been searching for a connection between the Scribes and this client list and had thus far found nothing aside from their being on the list itself. But if, as you say, the unifying factor *is* the list, it is borne by Inq, through her *signatura*." The Bailiwick addressed the young man stained in oily blood. "A second set would be thus unified through Ink. Once Aniseed had been willingly given one *signatura*, it would not take much for her to consider the ramifications of having more. And with both the Scribes...she could claim hundreds of humans, thousands, millions."

"But why?" Ink said doubtfully.

"Numbers," Graus Claude murmured. "Sheer numbers are enough to tip the balance and bring about this supposed Golden Age if humankind falls."

"And she believes in this Golden Age of the Twixt?" Ink said.

The Bailiwick's eyes smoldered under his brow. "What does it matter if she can bring about humanity's end?" he said. "I can imagine she would like nothing more."

Ink spread his hand over the photograph. "But if she has legitimate claim...?"

"These humans are not legitimate," the Bailiwick roared. "They did not fall under her auspice—she took them like the parasite that she is! If these were her legitimate claims, they would have been marked by region at the very least. No, she has collected this mass by insinuating herself into others' claims. She could never have amassed this group all at once on her own," he muttered, "but only because her ties are tenuous. By her very nature, her claims die."

Joy paled. "Die?" She waved her hands to whoa. "Wait a minute. What are we talking about? I thought we were talking about Aniseed and *signatura*."

"Yes, *signatura*," Graus Claude grumbled as he trudged down the hall toward the guest toilette. "Your people do not have *signatura* of your own, but you bear ours, which makes you our responsibility. They are the ties that tether us together, preserving the balance, keeping magic extant. Aniseed has been insinuating her own *signatura* upon others' legitimate claims, upsetting that balance? It is unimaginable!" His four hands became fists. "She has concocted diseases for centuries, but they have always been contained within the parameters of her auspice."

"*What?!*" Joy shrieked.

"Aniseed's auspice is *disease*. Death is within her purview," the Bailiwick confessed. "That is her native responsibility—balance, preserving nature's cycle, purging stressors like overpopulation. Bubonic plague, scarlet fever, influenza,

AIDS..." He grunted as they rounded the corner. "However, if she has changed her strategy from natural vectors to *signatura,* well, it's unconscionable, but she would most likely succeed in what I can only assume is her ultimate objective."

"To end the Age of Man," Ink concluded.

"Precisely." Graus Claude opened the door. "And most elegantly, I'll admit. Disease takes time to gestate and spread. It can take years—decades—before affected numbers attain critical mass, before causes are identified, cures discovered and disseminated. All this time slowly unraveling the skein of Man. I can only imagine her patience. And now you and Mistress Inq can provide a much-sought shortcut."

He cast his bobbing head toward Inq spread on the couch. "Aniseed's efforts have always been maddeningly brilliant, yet never to this scale. The numbers we are talking about... I doubt humanity would survive," he admitted. "The Twixt would be forced to bear witness to her coup de grâce, unable to uphold the promises that bind their True Names to their charges. It would be...catastrophic. Epidemic. *Pandemic!* Magic would fail. Our bonds, collapse. The paradox alone would drive a knife between our peoples and sever our worlds."

His four hands opened and closed, failing to express the magnitude of what he was saying. He stammered in disbelief. "The Council was created as a safeguard for both worlds— one cannot exist without the other. Balance is paramount. Aniseed has been a bulwark against humanity's intercession with a fair hand for years. While her past involvements have been detrimental, to say the least, all have required a natural vector—airborne particles, tainted water, fluid exchange.... But all that is unnecessary when the assault can be instantaneous, the culprit lying undetected—" his claw dimpled the back of one hand "—beneath the skin."

"Joy..." Ink whispered.

Understanding bloomed in the great toad's eyes. "She bears Aniseed's mark," he said.

"Impossible," Ink insisted. "I have not granted Aniseed my *signatura*."

"No," the Bailiwick said softly. "But Briarhook has."

Joy's insides iced over. Her legs loosened. She stumbled. He caught her. "Ink?"

"I am here," Ink said, although all his attention was fixed on the couch where Inq lay. Her eyes were closed and if she breathed, it was just barely. His sister lay naked, tucked beneath a clean sheet, her face washed, her hair pushed back— a gesture that Inq thought of as gentleness. Had she learned that from Kurt's hands?

The butler knelt next to her, the silver tray with its bottles, syringes and matted, black-stained gauze sat forgotten on the floor. He stared, intense and intent, on Inq's face. His arms moved carefully, with barely contained tension, the muscles bulging like the veins on the back of his hands—it was as if any moment he might tear through the wall with his fists. Joy stayed by the door.

"Is the seal intact?" Graus Claude rumbled. Kurt nodded and massaged the meat of Inq's left hand. "Good," he said, gesturing to Ink. "Then I leave you to your business. Miss Malone, I will arrange for you to be safely housed until such time as the Council has addressed this assault."

"Wh-what?" Joy stammered, staring at Ink, who had pulled his smoke-silver shirt over his head. Back bared, his *signatura* pulsed as it spun. The room filled with the scent of him: the rain of a coming storm.

"We should go," Graus Claude said.

"No. I have to go home!" Joy insisted.

"I understand your wish, but that is no longer an option," Graus Claude murmured. "Regretfully, as is often the way of these things, to be of two worlds, one can rarely have both. There comes a time when you must choose."

"Ink," Joy called to him as he rubbed his forearms with strong hands. "I *have* to go home. Dad... Stef..." They were on the phone. Right now! Her mind stalled. "It was only supposed to be a moment!"

"Graus Claude, please, take her home," Ink said dully as he withdrew his wallet.

The Bailiwick sighed deep disapproval. "Booking the flight, aside from the costs, will take time and explanation that we cannot afford," he said reasonably. Kurt repositioned himself and forced Inq's head back at a tilt. Ink turned and looked at his sister, determination on his face.

Joy stammered, "B-but I thought..."

"Come," Graus Claude urged.

"Joy..." Ink began, but Kurt snapped his fingers once, the sound cracking like a whip against tile. Ink dropped his head and flicked his straight razor open, quickly severing the tips of his first three fingers, holding his hand up like a brimming champagne flute. Kurt slid a finger into Inq's mouth.

Joy gagged. "What are you *doing*?"

Ink lifted his half hand and tipped his own substance into Inq's mouth. Kneading his biceps, he watched her jaw. Kurt pushed her throat in and down. Ink's cheeks hollowed. Inq's bulged, then emptied. Ink and Kurt shared a rhythm, feeding Ink into Inq.

"No..." Joy whispered.

"Come," Graus Claude said, resigned. "Now."

"NO!" Joy cried, scrabbling forward, but Graus Claude's four arms were faster, stronger. *"NO!"*

"Calm yourself," the old toad advised. "He's only lending her substance, the life that they share. Onto one, so, too, the other. It will not drain him completely—you shall have your master back."

She couldn't hear him—not really. She screamed as Ink's eyes drained.

Graus Claude seized Joy and ushered her down the hallway, guided by two of the Bailiwick's sweeping hands. Her screams eventually broke into whimpers and hot tears cooled by the time she sat in his office, weary and defeated. Her bathrobe felt damp and heavy. Hysteria ran on centipede legs under her skin. Her hands and feet tingled. She drank a glass of water without noticing.

"Miss Malone?" The Bailiwick's tone implied that he'd repeated himself more than once already.

"He'll be okay?" she asked weakly. "Both of them? You're sure?"

"They will be weakened, yes, but eventually whole—in no small part thanks to you." He tossed her a handkerchief and waddled around the desk. "It is you who are of present concern."

Graus Claude settled into his massive, thronelike chair. It creaked and groaned as it took his weight. "I will do my best by you, Miss Malone. On that, you have my word. The Edict has not been kind thus far and so I am taking it into my own...capable hands." He tried for a smile and clicked his monitor to life as she wiped at her face. "Let me tell you something, Miss Malone," he said. "I have known Master Ink for many, many years—too many to bother recounting—but suffice it to say that in all that time, I have considered him more of a service than a servant. A tool rather than an individual. He has expressed no motives, no desires, no wants or interests outside of his work, and for one such as I, I assure you that this constitutes an ideal business associate, although not one that I would invite to my dinner parties.

"Since your association, Master Ink has become both stubborn and distracted, moody, insistent, alternately ruthless, passionate and pathetically idealistic, rushing off at the least provocation and into quite a variety of reckless pursuits. In all ways he has become an abysmal worker." Joy tensed inwardly as Graus Claude exhaled through his nose. "However, he is now a *person,* one whom I can respect and admire, even if his manners are deplorably absent of late. I accept this as a fair price for having discovered there lies a soul within that perfect shell. Someone whom I would consider a loyal friend. There are not many afforded to someone in my position, and I value it beyond worldly riches."

Joy waited for some cue, but none came.

"You're welcome?" she tried.

"Yes, well, praises will be earned if we muddle through this alive," Graus Claude muttered as two of his hands began furiously composing electronic mail. "If our theory is correct, Aniseed may trigger her epidemic without the additional insurance of Master Ink's *signatura,* possibly achieving her critical mass on Mistress Inq's alone if she fears discovery." He shook his bobbing head in dismay. "And it may be all for naught—as I said, disease is well within Aniseed's jurisdiction, and that is what makes her a most valuable member of the Council."

"She kills millions of people and she's *on* the Council?" Joy snapped.

"Well, yes," Graus Claude said. "She has a great deal of status and a great many supporters within the Twixt, many of whom would like nothing more than to see Man's supremacy fall. However, we on the Council are charged with maintaining a balance between our worlds and she holds a position that is responsible for that equilibrium more so than most. Her crime is compounded by the additional abuse and trafficking of *signatura* as undeniable evidence of conspiracy to commit worldwide genocide, the likes of which the Edict protecting our human counterparts cannot abide." The Bailiwick paused from his typing. "At least, let us hope that remains the case."

"And what about me?"

The Bailiwick frowned. "What about you?"

"I have Aniseed's *signatura* because it's linked through Briarhook's, right? If she starts a plague or whatever, it'll happen to me, too!"

Graus Claude stared at Joy for an uncomfortably long time. "We have time," he assured her. "Fortune is on our side." He smiled mysteriously. "And I understand that you've been granted a Sir John Melton's boon."

Joy blinked. "A what?"

"A four-leaf clover," Graus Claude said, smiling, and Joy remembered it tucked in her wallet.

"Does that really work?" she said skeptically.

Graus Claude arched his brow ridge. "You tell me." His

third hand swept the mouse and made a few expert clicks. "Now, I can get you on a first flight back to your local airport by 5:15 a.m. I'm not certain I could do better, even with a chartered plane. That will simply have to do...."

"I can't take a plane home!" Joy said. "My father would kill me! He's expecting me to be in my bedroom *right now*—he's waiting for me to join him on a phone call to my brother."

Graus Claude pursed his lips. "Tricky," he admitted. "How does your father deal with disappointment?"

Joy grimaced. "The word *badly* comes to mind," she said. "Followed by *cardiac arrest.* Can't I wait for Ink to poof me back?"

"Master Ink will not be 'poofing' anyone anywhere any time soon," Graus Claude retorted. "Might I remind you the word I politely chose was *weakened* and that should be considered a gross understatement. However, as time is of the essence, I believe I have other avenues at my disposal," he said conspiratorially. "The Scribes are not the only ones who can slip the stream, so to speak."

Graus Claude's two hands typed furiously while his third opened a thin drawer and a fourth extracted a small, stained-glass box. Joy watched hands three and four dance a magician's wave, lifting the soldered lid and removing a small blue-velvet satchel. Unwinding its tasseled drawstring, he spilled a handful of soft, yellowed cubes into his hand, all while ticking and clicking behind his monitor.

"Knucklebones," he said quietly. "Originals." And he tossed them with a flourish upon the floor. Joy watched the dice wobble and land with chalky sounds. In the spill-off light of the computer, Graus Claude right-clicked the mouse and a laser near the floor bounced off the knucklebones like so many mirrors, creating a large geometric pattern that hovered above the rug. Joy stared at Graus Claude, who wore the widest smirk she'd ever seen.

"Observe," he said with almost childish glee.

There was a high-pitched hum on the edge of Joy's hearing, closing like the sound of an oncoming train. The light intensified, the dice trembled and Joy sat on her fingers to keep from covering her ears. The fractal pattern solidified, pulsed once and incandesced.

Someone appeared as the lights faded.

He shook out his umbrella and righted his felt hat, blinking a smile up at Joy.

"Hello," Dennis Thomas said, dusting his sleeves. "We meet again."

"Indeed." Graus Claude closed the box with a click. "Mr. Thomas has generously volunteered to escort you and, I understand, is a previous acquaintance?"

"Um...yeah," Joy said, slightly embarrassed that she couldn't remember whether she'd delivered the old man's message about his bier of roses to Ink.

"I thought a familiar face would be of some comfort, Miss Malone," Graus Claude said. "Fortunately, Mr. Thomas was both available and amenable at such short notice."

"Being an old widower often qualifies me as both available and amenable," Mr. Thomas stage-whispered with a wink. "But it's a pleasure to be asked to aid a damsel in distress."

Graus Claude laughed. "You always had a weakness for the ladies."

The man's eyes twinkled. "When they are both young and pretty, how can I refuse?" He took a couple of steps toward the stone basin, its softly burbling water spinning the lily pads on its surface. He inhaled deeply, relishing the scent. "Smells like her hair," he said and smiled an apology to Joy. "My wife. She died not long ago. She had the most beautiful hair."

There wasn't much Joy could say, but she was moved. "I'm sorry," she said, and Mr. Thomas pressed a hand to his heart.

"I am a proud fisherman," he said. "And proud to have had a fisherman's wife."

"And how is your daughter?" Graus Claude asked politely.

The old man shrugged, hand patting his heart. "She mourns. She is young and beautiful and has lost her mother. Even beauty mourns," he said. "But time is kind."

"Mr. Thomas is a fine man, an excellent porter and an old friend," Graus Claude explained. The rumpled man bowed humbly at the praise. "Miss Malone is in danger and cannot brook delay. I have adjusted your point of arrival to be just outside her domicile in order to avoid any unpleasantness due to the wards placed by Master Ink." The Bailiwick directed his blue eyes to Joy. "I trust in your singular inventiveness to explain how you were no longer in your room, Miss Malone. It is the best I can do under these circumstances."

"I understand," Joy said. "Thank you."

Graus Claude nodded to Mr. Thomas. "I have precise coordinates and the time of departure." He handed the old man a printout from the printer tray. "Eastern Standard Time," the Bailiwick said. "And many thanks."

"My pleasure, Old Frog," Mr. Thomas said and turned to face Joy. "If you'd allow me." The elderly man offered his elbow and Joy took it. He patted her hand in the crook of his arm. "It's like dancing the fox-trot," he said wistfully. "I hope you don't mind if I lead. My dearest Marion—how she loved to dance!"

Joy glanced uncertainly from Mr. Thomas to Graus Claude. The Bailiwick nodded his great head. "It's all right, Miss Malone. Dennis will get you home safely and well in good time."

"Tell Ink..." she started and didn't know how to finish. The grim determination as he'd chopped off his fingertips flashed through her mind. "Tell him to come see me soon."

Graus Claude patted her shoulder again. "I'll tell him," he assured her. "Go now."

Joy hooked a second hand over Mr. Thomas's arm. He placed his paper-soft palm, wrinkled with age, over hers. The hum of the knucklebones began again and the air hissed red.

"Listen for the song," Mr. Thomas said.

Joy frowned. "What?"

The octagram on the floor flared and rushed to meet her. There was a keen, high-pitched whistle deep in her ear. She shrank against Mr. Thomas and his hand squeezed her close. The sounds and lights died away. They stood on solid ground and his hands still held hers.

"You can let go now," she said.

She tried. He didn't. Joy frowned in the dark.

"This isn't..."

Mr. Thomas spoke over her shoulder. "Here she is, as agreed." Twirling her in a mock dance spin, he released her, stumbling, off-balance and confused. Joy spun to a stop, focusing on brown eyes in a brown face framed in orange fur. He kept speaking from somewhere behind her. "I slit the Scribe. I brought the girl. Our deal is done."

"Splendid," said the rich, warm voice. Joy's insides

churned. Polished mahogany eyes flicked over her shoulder. "Your payment." The dark woman offered him a stoppered classic Coke bottle. An unfamiliar glittery fluid sloshed inside its familiar shape.

Mr. Thomas accepted the bottle, fingers curling around the glass, and Joy knew for certain that she'd been betrayed.

"He'll know it was you," Joy said. She wasn't sure if she meant Graus Claude or Ink. Anger boiled off her tongue.

Mr. Thomas had the grace to look ashamed. "Graus Claude doesn't understand, but I believe you do," he whispered, stroking the bottle. "He cannot understand what we do for love." His eyes misted over; he wouldn't look at her. "She was a siren, you know. I miss her singing. It's still inside me." Tears trickled over his soft cheeks. "But time is unkind and I'm unable to forget."

Without another word, Mr. Thomas shook out his umbrella, opened it with a snap and, lifting it gently over his head, disappeared.

SEVENTEEN

"Don't be angry with Dennis," Aniseed said. "He is haunted by regret, burdened by memories. It is a vice, a weakness." Her eyes roamed over Joy. "And you can learn a lot about someone by knowing their weakness."

Joy shuddered. She was Ink's weakness. She, and Inq. And Aniseed had used them both. Through Mr. Thomas. And Graus Claude. Had he known all along? Had the Bailiwick sold them out? It was too terrible to consider.

Joy stared at her feet—she was on a concrete floor surrounded by giant, meticulously painted runes strung together like script spinning out into the dark. Strings of sigils wound outward, blurring into a shadowy distance beyond a familiar line of blue lightning. Mounted torches stood in a circle, catching glitters in the paint, chips of mica or glass. There were hundreds of *signaturae* here. Joy guessed that they were in a vast warehouse and that she was trapped. Again.

The tall woman shifted. Joy raised her eyes.

"I am Aniseed," she said formally. A dusty licorice smell wafted up from the floor where her hem dragged. Dressed, she looked regal. The furred collar about her neck and shoulders was a thick canopy of bright foxtails and her cloak trailed on the floor like a willow seeking roots. Aniseed was very tall, well over seven feet, and Joy thought she hadn't looked that tall lounging naked at the base of the Glendale Oak. Aniseed smiled as if she could read the memory of their first meeting in Joy's eyes.

And when she moved, it was with the sound of heavy wicker baskets.

"I know who you are," Joy said. However, it wasn't true. She'd heard the name, the abbreviated version of her past, seen her hideout at Dover Mill, met her underlings, Briarhook and Hasp, and even witnessed Graus Claude turn pale with rage at her deceit, but none of it had prepared her for the person standing before her now.

"Mmm. I knew the Bailiwick would need someone to fetch you once Ink was indisposed. It was merely a matter of enlisting the most likely candidates into my service with instructions to deliver you to me," Aniseed said. "Not much for me to do, truth be told, but far more energy than you are worth." Her eyes narrowed, lids sliding over carved orbs—a ship's displeased figurehead. "You are a slippery creature," she conceded.

Joy struggled between anger and fear.

"All this to kill me?"

Aniseed might have laughed, but the rasp of her wringing-twig movements drowned out the subtler sound.

"No, little one, this is not all for you—although you have become oddly instrumental in the ultimate design." Aniseed walked slowly along one of the outer whorls of runes. She looked like a diva but moved like an old woman. Creaking bones. Wooden canes. She stroked her collar with a slow hand.

"What I would like," she said, "is for you to call your master. I know that you can." Aniseed pursed her Cheshire cat lips. "I have need of him here, and the time is now abomi-nably short thanks to your involvement of the Bailiwick." She reached under her collar and extruded a tiny vial with a long glass stopper that looked like a tester for perfume. Her slender fingers crackled and popped as she opened it. "Call him and we may discuss options."

"For ransom," Joy guessed.

"If you'd like," Aniseed said. "He has something that I want, and now I have something that he wants." She lifted the thin bulb of glass and watched a single drop of brown fluid fall to the ground. It erupted in blue flame. Fire flickered and settled like coals in a campfire, merging into the telltale bar-rier shot with lightning bursts. Aniseed dipped the pipette back in its vial.

"Alchemical fire," she explained. "Developed for ascrib-ing *signaturae*, linking our symbols to human flesh. The for-mula was my personal design, one I was proud to present to the Council as a solution against further entrapment by hu-mans. It is an inherent element of both Scribes. Ironic, no?" Aniseed began walking in a stately circle. "It really makes no matter to me how this game is played, merely that it be-gins. I'll admit my preferring a slightly longer timetable, but I learned long ago to make do with what I have rather than mourn what I have not. Do you think your master feels the same?" She inclined a lofty finger. Joy might have imagined hushed mutters in the dark.

"Let us ask him."

What could she say?

Joy raised her chin. "No."

"No?"

Joy felt her hands shake. She curled them into fists. "You plan to kill everyone."

Aniseed looked mildly surprised. "Not everyone," she said. "Just the bulk of the infestation. Your people have grown far too numerous for your own good. And ours. The Edict requires a balance in the interest of symbiosis, for self-preservation, in case we *do* need one another to exist. Even I cannot undo that completely," she continued magnanimously. "However, I believe a shift in the balance is long overdue." She delicately loosed the stopper, clinking it against the glass sides like a bell. "It's nothing personal, you understand. Yours will be one death among billions, if that is any consolation."

Acid roiled in her stomach. This was too impossible to believe.

"You can't," Joy said.

"I can," Aniseed lilted, as if speaking to a child. "Call him."

Joy shook her head. She was shaking all over. A tremble shivered her voice. "No."

Aniseed flicked a drop at Joy, who flinched and started screaming. The chemicals ate her skin, burning her palm, her scalp and the tip of one ear. She pawed at the pain, smelling scorched hair and vinegar. Strange symbols danced like liver spots over her skin, oozing sickly and with malice. Joy whimpered. It *burned!*

"He should feel that," Aniseed said, recapping the bottle. "I am not familiar with the intricacies of having a human drone, but I hear that pain is a link as well as a good motivator." Joy touched herself tenderly—there were dark bubbles growing on her skin. Her eyes brimmed, but she refused to blink. She refused to call his name. It was what Aniseed wanted! And whatever Aniseed wanted, Joy wouldn't do. She stared at dark blisters through unshed tears.

"He will come," Aniseed said. "I have no doubt. He has

never bequeathed his mark before, but I am well versed at this game. I have not been able to tempt or exploit the Master Scribe, but that was because he has never *wanted* anything before. No wants, no weakness, no vice, no *needs*—he was little more than a pretty stylus on legs. But now he has you," she said almost hungrily. "His very first *lehman*. Yes, I have been waiting for an opportunity like you for a long time."

Joy sniffed, cradling her burning flesh to her chest, and fought back tears.

"You shouldn't worry about saving yourself," Aniseed confided as if sensing Joy's thoughts. "I don't need his *signatura* to bury you."

She walked over to a particular spot and faced Joy with a foxlike grin. "When the fires reach this symbol, here—" she pointed at a thorny briar rose at her feet "—the poisons I've concocted will alight in your blood. There's no escaping it. Should you walk out of here, I am already with you." Her wooden eyes held no light. "Should you survive this day, you are already dead."

Joy felt the tears spill down her face.

"Yes," Aniseed purred. "Cry. Your tears are precious to me." Her branchlike fingers reached, itching to catch the droplets. Joy shrank back. Aniseed wavered and then withdrew. "But, of course, these plans take precedence, and so... let us begin." The *segulah* straightened on the opposite side of the ward as if straining to hear something in the distance. "He should be here by now," she mused. "Nevertheless, why wait?" She suspended the glass stopper above the first glyph. The brown elixir caressed the edge of the glass, a drop of doom hanging, threatening to fall.

"*No—*" Joy rushed forward but the shock of the ward threw

her back. She hit the floor without feeling it, a million spasms throwing wild sparks in her brain.

She never saw it fall.

Afterimages winked above her eyes as creeping lines of white fire traced the first *signatura* like a cascade of dominoes: inexorable, inevitable. A second sigil flared. Joy's eyes filled with tears, willing it not to be true.

The world tore a seam.

Ink charged through the rent in the air and collapsed on the floor.

Aniseed stoppered the vial and tucked it away. "There you are," she cooed.

"INK!" Joy screamed. Sprawled on the ground, she couldn't even sit up, her muscles still convulsing madly.

"Welcome, young master." He'd fallen at Aniseed's feet. She knelt like a queen and grabbed him by the hair. "I have a proposition for you...."

Joy had never seen Ink's face in pain. He'd always been implacable, always in control. Now his gaunt face twisted as he gasped in weak shock, limbs flailing like any street kid cuffed by the cops. Bare-chested, he looked thin. Joy clutched her fingers, trying to make a fist, force her limbs to obey.

"Now," Aniseed said calmly, resting Ink's head against her knee. "I am certain you can guess what I am about to propose, but I request your indulgence." A third glyph flared behind her. Joy bent her knees, straining against the gritty cement. "As you see, the formula is already gestating, percolating in the veins of those mortals touched by the Twixt. There are certainly enough to create a sizable impact, although it was not until recently that I realized how much of my catalog could be made redundant with two simple additions.

"I had one, and at a bargain, but the other proved elusive. Without desire, there is little to tempt someone to the table. Yet not so elusive now... You desire her, don't you?" She gave a punctuating squeeze. Ink clawed blindly at her hand in his hair. Joy saw that his three fingers were whole, a thick ring of raised tissue showing where the pieces had been hurriedly fused.

"In the interest of full disclosure, I'll let you know that there is no cure," Aniseed continued, unperturbed. "I cannot undo what has already begun. However, I can remove a sigil from the web, leaving it untouched and unaffected—" she inclined her head delicately toward Joy "—pristine and pure, simply by breaking the connection—" she tapped her foot "—here. Simply put, I propose to exchange the lives of your *lehman* and yourself for the willing surrender of your *signatura*."

Joy struggled to sit, her limbs all pins-and-needles. He saw her from across the room split by blue lightning.

"Your answer, please," Aniseed said reasonably. "Time is short."

"They are coming," he whispered, his words slicing through the void to touch Joy. "They are coming."

Another glyph burst into flame.

"Don't," Joy cried out through the tears. "Don't do it! I'm already dead."

"Not yet," Aniseed said. "Not yet. That is for you to decide, Master Ink. Her fate is written in blood and stone. Deny me, and her fate is sealed," she breathed. "Foil me, and her fate is sealed. Kill me," she whispered in his ear, eyes on Joy, "and her fate is sealed."

"Joy."

As he said it, his arms fell slack, defeated.

She'd pushed herself into a half-crouched position, swaying on her one good hand and knees—she somehow knew what was coming. His body curled in one short, tight burst. When she saw the glint of metal, she knew it for what it was.

Ink stabbed the scalpel into the meat of Aniseed's thigh and then twisted, arm outstretched, flinging the instrument straight at Joy. The blade pierced the ward as if held by Ink himself and clattered with a dental-scraping sound against the floor. Sheathed in Aniseed's blood, it had passed through the barrier unharmed. Joy tensed and shot herself backward to pick it up.

Aniseed roared, bleeding amber sludge.

Throat exposed, neck peeled back, Ink's eyes sought Joy's.

"I give it to you," he whispered, sharp as a knife.

Aniseed's teeth tore through his throat.

Joy screamed.

Aniseed dropped his body. A black, oily pool quickly spread across the floor. She considered her stained hand dripping with gore.

"I should save a sample," she bubbled through black lips.

Joy screamed again. Kept screaming. She clutched the scalpel in fumbling fingers, trying to move, but her legs weren't working. She flopped against the floor, staring at Ink's head, which had lolled at a wet angle, gazing sightlessly at Joy.

His eyes ran.

Her brain couldn't contain it.

No! No! No!

The air rippled. The cavalry arrived.

Too late.

"Aniseed." Graus Claude led the pack. He wore ancient

armor of overlapping plates and a flat helmet, looking like a wide, squat samurai. He held a spear, two swords and a pike in his hands. "By the authority vested in me by the Council of the Twixt, you are hereby ordered to stand down and cease your activities immediately, to stand trial for your crimes against the Edict—" The flaring script on the floor split, igniting two new concentric circles. Graus Claude took note of them and added, "Or die."

The great toad was flanked by Kurt in a bulletproof vest and hakama pants, holding a gigantic sword, and Inq, who glared at the *segulah*, unarmed, unarmored and unafraid. Behind them stood a massive crowd of creatures clearly ready for battle.

"All of this over a stripling?" Aniseed sounded truly surprised as she considered Joy from across the room. "Well, well. Would that I could bottle that, too." The alchemist wiped her hand against her gown, adding Ink's bloodstain in sickly counterpoint to her own. "So be it."

Joy clutched the scalpel. Fear rattled her bones.

"You surrender?" Graus Claude asked. Kurt stood taut, ready to spring.

"Don't be ridiculous," Aniseed scoffed. "Do you believe I am a revolution of one?"

Out of the darkness, things boiled into being.

Both sides surged forward. Aniseed rose like a single spire in an ocean that crashed past her in waves. The shock of it jolted Joy upright as Kurt scythed through the first line of creatures with a wordless scream. Graus Claude opened his mouth full of teeth and roared like the devil. Joy felt the sound burrow deep in her chest. She watched chains and swords and sticks and weapons that were unfamiliar to her outside of museums raised to charge, and everything became quickly violent and bloody and loud.

Two armies crashed atop the burning floor.

"Joy?" Inq's voice cut through the chaos. Even if Joy couldn't see her, it had the same quality she shared with her twin. Joy felt bruised, guilty, bewildered. *Ink.* "Can you stand?"

Joy shook her head. "No." Her hip hurt. "Ink..."

"I'm coming," she called. Maybe Inq misheard. "I'll get you out."

"You can't," Joy cried. "There's a ward."

Aniseed called over the hubbub, a commander inured to the horrors of the field. "So tragic," she said to Inq somewhere. "The little bird weeps in her cage." She gestured with her black, bloodied hands. "But I fear I have broken the key."

"SHUT UP!" Joy screamed.

Inq emerged from the fray, spattered with gore but otherwise heedless of the carnage surrounding her. It was as if she was on the dance floor, wading through bodies that parted before her—unknown and undaunted—as she made her way forward. She walked with a strut as the world moved.

"Don't be ridiculous," Inq mocked. "She's one of mine."

And she passed straight through the barrier without breaking stride.

Inq knelt over Joy, who stared, unbelieving.

"Kiss kiss," Inq said soberly and touched Joy's lower lip. "I marked you, here, when I saved your life." Joy reached up and hugged Inq around her neck, happy and sad and relieved and terrified. "I hope you don't mind."

Inq pulled them both to stand. Joy staggered and nearly dropped the scalpel.

"Why do you have that?" Inq asked.

Joy stared at it stupidly. "Ink gave it to me."

"Can you use it?"

"Yes," Joy managed. "But only to erase."

"Erase?"

"And heal."

"Heal?" Inq frowned. "Who?"

Joy swallowed. "You," she said, "and me." There was a shriek by the ward as a vermillion scaled serpent went down. "Please," she begged. "Bring me to Ink!"

"Stay out of the way," Inq said. "You're safer here."

"No, I'm not," Joy argued. Panic bubbled through the electrochemical shock. The *signatura* still burned, doom light snaking toward the spot where Aniseed had mocked her: the pictogram of Briarhook's rose. It linked the brand on her arm to Aniseed's curse in her blood. Joy looked at the scalpel. Could she cut through the ward and then cut all the glyphs? Doubtful. If she stepped one foot into that chaos, she'd be dead within minutes. What did she have? She felt the blade in her hand and pushed past the tears. *He gave this to me.*

That. And his *signatura.*

He gave it to me.

Joy threw off her robe, stabbing the scalpel through her shirtsleeve, and tore near the seam. Fabric snarled as she yanked her arm free.

"Get me Ink's body."

To her credit, Inq did not pause or ask questions. She simply started walking.

Inq crossed the barrier. Joy caught a glimpse of a nail-studded club aimed at her skull, but a tongue shot forward, stuck to the man's head and yanked him backward. Jaws slammed shut. Graus Claude sank on his haunches and started chewing.

Joy shuddered and rubbed her bare arm.

Inspecting the raised callus of her scar, Joy tried to remember what it felt like to heal her hand, and she simultaneously tried to ignore how close the fire must be to Briarhook's *signatura*. She could try to escape, cross the battle and break the script, or she could remove the mark on her own flesh before the fire reached it. It wasn't brave to stay inside the ward, but it wasn't as stupid as trying to leave it. Joy swallowed, thinking back. *Remember: No Stupid.*

Ink knew that he could not save her, but she could save herself.

Pressing the thin blade flat against her arm, Joy scraped a slow, even line toward the scar. Where she hit it, there was no pain, just a slippery sensation as the tip of the scalpel passed easily beneath her bubbled-over flesh. Joy kept the blade steady as the thick skin peeled away like a curl of whittled wood.

Joy carefully sheared the *signatura* from her body amidst screams and snarls and clanging brass. It was agonizingly slow. Her fingers tightened on the grip. Roughened skin split. Her palm stung with sweat. There was no room for distraction, but it was hard to ignore the wet, breaking sounds and the cries cut short just outside the ward. Hot smells scraped her nose and salted her eyes, smelling of spice racks and copper and campfires and blood. Somehow, it smelled too sweet to be death.

But she was alive. Still alive. With moments to go.

Her vision narrowed to the last few millimeters of skin-on-skin, the imminent hiss of fire clawing at her nerves. Joy half expected to feel a surge of hot sickness, as if she might spontaneously combust along with the glyphs. It was just a matter of time she didn't have.

Joy forced herself
to slice
the last bit
free.

A perfect stenciled rose floated to the floor—a couple of layers of crinkled, peach-colored skin. Something inside snapped, followed by a sense of relief. The mark next to Briarhook's caught fire. Joy exhaled.

Safe!

Feeling flooded back into her body, leaving her weak. *Safe!* She was free of Brairhook's *signatura*—he had no claim on her.

Kurt exploded into view, snarling and red-faced, his eyes fixed on Aniseed—all cool, calm austerity gone. It scared Joy back a step. Kurt aimed himself at the *segulah* with single-minded fury.

Graus Claude sat nearby, holding his weapons in a defensive, four-cornered shield as he chewed.

"Graus Claude!" Joy shouted and was satisfied to see his bright eyes flick through the electric fence of runes. Her tongue probed her lower lip, trying to find Inq's mark. "Where is Inq?"

His eyes swerved back and he turned his massive head thirty degrees, pointing with the tip of his spear. Joy saw her.

Inq held her hands flat and tight, like fins, spinning in what Joy first thought was some sort of martial art. A large, boarlike creature rushed her and burst, a slash splitting his torso, erupting and vibrating blood. It happened a good two feet away from where Inq stood, looking grim.

Inq swung her forearm through the air and another attacker's face shattered with the sound of chain saws grating bone. Her face remained smooth, her eyes dark and deadly. Inq fought as if her arms were swords and her skin was armor plate. She hadn't physically touched either foe.

I don't need tools at all.

Joy felt herself grin. "Her weapons are invisible!"

"Of course," Graus Claude spoke through a full mouth. "She's a woman."

Joy laughed, hysterical, raw. But how could she remove Inq's mark when it was invisible?

A grayish blur flickered and jumped. Ten, then twenty, then fifty flitted about the battlefield. A flurry of wings tugged at her eyes. *Flash! Flash!*

"Second wave," Graus Claude grated as he easily parried something thrown.

Joy recognized the aether sprites using their *locqui* to maneuver about the room. The violent twist of a head dropped the soldier who'd raised a sword against Kurt. A plated anteater lifted, disappeared and dropped thirty feet to the right as a hunk of red, blistered meat. The sprites moved among Aniseed's troops, cracking necks and weapons and limbs as they came.

If Aniseed minded, her face didn't show it and she clearly did not intend to withdraw. Two rings of *signatura* now burned on the floor. Countless humans infected.

"Stop! Stop Kurt!" Joy called out to the Bailiwick. "He can't kill her! She might know the only way to stop this!"

But Graus Claude squatted, chewed and didn't move.

"Impossible," he mumbled. "There's no stopping him now."

Joy quivered. Her body felt heavy and cold. Everywhere she looked, those with the Council seemed to be winning, but what good would it do if humanity died? Another line of fire, a new ring aflame: three wicks simultaneously burning. Joy caught another flare in the distance. Four.

What could she do? She squeezed the scalpel in her hand. She could erase things. She had Ink's *signatura*. And Inq's. But what could she do with them? Joy squatted down and tried drawing the swooping mark of Ink's True Name. The thin blade stuttered over the concrete, but left no trace on the gritty gray floor. Joy pressed her palm to it, pricking the spots of her third-degree burns. Nothing. She scraped the edge of the blade gently against her lip. No mark. No ideas. Nothing.

I have to save Ink.

Joy stared at her prison. She touched the blade to the barrier and it cut a small hole. Lightning grabbed the pinpoint like a Frankenstein prop. She withdrew. It sealed over. Aniseed glanced in her direction and smiled.

"If you dare, little stripling," came a whisper of branches slicing through like winter wind. *"Come for me. If you dare."*

Anger filled her, hot and reckless. She wanted to slice that Cheshire grin right off Aniseed's face. She could do it—she'd watched Ink pierce the barriers, seen him cut the witch with the scalpel, but there was a battle raging between them. Unprotected, Joy would likely die the instant she stepped beyond the ward.

And it sounded like Aniseed *wanted* her to try—and anything Aniseed wanted wasn't something Joy would do. Aniseed used people's weaknesses. Hers was Ink.

Joy frowned. It was a distraction. A tangent. *No.* Joy turned her back on the *segulah* and her war. Both Aniseed and Ink knew that there was something she could do with the scalpel and the *signatura*, but she couldn't figure out what!

Joy swung the blade, feeling helpless. She had to try *something*. She couldn't just stand here!

There was a grunting snarl as Briarhook passed the barrier, close enough that his quills brushed the wall. There was a thick metal plate riveted to his chest, the edges crusty with dried pus and blood. He brandished a hooked spear that he slammed into someone's chest. His piggy eyes spied Joy.

"Lehman!" he snorted. "I fight. See this? Fight for my heart! Tell Ink, you! I fight for my heart!" He shook his head as if tearing meat in his teeth and charged deeper into battle.

Somewhere in the center of the mass, Kurt gave an inhuman howl as he hacked his way toward Aniseed. Bodies fell. Blood splashed. His eyes were fever-bright with madness. Watching, Joy suddenly understood: Kurt had been training and perfecting himself for this moment, for the day when he would finally kill Aniseed. It was written on his face in smears of blood. Graus Claude was right—there was no stopping him now.

But there had to be a way to stop her.

Above the fray, Aniseed finally deigned to acknowledge Kurt. She touched her fingertips together, mocking his rage by smiling. The entire room moved with a sudden change in pressure, pressing lungs and feet flat.

It began raining apes.

They fell from the rafters—hairy, screaming, caped and helmed, with long tails fluttering behind them like kites. Their arms ended in thick, knobby bone and they pummeled whatever they landed on, full force. Backs snapped. Shields burst. Skulls crushed like hollow chocolate eggs. Hooting cries filled the air. The battle boiled like oil.

Graus Claude turned his weapons inward, making a tepee-shaped cage against the onslaught from above. Kurt fell under three of them and Joy held her breath. Inq split one before it even hit the ground, a red flash dissipating into a fine pink mist.

Joy couldn't see Ink. His body. His eyes. He was lost somewhere in that mess, trampled underfoot. Joy's hands fisted impotently. Fingernails dug into her palms. And she still couldn't think of what to do.

She had no idea when Inq's glyph would catch fire.

Someone in the back raised a round metal shield—a pitiful defense against this newest attack. A large man draped in matted furs raised a long-handled hammer and swung its square head down with a grunt. A gong sounded. There was a great shout, an invocation.... A clap of lightning split the air, rattling teeth and raising every hair in the room. The ceiling filled with a cumulous mist and enraged riders on horseback galloped down from the clouds, sloping in at sharp angles out of the gathering storm. Ravens and eagles and bright white swans flew over the charge like royal banners. Wild hair flying, swords and shields at the ready...

Lightning flashed. Thunder boomed.

It was the third and final wave.

"Filly!" Joy cried. Although she could not make out which of the face-plated women might be her friend, she took strength in the familiar flying blond braids and bony capes, their weapons held high amidst whooping battle cries.

Joy peered around the warded wall, squeezing the scalpel in her hand, swearing to herself. There *had* to be something here! Something she could erase. Undo. Unmake. She had Ink's *signatura* and she could use it. *How?*

She moved her arm experimentally, mimicking Ink's slashing a hole in the world—a swooping gash rendering space and time apart.

There was no cut, no tear in the universe, but the mark

itself flared briefly. A great snap echoed inside her. It was shocking, the loss. Some people beyond the barrier knew it—felt it—and a few nearby stared. Joy realized that there were suddenly many eyes upon her.

Joy centered herself. She felt...looser. Alone. Blinking, confused, Joy suddenly realized that there was no answering flash in her eye. Nothing unusual happened, which wasn't usual. It had been a long time since she'd felt "usual" and now it felt strange.

Ink's *signatura* was gone, his claim on her with it.

Inq's voice sliced through the war zone like a bell.

"Again!" she commanded. "Do mine!"

Four glyphs flared in doomsday fire.

Joy needed no encouraging. She drew three concentric circles, imagining them as a bull's-eye, glowing. It appeared where she'd carved it in midair, and an answering ripple tickled like a heat wave in reverse. The *signatura* collapsed inward, pushing Joy bodily back. Again, the internal snap. Again, the moment of odd freedom.

For a glimpsed moment, Joy saw: everyone had noticed it now.

Aniseed's mahogany face constricted in fury.

"You!" the *segulah* screamed. The word punctured through the clamor. But Joy smiled and spun the scalpel. She had the answer. One more *signatura* to go.

It hadn't been given. It had been forced upon her, much like Briarhook's brand. Joy remembered Graus Claude's words: *while marks are given voluntarily, they are not always received that way.*

Holding the scalpel at eye level, Joy drew a long, pointy petal, pausing to circle a seed in its center like the iris of an eye. She purposefully faced the ward, knowing that Aniseed could see her. Knowing she couldn't stop her. Joy drew one giant eye-petal, then two, three....

"STOP!" Aniseed shrieked. The ward incandesced, a wall of lightning flame. Something—or maybe many somethings—swarmed the opposite side, trying to get at her, exploding on impact. Joy could smell burning flesh and smoke through the crackling cage. She ignored it. Kept going.

...four petals, five, six...

The roaring quieted, blue-lightning geysers slowed to sparks. Joy could see the battle raging and hear the horses scream. Aniseed seethed above it all.

Joy flashed her a smug look, the one her dad hated most.

Aniseed dove, clawing headlong through the fighting as if the figures were nothing more than toys, her hands growing larger, her back lengthening in a surge. The sound of straining wood became a deafening roar as Aniseed swelled, becoming more and more the tree she resembled, awesome and gloried and ancient.

Coming for Joy.

A giant hand pierced the ward, three-foot fingers extended—

Joy was trapped within Aniseed's barrier. Nothing could keep Joy safe from her. But she could keep her family, her friends and the rest of humanity safe.

She could do that.

Joy stubbornly drew the seventh petal and curved up the eighth.

Fingernails descended, barbed and ringed in white-hot fire. The lightning prison filled with the smell of smoke. Joy crouched, whipping her head out of the way, and nearly dropped the scalpel.

I won't make it. There isn't time!

Joy wavered.

"Finish it!"

She didn't know who'd said it, but her hand obeyed, completing the last curling motion of Aniseed's *signatura*. The star anise pictograph flared once. Another bodily snap. Another release. Joy's skin tingled.

Aniseed screamed.

Joy flattened, hugging the floor. Through her hair, Joy saw Kurt standing in triumph encircled by sharp-feathered bears. He had shoved his sword upward, deep into the inhuman body overhead, piercing the *segulah's* wide throat.

Aniseed and Joy shared an expression of raw shock.

A paw slammed into Kurt's middle and pulled out something wet.

He fell.

Joy screamed.

Aniseed's body crashed down.

Horses reared, shrieking, and those creatures around them continued to fight, pounding, slicing and slaughtering whatever still stood, but the tide had turned. There was an angry flicker as simian troops bounced into the rafters, the clouds dissipating as arrows stopped flying and battle cries slowly sang out of breath. The blur of wings stilled, materializing into bony gray bodies that hovered gravely over the fallen. Weapons dropped, empty hands raised—including hooves, paws and claws—and all those who surrendered fell to their knees.

A robed figure colored like some exotic deep-sea fish scattered fistfuls of powder that settled, crackling, onto the warehouse floor. The fires extinguished. Joy could hear its hush under the painful, crumpled moans.

Graus Claude clambered forward with a clatter of armor,

the *plonk* of his spear butts measuring his step. Bowing his head, he wove his hands in silent benediction. Heads dipped down, fists clenched solemnly over hearts, and the Twixt prayed over their own.

Joy stood in the ghostly emptiness as the torches smoldered, the warehouse slowly growing darker by degrees. The ward remained, an obedient, crackling electric fence. Joy knew that she could cut her way out, but she felt like an intruder on whatever had just passed. Whatever else she'd become, she was still human.

Feeling helpless, she fiddled with the scalpel. Silence folded over the warehouse like a coarse blanket. Inq emerged, the crowd parted, her face and torn corset flecked in blood, and her eyes pierced Joy's as blue lightning flickered past.

"Did we win?" Joy mouthed.

Inq's disembodied voice sliced through the quiet and answered solemnly.

"Yes."

Vambraces rose, mouths opened and fists pumped the air.

"Victory!" the voices yelled. Swords and hammers and shields clashed, joining the chorus, chanting, *"Victory! Victory! Victory!"*

But to Joy, it was hollow.

Ink was dead.

EIGHTEEN

THE CROWDS DISPERSED, TAKING THEIR WOUNDED ON STRETCH-ers, over shoulders and dangling from claws. Some of them moaned, others glared and far too many were covered with cloaks, now shrouds. The rebels formed long lines, escorted by stocky, well-armed guards.

A small knot of stragglers approached the barrier and Joy sliced herself a door to meet them. The air was warm and smelled like burned meat.

Inq offered her hands, which Joy took with only the slight-est hesitation, remembering the thrown ripples that buzzed through bone. Inq placed a chaste kiss against each of Joy's cheeks.

"I'm so proud of you," Inq said. Joy shrank back. She didn't feel proud. She felt carved out and confused, cowardly and weak. Inq squeezed her fingers. "Thank you for saving me."

Joy swallowed nervously, eyes tearful. "Fair is fair."

"Let's go," Inq said and opened her hands, creating a giant vertical whirlpool of concentric ripples in the air. Graus Claude switched his spear to another of his hands and of-fered Joy one as condolence.

"After you," he intoned, but kept a protective grip on her as they passed through the breach. It seemed he had no intention of letting her travel without him as her personal guard. She was deeply grateful.

Graus Claude entered his own foyer with a hearty sigh. Unfastening the buckles across his chest, he clambered past, removing his helmet and armor plate while gathering his weapons together in one fist.

"No room, blast it," he muttered, lumbering down the hall. "And I might as well turn this water closet into an infirmary, while I'm at it. Place a little glazed tile with a Rod of Asclepius right here?" He gestured with a claw and glanced at Joy, who stood awkwardly behind him. He sighed. "I'm joking, Miss Malone." He gestured into the washroom with a resigned expression. "Go on. The others will join us momentarily."

People were crowding into the small antechamber. Joy stayed in the doorway until she saw him.

Ink.

Filly carried a double armload of what looked like an empty wetsuit. Joy seized his arm, slack and boneless. She whimpered deep in her throat.

"Hey, now, move," Filly said and marched into the ultra-feminine toilet, depositing Ink's body on the available settee. Joy sank next to him on the ottoman, staring blankly at his ragged skin, his torn throat, his empty eyes. *Ink.*

Filly knelt next to Joy, a sharp-eyed raven perched on her shoulder. It hopped from leg to leg as she leaned forward.

"It was a good battle," Filly whispered encouragingly. "But I'll not be claiming him yet." She winked at Joy, patted her arm and stood in the center of the floor. "Tell Skögul and Hildr that I'll return shortly." The blonde horsewoman lifted her chin to the ceiling and raised one bright vambrace in salute. Joy's hair billowed out in static currents. Ionic crackles smelled like Ink.

Filly spoke a sharp word. Lightning crashed. Gone.

Joy sat alone with Ink's body.

She turned his face toward hers, feeling no resistance. He puddled under her fingers, his neck attached by barely a hand's width of skin. She brushed the hair out of his face, oddly thankful that his eyes were closed. She touched his thin lips lightly. They were cold. Her eyes spilled over.

"He'll be okay," Inq whispered over her shoulder.

Joy shook her head. "I saw him die."

"Looks can be deceiving," Kurt said as he entered the room looking whole and at ease next to Inq. His Kevlar vest was nothing but tattered, wet shreds, but his voice was a smooth tenor, totally at odds with his bulky body.

"You...?" Joy rested her hand on Ink's chest. It seemed impossible, hopeful, a trick. She grasped for something to say. "You can talk?"

"I can now," Kurt said simply. Inq gazed up at him like a kitten with cream. He knelt by Ink's body. "Let me," he offered, holding the edges of Ink's wound closed. "I've had some experience with this."

"I know," Joy said. "Thank you." And she bent to work.

She tried not to think of the thing in front of her as Ink— the Ink she knew or how she'd last seen him: in pain and, with his last breaths, giving her hope. His skin had been mutilated, his body broken, the edges of his wound gouged by sharp, splintered teeth. Joy's pulse pummeled in her temples, making her squint. She could do this. She could fix this. She could make it untrue.

She carefully followed the ragged line with shaking fingers gripping the scalpel's hilt. Ink's pale skin sparkled with negative stars. She passed the halfway point, rolling over the Adam's apple—or, at least, where one should be—willing the seal to stay closed, to hold him together, to bring him back.

Leaning over his face—almost kissing-close—the smell of him filled her head, tears dripping straight from her eyes onto his. Embarrassed, she tried to shrug them away.

Joy sniffed. "I thought you were dead."

"I thought so, too," Kurt said. "But I couldn't die yet."

"You had to kill Aniseed first?"

Kurt's face hardened into a mask of scars and memories. "No," he said. "But that was all that I lived for." Joy spied Inq's fingers stroking Kurt's neck. He raised his head slightly and his voice softened several degrees. "Everything else is now an added benefit."

Joy tried to smile, but she felt sick. Ink looked so empty. She'd never seen him so helpless, vulnerable. She'd never even seen him asleep because he never slept. Or aged. Or died. *He didn't die. He won't die. He was never born; ergo, he can't die.* She slid the scalpel over his throat, and with his skin snagging the blade, her fingers slick and hot-pink-black, Joy closed the last inch with tears in her eyes.

The scalpel fell from her fingers and clattered against the tile. Ink's head rested in profile: she was looking straight at his ear. Her ear. Joy felt his touch on her face like a ghost.

"Nicely done," said Kurt.

Joy stared. Ink didn't move.

"Don't worry," Inq said. "He just needs a little more juice." Joy blinked, uncomprehending, at the vacant flesh under her hands. Inq brushed back a lick of black hair and sighed. "I know my brother's one for theatrics, but I'm not too keen on hacking off my manicure." She waggled her fingers, still unblemished with nails or knuckles or fingerprints. "Besides, there isn't enough to split between us right now. Don't fret, it only takes a little patience. You'll both learn. In time." Inq grinned. "In the meanwhile, I'd best get ready to grovel."

"To who?" Joy blurted.

"Our creator," Inq said and shrugged off Joy's shock. "Ink doesn't know. To be fair, I *was* made first." She held up a finger and shushed. "Don't tell him, okay? It'll be our little secret."

"But...he'll be alive?" Joy asked. "Safe?"

Inq grinned. "I'd bet my life on it."

She offered to help Joy stand. Joy needed it. Inq swung their hands together like little girls at play.

"You know what this means, don't you?" Inq asked impishly.

Joy shook her head, still dazed, "Humanity's safe?"

"Well, yes, that, too—" Inq said. "But, better than that, this proves that *I* was right!" She winked. "Even Graus Claude thought it was a bad plan, us bringing you on board, but without you we might have lost..." her eyes sought Kurt "...everything." Her face lost some of its merriment. "And nothing's worth that."

She widened her left hand and a small ripple appeared by the sink. Rummaging inside, she withdrew a plastic saline bottle riddled with Sharpie hieroglyphs. She handed it to Joy.

Joy inspected the bottle. "What is it?"

"A bad trade," Inq said. "Not worth the price. But still..." A drop clung to the inside. It sizzled with color. "It had its uses." Inq smiled ruefully. "I suppose, in the future, I'll have to choose only those with the Sight," she sighed. "They'd better be ripped."

Joy held the bottle as several things slid into place.

"The Cabana Boys?" Joy asked.

"Every one of them," Inq said. "Without it, they couldn't see me." She made air quotes with her fingers. "'Invisible Inq.' That's why I went to the *segulah* centuries ago—to get this on tap. It's rare and, generally speaking, the Twixt doesn't approve of cross-border bondings. In the past, it's led to all sorts of trouble—" she sidled up against Kurt "—but, then again, they weren't big on using proper protection."

Kurt coughed. Inq dimpled. Joy reddened and held up one limp hand.

"But Ink..."

"He'll be fine," Inq insisted. "Trust me." Her expression grew vulnerable. "Please, Joy. Trust me." Joy felt herself nod, and Kurt lifted the limp body from her grasp. Joy's hand lingered on Ink's—her hand, now his, their hands—until the butler moved sideways, breaking the touch. She felt its sad echo on her skin. Numbness followed.

"Thanks again, Joy," Inq said. "It was nice being your mistress for a while." She squinched her nose playfully and pulled Joy into a hug. But she didn't feel real, Joy realized. None of it did. It was as if the world was peeling at the edges, collapsing, folding her outside. The colors looked thinner, dimmer somehow.

"What's happening?" Joy whispered.

"No one has claims on you anymore," Inq whispered back. "When you drew the *signatura,* you erased our marks on everyone, everywhere." She pulled away, eyes shining, and tapped the tip of Joy's nose. "You've given me a lot of work to redo!" Inq spoke a little louder. "What Aniseed did—it tore at the Twixt. It's dangerous for you here. Without a *signatura,* without protections, you cannot stay. The Twixt isn't a part of you any longer. You have to go home."

Joy didn't know what to say. Inq tugged her arm, pulling her close. Joy worried that she might kiss her again. Instead, Inq breathed something softly into her ear.

"Just remember—you caught his eye before he cut yours," she whispered through a smile. "And *that* was no mistake."

With that, she let Joy go, stumbling to understand. Joy tried to form words, but the black-lace figure retreated as Graus Claude stepped between them.

"Do not worry yourself about Master Ink, Miss Malone," the Bailiwick assured her in a drowsy sort of voice. He wore a comfortable set of clothes under his expensive smoking jacket. There was a neat bandage taped around his neck like a gauze ascot. "Miss Invisible and Kurt have him well in hand."

"How can Kurt be alive?" Joy said. "I saw him fall. Aniseed's body crushed him."

"Yes, well, Kurt is an unusually hardy specimen, but even stubborn human determination fueled by revenge can only go so far. Kurt is...not merely mortal any longer," Graus Claude said with bare honesty. "He came from a line who knew the Old Ways, and knew me and my kind for what we are." Graus Claude's bright blue eyes unfocused as if remembering. Nostalgia looked weird on him—like finding her grandfather drunk.

"When his mother came to me invoking the True Names, I said that I would save her son from the sickness that ravished their village. How could I refuse?" he asked rhetorically. "I said that when he came of age, he could work off his debt to me."

"So you healed him?"

"I? No. I did what I could. I removed the affected organs and bound him to me. But it was Aniseed's blood that was the panacea, Fate's reversal, erasing all injuries that were, at root, her cause. So, bathed in blood, Kurt emerged as good as new, by his own hand, no less. It is what he has always wanted." He made a small adjustment of his lapel. "They are scouring the floor with it as we speak, soaking the glyphs, thus eliminating whatever devastating thing she'd designed for this night." Graus Claude added conversationally, "She was the originator of the Great Pestilence that killed his family and millions more, after all." Joy stared. He sighed, disappointed. "Modern references call it the Black Plague."

Joy shook her head. "But the Black Plague was hundreds of years ago!"

"Naturally, I extended his life," Graus Claude said with twin shrugs. "It was a very large debt."

Joy tried to move past him. "But Ink..."

It is very hard to sidestep a six-foot, four-armed amphibian.

"It is time to take you home," Graus Claude said with a spark of his old self as he tugged a bellpull, "the way I should have originally."

"Mr. Thomas..." Joy said.

"...is dead," Graus Claude finished. It clearly cost him to say it, to know treachery in a friend. The Bailiwick wiped two hands against his chest. "As I said, loyal friends are rare for one such as I." He placed a mottled hand upon her shoulder and smiled wanly. "Very rare, indeed."

Inq reappeared in the hallway.

"You rang?"

The Bailiwick raised an eye ridge. "Yes. Very well," Graus

Claude said. "It was an honor and a pleasure to know you, Miss Malone." He said it with a finality that Joy found both frightening and sincere. "I promise that you and your patrons will come to no further harm. The Council will assure it. Consider yourself and your family under a new Edict."

She felt herself nodding.

"Okay," she said.

Taking Joy's hand gently in his shellacked claws, he lifted her knuckles to his lips and pressed a kiss there. He glanced at the scalpel she still held in her right hand.

"I will return this to Master Ink." It was a gentle command she did not want to obey. Joy tightened her grip on the scalpel. Graus Claude's deep voice purred over her knuckles. "It does not belong to you, Miss Malone," he prompted. "Let it go."

Joy relaxed, rotating the handle between her fingers before awkwardly placing it in Graus Claude's waiting palm. She kept her hand there, holding on to its realness, its powerful link to Ink, hesitant to...

"Let it go," Graus Claude whispered.

Joy let go.

"Good," he said with a gentle squeeze. "And goodbye."

He lumbered aside, head swinging low.

She let him go. She let it go. She felt like she was letting it all go. Joy stood in a downy, careless fog, watching the world origami away.

"Ready?" Inq asked.

Ready? Ready to go? Now? But there's so much...

Let it go.

Sometimes, she thought to herself, that's how it ends.

"I'm ready," she said.

Inq took her hand. They slid through sudden ripples, stepping into Joy's room.

"Joy!"

She nearly jumped out of her skin as her father flung open the door. Inq lifted her hand like the flat of a sword. He looked about ready to shout again.

"Dad...?" Joy said stupidly, her brain rushing to adjust.

"When I say, 'Do you want to say hello?' what I mean is, 'Pick up the damned phone so we can have this conversation together!'" He thrust one of the wireless receivers into Joy's right hand and a tall glass of soda with lemon into her left. The ice hadn't even melted. The cold soothed her raw skin. "I know we don't usually talk like this, but we do starting now. This is important. This is family," he said. "Don't make me go through this alone, Joy."

Joy nodded weakly. Inq relaxed.

"Okay, Dad."

Inq hesitated, about to say something, then changed her mind, winked, blew a kiss and disappeared.

He looked Joy over, searching for something. "And after this, we're going to keep talking. We're going to talk about you. And me. And you're going to talk to your mother. And we're going to talk about everything. Get it all out there. All right?"

Joy couldn't help thinking, *Not everything,* but somehow managed a genuine smile. "Yeah. All right."

"All right." Her father wrapped her in a squeeze and led her down the hall in a one-armed hug. She hugged him back as he dialed the phone. He pulled away slightly, rubbing her bare left shoulder.

"What in the world did you do to your shirt?"

* * *

The door clicked closed. Joy stared at her room through the eyes of a stranger.

It was quiet. No noise. No ringing phone. No strange notes. No monsters. No weird ripples. No sounds of battle. No creaking wood. No rumble of Graus Claude. No crisp, clear voices. No Inq. No Ink. No one.

She was alone.

It was a trembling quiet. It was the first pause of nothing at all.

Joy collapsed on her bed, curling into a tight ball of misery. She smashed her pillow to her face, soaking it thoroughly with snot and tears. Dad was fine, Stef was fine, but she was anything but fine. She wanted the power to erase again, to make it untrue, to take the scalpel and cut reality apart: the nightmare of a perfectly normal day in a perfectly normal life.

One without Ink.

She cried the rest of the night.

Joy stared at the ceiling. She was wrung dry and hollow. It was dark. It was quiet. It was 4:00 a.m.

She reached out a hand to touch something invisible, willing fingers to materialize in midair and pull her up and away. She searched for images in the shadows: a flash of silver, a straight razor, a ripple of air, an ouroboros, a gleam of all-black eyes.

She wanted desperately to pull it back. She wanted desperately to let it go.

Joy recognized this feeling.

Getting up, she slid open her top dresser drawer. She took

out an envelope from the bottom of the stack and, unfolding its familiar creases, reread the first letter from her mother. The handwriting spoke in a voice that Joy could still hear in her dreams. The tears flowed freely.

She hadn't let it go. She'd never let it go. And, she suddenly realized, she didn't have to.

Joy sat on her bed with the letter and the ticket in her hand and sent a text message since it was three hours earlier in L.A. Joy didn't trust her voice just yet, but she could hit the keys.

i love you mom. i miss u. a lot. always—joy

NINETEEN

On May twenty-third, Joy sat contemplating her hands. The burns had healed to soft, dark patches beneath her artificial suntan—a gift from Stef for her week-long visit to California. The scars were almost unnoticeable unless she really looked for them. She looked for them often, if only to assure herself that it had all been real and not some crazy dream.

Joy was seventeen today.

Life had become so *quiet.* There had been no strange messages, no texts, no monsters at the window or knocking at her door. She hadn't missed that part—but she missed Ink. She missed him like an ache, like a bruise coating the inside of her body. She thought the feeling would fade, but it hadn't. It just sank deeper, becoming more a part of her every day.

She'd looked for him in every shadow, every doorway, every corner at school, half expecting him to appear at the Carousel or in her kitchen or Hall C. Joy waited for the world to slice open with the scent of rain. It never did. She went to bed empty and fitful and sad. And when she dreamed, she dreamed of Ink, but then she was the one who was invisible—he could not see her for all her screaming and he simply walked away. She woke half expecting to see him there.

Joy rehearsed what she would say, what she would do,

when she finally saw him. But now it had been too long, the words becoming jumbled in her heart and head. Now she just wanted to *see* him. She felt for the one-armed shirt under her pillow and bunched it against her face, breathing it in, trying to recapture his scent, as if it might somehow invoke him again. It smelled faintly of salt water—of storms and tears.

She'd gone through stages, like the ones in Monica's pamphlets. She'd passed denial and went straight to prayer, circling angry several times, before feeling hopeful, then helpless, then numb.

Stupid things kept reminding her of him, and it was a fresh hurt every time. Butter knives reminded her of him. Notebook paper reminded her of him. A milk jug in the refrigerator. Rain and loud music. Glow sticks and her pillow...

Her own hands reminded her of him.

It was a slow recovery.

Ink had infused her. It was excruciating. And when she blinked, there was no longer any answering flash in her eye. Nothing to prove that he'd ever been there. Nothing to prove that they had ever been real.

She pushed a little on the burn scars, trying to eke out a pinprick, a dull needle of pain. But it had been too long. She'd healed without meaning to. Time was unkind—it healed things without permission.

Joy was seventeen, and tomorrow she was headed to L.A.

The phone rang.

"Are you coming?" Monica said. "We've got a whole Birthday Girl send-off planned, but can't start without the Guest of Honor!"

"I'm coming," Joy said, fastening her bracelet. "Be there soon."

"Look for the giant Over the Hill balloons."

Joy groaned, "You didn't!"

"Didn't I?" Monica said archly, "Just wait'll you see the cake! Totally NC-17!" Monica was a firm believer that the quickest way to get over heartbreak involved lots of smarm.

Joy chuckled despite herself. "You're evil."

"And you're welcome," Monica said. "Now get moving." She hung up and Joy thumbed off the phone, looking around for her knit sweater.

"Joy."

Ink stood inside the closet door, the mirror ignoring his reflection.

Her heart stopped. Joy wanted to launch at him, but something in the way he stood told her *No.* He was paler, weaker—not just how he stood, but *him*, a faded sort of out-line, a ghostly presence not quite in this world. Joy hadn't seen him since Graus Claude's, but she'd pictured him, how he looked, trying to keep him fresh in her mind, trying not to forget how he held himself, how he smiled, how he smelled. And now he was here. Really here.

Ink.

It crushed her, holding back, sitting still. Only her mouth moved.

"You're okay."

"I am," Ink said with a nod. "Thanks to you."

Their pause stretched—a silent, wrenching thing.

"Ink—"

"I was uncertain whether or not to come," he said quickly. "I thought, perhaps, it would be best to let you be, let you live your own life, free of me and my kind. But then I thought that you would want to know what had happened. That we owed you that much."

Joy shook her head. That didn't sound right. He didn't *owe* her. What had happened? What was wrong? Didn't he remember? Didn't he remember *her*? Or had he let it go? She hadn't considered the possibility that he might not *want* to come back.

Her hands hadn't budged from their nest in her lap, hot with sweat and nerves and wanting. Why couldn't she move?

"I came to tell you that I am well. Inq is well. The Council renounced Aniseed's followers and reaffirmed their position preserving our ties with your world. Aniseed's work is destroyed. Her network abolished. Her poisons neutralized. She is dead," Ink said. "Your family is protected under the Edict and I have formally and publicly renounced our association, so no one from the Twixt should ever contact you again." He spoke flat and businesslike. "Kurt sends his regards, and Graus Claude his regrets." He paused, blinking owlishly. "That should be everything."

Ink's eyes were open and empty as a starless night. He sounded bored, tired.

"Our 'association'...?" Joy said.

"Was a mistake."

Joy stood up. He looked curious, and maybe a little afraid.

"It was *not* a mistake," she insisted. "That first night, the night at the Carousel, *before* you tried to take my Sight...that was no mistake. And don't you dare say that it was." It was as if he wanted to look away, but was frozen, unblinking. "I was *born* with the Sight, Ink," she said, voice trembling. "So tell me, why were you the first person I'd ever seen from the Twixt?"

They stared at each other. His answer slipped through his lips.

"Because I saw you," he confessed. "And I couldn't look away."

Ink snapped into sharp focus, his eyes digging deep. He was *here*. And when he spoke, his voice shot to her core.

"It hurts everywhere," he said, sounding surprised.

She was in his arms and he was holding her, squeezing hard.

"It hurts everywhere," he said again against her skin. "I can't pull you close enough."

Joy wrapped her hands around his neck.

"Try."

He buried himself in her, filling the empty nooks with more of himself, burrowing into the spaces between her neck and her hair, drinking in Joy like a drowning man. She turned her head and kissed him. He kissed her back, worshipping her closeness with soft lips and warm skin, his hands kneading her back and clenching her hair.

"Joy," Ink whispered. "I miss you. I miss that part of you," he pressed her to his chest, "here."

"I've missed you," Joy whispered back, "everywhere."

"But this is your life." Ink struggled to say it, pushing back an inch that felt like miles. "I was never meant to be part of it."

Joy refused to submit, refused to let go now that she had him there with her. She bunched her hands in his smoke-silver shirt. "I didn't know what drawing the *signaturae* would do!"

"It saved everyone," Ink said, touching the tiny hairs of her eyebrow as if he'd forgotten what they looked like and was trying to memorize it now. "Erasing our *signaturae* broke Aniseed's claim. It freed them. It freed you."

"I don't want to be free of you!"

There. She'd said it. Joy's heart slammed under her skin. Ink hovered in that moment.

"You cannot mean that..."

"I do!" Joy said and tightened her grip on him, afraid to let go. "You asked me what I want, and I am *telling* you." Her voice warmed, the words growing surer. "No accident. No mistake. You chose me and I choose you."

He wanted this. Badly. It was written on his face.

"Joy..."

"Please." Joy squeezed, reminding him, tangibly, of what they had together. "Please, Ink, choose me."

"I did," he confessed. "I do." Ink rested his forehead against hers, his black eyes slipping closed. "But you cannot ask me to risk you again."

"I'm not," Joy said. "I'm asking you to give me what I want."

The bareness of it hung fragile and tender and wild and frightening. Joy held her breath in that soap-bubble moment.

Ink's face lifted, daring and shy.

"Yes," he said tenderly. "Yes, Joy Malone. But you don't need my mark to be mine."

Joy almost laughed. Almost. "I 'don't'?'"

"No. You don't," he said. "I do not bear your mark, and I am yours." He touched her face softly. Joy's senses rose to meet him. Ink wiped a thumb wondrously over her cheek. "It is...a feeling we share that needs only to be named."

"Ah," she said, stroking the back of his neck. "Names are powerful things." She couldn't stop smiling. "And what would you call this feeling?"

Ink smiled. Dimpled.

"'Joy.'"

EPILOGUE

THERE WAS SOMETHING ON THE NIGHTSTAND IN HER MOTHER'S guest room.

Joy flung off the blankets. Hours of jet lag and late-night talking had made her brain woozy and warm, but she came instantly awake when she saw the box. A wide ring spread across its polished wood surface, hand-carved, intricate and deeply detailed. She traced it with her fingers, exploring the grain.

An ouroboros. Infinity etched in black.

It felt permanent. Enduring.

Indelible Ink.

Lifting the lid, she found a note and a glint of silver tucked inside.

This is yours.
Happy birthday, Joy.
I love you.

Joy picked up the silver scalpel and smiled.

* * * * *

ACKNOWLEDGMENTS

This is where I utterly fail to adequately thank all the amazing people who not only brought this book to life, but helped me become a better writer and not a certifiable lunatic in an off-the-shoulder, floor-length straitjacket. Big, huge helpings of thanks to my agent, Michael Bourret, who saw magic in these pages, and to my editor, Natashya Wilson, for unearthing the true world of the Twixt. Thanks to the Harlequin TEEN Dream Team: Jenny Bullough, T. S. Ferguson, Amy Jones, Nicki Kommit, Jane Ludlam, Sandra Latini, Gigi Lau, Fion Ngan, Michelle Renaud, Mary Sheldon, Annie Stone, Larissa Walker, Lisa Wray and also Anna Baggaley of the U.K. Mira Ink team for their shared brilliance in making this dream a reality. Particular thanks goes to Mario Sánchez Nevado who created the stunning cover art.

Thanks to my critique partners, beta readers and many good friends who humored/challenged/cajoled/comforted/cheered/harangued me out of love and deep commitment to my sanity and success; especially Deva Fagan, Angie Frazier, Maurissa Guibord, Susan Van Hecke, Mark Apgar, Jenny and Matt Bannock and Michael Owen Miller. Special acknowledgments go to Brigid McCarthy for sharing her expertise on Olympic-level gymnastics and the folks at USA Gymnastics for helpful tips and tricks. To my online communities including the Tenners, the Elevensies, Fangs, Fur & Fey, The Enchanted Inkpot, SCBWI and Verla Kay's Blueboarders: I couldn't have done any of this without you along the way!

Finally, I can't thank my family enough for everything they are to me—you are my magic! Love to my parents, Holly and Barry, Harold and Marilyn, my siblings, Corrie, Rich, Adam, Michelle, Shari and David, my incredible kids, Maestro & The Pigtailed Overlord (yes, Mommy's talking to you!) and, of course, to Jonathan: all of this (and more) is thanks to you. I love you more than chocolate mousse!

Now can someone please loosen these straps?